'Yiyun Li is an important and gifted writer' Marilynne Robinson

'Yiyun Li is one of my favourite writers, and *Must I Go* is an extraordinary book' Meg Wolitzer

'Li's prose in *Must I Go* is hard to fault. The grain of every sentence feels measured, each word jealously dispensed' *Spectator*

'Lilia Liska is a memorable creation – "as hard as the hardest life" – whose sharp judgements and shrewd, if harsh, insights into life ring with the painful candour of truth. As Lilia bravely declares: "Happy people have no use for words"' Joyce Carol Oates

'Yiyun Li has crafted an epic story of a life full of regret, but also of hope and perseverance and the importance of passing down our legacies' *Vulture*

'A titan of contemporary fiction returns with a provocative new novel ... Arresting and meditative ... Li is as fearless and incisive as always, plumbing fathomless emotional depths as she excavates the kinetic mind of her protagonist, a stern woman with shocking secrets who resists easy categorizations. Li is a truly peerless voice in contemporary fiction, and *Must I Go* is another unforgettable entry in a long career of excellence' *Esquire*, Twenty Best Summer Books of 2020

'Like she did in her 2019 novel *Where Reasons End*, Yiyun Li creates a sensitive, strange and heartbreaking account of maternal love as Lilia processes the losses she's experienced in her life' *Time*, Best New Books to Read in July 2020

'The MacArthur "genius" grant recipient's sixth work of fiction is the elegiac story of octogenarian Lilia, who's outlived three husbands and had five children, one who died by suicide. Now residing in an assisted-living facility, Lilia probes her past with a clinician's objectivity, trying to answer the question she's never stopped asking herself: why did her daughter take her own life?' *O, The Oprah Magazine*, Best Summer 2020 Books from Authors Around the World

'There is no writer like Yiyun Li, no one in contemporary literature who is as masterful at digging into the uncertainty of our existence on this earth. And *Must I Go* is sheer brilliance. Lilia Liska is one of the most arresting, strangely funny and complex characters I've ever met. In constructing a narrative that allows us to look into the past in order to reckon with what comes next, Li does something truly transformative. She remakes our world for us, so we can figure out how to keep living in it' Kevin Wilson

'A portrait of resilience like no other, *Must I Go* takes Yiyun Li – and the reader – into entirely new emotional territory. Bracing and almost unnervingly perceptive, this is wisdom literature for our time' Gish Jen

'I missed both Roland and Lilia when the book was over' *Irish Times*

'*Must I Go* affirms the complex bonds of divergent characters who learn to navigate through loss' *NPR*

ABOUT THE AUTHOR

Yiyun Li is the author of three previous novels, *Where Reasons End, The Vagrants* and *Kinder Than Solitude*, and two short-story collections, *A Thousand Years of Good Prayers* and *Cold Boy, Emerald Girl*, as well as the memoir, *Dear Friend, from My Life I Write to You in Your Life*. She has won literary awards including the Frank O'Connor International Short Story Award and the *Guardian* First Book Award, and was listed among *Granta*'s Best of Young American Novelists 2007. Her stories have been published in the *New Yorker*, *Paris Review* and elsewhere. She is a MacArthur Fellow, a recipient of a Windham-Campbell Prize and a professor of creative writing at Princeton University.

Must I Go

A NOVEL

Yiyun Li

PENGUIN BOOKS

PENGUIN BOOKS

UK | USA | Canada | Ireland | Australia
India | New Zealand | South Africa

Penguin Books is part of the Penguin Random House group of companies
whose addresses can be found at global.penguinrandomhouse.com.

First published in the United States of America by Random House 2020
First published in Great Britain by Hamish Hamilton 2020
Published in Penguin Books 2021

003

Printed and bound in Great Britain by Clays Ltd, Elcograf S.p.A.

The authorized representative in the EEA is Penguin Random House Ireland,
Morrison Chambers, 32 Nassau Street, Dublin D02 YH68

A CIP catalogue record for this book is available from the British Library

ISBN: 978-0-241-97868-9

www.greenpenguin.co.uk

Penguin Random House is committed to a
sustainable future for our business, our readers
and our planet. This book is made from Forest
Stewardship Council® certified paper.

For Dapeng and James

and for Vincent, always and forever

PART ONE

Days After Love

"POSTERITY, TAKE NOTICE!"

The exhortation, or the plea, appeared twenty-three times in Roland Bouley's diaries. Every time Lilia read the line, she reassured him: Yes, Roland, I'm here, taking notice. If one of her children in their younger years had asked her not to ever die, Lilia would have spoken with equal certainty: I never will. But that was a promise made to be broken. Roland had not asked for the impossible, only the eternal. Who else could be his posterity but her?

The single volume of his diaries, over seven hundred pages, was the only book Roland had published. He had culled sixty years of entries, and left instructions to have them printed by a friend's press. He had left everything to Peter and Anne Wilson, his wife Hetty's favorite niece.

Lilia disapproved of the Wilsons. Resented them wholeheartedly. They had edited Roland's diaries from three volumes into one, inserting ellipses where records should have been kept intact. The first time she read the book, and Peter Wilson's introduction that justified the culling, Lilia had sent a letter to Aubrey Lane Press, the address a P.O. box in Dartmouth, Nova Scotia. What arrogance to say that Roland's journals were "at times repetitive." *Life is repetitive*, she wrote. *Loyalty to a dead man should be the editor's foremost requirement*. She had received no reply.

Three volumes into one: These people might as well take a second job as cooks, whisking and reducing Roland's lifework into a bowl of gravy. In his introduction, Peter Wilson flaunted his editorial skill, praising his discretion in deciding what to omit and his moral integrity in respecting Roland's wishes without causing undue distress for the family members.

What distress? What family? Hetty had not given Roland any children. More than half of the finished book was about Roland's marriage. If the Wilsons thought that, by omission, they could make Hetty the center of Roland's life, they had made fools of themselves. Anyone reading Roland's diaries would know that Sidelle Ogden was the only one for whom he had made any space in his heart. That, for a man who had mostly only loved himself, was a feat.

Lilia did not mind. A woman's value, in her opinion, was not measured by the quality of the men in her life, but by the quality of the women in the lives of those men. Lilia, though she appeared only briefly in Roland's journals, would have made any woman proud.

Lilia had met Roland four times in her life. Had she told people that she had been rereading his diaries for years now, they would have called her crazy—man crazy, book crazy—but how wrong people often were. A story is not always a love story. A book is much more than just pages of words.

But the world was full of people like the Wilsons who understood nothing. They thought that they were humoring Roland by putting some pages of his diaries into print. They felt no qualms about forgetting Roland. Typical of him to entrust his posterity to people who dedicated so little of their lives to remembering him.

"I-M-B-O-D-Y," LILIA SAID, SPELLING HER NAME OUT FOR the two children. Patience was not her virtue, but if she had enough to live for eighty-one years, there was no reason she could not spare some for the third graders. Or were they in second grade? It didn't matter. She would long be dead before they would grow up into something remotely interesting. Though even that meager prospect was not guaranteed. Lilia was the oldest among six siblings, and she had raised five children, who had given her seventeen grandchildren, so she knew what would happen to the young. Yes, they start out warm and pure like a bucket of fresh milk, but sooner or later they turn sour.

Lilia had many verdicts to deliver when it came to children. One of the most dire she had given to Iola, her great-granddaughter. If Iola were someone else's blood Lilia wouldn't have minced words. Born to lose, that was what the girl was. Though of course Lilia would not say so to Katherine, Iola's mother. At Lilia's age all the other grandchildren were the garnish on her life, but Katherine, who had not been an essential ingredient to her own parents, would remain essential to Lilia for as long as she lived.

The week before, when Katherine had come to visit, she had gone on about Iola for so long that Lilia had no time to ask Katherine about her own marriage, which was seemingly heading into dangerous waters. Having predicted such a course, Lilia considered it her due to be kept informed of every deterioration. The *Titanic* would have been a dreary story if all we were allowed to know were its departure from the harbor (like a virgin) and its burial at sea (in its bridal gown).

And poor Iola. Chances are, she would turn out not to be enough of a ship to be wrecked by life.

Here was Iola's latest failure. A playmate's father, a real estate developer, had put his kindergarten-age daughter in charge of naming the streets and cul-de-sacs with her friends' names. Only two girls from Iola's playgroup had been left out.

What kind of parents would do that, Katherine complained.

What's the matter with not having a street bearing your name? Lilia tried not to point out that, had Iola's name been chosen, Katherine would have thought the idea ingenious. "Iola" had too many vowels for a too-short name. Too unconventional. But Lilia had kept these judgments to herself. What's the other girl's name? Lilia asked. My goodness, I hope her last name is not Cooper, she said. It's Minnie, Katherine said again, spelling the name with the same impatience Lilia now spelled out "Imbody" for the young visitors.

"Make sure it starts with an *I*," she told them. Lilia had kept her second husband's last name. Not that Norman Imbody was that special to her, but she had liked how the name sounded, and would not give it up for Milt Harrison. "Mrs. Imbody," Lilia said now. "Call me Mrs. Imbody."

Gilbert Murray would have comforted Katherine, saying that Iola was too precious a name to share with a street. Norman Imbody would have matched Katherine's dolefulness and lamented, most unhelpfully, that the world is not a fair place. Milt Harrison would have made up a ditty with the chosen names, Rosalie, Natalie, Caitlin, Genevieve, all of them given their mishaps.

Some women specialize in marrying the wrong people. Lilia had not been one of them. But all of these husbands were gone, the memory of their large hearts and small vices no more than the vanilla pudding at dinner: low-calorie, no sugar, with barely enough flavor. Who'd have known that she would live to see a day when food prides itself on offering as little as possible?

Lilia had to be strategic with Katherine. Like her mother, Lucy, she was an expert at making a life out of disappointments. Lucy had taken her own life at twenty-seven, two months after giving birth to Katherine. In earlier years Lilia had imagined showing off any little accomplishment of Katherine to her dead mother. Look at baby Katherine's new teeth! Look at her soft curls! Look how much you've missed. Lilia had never fought so fiercely with someone on a battlefield called cuteness.

And now Iola seemed to be catching up, her share of disappointments enormous for her age. Where did all three of them get that trait? Not from Lilia. She did not have a porous heart, and that, she knew, was the condition disappointments needed as a breeding ground. Could it be their inheritance from Roland? Though he himself would've been the first to protest, insisting that he was born without a heart.

No books written, no offspring—at least no one legitimate. And if there were bastards carrying my blood, they were not known to me, Roland wrote in his diary. 5 June 1962. *No woman's warmth enough to melt my heart, if, of course, there is a heart inside me.*

No, Roland, so much was unknown to you: your daughter's birth, your granddaughter's birth, your daughter's death.

"MRS. EMBODY, IS IT OKAY IF WE RECORD THIS INTER-view?" The boy in front of Lilia checked his notes before raising his face, the black and white of his eyes giving her a shock. One only saw droopy lids and fogged-up eyes these days at Bayside Garden.

The children were still here! Surprise, surprise, Lilia thought, how nimbly the mind travels in the time it takes a body to get itself uncomfortably settled in a chair.

This was one of those days when Lilia wouldn't mind playing truant from life. Coffee lukewarm at breakfast (and weak, but that was a given, as the kitchen only offered coffee as weak as the legs of the men in residence); Phyllis taking a seat next to Lilia (uninvited, though anyone sitting next to her fell into the category of the unwelcome); Mildred, sitting across from Lilia, talking about what to buy for her granddaughter's birthday (who cares); Elaine demanding everyone's participation in an oral history project led by a nearby school. The head teacher was her niece, Elaine announced.

Lilia had decided a little distraction would do her good. Now she could see it was a mistake. "Call me Mrs. *Im*body," she said. "Did you spell it wrong?"

The boy looked down at his pad. The girl next to him raised an innocent face. "Is it okay if we record this interview, Mrs. Imbody?" the girl said.

Lilia gave an impatient consent. The flyers advertising the morning activity had promised cookies, clementines, and hot chocolate with marshmallows. She imagined Jean and her assistant in the kitchenette next door, peeling and sharing a clementine. Infringing on the residents' rights. A theft, strictly speaking, though no one here was strict with petty crimes. When you're closer to death, you're expected to see less, hear less, and care less.

Care less until you become careless, and that's when they pack you off to the next building. The Memory Care Unit: as though your memories, like children or dogs, were only temporarily at the mercy of the uncaring others, waiting for you to reclaim them at the end of the day. You have to be careful not to slip into the careless. The care-full live, the care-less die, and when you are dead you are carefree. "But who cares?" Lilia said aloud.

The boy studied Lilia's face. The girl patted him on his back. Lilia leaned over to take a look at the girl's ear studs. "Are they diamond?"

The boy looked, too. "Do you know there's a diamond called Hope?" he said, addressing the air.

Normally Lilia would remind the boy that it was rude to speak when a question was not addressed to him. But somewhere in her body there was a strange sensation. Sixty years ago she would have called it desire, but now it must be as wrinkled as she was. The memory of desire.

"These are crystal. My cousin in Vancouver made them for me," the girl said.

Lilia turned to the boy. "Those crystals. Cheaper than your Hope, aren't they?" Hope, the diamond, had been the subject of a post-lovemaking talk Roland had had with a woman, as recorded in his diaries. Like Lilia, this other woman had been reduced to a single capital letter in the book.

Lilia herself, "L," had appeared in the diary five times. The first time was on page 124, and Peter Wilson had added a footnote: *L, unidentified lover*. Unidentified—nearly all Roland's lovers fell into that category, and Lilia often wondered if some were left out. It would've been a sting had she not found herself in the book— there would've been no way to tell which man had edited her away. To be erased, intentionally or haphazardly, would have upset her equally.

"My mom took me and my brother to see the diamond last year," the boy said. "In Washington, D.C."

"Did she?" Lilia said. Put a woman and a diamond together and you get a thousand stories, all uninteresting. "I bet you a hundred dollars that your mother is one smart woman who knows how to raise good sons."

"I don't have a hundred dollars."

"I don't either. It's just an expression."

"But my mother died."

The girl looked around, searching for an adult who might intervene.

"I'm sorry to hear that," Lilia said. "But it's okay. Everybody dies. It's not up to you and me to say when."

The boy's face, not expressive to start with, turned oddly flat.

"Mrs. Imbody, can we start the interview?" the girl asked.

Mrs. Imbody, Lilia thought, has no use for obedient little girls.

The interview was shorter than Lilia had expected. Five questions, all harmless and uninspiring. Where and when were you born? What was your family like when you were a child? Who was your favorite teacher when you were in school? What was your hometown like when you were a child? What's one thing you've done that you're proud of?

"One thing I'm proud of? Hard to choose. There are too many. How about I once knew a man whose friend tried to borrow that diamond of yours"—Lilia nodded at the boy—"for an exhibition."

"Did they get it?" the girl said.

"She. I said she tried."

"And they wouldn't let her borrow it?"

"Her country," Lilia said. "Which happens to be Canada."

"My dad is from Canada," the girl said again.

"Well, they wouldn't let Canada borrow it," Lilia said.

"Why?"

"Ask your friend here."

"I don't know," the boy said.

"I thought you saw the diamond with your own eyes."

"My mom took us," the boy said.

And your mom is dead. "Can you do me a favor?" Lilia said to the girl. "Run to the lady there—yes, the one standing by the cart. Ask her if you could help her."

Lilia moved closer to the boy when the girl went away. "How did your mom die?"

"From a heart problem."

"What kind of heart problem?"

The boy shook his head. The black and white of his eyes never for a moment blurred. Dry-eyed-ness was a virtue Lilia endorsed. She thought of pulling the teacher or her young assistant aside and asking if the boy's mother had killed herself (and if so, how). A death from a heart attack and a death from heartbreak were different. It was essential that whatever happened should be told just the way it happened.

After Lucy died, Gilbert had wondered if they should tell people that it was from a sudden illness, some complication from being a new mother. No, Lilia said, we don't lie about death. When Katherine was old enough to ask about her parents, Lilia had said that Steve, her dad, had not been qualified to be a father, and Lucy had been ill. She understood that no doctor could help her so she took care of the matter herself, Lilia said. She knew she could trust us to take care of you. People will say all sorts of things about those who've committed suicide. But, Katherine, your mom was a brave woman.

Katherine, barely six then, had not asked for more detail. She hadn't later, either, and Lilia had not brought up the subject again. But on family TV nights, whenever a suicide joke came up in a sitcom, Katherine would laugh, more loudly than Lilia, as though they were in a competition. It was one of the few moments when Lilia recognized Lucy's willfulness in Katherine. Between themselves they rarely mentioned Lucy's name. For Lilia, this family life after Lucy was a new one. For Katherine, the only one.

Jean clapped her hands to herd the residents toward the snacks. Lilia prompted the boy to thank her for the interview. He did, and instantly began rolling on the rug with another boy.

From the corner, on a baby grand piano left to the facility by a man who had lived to 104, someone started to play, tentatively at first, and then, when even the noisiest boys calmed down, more boldly. Frank moved close to Lilia and told her that it was a Bach minuet. Frank took pride in his knowledge and could not refrain from sharing it with Lilia whenever he deemed it necessary.

Ever so expectedly, it was Lilia's girl interviewer who was enchanting the roomful of people. Always eager to be more than what she is, Lilia thought. Those who had finished their snacks were looking for a spot to sit down. Walter, one hand on his cane, was conducting with the other arm. When you're closer to death, you don't need much of an excuse to play at being alive again.

Lilia walked around the room, looking for the boy orphan. He was sitting under a table, on which sometimes cut flowers would be on display but today the vase was empty. Again his face took on that obtuse look. Lilia beckoned him, and he did not move.

The world might not love the boy. The world might never be in love with him. But that was okay, because there was a secret, which nobody but Lilia could reveal to him: Let me tell you something that most people don't know. They'll expect you to always remember the sweetness of being your mother's child or the bitterness of losing her. They'll bring you replacements, thinking they're doing you a favor. But trust me. The days after love are long and empty. It's up to you and me to make them less so. Those others, they are of no use to us.

LILIA, YOU'RE THE KIND OF GIRL MY FUTURE WIFE WOULD disapprove of.

Roland had said that to Lilia the second time they met, the day Lucy had been conceived. Sometimes Lilia thought she could recall the exact tilt of Roland's head and the expression on his face when he said it, but when she tried harder, the man she imagined began to look more like Humphrey Bogart. How do you remember a moment as precisely as it happened sixty-five years ago? Roland's words were all that Lilia had. And Lucy, though Lucy too had become a memory. Nothing about her could be forgotten, but if Lucy had left a book, Lilia would have never opened it.

Every time Lilia turned to page 154 of Roland's diaries, she relished that line: *L—the kind of girl my future wife would disapprove of.* Roland had a habit of repeating things in his diaries. The same verdict was delivered again two pages later, though this time Lilia was mentioned alongside several other women, all of them deemed unsuitable as his wife. All went by single letters.

Roland spared no one from his repetitiveness. There was G, a ballerina, who showed up three times within ten pages in 1943, and in all three entries Roland had compared her to a pinwheel that would not last a month or two. There was S, "a doll who mistakes sentimental for romantic," and the short-lived affair (three weeks in 1956) was twice called "a bath taken out of self-hatred, in the tepid water already used by another body, with a stranger's suds clinging to one's skin." In 1972, C was said to be "widowed just at the right time." This was repeated a few pages later, with the additional words "C is a godsend. I am a godsend to her, too." But C disappears within the next twenty pages, while Hetty has another fifteen years to live as Roland's wife.

On that day, when Roland spoke of his future wife to Lilia, he had been sitting in the hotel bed and smoking what he said would be the last cigarette. It was late afternoon, and the fog from the Pacific was coming in. The Golden Gate Bridge, framed by the west-facing window, was half suspended in the mist, and it would soon become invisible when the night fell. Lilia was incredulous that they were there alone. It was a perfect movie set for a perfect love affair. He was worldly and handsome, she was young and seductive. Where were the people who should be busying themselves around them with cameras and lighting?

Why so quiet? Roland asked when Lilia didn't reply. I meant it as a compliment.

Why would your future wife disapprove of me? Lilia asked.

Why else would I marry her?

Later, when Lilia was getting ready to leave, she asked him when their next meeting would be.

Why? Roland said.

Because there's always a next time, Lilia said.

Nobody can guarantee that, he said. I could be run over by a streetcar the moment I step out of the hotel. You could fall in love tomorrow and be married by Saturday.

But things like that don't happen to us.

Why not? What makes you and me different from others?

We aren't nice people, Lilia said. Tragedies only happen to people nicer than us.

And love at first sight?

To fools.

Roland laughed. You're the kind of girl who could charm Sidelle Ogden, he said, when she's in the mood to be charmed.

On that day Lilia didn't ask herself why Roland mentioned Sidelle. Later she would understand two things: Roland's need to talk about Sidelle with someone was urgent, and Lilia mattered so little that she might as well be the headboard.

The kind of woman who is a cross between a nymph and a witch, Roland had said when Lilia asked what Sidelle was like.

This did little to help Lilia. Yet what did she fear? She was sixteen. Sidelle, even though Roland did not reveal her age, was much older. The younger woman always wins.

I don't see why I should care about charming Miss Ogden.

Mrs., Roland corrected her. There used to be a Mr. Ogden.

He died? Lilia asked.

He did, unfortunately.

You must be happy.

Happy? No. I appreciated Mr. Ogden as much as Sidelle. I would even say we both have to bear the unbearable loss. But of course you're too young to understand that.

You didn't think of me as too young to be a lover.

You don't think of yourself as too young to take a lover, Roland said. Look, I don't mean it lightly when I say someone can charm Sidelle. Or that someone would be disapproved of by my future wife.

Have you said these things to other girls? Lilia asked.

As a matter of fact, I have not.

What do you say to them, then?

Oh, different things.

Lilia thought for a moment, and asked again, Why would I want to charm Mrs. Ogden? She's probably old enough to be my mother. I didn't even care to charm my mother when she was alive.

Lilia's mother had died the month before. A more dutiful daughter would not have allowed a dead mother to enter this conversation, but what other woman did Lilia have in her life to call on to battle Sidelle Ogden?

You don't charm Sidelle as you would charm your mother or your aunt, Roland said.

But as your mother or your aunt?

Don't be clever. All I'm saying is, I could see her being tickled by you.

Would that make you want to marry me? Lilia said.

You, Lilia, or you, a little girl from California?

What's the difference?

I can't possibly marry a little girl from California.

But if I'm only me, if I'm only Lilia, you would marry me then?

You're too young to think about marriage.

In the old days girls my age would've had children by now.

In the old days I'd have long abandoned you, Roland said. Don't come here again. I know where to find you. Let me be the one to make decisions, will you?

So there were, Lilia calculated, future possibilities. Is that how it works with Mrs. Ogden, too? she asked. That you're the one to make the decisions?

Listen, Lilia, Roland said. Between you and me, let me always be the selfish one. There's nothing else I would ask of you, I promise.

POSTED IN THE ELEVATORS AND ON THE BULLETIN BOARDS of each floor were flyers announcing an upcoming memoir-writing class. "Wisdom to share, memories to preserve, discover the inner writer" and so on and so forth. It was the talk of the day. Lilia could already guess who had signed up, who would be coerced to attend, and who would refuse only to regret it later. The class would run for eight weeks, and the announcement called it "perfect timing," ending just before the holiday season, as everyone would produce "a precious record," "a priceless jewel," "a special gift for the special ones."

Eight weeks! Long enough for any one of them to drop dead from an accident. Or for one person to fall in love with another person, though love was a trickier business than death. The week before, Calvin's children had terminated his contract abruptly and whisked him to Portland, Oregon. Bewitched, they had said of him. At least that was the word reaching Lilia's ears, as though she had gone out of her way to cast a spell on Calvin so that he would strike them all out of his will and put Lilia's name in instead. Foolish children, foolishly vigilant. At that reunion in the next world, she would be busy enough without Calvin tugging at her elbow. He might insist on introducing Lilia to his wife. Would she be glad to see him again, or would she scurry away, hiding her face in her shawl and upsetting a drink in someone's hand while fleeing? You never know who a person really is when she is alive. Dead people will have more surprises for us.

Lilia imagined her parents, her three husbands, some of her siblings. Lucy? Oh, Lilia, let's not go there.

It must be a chaotic puppet show up there, every figure pulled by too many strings. If she went, Lilia thought, she would have to bring a pair of sharp scissors. *Snip snip snip.* What she wanted was to sit under a tree, on a bench, with a sign that said, DO NOT DIS-TURB. If only god had been considerate enough to install such a bench for Eve at the beginning. You know god is a man because he thinks a woman is always waiting to be approached.

No, at that party Lilia would make her stance known. Nobody would disturb her, except Roland. If a man approached a woman sitting next to a sign saying DO NOT DISTURB, it would have to be Roland.

"What do you think?" Dolores asked. She had taken the seat next to Lilia before some man could.

"About what?" Lilia said.

"The memoir-writing class. Won't it be fun?" Dolores said.

Isn't it enough, Lilia thought, that already most of them sit around doing nothing but reminisce about the good old days? To spend extra time spelling them out—what lengths do people go to to make themselves believe that they have lived a memorable life?

"There's so much we can talk about. I for one already have several ideas brewing," Dolores said.

"And we can all look like mutton dressed as lamb?" Lilia asked.

Dolores did not look as though she had comprehended Lilia. Was it the wrong idiom?

No need to cry over cracked eggs, Lilia's mother had said shortly before she died. Her hip bone had fractured, but no one expected her to die that night—not from the broken bone but from an injury to her head. Earlier that day she had gone up to the attic. Looking for a pair of overalls, she said when Lilia's father called from below, demanding to know what she was after. Make a list of what you need, he said. Hayes or Jack can get them for you.

He had not understood that her journeys to the attic, increasingly frequent in that last year of her life, had been a protest. There were other places on the ranch if she had wanted simply to escape her husband. Instead, she insisted on climbing up to the attic, but only when he was around. When she slipped and tumbled down the ladder, he said that a lesson must be learned.

No need to cry over cracked eggs, but who was crying then? The jumbled idiom had baffled Lilia. She was the only one to stay at the hospital. Her father, having predicted little emergency, had forbidden her younger siblings to accompany them, and he himself had left for home just in time for supper. He was a man of strict routine.

Perhaps her mother had been consoling herself. All women must have spoken to themselves words unheard by their husbands.

"So you will say yes?" Dolores said.

"To what?" Lilia asked.

FIVE YEARS AFTER LILIA'S MOTHER MARRIED HER FATHER, an uncle of hers died and left her and all of her female cousins a small amount of money each. Long after the money was gone, Lilia's father had still not tired of complaining. The uncle, who had never married and had not left Missouri for the west as several of his siblings had done, kept a tobacco shop and only sold it toward the end of his life. A bad deal, was what Lilia's father called it, because no one would hesitate to cheat a dying man. At least he could have arranged for a family member or two with some brains to help him, Lilia's father said. His audience all knew that he was thinking of himself as the ideal candidate, and they all knew that he had no business sense.

The money, equally divided among the old man's nieces—he had not included any nephew in his benevolence—had not been much, and Lilia's father had thought of that as an insult to the ones who could use some real help, Lilia's mother among them. That money was only a pittance to Cousin Essie, who had married into a Greek family developing estates in Sacramento, so why include her? Or Cousin Maude who wasn't even on speaking terms with most of the family? Surely it's good for anyone to be thought of by a man who's about to die, Lilia's mother had replied once. He looked at her contemptuously, and she looked back blankly, as though to say she had given him a genuine answer to the questions he had asked.

Such a trick you could do with money. Lilia's mother had met the uncle only twice when she was small, and she had had little recollection of him. But he had successfully turned himself into a residential ghost in Lilia's family. Maybe in the families of other cousins, too. Money always makes a good ghost story.

What Lilia's father had deemed unforgivable was that Lilia's mother had kept the inheritance from their household, where every corner was in need of money, every child's arrival a threat to the bank account. Without consulting anyone, Lilia's mother signed up for a writing course at a correspondence school, with the hope of making some money if she could publish stories—at least that was what she had said to Lilia's father.

Lilia was four then, Hayes two, the twins mere sucklings. Jack and Kenny would come along in a few years, and all of them would listen to their father's lament until the woe became their own (Hayes and Jack) or a private joke (Lilia, Lucille, and Margot). Not Kenny, though. He had been eight when their mother died. Some people blamed this early loss for his going to the wrong side of life. But there are many motherless sons. Not every one of them rushes through life until landing behind the bars.

Lilia did not have any recollection of her mother's literary pursuit, but she had saved the folder of papers before her father could burn them along with the letters her mother had received and bundled by year, most of them from two school friends. Lilia did not know the two correspondents. Perhaps those long letters from her mother to them had survived, though what could she have written? Lilia was not a sentimentalist, but even a sentimental woman had only so much to say about a ranch life that rarely changed from day to day, season to season. Husband and children? It was away from them that her mother had been running in her letters. Lilia thought about Peter Wilson's complaint about Roland's repetitiveness. Show me one person who has not lived in repetition. Only many people, unlike Roland or her mother, dare not keep a record.

It remained a mystery where Lilia's mother had got the idea of taking the correspondence course. She had been a dreamer, no question about that, but why not dream about something more concrete. She was a handsome woman, and never went out to the vegetable garden or to milk the cows without combing her hair carefully and arranging a spray of bridal wreath or a cluster of as-ters in her hair. Her short-lived enthusiasm for writing stories was, for a time, replaced by an interest in sewing. She made clothes for herself and her children, a bit fanciful for anyone living on a ranch, and when the boys were old enough to grumble, she gave up sewing, becoming more distracted by the day.

What a bunch of disappointments they must have been for her mother. Someone—a ranch hand, a shop owner, a traveling salesman of ballpoint pens—should have fallen in love with her and provided her with another dream, but she had remained a faithful wife, ever impractical while enduring a practical husband.

When Lilia's mother was alive, and especially when she was within earshot, Lilia's father liked to repeat the tale of her literary failure. He acted out his agonizing over the monthly remittance to the school in Chicago. All humbug, he said, but she had become so absentminded. The way she fed her chickens while thinking about princes and castles, he said, he could've married another woman and had another litter of children and she wouldn't have noticed.

I wish you had, Lilia's mother once replied. Lilia's father and his friends, who had been throwing horseshoes, all paused, while she placed a jug of punch on a bench, as though she had just made a comment about the weather.

Most men are undertakers of their women's dreams. And, of course, most women are undertakers of their men's dreams, too. But for Lilia's father, there was the extra obsession that he kept exhuming what he had buried. He was never violent, and he did not drink excessively. A man with little capacity for joy or vice, he derived his only pleasure from tormenting his wife with a tale in which he did not have a place. And she did that to him, too.

"I'VE LIVED A LONG AND GOOD LIFE AMONG HUSBANDS and children and gardens. I've lived a self-contained life. I'm what you call a happy woman."

What nonsense! Lilia erased the words that she was writing in her mind. All good lives are self-contained. All happiness, too. Who wants to pull open that drawer called life for others to see? Here's how I've bundled up some old flame in wrapping tissue. Here's where I've placed husbands, separated by dividers. Here are children and grandchildren, all fitted together like Lego pieces. Parents and siblings? Their photos are stacked up there. The dried flowers covering them are forget-me-nots. And now, have you had enough of the view? Lilia laughed when she imagined herself shutting the drawer to a pair of gawking eyes. No, the better thing was not to open it for anyone.

Dolores had asked Lilia again to join the memoir class. Imagine what treasure you can leave to your children and grandchildren, Dolores said.

Other than her collection of baubles, Lilia had not much to bequeath to her children and grandchildren. Photo albums they could share among themselves, and Lilia suspected that one day, sooner rather than later, they—her grandparents, her parents, aunts and uncles, long-lost cousins, her siblings, and herself—all of them would end up in antiques shops. A customer might finger the pages while thinking about a lover or a family trouble. Another customer, out of habit, might look at the price tag and put down the album without opening it. In time the dead no longer remain individually dead. You're all bundled together, and no one is deader than any other.

Lilia did not believe in that nonsense about keeping the dead alive through love, but she wouldn't mind having someone to keep her from being generally and generically dead. Family members you might be able to trust for a short time. A year, perhaps two years at most. Then what? Sometimes it's the unexpected people, those you've forgotten or those you've never met, who keep you from oblivion. Look at Roland. And Sidelle. Were it not for Lilia, they would not have survived their deaths. (Sidelle wouldn't have cared, but Roland would've suffered in his grave.)

After Lilia's death, who would do that for her? And for them all?

If there was one thing Lilia had been unwilling to leave to her offspring, it was her own life story. They knew bits and pieces, from being parts of it, but what she had not intended for them to know would never become their possession. Let her past remain unknown and burned to ashes with her. Let her offspring gather on a rented boat and scatter the ashes into the Pacific. When Lilia had first let her children know that this was her wish, they had questioned her. Her two latter husbands were buried next to their first wives. She could see that her children thought it appropriate that she be buried next to Gilbert. They didn't understand that Lilia had only her own heart's orders to follow, but then she couldn't really blame them. She never cared for her heart to be known. Every time Lilia heard the phrase "the key to my heart" she laughed. A lock only invites a burglar.

Understanding or not, her children would do their best to send her off, Will calling his pals to arrange a discount for a boat, Tim dragging his family back from Tacoma, Carol and Molly making everything look as sentimental as in a movie. Katherine and Iola? They would look out of place among the family, but they were the two people who would miss Lilia the most. She would miss those two, too, if a dead person could miss the people left behind.

Halt, halt, easy now. Better not to go down that path.

Lilia would not mind ending up landlocked in the backyard of 23 Roosevelt Road. Gilbert and she had bought the house in 1956. Orinda, separated from San Francisco by the Bay and further by the Caldecott Tunnel, was hardly a town then. His parents mourned as if their son was to move to another country. Lilia was disappointed about leaving the city, though this she did not show; and what she decided not to show, Gilbert would never have guessed. He had set his heart on a three-story house with a large backyard. He wanted something concrete and affordable, so why not let him have it. She herself could make a life anywhere.

Lilia never liked the phrase "rest in peace," a saying, she believed, invented to make death sound both ordinary and rewarding. What about "rest in oblivion"? Less pressure for both the living and the dead! Still, if she wanted to give an RIP version of her life, that house would tell her stories. There she and Gilbert had raised five children, a granddaughter, plus three puppies and generations of hamsters. She had made a garden, where the dogs and hamsters had been buried. They had received the policemen in the living room when they had come with the news of Lucy's death, insisting that everyone sit down, as though that would have made any difference. In the last months of Gilbert's life he had slept in the living room, but when he was near death he asked to be removed to the hospice. It would be good, he said, that he died elsewhere so as not to dent the house's value. Who cares about the house's value now? Lilia argued. He said the house was the only thing he could leave her, and he wanted it to be in its best possible condition.

Gilbert, Lilia knew, wouldn't have minded that she remained his widow, but she had not liked to live as a widow. She had held on to the house when she remarried, and true to Gilbert's wish, the house, sold in the summer of 2007, would sustain Lilia as long as she didn't live forever. In an ideal world it would make sense for her ashes to return to that place, but Lilia could not insist on nourishing a stranger's garden after this life. People there might think of her as an intrusive ghost. The truth was, her ghost would have zero interest in them. But put a ghost in any story and you'll get many volunteers to be haunted!

Ah well, off she'll go, to the water.

"What are you doing?" Nancy said.

The door, which Lilia had kept ajar so one of the girls could come in and change her sheets, had been pushed open. Nancy was harmless, and Lilia had nothing against her except that Nancy thought of herself as a darling Shirley Temple. Lilia had always resented that dimpled starlet with her shiny shoes and saccharine smile. She had once told Nancy that, as a child, she used to fantasize about cutting the curls off the little dolly. It was not true, but Lilia had wanted to hear Nancy gasp. And Nancy more than gasped. She told Lilia that her older sister, who was not as pretty as she was, had once sheared all the curls off Nancy's head when she was taking a nap. Even my mother cried, Nancy had said.

Lilia looked at Nancy, waiting to hear what she wanted from her. "Why were you flapping your hands like a bird?" Nancy asked. "I was invited to watch a documentary the other day and they said that was a sign of autism."

"I didn't know you were interested in science."

"Dale invited me. You know how he's always into these things."

"I don't know," Lilia said. "And I'm too old to have autism."

"Then why were you doing this?" Nancy asked, turning her own arms into a pair of undulating wings.

"Pretending to scatter ashes," Lilia said. "Cremains."

"Whose cremains?"

Lilia took on a thoughtful look, prolonging the moment before Nancy's gasp. "Mine," she replied finally.

Nancy gasped. "That's morbid, Lilia! Besides, you can't scatter your own ashes."

"Why else would I be pretending? Do you pretend to be your husband's wife? Do you pretend to eat your food at breakfast? Do you pretend to sleep in your own bed? You can, however, pretend that you sleep in a coffin."

"I don't know what you're talking about," Nancy said.

"Pretending is a way to do things that otherwise you don't get to do."

"Including things we could do in the past but no longer can?"

Nancy said, looking coy as though she were blushing. She was not, Lilia decided. It was just the rouge she wore. "Oh, Lilia, I need your advice. Should I say yes to Dale?"

"Did he propose to you?"

"No, but he asked if we could spend more time by ourselves."

"What are you going to do?"

"We can watch some programs he likes. Take walks. Do you know he has ten siblings? The only one who didn't live to ninety was their littlest brother."

"How old is Dale?"

"Not that old. He has good genes. Do you know he was a policeman before he became a private detective? I thought the lady who used to visit him was his wife. Turned out she was only a neighbor. Peggy Horn. When her husband was alive, he and Dale were not on speaking terms."

"Was she being naughty with Dale? Were they caught by her husband?"

"Lilia! Dale is a good man," Nancy said.

"We can't really be sure about that," Lilia said. "Why did she visit Dale then?"

"He didn't know! She insisted on visiting him."

"Maybe she was doing that to annoy her husband in his grave," Lilia said.

"You always make people sound weird," Nancy said.

"Why isn't she coming anymore?"

"She died in April."

"Is that why Dale wants you to be a special friend, now that Peggy Horn is gone?"

Nancy closed her eyes. Lilia had noticed that when Nancy didn't want to answer a question she would blink in a slow-motion manner. "If I don't say yes he may ask another person," Nancy said when she opened her eyes. "It's not that I'm particularly fond of Dale, but I don't want to see him sit with someone else after he already asked me."

"By all means say yes!"

"You make it sound like an engagement."

"Trust me, I've married three times and it's always fun to say yes," Lilia said. Even Hetty, that woman made of marble, must have felt a moment of thrill when Roland proposed.

ETWEEN FURNITURE AND GARDENS, LILIA HAD ALWAYS preferred gardens. This was not a confession. Nevertheless it was a fact worth sharing aloud with her room, for which she had no fondness. The dresser and the armchair, from her marriage with Gilbert, had moved in with her. Some other furniture had been shed like skin when she married Norman and again when she married Milt. The move to Bayside Garden, however, was not about shedding skin, but cutting loose a few fingers. No, a limb or two. Lilia had not let herself feel sentimental. Having outlived her three husbands, the table and the chairs and the buffet and that old armoire Gilbert's parents had given them as a wedding present had taken on a kind of coldness. Like friends and family all of a sudden looking distracted after throwing the flowers onto the casket. They were thinking about their suppers, or their toes pinched by new shoes in need of breaking in, or the dry cleaning fee for their black suits.

What Lilia did miss, when she moved around her room or watched the world from her seventh-floor window, were her gardens. They were what she had to surrender with each move. Gardens never uprooted themselves for anyone. A garden stays put, nonchalantly and disloyally blossoming for the newcomers.

"If I want to write about my life I would write about the gardens," Lilia said. No one was listening, and that was what she wanted. Lilia had two voices, one for other ears, one for her own. She was not alone in this, but people often made the mistake of letting the latter voice bleed into the former. A sign of weakness, or a sign of aging—Lilia allowed neither. The voice she used with her fellow residents was the one she had long settled on between the world and herself—one size fits all! When her children called, she sounded friendly, accommodating, cheerful, busy—whatever would put them at ease. The tricky case was Katherine. Lilia couldn't be merely fuzzy and warm and absentminded, like a grandmother; and she couldn't be demanding or polite or passive-aggressive, like a mother. Katherine was Lucy's daughter before she was Lilia's granddaughter, and it was on Lucy's behalf that Lilia brought up the girl. But how do you speak to a granddaughter in her dead mother's stead? Can the responsibility to the dead ever be replaced by the responsibility to the living?

A mother is always a cautionary tale for a daughter. Lilia did not mind if Carol and Molly treated her as one. Lucy? But it was too long ago, and Lilia did not want to think of herself in Lucy's eyes. Lilia's own mother, greedy for happiness that would never be reached, had settled for the rapture of misery. Even when she should have felt contented, she had wasted no time in feeling the injustices done to her. For instance: Kenny as a baby, rosy-cheeked, sleeping in a white wicker bassinet under the weeping cherry in their garden. Lilia calculated—she was eight then, so her mother was thirty.

Let's hope he doesn't break too many girls' hearts when he grows up, her mother had said.

Even at eight, Lilia could see through her mother. She was hoping for the opposite. The many hearts Kenny would destroy would make his mother proud.

But by then there won't be a place in his heart for his old mother, Lilia's mother added, kissing each of the baby fingers. Lilia looked on with abhorrence. Her mother was only waiting for Kenny to get older, as the witch waited for Hansel to fatten up. Lilia and her other siblings did not give their mother the same appetite.

They all had mothers to judge or to love, but not Katherine. She did not know where her life came from.

I'm the oldest of six children. My father's side came to California from Lithuania. My mother's side came from Missouri. We are: Lilia, Hayes, Lucille and Margot (twins), Jack, and Kenny. Our fa-

ther liked a big family so our mother gave him that. She tried her best to love all her children. She only achieved that with one of us, and I believe she chose the wrong one.

Erase? Erase, yes. Lilia did not like that her mind was making up its own mind to talk about these things as if for an audience. Lilia never cared for the stage, not out of shyness or timidity but because the stage was a set thing, and anything set bored her.

Most people live on a stage, though. Some feel they are pushed onto it. Others constantly seek it. Life would have been bleak for Roland if not for all those people he imagined were observing him with admiration or envy. Did he count Lilia among them? As much as he counted other women who had once been known to him and then forgotten?

On the way back from the pub David said, I didn't realise you knew so many people in this town. Have you visited before? No, I said, and I don't know any of them. The point is, I explained to David, they see me greet people and think to themselves, look at that lucky bastard with so many friends. Then when I greet them they will think themselves lucky because they now appear to be connected to me.

That entry from July 1929 — Lilia did not have to open the book to remember it, though she liked to reread these words. Roland had written it when he and his friends traveled to Prince Edward Island. Those people whose eyes he had so cherished had long been dead. It was his fortune that someone was still here, watching him, seeing him, seeing through him, but with fondness, so he wouldn't feel that he was strutting around naked. (Oh but, ho-hoho, he would've loved that.)

Longevity is required for loyalty, and true vindictiveness is like true loyalty, neither of which you can boast of unless you have outlived the shelf life of those perishable feelings called love and hatred. To live a long life is to weed out the people who do not deserve either loyalty or vindictiveness. Lilia always preferred those flowers that blossomed all season long.

DEAR ROLAND, I'M SORRY THAT YOU NEVER LEARNED *about the birth and the death of your daughter. She was very much your and my daughter: good-looking and difficult.*

Time and again Lilia began this letter in her head whenever she reread Roland's entries of February 1946, but she had never written it down until now. He was sailing from England to Canada, toward his future bride. Lilia was a week overdue with Lucy. She didn't mind carrying the baby longer. Her mother-in-law and women like her would pay close attention to the calendar when a marriage happened hastily.

What if Lucy had died as an infant? You hear such stories, babies stillborn or having only a brief life. Of course, Lilia might have died giving birth, but she was not the kind of woman who would die in labor. Just like the mares—one look and you'd know which would be the troublesome ones at foaling. You can't explain that to people who don't understand. Some creatures are just born with more life in them.

But suppose Lucy had never really lived but for the short period in Lilia's womb? Would it have been felt by Lilia as a punishment? Or a liberation? The slate between Gilbert and her would have been wiped clean. What would have become of their marriage then?

An untimely death always has mystery in it. And hypothetically untimely death? Lilia might have set out to look for Roland. But equally possibly, she might have forgotten him. Perhaps Lucy lived so Lilia would remember Roland. And Lucy died young so that there was no way for Lilia to forget Roland. There was no way to get even with him, was there? To be forgotten was a defeat. To be doomed to remember someone was a defeat, too. Lilia hated to be defeated.

Lucy broke many hearts. Except Roland's. He was not heartless, but he would not let his precious heart receive even a scrape. Poor Lucy. No, poor Gilbert. Having his heart broken when someone else should have suffered in his place.

Oh shush! There was no reason to get upset now, except Lilia felt funny this morning. Indigestion, heartburn, palpitation, but not one of them was quite what she was feeling. Perhaps she was simply disturbed by the conversation at breakfast about the writing class. The instructor, a Kurdish-Iranian-American woman, was said to be fiercely funny by some, hard to follow by others, impossibly impertinent by Elaine.

"Too bad you're not taking the class," Dolores had said to Lilia at breakfast. Repetition was the only aggressive behavior Dolores had mastered (or retained), a weak weapon, like a toy knife in a toddler's kitchen set, yet it left a mark on Lilia. No, no blood drawn, but who knew the leathery skin of old age could become sensitive to nuisance?

"I'm glad you're enjoying it," Lilia said.

"I sure am," Dolores said. "I only wish you were part of it, too."

Lilia imagined Dolores as a plump, well-dressed, golden roasted turkey looking pitifully at a wild turkey outside the window and saying: Too bad you have to walk in the darkness by yourself. The thought braced Lilia for a few more sympathetic words from Dolores. If Lilia were to trek anywhere down memory lane, she wanted to do it alone.

Dear Roland, I'm sorry that you never learned about the birth and the death of your daughter. She was very much your and my daughter: good-looking and difficult. Lilia reread what she had written, and added: *But unlike you and me she didn't know how to make use of these traits.* The words didn't really say what she wanted to say, but they came close.

PART TWO

———

Days Last Past

ANOTHER BIRTHDAY. ALL BIRTHDAYS ARE ACCOMPLISH-
ments, but this time someone was turning ninety. The birthday
boy, a retired philosophy professor from Stanford, would deliver a
lecture on the day. "We don't have to invite an outside speaker this
fall," Jean said when she made the announcement.

"As though she needs to worry about her budget," Lilia said,
loud enough for Jean to hear. Bayside Garden had a well-endowed
performance series. The only unsuccessful presenter during Lilia's
residency had been a mindfulness expert—more than half the audience fell into uncomfortable sleep. The best had been a twelve-
year-old boy, who had won second place in an all-state magician
contest in Sacramento. Such a handsome young man, his dexter-
ous hands and shy smile just the right combination to enchant his
audience. Some asked him to repeat the same tricks. Others demanded he reveal the secrets. The show, scheduled for thirty minutes, had lasted an hour and a half.

"I like birthdays," Nancy said. "I share mine with Julius Caesar.
I remember my father told me who Julius Caesar was on my seventh birthday."

"I share my birthday with Barbara Bush," someone said. "But
she's older than me."

"If you think about it, we never ask ourselves whose death date
we'll be sharing," Lilia said. "That's one thing I would die to know."

The day after her mother died, Lilia had accompanied her father to the funeral home in Vallejo. As they left, she noticed the
unusual crowds in the street. Women wept. Men, too, some quietly
taking off their glasses and pressing handkerchiefs to their eyes,
others baring their wounded faces to the sky. At the next block a
black maid threw open a third-floor window of a boardinghouse.
He died, she wailed, he died. That night, listening to the news of

President Roosevelt's death, Lilia wished her mother had lived a day longer. All those tears shed and her mother didn't even have a drop to herself.

"Let's focus on the birthday party," Jean said.

"We should throw confetti," Lilia said. "We should all blow horns and shout surprise."

"We don't do anything like that here, for health and safety reasons," Elaine said. She had moved into Bayside Garden a month after Lilia, and the first time she had introduced herself, she had said emphatically that her strength was to be a leader. If you think I'm not good at listening, it's because I haven't met many people whose opinions are worth listening to, Elaine said. Lilia laughed out loud, and laughed again when she realized that the other people only nodded, perhaps out of politeness. But sheep are polite too, following one another to the slaughterhouse, not questioning anything.

"Mark Twain died on his birthday," Owen, who sat at a nearby table, said aloud.

Frank, that encyclopedia in residence, said Owen was wrong. Mark Twain didn't die on his birthday, but Halley's Comet was in the sky on both his birth and death days. "I bet you knew it," Frank, who never sat far from Lilia, said to her.

Lilia wanted to make a joke about death days, but before she could come up with something clever her heart seemed to skip a beat. It didn't. It was that sudden emptiness, which was Lucy's doing. It was worse than having your heart broken. If someone broke your heart, you could still gather the pieces and glue them back, or just leave them scattered around, evidence of what was once your heart. But Lucy's trick was to make that heart disappear. Like the boy magician. Anything could disappear when he put it in a hat or under a handkerchief. But he gave back whatever he vanished.

Lilia turned her mind to other deaths, some recent, some in the remote past. That emptiness could be as fatal as a heart attack, and she had trained herself, faster than the most experienced first responders. Enough people had died on Lilia. But they were more or less in the right order, and the pains they left were the tolerable kind, losing their sharp edges with each month and each year passing. Her grandparents, her parents, some of her siblings, her husbands. And Roland. She didn't count Roland as dead dead, but he, like the others, let Lilia move her fingers around until they could feel the outline of that heart. Yes, back here again, sturdy, almost stone-hard. Oh, that heart. It did play the vanishing trick on her once in a while.

A FEW MONTHS BEFORE THE DEATH OF LILIA'S MOTHER, Lilia's father had joined Mr. Williamson in an investment. The idea of combining their ranch with the Williamson Inn as an attraction had been Mr. Williamson's. With the return from war of sailors and soldiers, he had reasoned, and with the guests for the international peace conference in San Francisco, they could start a business of lodging and horseback riding for those who needed a break. Once established, they could advertise it to the locals as a place for weekend outings and family gatherings.

The inn and the ranch were close enough to the city, yet far enough to claim the idyllic-ness of the countryside. Both had been established early enough to claim being historical; both families had been in the state long enough to be called true Californians. The prospect, no doubt dangled by Mr. Williamson as bait in front of Lilia's father, was presented to the family at supper. California is the future, but exactly for that reason, a ranch that brought back the past would be appealing. When everything changes around us, Lilia's father said, we can make a fortune from not changing. The words must have been fed to him by Mr. Williamson.

Why is that, Hayes asked, not questioning but giving their father an opportunity to go on talking. A few months short of turning fifteen, Hayes had already begun to think of the ranch as his. Nothing had been said in the family, but Lilia suspected that their father had made some sort of promise to Hayes in private.

People have fancies about the old time, Lilia's father said. And we can make money out of their fancies.

Mr. Williamson's sales pitch, Lilia thought, word for word.

Sounds like a great idea, Hayes said. What do you think, Ma?

The children turned to her. They knew their father didn't need anything from her but to say it was a good idea. They knew, too, that Hayes had spoken twice because of her silence. With a shrewder mind than their father, Hayes was on good terms with both his parents and his siblings. Lilia respected him for his calculation.

Their mother shrugged, cutting a potato into two perfect halves.

People go in for that kind of recreation, Lilia's father said, raising his voice. That you don't know how to enjoy life doesn't mean others don't. After years of marriage, Lilia's mother still held some power over her father in her expressionless face, which made Lilia pity him. He still did not understand that the more provoked he appeared, the more powerless he would look in front of his wife and children.

Lilia knew that her mother would not bother to voice her objection. We're doing fine, Lilia said. Why do we have to change just to help the Williamsons out?

The inn, which once bore the majestic name of the Empire Inn, had been built by Mr. Williamson's great-grandfather, and it had served well the travelers between San Francisco and the mining towns up north. But by then it had more stories to boast of than prosperity. An inn did not renew itself every year like livestock or vegetables.

Young lady, nobody is asking your opinion, Lilia's father said. He could've said something nastier, but Lilia had turned sixteen the month before, and he felt it necessary to give her some respect as a grown-up woman.

You know what's best, Lilia's mother said placidly, looking around the table at each of her children, pausing just long enough, Lilia thought, to register their names and ages. She would have given them the same look had there been an earthquake that had destroyed everything but spared her children's lives. So you're all here—that look would have said—and I still have to find a way to mother you till we are freed from each other one day.

Lilia's mother had married the wrong man. It was like boarding a train that never takes you in the right direction, let alone to the destination you have in mind. The farther it travels, the less point there is in going on, and the lesser in getting off. What was unforgivable, though, was that she was the kind of woman for whom any husband would be the wrong husband. Why marry, then?

Lilia's mother had hoped that Lilia would go into nursing, but she had had no interest in alleviating other people's suffering. Her beauty would have been a waste in a hospital ward, as her mother's was a waste on the ranch. Instead, Lilia had set her heart on enrolling at a secretarial school in the city. When she saved enough money for a place to live she would leave the ranch, and once she finished her training she would wear heels and lipstick every day to work, living in a room paid for by her own wages and going to movies with men who knew the world like the backs of their hands.

The Williamson-Liska venture turned out to be more than just a retreat for innocent souls, though Lilia's father refused to admit that he had assisted the immoral sailors and soldiers and their girls, who were temporary and interchangeable to those rowdy young men. The reputation of the place must have traveled fast. Some of the girls had become returning customers, bringing different men with them and calling themselves by different names.

Lilia and her siblings had much more to say to one another now. The dinner conversation, supervised by their parents, was drab as ever. But promiscuousness penetrated like mold, its spores in the air, its odor in every room—except it was not mold, but something more captivating. Even Kenny absorbed the excitement like a greedy sponge. They were resourceful children, and they competed to make anything out of what little they had access to. Their father's misjudgment and the regret he would not voice only added to their pleasure.

The most salacious encounters happened over at the inn. Other than Lilia, the children were forbidden to go near it. She observed the girls walking up the staircase and studying themselves in the mirror on the second-floor landing. Some looked more experienced, others only a year or two older than Lilia. None was as pretty as she was. You could see that in the young men's eyes, but Lilia did not need their confirmation. The mirror was her truest friend.

Where were these girls from? What kind of lives did they have before arriving at the inn? One afternoon when she was saddling Dee Dee for a girl named Betsy—the young man who had come with her was sleeping—Lilia asked Betsy about her life. It was her third visit to the inn, and she seemed eager to talk. She said that she did not have parents. She was raised by her grandparents in Butte, Montana, and after they died she had sold everything and boarded the train for California. Did they tell you who your parents were? Lilia asked. Betsy said, Not really. In fact, she wasn't sure if they were her mother's parents or her father's. Do you have siblings? Lilia asked, and Betsy said no, she was left to her grandparents as an infant. The thought of being an only child fascinated Lilia, like being the only horse or the only cow on a ranch. How do you fight for anything if you are the only one? Betsy, who was not pretty but sweet, did not return after that day. Lilia imagined her falling in love with a soldier and getting married. But would that be it? Lilia wasn't sure. She made up a second story, in which Betsy was murdered because a girl like that, without anyone to watch out for her and without the upbringing to teach her how to fight, could end up badly.

All visitors were an education for Lilia. From watching the girls she had learned to narrow her shirts at the right place. She had chosen ribbons of different colors and shades that would go with her red hair, emerald green on foggy days, mint green or creamy white on sunny days. From serving the men she learned to be playful but keep a crucial distance. Still, she felt listless. And this feeling was strongest when some of the men would let their fingers linger on her wrist when she handed over the reins, or else they would whisper a few words of endearment when no one was around. They all wanted her, she knew, but their wanting her did not make them more attractive. Hunger and appetite were two different things. Those men, who were mere morsels, wanted Lilia to feel as hungry for them as they felt for her. But she had no use for hunger, which only destroyed appetite and led people to tasteless errors. Yet within a short time after the business opened, her appetite had been sharpened. For what, though, she wasn't entirely sure.

The week before Roland and his friends visited the ranch, Mr. Williamson's daughter Maggie had come down with German measles, and the two girls hired to clean the rooms caught it from her. Mrs. Williamson, nursing the quarantined girls, had sent her younger children to stay with her cousin and was in dire need of a female helper. Lilia's twin sisters, Margot and Lucille, were not old enough to be allowed to witness the soiled side of love, and after haggling with Mr. Williamson for a higher rate than the two regular girls were paid, Lilia agreed to fill in.

It was a busy weekend. Some sailors had asked to pay a fraction of the price for a shorter stay. A couple hours, one of them said, good deal all around. Lilia's father was paid by the visitors coming for horseback rides. Not every young man was interested in bringing his girl over at extra expense, and the unevenness of what the two partners made was never addressed. Lilia's father was the kind of man who always trusted the judgment of people outside the household, which he easily took as his own judgment. And he would do more for anyone in the name of friendship than for his own family. Mr. Williamson, beady-eyed, had worked it out all for himself.

What was worse, to have a fool as a father, or a mother who had married the fool and given you life?

On the day Roland arrived, Lilia was in a dark mood. By the time Mr. Williamson led him and his friends upstairs, late in the afternoon, she was already worn out by having changed the sheets and pillowcases multiple times and having to breathe in other people's sordidness. She heard Mr. Williamson apologize, saying they only had two rooms and an extra in the attic left. Let's take a look, someone replied, and then said something in another language. Lilia did not recognize the language, but whatever the man spoke, even in another tongue, did not repel her as the sailors' words did. The man spoke the way movie stars did, unhurried because they had all the money and time in the world.

Four men followed Mr. Williamson into a room, three in dark suits and one in a cream-colored suit with a matching fedora. Lilia knew right away that the man in the light-colored suit was the owner of the voice she had heard. He dressed to stand out among a crowd.

Are the other two rooms like this, too? he asked.

Lilia had slipped into the room just before their entrance. She looked up as though caught in surprise, her hands arrested in the middle of arranging a bouquet of larkspur. Lilia's mother had loved wildflowers, arranging them in jars on the windowsill or wearing them in her hair, not to impress men but to make the flowers her allies against them. Lilia had decided that flowers in her hands would be more welcoming to the right men.

Yes, Mr. Williamson said, but I can bring in a cot if two of your gentlemen don't mind sharing a room for one night. Tomorrow we'll have vacancies.

I'm afraid these rooms are too small to be shared, the man said.

Lilia laughed. Even the dullest among the foreigners looked at her. Hello, the man in the light-colored suit said, what's so funny?

Of course three rooms are not enough for the four of you, Lilia said, unless one of you were a lady.

How do you know we can't make do with the rooms? the man said to Lilia. These gentlemen, like myself, have come from war zones. We've all seen worse.

She looked the men up and down. You're not dressed for war, she said, and you're not here for war. Besides, you yourself said these rooms were too small.

Mr. Williamson told Lilia that her father must be waiting for her to get supper ready. He tapped the face of his new wristwatch and looked at Lilia sharply.

Mr. Williamson, remember I'm to be here all day? Margot is cooking today.

The man spoke with his friends. One of them, a short man with chubby cheeks and dark bags under his eyes, seemed alarmed. *Non*, he replied when Lilia's friend—who else could he be but her friend, having already exchanged words and smiles with her—said something to placate him. *Non*, he insisted, and the other two men shook their heads, too, with resignation.

The man argued courteously in the foreign tongue. He had a narrow face, shaved to a blue shade. She lingered, rearranging the flowers and taking one out to put behind her right ear. She'd like to see how this man, who had introduced himself as Roland, managed to get what he wanted. He looked like that kind of man.

The short man looked sterner. Roland sighed and asked Mr. Williamson where the horses were kept. Some riding might put these gentlemen in a better mood, he said.

What's so difficult? Lilia said. If you need one more room, we can put you up in our house.

You can? Roland asked.

Lilia recognized a light in his eyes—he wanted the room desperately. Oh, but one of you would have to put up with the inconvenience of staying separately from his friends, she said.

Five minutes' walk only, Mr. Williamson said, and offered a discount for the backup room.

Roland spoke to the foreigners again. They seemed unconvinced, but he pressed on with his gentle voice until they agreed. Lilia pretended to be burdened when Mr. Williamson asked if she could show Roland his room. By sending her, she knew, Mr. Williamson would bypass the trouble of facing Lilia's father.

He had not been quite himself since her mother's death. A loveless marriage still made him a genuinely bereaved widower. And like a grieving husband he started to neglect his duties. A week ago he had left a bag of oats untied in Beau's box. If not for Hayes, who had begun to trust only himself when it came to the ranch, Beau would have devoured the oats and burst his stomach. Not wishing to undermine their father's authority yet, Hayes told only Lilia of the error and said they would have to be more careful in the future. Lilia was not particularly close to Hayes, but the two of them had shared their parents longer than the rest of their siblings. One day he would reign as their father had in this decrepit kingdom. She hoped he would marry someone more suitable to be a wife and a mother than their own. A dreamless woman, so that he wouldn't have to murder her dreams.

Lilia's father said the only room he could spare was the cottage near the stable. What about the guest room upstairs, Lilia said.

Right away Roland said he didn't mean to intrude on family life.

There was no guest room in the house, but to offer what was not there was a way to make a fool out of someone. People felt gratified or flattered. That Lilia was offering something that she did not have would never occur to them. It was like a game, with its rules only known to Lilia.

And they often gave something in return. Something they did have.

Here, no one will intrude on your quiet stay, Lilia said after she showed him the cottage, which had a small sitting area and a cot in a corner. It was clean enough.

How's your business here? Roland asked, watching Lilia change a set of bedding.

Good, Lilia said. How did you find us?

I saw an ad in the paper. I thought I would bring my friends for a change of air.

What are they?

You mean, who are they?

They're foreigners, no? Which countries are they from?

Europe, Roland said.

They've probably stayed in better places.

Nothing wrong here, Roland said. They've had a war there.

Are you from Europe, too? What are you?

Who am I, you mean? I'm Roland Bouley. I'm from a lot of places. And who are you?

I'm Lilia Liska, from Benicia, California.

You make it sound like a poem. Or a song. Have you practiced?

Lilia had never had to introduce herself to anyone like this. People in her world were those who knew her name (and her parents' and her grandparents' names). The visitors to the ranch did not mind not knowing her name. Men liked how her face and her body looked. They would put their arms around her waist or press their lips on hers if she let them, but most men did not bother to fake curiosity, just as they did not bother to hide their desires.

Why do I need to practice being myself? she said.

You're a natural poet, then.

Who needs poetry, Lilia had said on that day, and she now said it again aloud: "Who needs poetry?" Lilia had too much life in her to be contained by rhymes and rhythm, pauses and stops. The next two nights she had slipped into the cottage—perhaps other women, weaker and more sentimental, would remember the time spent with Roland as poetry, but calling it poetry would be like reducing an endless field of poppies and lupines to patches of yellow and purple. Once, a visitor did just that. He came by himself and stayed for a week at the inn. Several times Lilia had tried to strike up conversation, but he had not looked at her as he had looked at the flowers. She scoffed at him then. Why settle for something dull and dead on a small canvas, when you can have the live and the real?

12 MAY 1945.

An outing planned with Mr. T and his two colleagues, but I
have promised myself this is a personal diary and no work
is allowed to enter this space.

15 MAY 1945.

We came back to the conference yesterday. A pleasant
surprise at a true Californian Ranch. L: vivacious,
refreshing, young (how young?). And audacious. While
shaving this morning I could hear Mr. Dalsin explaining
the word audacious. My mind started right away to
conjugate. *Audeo, audes, audet, audemus, audetis,
audent.*

Who, between L and myself, is risking more? Who is
daring whom? But these questions need not be answered.
We have returned to a global stage where L has no place. I
could not even feign melancholy at the farewell yesterday,
clandestinely carried out before daybreak. She and I said
things to each other, sure, but things are always said when
two people lie in a bed meant for one, more intimately
than two people sitting at the smallest table in a restaurant.

L looked perfectly willing to believe that we would
meet again. Such confidence. She is too young to under-

stand that it is almost always a miracle that two
people meet. I, too old to be taken hostage by any miracle.

"But we did meet again, didn't we?" Lilia retorted, as she often said
to Roland when she reread this page.

On Monday afternoon a visitor, someone's daughter, brought in a giant bouquet of flowers to the dining room. They were from a wedding she had attended the day before—it took no time for Deb to find it out. "Can you guess how much the family spent on the flowers—eighty thousand dollars!"

"You must've heard it wrong," Frank said. "Must be eight thousand."

"I double-checked. My late husband was an auditor. I'm good with numbers."

"I had a client once who asked my wife and me to design a garden that would bloom all year round in white," Michael said. "Guess what her budget was? Three hundred and fifty thousand."

To feel incredulous as though there was still much to marvel at about life—Lilia wondered if by growing old, by forgetting, by pretending, they had reached the point where the world was new all over. New in what way, though? The world is your oyster but once. The second time all you have are the oyster shells, ready to be ground into powders to fertilize someone else's garden.

The brochures advertising Bayside Garden boasted of the intelligence and the longevity of its residents: an average age of eighty-seven, with sixty-seven percent having advanced degrees. Yet Lilia, below average as measured by those criteria, could easily understand the boundless strangeness of life, which seemed equally boundlessly inexplicable to her peers. It took her some effort not to point out that everyone present must have done something similarly nonsensical. Didn't Bill spend an enormous amount of money to buy his two sons VIP tickets to a Giants' game, but they left the game still not on speaking terms even though the team had won that night? And everyone had heard Gwen yelling on the phone at her sister in New Jersey, who called every time the weather forecast looked ominous on that coast. I told you before and I'll tell you one more time—Gwen, who was in general on the quieter side, would raise her voice—there's a solution. One word: California. What? What about earthquakes? We sleep through earthquakes all the time. A big one? No, it won't happen while you and I are alive.

Gwen, Lilia said once, can't you understand that your sister doesn't need your advice, doesn't want to die next to you, but only wants you to listen?

You don't know half the history between us, Gwen replied.

So? Lilia thought. History is like a credit score. Do you live your life in constant consultation with it? You take this or that action, the score gets better or worse, and you live with the result.

Lilia's decision to move to Bayside Garden had baffled her children. She was healthy and self-sufficient, and she could see that they had envisioned a different scenario for her, living an independent life until the very end. What they did not understand was that she had no use for solitude. No, she was not afraid of being alone, but she preferred to be alone among people.

Rightly remembered, everyone is a curio decorating someone else's mental mantel, Lilia quoted to herself Roland's words. They often put her in a lenient mood toward her peers at Bayside Garden. They might not become a stately bust or a peacock feather or an antique vase, but together they would make a good collection of marbles. (Don't you lose them, Lilia.)

Though what does "rightly remembered" mean? Timely remembered? That would explain Roland's recording his life in such detail, but what is timely remembered can be timely forgotten, too. Or, perhaps all things timely remembered are wrongly remembered, and it's only when we pass a certain point, after we forget those things, that we can re-remember them and call it the right way. When does that happen? Middle age? On becoming a grandparent? After an unexpected death? Or an expected death? Hello there, Lilia imagined asking everyone she met. Have you walked through that door already? What door, the person would ask. That door, she would say, the one that opens only once, and when you enter you cannot return. The person might be confused, or incensed, or, if he had a good sense of humor (fat chance), he would say, do you mean the door between life and death? Pah, she would answer. The door you're talking about is far less interesting than the door I have in mind.

Lilia had not passed through that door yet. There were so many things she hadn't forgotten. She knew this with the certainty that she knew her own name and age and the first day of her last menstrual period, which at her checkups she was still asked to fill in on the questionnaire. *Oct. 19, 1987. (Black Monday)*, Lilia would note it. No one ever asked what the parenthesis meant. You would think people would have a decent level of curiosity.

Rightly remembered, everyone is a curio decorating someone else's mental mantel. Those words described an encounter with another woman, which had happened in the same month Lilia had met Roland. He was in a San Francisco pub with a few friends, and a queenly woman with a flawless accent and an enchanting manner came over and asked: Would you mind if I took this chair?

The group of friends competed to consent. You're not from this part of the world, ma'am? one of them asked.

No, I'm from across the Bay, the woman said. Oakland.

Roland wrote that subsequently he had been informed the woman was one of the Mitford sisters. When Lilia read the entry it had been decades later—even then she had had to go to the library to look up the Mitford sisters. Mrs. Anderson, the librarian, had been elated by Lilia's questions. Mrs. Anderson was Lilia's age, and had received a Ph.D. in Russian literature but worked in the local library till the week before she died. Once a year, Lilia asked Mrs. Anderson about a Canadian author, Roland Bouley. He had told her, when they first met, that one day he would become a well-known author, and she should watch out for his name. Mrs. Anderson, though never asking Lilia for an explanation, had taken up the search as a kind of professional challenge. How strange that one woman's obsession could become another woman's, but those who pick up fragments of other people's lives must be the loneliest ones. The Andersons did not have children. Mr. Anderson practiced family law for a day job and coached Little League after work and on weekends. Perhaps Lilia's constant questions and requests were exactly what Mrs. Anderson needed. When she eventually found Roland's diaries—god knows how she did it, patient and persistent woman she was—she ordered two copies, one for Lilia, one for herself. Did you know the author? Mrs. Anderson had said after she told Lilia that she had paged through Roland's diary. He's a distant cousin on my mother's side, Lilia had replied. One of those relics of our century, wasn't he? Mrs. Anderson had said.

Mrs. Anderson might have never found Roland's diaries. But then Lilia might have never met Roland. A different sequence of events, yet life would be the same, full of strange things that can't be remembered rightly.

People are like flowers. Some are born rare species, and they are assigned certified gardeners, and people line up to catch a glimpse when they bloom. Some demand cultivation and maintenance even though they live in an ordinary garden. Some are as common as lupines and poppies. Yet in the end all flowers blossom for the same purpose, and none of them last unless you press them between pages. Once preserved, they take on a gray tint, half transparent, with the lifeless thinness Lilia had always pictured Hetty Bouley's skin to have. Lilia had never met Hetty, but she'd learned from Roland's diary that it was one of Hetty's hobbies to press and preserve flowers. Imagine the sixty or seventy years of flowers Hetty would have left for Roland. No, Lilia could not imagine. There was something wicked about it. Marianne, whose room was across from Lilia's, had once invited Lilia to see her pressed flowers, a hobby begun, Marianne said, after her husband's death. It took great discipline for Lilia not to call Marianne a serial killer of flowers. Well, she shouldn't chastise Marianne, who was a minor criminal compared to Hetty.

Sidelle Ogden died in 1969. Hetty Bouley died in 1987. But as long as Roland had lived they must have retained some realness. That thing people say about memory keeping the deceased alive— there's no harm in believing in that nonsense just as there's no harm switching to another brand of toothpaste because you like its commercial. When Roland was alive Sidelle and Hetty must have been like flowers that still bloomed in the sunroom of his mind. But they had become dead specimens in his diaries when he died.

He would, too, once Lilia died.

Oh, Roland, someone had better come and inherit you before we become flowers pressed between pages. We can't be as dead as Hetty.

ON THE DAY ROLAND AND HIS FRIENDS VISITED, AFTER Lilia showed him his room, he had walked with her to the stable. He asked about the land, the weather, and the history of the region. One of his friends, he said, wanted to botanize. To what, Lilia asked, and Roland replied that his friend was interested in collecting some plants.

We have plenty here, Lilia said, pointing to her mother's garden. It had gone wild since her death. As it went toward its irreversible deterioration, Lilia felt the kind of pleasure similar to that of seeing someone, with bad eyesight, hard of hearing, slow in movement, being stolen from by a pickpocket. Could Lilia raise her voice on behalf of the victim? Sure, but why would she? When such a thing happened in a Charlie Chaplin movie you were supposed to laugh.

Lilia was waiting for the day when the garden would become a complete eyesore, and her father would have to order them to hack down the plants and set them on fire. No, Lilia would refuse to feel sad to see the garden go. Her mother had not had much in life, and she should be allowed to take her garden with her.

What had surprised Lilia, though, was that the twins, Lucille and Margot, did not lift a finger to save the garden either. Lilia could understand Lucille—anything Lilia did not do around the household Lucille would not take up as her responsibility. She was all about fairness, but how could she not see life was not meant to be fair? Lilia was older, taller, prettier, and no matter how much Lucille resented these facts she could do nothing to change them. But Margot? Margot had a soft heart. She had cried the most of all of them after their mother died, and she alone had saved a few articles of their mother's clothes when their father told them to bundle things up for the secondhand shop. Margot would surely have adopted the garden, so Lucille must have forbidden her to do so. She needed Lucille more than she was needed by her, and between a dead mother and a live sister she had to choose.

To botanize, Roland explained, requires visiting native plants in their native habitat.

Native habitat—they were not the kind of words Lilia or anyone she knew would use. Why do you even care? she asked. Only native animals need the plants, and you aren't one of them.

Roland studied Lilia. Till then, she knew, she had looked to him not much different from a native plant. Of course we aren't animals, he said. But we do things animals can't do.

Like being able to botanize?

Precisely.

And feeding on animals we raise? Lilia said.

What a good observer you are, Roland said.

Who feeds on us?

Who?

Animals, Lilia said. She had once seen a mountain lion jump up almost to tree height to catch a bird, and she had wondered if a small child playing in the tree would also have been torn to pieces. A coyote had taken a kitten from the barn when Kenny had just begun to crawl, and their mother had been consumed by the fear that the coyote would come back, taking Kenny next.

In some places, maybe, but in most places people feed on people. We're cannibals who don't recognize our lot, Roland said. But it's also that lot that allows us the capacity for happiness.

Our dogs are happy, Lilia said. And they don't eat each other.

Not happy in the way you and I can be, Roland said.

Lilia liked how he talked, chewing hard on each word, too greedy to give them away lightly. She shrugged, all the same, as though bored by his nonsense.

You're a bit young to understand, aren't you? Roland said.

Are you calling me stupid?

By all means no.

Then you're one of those men who think it's okay for girls to know nothing when they're young, Lilia said. And when they are no longer young you call them stupid.

Roland laughed. You surely know a lot.

And I know what makes animals better than us, Lilia said. Devils feed on our souls, not theirs.

And who feeds on devils?

Lilia hesitated. God? she said.

Roland laughed. Annoyed, Lilia asked when he wanted the horses to be ready. He brushed a piece of hay from her hair. I'm not laughing at you, he said. Only you remind me how hard those fusty theologians worked without understanding half of what you've intuited.

I don't understand, Lilia said. I'm not educated enough for this conversation.

It isn't so much a question of whether a person is educated enough to understand the world. It's whether a person understands the world enough to be able to make something out of a life.

And you're saying I do? Lilia said.

How else can we be happy? Roland said.

The conversation was interrupted then when Roland's friends joined him at the stable. The man who had wanted to botanize turned out to be a Pole working for the Soviet Union, but Lilia would not learn this until years later when she read Roland's footnotes to this visit, which explained in vague terms that his endeavor was undermined by the betrayal of the Pole and his associates. What endeavor? It frustrated her that she would never find out. Had Roland been doing something illegal? He had brought these people to the inn and encouraged their stay. Mrs. Anderson could not find a record of a Roland Bouley attending the United Nations conference in 1945. Perhaps he was a spy, or a double agent. What a shame then that nobody got to hear his stories. They didn't matter to the world. And what the world doesn't care about, it wipes clean. People would say, Oh, forget about them. They're water under the bridge now.

Lilia did not believe in such nonsense. And Roland did not, either, or else there would not be a book full of his words in her hands. And who belongs to the water in any case? You don't drown people when they are alive, but you especially don't drown them when they are already dead. Lilia remembered the tales from her great-grandparents, about the floods of '61 and '62: whole camps, with tents and their inhabitants, swept past; entire towns submerged; miners clinging desperately to tree trunks, singing folk songs in their mother tongues; cattle, horses, mules, dogs and cats, you name it, they were all in it together. Each retelling drained more horror from the flood, the way that the bones of an animal, after many seasons, become pristinely white.

Yet there was one tale Lilia never forgot, about a cemetery in the flood, all graves flushed open, caskets bobbing away. Had those caskets been built sturdily enough to float? Those bodies: Were they liberated, or still imprisoned in the caskets? Lilia did not believe that the dead rest in peace, but the dead should not be forced to share a flood, or an earthquake, or any kind of catastrophe, with the living. Lilia had long ago settled on her choice of cremation. She had told her children that it was more fair for all that she was not interred with any one of her husbands. What she really dreaded was to be confined to a single place, where you can always be found again.

UNLIKE LILIA'S OWN CHILDREN, KATHERINE VISITED regularly, oftentimes bringing Iola. A granddaughter, parading the hallway with a great-granddaughter in tow, never failed to inspire envy and jealousy among Lilia's peers. She was touched by this devotedness, though not without pity. Wouldn't it make more sense that children, when they grow up and have their own families, should become less of their parents' children? But Katherine was never anyone's child. A child, you let her go or she let herself go, but with a middle generation missing, a grandchild lingered in a grandchildly way.

Lilia thought highly of loyalty as a virtue, but not Katherine's kind, which was a character flaw. Katherine's loyalty was like her smile—you know she chose them because they were the easiest ways to accept defeat. As a little girl, she smiled readily, when a neutral situation did not request her to, or worse, when she was frustrated or embarrassed or in physical pain. How odd, this one doesn't cry or throw a tantrum like a normal child, Lilia remembered thinking then; like there was a photographer only Katherine could see, who prompted her to smile in all situations.

During her teenage years, Katherine had not been difficult, and she would still follow Lilia around, going to the grocery store with her, weeding next to her in the garden, rocking herself on a stool when Lilia cooked, all the time chatting about her schoolmates and teachers, never choosy with details, seldom with malice. She had many friends, but none too close. She did not spend hours studying herself in the mirror. She did not sulk. Everything Lucy had been, Katherine was not. The sweetest child we've brought up, Gilbert would say, as though incredulous that life could still treat them with such generosity after Lucy's death. But sweetness was never a commendation for any girl. That Katherine did not seem to hide anything as most children do—this had worried Lilia. What if they were bringing up a child who did not understand her right to secrets?

It annoyed Lilia that so many Bayside residents adored Iola unabashedly. She was the least eye-catching girl from Roland's line, his blood three times diluted. Lucy had not been perfect. Her eyes—Lilia's eyes—were disproportionally large for her face, which was narrow like her father's. Conscious of that flaw, Lucy had studied the movie stars in the magazines until she settled on Dana Wynter, whose press shots Lucy would show the hairdresser. Katherine's beauty was less striking. If Lucy could be called a piece of artwork—a piece of work she surely was!—Katherine was a decent replica. Everything about her was less sharp. The angle of Lucy's cheeks was softened in Katherine's face (and Roland's jawline almost gone). Katherine's eyes were not as cold as Lucy's icy blue, but rather a bluish gray.

Iola was no more than a china figurine, pleasing in her cuteness—but that cuteness would mean little once she outgrew her little-girl-hood. More unforgivable, however, was that Iola was a child without depth. Lilia believed that a person was either born with that trait, or without, but Katherine never understood this. She, like many fellow mothers at Iola's school, believed that by making her daughter *do* things, she would one day help the girl overcome that fatal inability to *be*.

"Welding?" Lilia said. For a six-year-old, Iola had a schedule that required professional management. Ice-skating, dancing, acting, violin, art, with the recent addition of an eight-week welding class, as Katherine had just told her. "What are you raising her to be, a blacksmith?"

"Different things, Grandma," Katherine said.

"Welding sounds disreputable for a girl. What's next? Butchering? Tanning? Wheel-making? If you want her to be useful I would suggest weaving, knitting, embroidering, or egg-painting."

"Egg-painting sounds so nineteenth century."

"My mother, your great-grandmother, won a contest once when she was in grade school."

"I know, I know," Katherine said. "Iola is a hundred years late for that activity."

"Welding sounds medieval," said Lilia.

Welding, Katherine explained, was part of a school program designed to empower girls. Lilia's other children must have endured (or were still enduring) these nagging concerns of parenting. But her policy, when it came to her children's lives, was "don't ask, don't tell."

"It's between welding and coding, and I don't want Iola to have too much screen time," Katherine said.

Poor Katherine. She lived so timidly. Already her face showed the wear and tear of motherhood that you would associate with someone who had raised seven children. A heavy-hearted child, Katherine's kindergarten teacher had once commented—that, despite Katherine's constant smile. Lilia wouldn't mind tying a bouquet of helium balloons around that heart.

Katherine studied the pictures—children and grandchildren, but no husbands—Lilia kept on the dresser, taking her time, a sign that she was getting ready to ask Lilia for something.

"How's your marriage?" Lilia said.

Katherine gave a laugh. Now things were getting worse. Nothing good could come out of Katherine's laugh. "What's your plan for Thanksgiving?" she asked.

"No plan yet," Lilia said. "Are you thinking of inviting me?"

"I was hoping someone already invited you."

"Meaning one of my children?"

"Someone will invite you, right?" Katherine said. "I can drive you."

"Thank you, but no, you don't have to worry about that."

"The thing is," Katherine said, "I was wondering if Iola and I could come with you."

"I can make a few phone calls, but why? What's going on with you and Andy?"

"Oh, nothing new. I offered to go to marriage counseling with him," Katherine said. "But he said the whole marriage counseling business was a scam."

He had a point, Lilia thought, though as a rule she never sided with Andy. He worked as a marketing manager at a tech company; he'd had a failed marriage but no child. Lilia had not felt that it was her place to say anything when Katherine dated him. The first time Lilia met Andy, she had counted. He had only said three sentences that were not about himself during the two hours of the meal, and he had been the one talking nonstop.

"I know this feels like a big terrible thing now, but forty years down the line you may not even remember his name. You certainly will forget his face."

"It's my marriage we're talking about," Katherine said.

"Forty years is a conservative estimate," Lilia said. "Give it a few years. Listen, I've lived long enough to be a three-time widow, and I can tell you this: If you want a long-lasting marriage you don't start with love, or obsession, or any of that silliness. You can certainly end with all those things. And you'll be happier. Trust me, next time you'll begin in a different place."

"Next time," Katherine said. "You make it sound like buying a new pair of shoes."

Shoes are better friends than men to women, but Lilia reminded herself she should be gentler with Katherine.

LILIA'S EXCUSE TO GO TO SAN FRANCISCO WAS FLIMSY, and anyone who cared to point it out could have done so. She deserved a break, people would think, as she had been working so hard when Maggie Williamson and the two other girls were sick from German measles. Even Lilia's father, for whom rest was not a word in the dictionary, did not say anything, but asked if she needed some money for the day's outing. Surprised by his generosity, she said no, which she later regretted.

Lilia told everyone that she was visiting a jeweler to see to the ring her mother had left her. The ring was of pure gold, its dull hue an endorsement of its purity. It had been Lilia's great-grandmother Lucille's before she had given it to her eldest daughter, Lilia's grandmother, who had then passed it to Lilia's mother, also the eldest daughter.

The ring did not have an excessive value but it had come with a story. Great-grandmother Lucille had set out from Missouri to California with her husband two months after their wedding. He was a physician, drawn to the west, he had told people, by the stories of people dying in the gold mines due to the lack of medical care. He had not mentioned his interest in prospecting, which eventually would fail him as it would fail so many men of his ambition, costing him much of the fortune he had made as a doctor around the mining camps.

It took them eight months to reach Blanco Bar, and she had dispatched letters to her family, detailing the traveling. Later in her life she had got in her mind the idea of publishing the letters as a travelogue, but her correspondence had been lost after her parents' deaths. Lilia's mother must have been infected by the same bug, wanting to write a book herself. Who would read their books? Perhaps they never dared to ask themselves that.

The day after Great-grandmother Lucille's arrival, a miner visited the inn where they were staying. He brought out a ring he had made himself. He had nearly died the previous year in a flood when the dam broke, he explained, if not for a felled tree that grabbed him from the current. He had made a ring, the gold coming directly from the ore, and he promised himself that he would give it as a present to the first lady he saw after the flood.

The story, like so many stories Great-grandmother Lucille passed on to her children and grandchildren, was shared by them— but the ring Lilia did not have to share with anyone.

Why do you need to see a jeweler, Lucille asked before Lilia left that morning.

It's my business, Lilia said.

Are you thinking of selling the ring? If you are, I can buy it from you, Lucille said. As the namesake of Great-grandmother Lucille, she had always thought she had the right to the ring.

How can you think so low of me? Lilia said. The ring will stay in the family.

What do you even care about this family? Lucille said.

Lilia measured the distance between herself and Lucille. She did not think Lucille would grab her purse by force, but with a girl like Lucille you never knew. If you want to buy the ring, Lilia said, where would you get the money?

I can ask Hayes for a loan.

Lilia laughed. They both knew that Hayes, like their father, would not part with a penny.

I'm not selling it, Lilia said. You should stop thinking about what's not yours.

But why are you taking it to a jewelry shop? Lucille asked.

I want to see if they can make it into a pendant for me.

Lucille glanced at Lilia's neck. They were not the kind of girls to wear a necklace or a pendant, she knew Lucille wanted to remind her.

I may be able to wear it when I move to the city, Lilia said.

Lucille stared at Lilia. Lilia wished she could pinch Lucille, hard, and warn her about that look in her eyes. It was among the things that had driven their mother into a constant state of absent-mindedness: their father's nagging, the boys' unintelligent bickering, Lucille's harshness with everyone, Margot's tears, the dangers threatening Kenny's happiness.

So this is how things are, Lucille said. Now that Mother is gone, everyone is looking for a way to leave.

Hayes will never leave, Lilia said. Jack may stay. Kenny is still young. Neither you nor Margot will leave, at least for some time.

You don't understand, do you?

What don't I understand? Lilia asked.

You live with your head in the clouds, Lucille said. Just like Mother.

Lilia looked at the cloudless sky. The rainy season was over, and here were the long sunny days ahead. Better than keeping my head in the chicken coop and the laundry tub, she said.

Can't you see your responsibility now?

We all have our share of chores. I do more than anyone, Lilia said.

I'm not talking about chores.

Are you saying it's my turn to make this a happy family for everyone? Mother didn't.

Without saying anything Lucille left with stiff strides.

Lilia resented that she was not the one to have walked away first. On the bus, though, she realized that the look in Lucille's eyes was that of terror. Lucille, despite her sternness, was fiercely loyal to the family. Anyone defecting would crumble Lucille's world, including their dead mother. But what could Lilia do for Lucille or anyone? She looked at the fields outside the bus, so much prettier if you didn't have to toil in them. The same mother had raised them all. With the quarrels and fights among themselves, they had nevertheless shared a family life. Orphanhood they could not share.

Lilia turned her thoughts to Roland. In his eyes, the green hills and the blue oaks and the marshes would make California a poetic place. Why would she want to get stuck in a family that she had always wanted to leave behind, when she could be a pretty and carefree girl from California?

AT THE HOTEL FRONT DESK LILIA WATCHED THE RECEPtionist place a folded note to Roland in a cubby that had the number "706" underneath. When she returned, she would check that cubby first to see if it was empty. She was in town for an errand, she had written on the hotel stationery, and she would stop by at three o'clock to say hello if he happened to be around. The paper, gilded and watermarked, made Lilia feel cosmopolitan, and the receptionist's unquestioning agreeableness reminded her that not every encounter in the city required her to use her vigilance as though she was dealing with an unruly horse.

She asked for directions to the opera house. Since the weekend Roland spent on the ranch, Lilia had followed the news about the conference in the papers, which Mr. Williamson subscribed to for the guests, though rarely would someone open them. Most of the guests came to be away from news, of war or peace.

What are you looking for? Maggie had asked. The Williamsons, like Lilia's family, were the kind to rely on the wireless for news.

Lilia said she was looking to see if there were any jobs she could apply for.

Are you serious about leaving? Maggie asked.

Why not? Lilia said.

Maggie sighed and said she could not imagine herself doing the same.

You're not thinking of spending your whole life here? Lilia said.

They had been sitting on the back porch of the inn then, a Monday afternoon, slow for business. Maggie looked around. What's wrong with here? she asked.

God help her if she cannot see anything wrong. But don't you want to have something better? Lilia said.

Better how? Maggie said. Even if you find a job in the city, you still have to have a room and a bed, and you have to cook and wash and go from chore to chore, no?

If Maggie were Lilia's sister she would've given Maggie a knock on her head, calling her an idiot, but Maggie was a loyal friend. You can come and visit me anytime, Lilia said. You can stay with me if you need.

Maggie nodded as though she understood the invitation. Lilia might as well have said, I'll save you a seat in that movie theater called paradise when you have a day off from your boring life. Maggie would have nodded the same way.

Do you think you'll marry soon? Maggie said.

Why? Do you want to marry? Who can we marry? We're still young.

No, not me. Not yet. But my ma wondered if you would get married one of these days.

Mrs. Williamson was no more than a nuisance. But Maggie's imagination didn't even stretch beyond her mother's harmless malice. If Maggie were told about Roland, what would she have said?

Lilia reached the opera house around lunchtime. She was hoping that the delegates would be released into the sunshine for a change of air. A British diplomat had been quoted in the newspaper about the sessions running until late at night, the delegates' brains fogged up by cigarette smoke and sleep deprivation. Perhaps her own visit would offer a break that Roland dearly needed. Refreshing, he had called her the morning before they parted.

The street in front of the opera house was lined with people. Inside, Lilia knew, there were women and girls, but they were the wives and daughters of rich people from San Francisco, dressed up extravagantly to showcase the hospitality of the city. Lilia had seen their names and photographs printed in the society sections in the newspapers. They called themselves volunteers. One of them had been quoted, talking about "the historical contribution" of San Francisco to "the golden future of mankind." The word "golden" was used often when people talked about the peace conference. Lilia wondered if the fashion would catch on, with shops and restaurants and laundry detergents and men's shaving creams soon all renamed with the word "golden" in them.

A policeman on a horse gestured for the crowd to stay behind the cordon. A boy, not much older than Kenny, hung on to the shoulder of his friend, a Chinese boy, both wearing sailors' shirts, hair parted the same way. Clean and neat boys who still had mothers offering love and care. Kenny was no longer one of them. In the past few weeks he had transformed himself from his mother's son into his father's. Lilia resented seeing them on the porch, his father passing a half-smoked cigarette to Kenny to finish. How could two selfish people be drawn so close by mourning?

Lilia pushed through the crowd to the boys and asked them what they were waiting for. The pale-skinned boy said that a few veterans on stretchers would arrive soon according to the news, and they were waiting to salute them. Lilia withdrew from the crowd. She did not want to see anyone maimed by the war.

A young man caught up with her around the corner. Do you also work for the conference? he asked.

Lilia had put on her best outfit for the day: a tweed suit that she had saved for a year to buy. When she had shown it to her family, her father had said it made her look twice her age, and her mother had nodded absentmindedly and said the color matched her eyes. Refusing to accept defeat, Lilia had walked to the inn and shown it to Maggie and Mrs. Williamson. Maggie had only offered the most banal praise, but her eyes spoke more articulately of admiration and envy. Mrs. Williamson had not been able to find much fault, so she had told Lilia she had better sew the buttons on one more time to secure them.

Lilia pulled back her shoulders, conscious of the newness of the jacket. Do you work for the conference? she asked.

Indeed I do! the young man said. In a way.

Lilia nodded, and began to walk again. Wait, he said. Do you want to have lunch together? There's a good deli around the corner.

Why not, Lilia thought. She was hungry. There was no point acting like an agitated fool, wandering in the city and looking for a man who was not expecting her in the first place. (But was he not? Lilia wasn't sure. Roland had mentioned the name of his hotel twice. He wouldn't have done that if he didn't want to be found.)

Once they had put down their food on the table, Gilbert Murray—for that was the young man's name—said he knew Lilia was too young to work at the conference. Lilia looked into Gilbert's blue eyes. Whatever age he was, he had no idea how young he was. A boy named Jimmy Campton from Hayes's class, who had been sent to the Youth Authority for some crime, had been working at Benecia Arsenal for the past two years alongside German and Italian POWs. Gilbert, Lilia thought, looked like a little brother of Jimmy's, for whom she had had a moment of fancy, but that was before Roland.

At lunch Gilbert talked about the importance of the conference. Two billion people represented, he said, eighty percent of the population on earth. Can you believe that? We're making history, right this moment, right here in San Francisco. The whole world is watching us now.

He must have memorized these numbers and words with the hope of impressing a girl. What difference does it make, two million or two billion? The only things that matter happen between two people. If he was smart he would know better than to drag in strangers to woo a girl.

And you, Gilbert said, are you visiting the city?

Visiting a friend, Lilia said. I'm meeting him at three o'clock.

Oh, Gilbert said, looking down at his wristwatch.

A family friend, Lilia said.

Oh, he said, looking up.

Poor boy. He was too well-mannered to inquire further, so Lilia showed the ring to him. Before my mother died she asked me to give this to her friend, Lilia said. It happens her younger brother is in town.

Gilbert looked hesitant, not knowing if he should take the ring from her, or perhaps not knowing how to express his sympathy for her loss. Lilia would have dismissed him as dull, even tormented him with some jokes, had it not been for that eager look in his blue eyes. It was a look different from the hungry look in the eyes of sailors. Different, too, from Roland's eyes. Here's someone who doesn't know how not to treat anyone with a gentle seriousness. Two billion people around the globe, Lilia thought, and he would not mock any one of them.

So, what do you do at the conference? she asked.

In no time she gathered enough information. Gilbert had turned twenty in March. His two older brothers had fought in the Pacific, but he himself was not called up. Lucky for you, Lilia said, but he only looked at her strangely, saying that he would rather be fighting for his country.

Isn't it good enough that you're serving the country by serving the conference? Lilia said.

Oh yes, Gilbert agreed. This is not the war, but it's historical.

Lilia looked at his wristwatch and tried to read the time upside down. It was still early.

Gilbert worked at a printing press, and this was a busy time for them. Two weeks ago, he said, when the *Daily* was about to go to print, he had caught a mistake in the headline, which had turned "United Nations" into "Untied Nations." Mr. Dupree, his boss, had been pleased with his performance and had promised a promotion if Gilbert kept up the good work. Mr. and Mrs. Dupree, Gilbert explained, were like a second pair of parents to him. He had begun to work for them right after he turned seventeen.

Why, Lilia asked, don't they have their own children?

No, Gilbert said.

Why don't they have children?

I don't know.

Don't you want to know? Lilia asked.

No, why should I?

I always want to know things.

Things? Like what?

Why people get married. Why they have children, or don't. Do you think Mr. and Mrs. Dupree didn't want children, or they couldn't have children, or maybe they had children but they died young?

I don't know, I don't want to pry, Gilbert said. And then, as though he was granted some permission by Lilia, he asked: Do you always ask people questions this way when you meet them for the first time?

It doesn't sound polite to you? Lilia said. So people should have small talk when they first meet? If you ask me, small talk is for neighbors and families and maybe, in your case, coworkers. You don't waste your life having small talk with strangers.

I've never thought of it that way, Gilbert said.

The world would never expand for a polite person like you, Lilia thought. She was going to make the pronouncement and then stopped herself. He was too easy a target, his face as innocent and helpless as a three-day-old foal's. Besides, he did go out of his way to speak with her in the street.

On the way out of the deli Lilia opened the *Chronicle*, left by a customer at the counter, to Mr. Williamson's advertisement. If you ever want a riding lesson you can find me here, she said.

BUT YOU COULD'VE MISSED ME ENTIRELY, ROLAND SAID
later that afternoon. I could've been at a meeting. I could've gone
out with friends and colleagues.

You could've refused to see me, Lilia said. She could've been
on the bus now, knowing her wild dream for the day had come to
nothing. But so what? It would've only been one day of her life
lost. There would be other days, and there would be other men.

She huddled in an armchair, wrapped up in Roland's robe. She
wondered if there had been another woman's body in it before, but
that hardly was worth her attention. She was sitting here now. He
was sitting up in bed with a stack of pillows behind, a cigarette
slowly burning to its end. He didn't turn to meet her eyes. He knew
she was watching him.

Lilia, you really are . . . Roland said.

Crazy?

Irrational.

But here we are, and you were happy to see me.

Happy? That's quite a word to aspire to.

You didn't turn me away, Lilia said.

Does that mean anything? Roland asked.

Lilia looked around. Does this mean nothing, she asked, but
before Roland answered she laughed. How serious you look, she
said.

You're too young to understand the seriousness of anything, Roland said. I've lived long enough to know everything has some consequence.

Consequence for you or for me?

You're not one of those girls entertaining sailors and soldiers. I
wouldn't feel concerned at all if you were one of them.

Oh, those girls, Lilia said. I know better.

Roland lit another cigarette. Perhaps he didn't think that she was much different from those girls. There's something you should know about me, she said.

Which is?

I take good care of myself, Lilia said.

And?

Men like you would hate it if girls like me complicate your life. But you won't be satisfied at all if we don't let you feel that it's you who has decided how our lives will turn out.

Goodness, I don't want to feel I've done anything to your life, Roland said.

But you want to feel that you've done something to another person's life?

There are always others. At my age you'd expect me to have met a few people, Roland said. Women, I mean.

But do you also say to them, Goodness, I don't want to feel I've done anything to your life?

All but one.

Who's she?

Roland laughed. What makes you think I'll tell you?

If you say there's a woman, you want me to ask. Then you have something I want, and you're in a good position because you can refuse me. People always play such games.

Go on, Roland said.

Well, only I don't think you want to be one of them.

Why not?

People play these games because they can't trust themselves. My great-grandmother had these stories of miners gambling away all their gold. It was not because they didn't have anything but because they didn't believe they were meant to be rich. She said they gambled to make sure luck was on their side. And that's when they lost. I don't know about you, but I can say I have not met many people who trust themselves as I do.

Is that so?

She could not tell if he was listening simply out of boredom, but why worry about that, when what she wanted was for him to see her again. And again. To be seen by him was different than to be remembered. The moment you want to be remembered by another person you give him the power to forget you.

Well, if you doubt that, you don't know me, Lilia said.

Show me what that trust can do.

I trusted myself that I would find you, and here we are.

But you do realize how improbable this meeting is. Nine out of ten men would hide from you.

You didn't.

What if I'm in a hiding mood next time?

Then I won't find you, she said.

What would you do then, with that trust of yours?

Nothing, Lilia said. If I know there's nothing more to us, I'll walk out of this room and by the time I turn the corner I'll forget you.

You make things sound easy, Roland said.

Lilia remembered Gilbert Murray reading Mr. Williamson's ad in the newspaper, more purposefully than one would read an ad for a shoeshine or a travel agency. Lilia had left Gilbert a path, just as Roland had left her a hotel name. Why make life hard? she said. If there're other women for you, there'll be other men for me, too. There will always be people. They're like bricks, and you build a house and live a good life inside.

A prison I would call it, Roland said.

Show me one person who's not in some kind of prison.

Where do all these thoughts get into your head, Lilia?

You thought I spent my life thinking about feeds and manures and cooking suppers and making beds?

And marriage, perhaps?

My mother used to say she was glad that I was born in a family like ours.

Because she saw that you could make a hell of troubles for others?

Tell me, had I been born into your world, what would I have become?

My world? There's not a world that's mine. But had you been born in another place, maybe you could've become one of those Soviet delegates.

Even as a woman? Lilia asked.

There are women delegates, Roland said.

What are they like?

Older than you. Not as pretty.

Have you thought of doing this with them? Lilia asked, pointing to the untidy bed sheet with her raised chin.

Roland laughed. Oh, Lilia, don't play dumb.

The woman—the one whose life you do want to feel you've done something to—is she prettier and older than me?

I see you haven't forgotten her, Roland said. She's older, yes, than you and me combined.

And pretty?

Pretty can be used to describe a million women. Not Sidelle Ogden.

What was wrong with these men, Lilia thought, who liked to talk about millions of people. Perhaps Roland was not much different from Gilbert. They had to rely on a number too big to imagine to make any small point.

Roland went on telling Lilia a few things about Sidelle.

Will I meet her one day? Lilia asked.

It's time for you to know a thing or two about men, Roland said. I know you are clever, but there's always something new to learn.

Teach me then.

Roland explained that a man would fit women into different slots in his life. It's like furnishing a house. Some women are good furniture you've inherited, he said, so you put them there for all to see. Others are perfectly nice, like wallpapers and curtains and umbrella stands, but easy to replace. Some are impulsive purchases, and you really want nothing to do with them afterward. Some are fine things you enjoy once in a while. And then there are necessities, like washbasins.

Which slot does your Mrs. Ogden fit into?

What you should ask is where you yourself fit in. You can't expect to be everything for a man. In fact, you must avoid that aspiration at all cost.

Then, what do I want to be for a man? What am I to you? Lilia knew well that she should not have asked. But she wanted to know.

Rubato.

What? Lilia asked.

I don't know what you want to be for other men, Roland said. You figure that out yourself. But I'll always think of you as my *rubato*.

What is that? Lilia said. In which room do you keep it?

Unfortunately, it doesn't fit into any room in any house, Roland said. *Rubato tempo*, it's stolen time. Robbed time if you translate literally from Italian.

Well, I would say stolen time is better than a stolen wallet, Lilia said. Lucy, by then, had already existed. This Lilia had liked to think about over the years. Roland had stolen from her, but she had, too, from him.

GILBERT WAS THE ONLY ONE WHO HAD KNOWN ABOUT Lilia's pregnancy. He had to be told, since he wanted to marry her. The engagement and the wedding, speedy to the point of perfunctory, did not surprise the Williamsons and other neighbors. They had agreed that after the death of Lilia's mother, the family would not hold together. She had been scatterbrained, they said, but that didn't mean she hadn't done her job. Lilia always acted like she was destined for something better, except a man still with the baby fat on his cheeks didn't sound such a fancy choice.

Lilia did not need Maggie to tell her these comments, as none of them was unexpected. Still, Maggie took her time reporting them. Lilia could see sympathy and pity and a little pleasure in Maggie's eyes—the marriage didn't in the end prove Lilia superior.

Lilia told Gilbert that the pregnancy was the result of a night spent with a visitor to the ranch—the only time she had done so. It was near truth, and Gilbert did not press to know more. Lilia thought he was both sweet and admirable for this. She vowed to herself that she would never lie to him (unless absolutely necessary). She wanted a marriage made by herself. Unlike her mother's. Unlike many other women's.

After Gilbert came to ask Lilia's father for her hand, he told Lilia that she and her siblings were all brave children, living on the ranch the way they did. Lilia found the comment irritating. His own parents managed a pub in inner Richmond, which didn't make them any more aristocratic. She objected, and Gilbert apologized. He didn't mean that they lived in poverty, he said, but that the children were brave to carry on without their mother. That, too, bothered Lilia. But then she met her future in-laws, and understood what had prompted Gilbert's comment. He was the youngest child of the family, but unlike Kenny, Gilbert had not only both parents' love but also devotion from his two brothers and two sisters. Gilbert would become a lost lamb if their love were obliterated by a calamity. They treated Lilia with politeness, but she could sense a secret conversation in their exchanged looks. Let them think the hurried marriage was unwise. Lilia had not forced Gilbert to marry her. Your lamb, she wanted to say to the tightly smiling Murrays, did not get lost. He only found himself a greener pasture without your help.

If we haven't all died by killing one another, Gilbert liked to paraphrase President Truman, we must live together peacefully. The baby would be their first to be born in a golden time, he said, and they would have more children, all of them with a bright future. Lilia suspected that his marrying her with such magnanimity was part of the dream he was infected with at the UN conference. He never tired of talking about the eighty percent of the world population loving one another. Roland would have made fun of Gilbert, but he made fun of everyone. At the San Francisco hotel, when Lilia asked him about his work, he had made a show of mocking the Soviet delegates along with the British. He imitated some bigwig from China who had given what the newspaper had called an important speech, and he laughed at the Americans, the Canadians, the New Zealanders, the Australians, the South Africans, and above all, the French.

But which country are you working for? Lilia had asked.

Canada, America, Britain, what's the difference? I work for world peace, he replied, but you've got to laugh about that like you laugh about any country.

What's so laughable about everything?

When you go to a circus show like this, where people take themselves so seriously they don't even know they're part of a circus, what else can you do but laugh?

Are you sure it's a circus show? Lilia asked.

'Tis so, Roland said. 'Tis so. Why, did I break your little patriotic heart?

Lilia said she didn't see why she would be bothered by his attitude toward any country. As long as there is not going to be another war, she said, my brothers will be okay.

But there will be, Roland said. Mark my words.

Then, what are you doing here?

You can't prevent a war, Roland said. Like you can't stop a storm coming. But at least you can have a sense of where it comes from.

So you're like a weatherman? Lilia said.

You could say that.

Are you good at what you do?

I know a thing or two before others know. I have good instincts.

Lilia wondered how much she could trust Roland's words. Perhaps he did know a thing or two, including not staying around to learn what would become of her. When she had come to the city with another excuse, two weeks after her visit to the hotel, he had left, this time not leaving a trace for her. Later she thought about how, or whether, to write him about the pregnancy. She supposed there was a government agency she could send a letter to, to be forwarded to him, but what was the point. He knew where to find her but chose not to. Gilbert did, so Gilbert it had to be.

Was there ever another woman who had borne his child? Lilia did not believe so. In February 1946 Lucy was born—Roland was crossing the Atlantic then, to join his future bride, Hetty. Lilia had seen movies of glamorous people on such ocean liners, the women wearing something that could flutter in the sea breeze, the men dapper. Some of them must have had to bow out of life while not yet ready, sunk with the *Titanic* or struck by a cold turned pneumonia. But Roland was the kind of person who could never be aboard a sinking ship or a crashing plane. He had died an old man, hardly a tragedy.

In the right mood Lilia would allow Roland to be a movie star, the same role she had given him when she was younger. The right mood: not a sentimental one, but one that Lilia—an actress sharing a scene, an audience watching it—could enter and leave freely as she had not been able to in the past. Lilia had lived long enough to know a movie is no more than a lollipop. A lollipop does not cure insomnia or kill pain.

LILIA'S FIRST PREGNANCY WAS DIFFICULT, THE MOTHER-
hood harder than what she remembered her own mother's had
been. But being young, being doted on by a new husband, and
being confident that the baby's father hadn't entirely vanished
from her life—all these made Lilia contented enough. Her beauty,
like her temper, had softened, which many people had noticed
and commented upon.

Lucy was a colicky baby. You would expect that, just as none of
Gilbert's children would be so difficult as infants. But Lilia and
Gilbert had accepted all those sleepless nights and exhausted days,
he out of love for his wife and humankind, she out of her respect
for his love, and the memory of someone absent.

Those early days of a new marriage—you could always call
them happy memories. Picnicking on the bench in front of the
opera house where Lilia and Gilbert had met. Moving out of his
parents' house to their own place, rented yet still making them feel
legitimately grown-up. Listening to Gilbert talk about his work at
dinner, even though one day was much the same as another. Taking walks with Lucy while pregnant with Timmy. So soon—Lilia
remembered feeling dismay, but she had concealed this feeling
from Gilbert, who was overjoyed. Poor man who didn't mind being
a replacement. He deserved a baby of his own.

People peeking under the muslin shade on the pram were often
in awe of that angelic face, framed by the bonnet. Such a beautiful
baby, just like her mother. Lilia could not see much of Roland in
Lucy then. It was the best for everyone. There was no reason for
Gilbert to be reminded constantly of the baby's origin. There were
days when even Lilia didn't think about Lucy's real father. Still,
when she cried tirelessly—in Lilia's arms, in Gilbert's arms, late

into the night, too early in the morning—Lilia wondered if this near-blind rage was Roland's punishment for her, for not at least informing him of the birth of his daughter. But such a thought put Lilia into a rage, too. She had given birth to Lucy. No one—not Roland, nor Gilbert—would have any right to tell her for which father Lilia was raising Lucy.

When Timmy was a little over two Lilia again became pregnant. Another child would be a strain on their finances, and Lilia thought about finding a job. Her twin sisters were both out of school now—Margot training to be a nurse, Lucille working on the floor of the Emporium. Lilia could learn typing and shorthand, but discussion ended when Gilbert was offered a promotion at the printer. Mr. and Mrs. Dupree had decided to move back East for some time, to be closer to her sister, who had just lost the last of her three sons, this time in Korea.

Lilia was not close to the Duprees. Mrs. Dupree was like a second mother-in-law, but unlike Gilbert's mother, she did not have any grandmotherly tenderness toward Lucy and Timmy. Still, what sad news about her sister. Imagine sending little Timmy into a war, or Lucy as a soldier's widow. Had Lilia been a sentimental woman, these possibilities would have made her despair. But Roland had said no war was ever going to be the last war. She'd better prepare herself.

So much for your talk about world peace, Lilia said.

Gilbert sighed and agreed that he had been shortsighted. But we all believed in peace at the San Francisco conference, he said. If only you had been there.

She was there. She had seen the Arabs in their long white robes and the Indian women in their colorful garments. She had seen the foreigners at her father's ranch, though she had not seen them through Gilbert's eyes. You would think life would be particularly cruel to a man like Gilbert, but no, it had been extra careful with him. He didn't lose either brother when so many brothers had been missing or killed in action. He didn't have to please a difficult boss. He never understood what it meant to wake up some days, knowing himself to be loved but still feeling lonely. On those mornings, Lilia would stay in bed just a few minutes longer, taming her heart as though it was a difficult horse. Here's your apple of a house, a good husband, and two cute children, she would offer with an open palm. And let's be good, easy now, easy now.

Oh well, I'm older and wiser, Gilbert said.

Two billion people loving one another unconditionally, Lilia thought. How fast that future for mankind had lost its golden hue. Roland was right. You either choose to be in that circus, or you watch the acrobats and clowns taking themselves seriously. But Roland laughed at everyone. Lilia would still applaud because some people's feelings should not be hurt. Aren't we all older and wiser now, she agreed with Gilbert.

And I haven't done so poorly, now that Mr. Dupree trusts the business to me, Gilbert said.

Lilia bent over to pick up a rolled-away ball so that Gilbert would not see the impatience in her eyes. This, she thought—to manage a tiny printing press—is the limit of Gilbert's ambition.

A few weeks later, Lilia received a letter from Roland. He had sent it to the ranch. Kenny and his friends were coming to the city for a Friday outing, and he stopped by to drop off the letter, showing little curiosity at the Canadian stamp. If anyone at home had noticed that, Kenny did not mention it. Lilia gave two half-dollars to Kenny, and told him to treat himself to something nice.

Bills arrived regularly in the mail, but nobody ever wrote Lilia. She remembered the days when her mother had gone to the mailbox the moment the postman left. Lilia had pitied her mother, perpetually waiting. What if there were a fire and the letters were burned in the mailbag—no one would know what was lost. What if her friends woke up one morning and realized that it was pointless to write—all those words would make no difference to their lives. Waiting for a letter is worse than waiting for happiness. The latter may never happen, but you don't allow yourself to believe that. A letter—when it's not coming it means too much, but once arrived, it never brings enough.

Even Roland's letter was no exception. That he had written meant he hadn't forgotten her, but between that fact and happiness there were a thousand questions. What made him send the letter? Had Lilia been a feebleminded woman she might have believed that it was the pull of Lucy, his blood; had she been blindly proud she might have thought of herself as the magnet. But neither made sense to Lilia. And why on earth did she allow herself to think of happiness upon receiving a mere one-page letter?

Lilia thought of her marriage as a happy one. Keeping a house and raising children were rarely tedious tasks for her. She had been born to do things, like the horses were born to toil. What bothered her was that she had stopped watching herself from someplace hovering above. Before there had always been two Lilias: one studying herself in the mirror, and the other watching the girl inside and outside the mirror with the same interest; one speaking to a sailor with a pouting face, and the other watching the half-smile hidden underneath. In every moment she had had with Roland there was the other Lilia, assessing herself and Roland. But that Lilia had vanished, and now when she went to the market or exchanged news with her neighbors, when she fed Timmy or played with Lucy or, even, when she lay in bed with Gilbert after the children fell asleep, she felt she could live this life with her eyes closed. A good neighbor, a good wife, and a good mother. Good enough for everyone.

She read the letter again. She missed the thrill of being two Lilias. Was that what she wanted as happiness—knowing that she had the freedom to go from one Lilia to the other? But did that mean then that she did not have real happiness even in a happy marriage?

Lucy clamored, wanting the letter, and right away Timmy made the same demand. Lilia shushed them. When neither child gave up, Lilia screamed.

Mrs. Murray, are you all right? someone called from outside. Mrs. Nelson, of course.

Lilia gave Lucy a stern look, whose small face looked frosty and her eyes more gray than blue. It baffled Lilia that Lucy could in an instant turn into this strange child. If Lilia had had time she would have shaken Lucy's shoulders and said something sharp. But Mrs. Nelson called out again, and if Lilia didn't answer, that woman would be knocking on their door the next moment.

Lilia went to the window, her upper body stretched outward so she could see the end of the street. Mrs. Nelson from next door was standing on the sidewalk, looking concerned.

I just tripped on Timmy's ball, Lilia said. Don't worry.

Don't lean out of the window, Mrs. Murray. You must take care of yourself now.

Lilia wondered if Mrs. Nelson spent her days by her window, watching for any sign of change in the bodies of married women. Or perhaps her attention was even more astute when it came to the few unmarried daughters on the street? That Lilia was too young to be a wife or a mother of two children was Mrs. Nelson's opinion, which she had expressed to other neighbors. Some of them had passed the judgment on to Lilia.

Yes, I will, Lilia replied, and then said she must be off to get Timmy to nap. If Mrs. Nelson could notice the change in Lilia's body, would Roland, too? Oh, Lilia, she laughed. In his letter Roland hardly said anything worth hoping for. You're not sixteen anymore.

WHERE'S THAT LETTER FROM ROLAND? THE PROBLEM with walking down memory lane is that you want to find that very thing the moment you think about it. But life is never arranged accordingly. If there was a memory lane, it would not look like one of those shaded drives leading to a grand country house seen in films, maintained by diligent groundskeepers, flowers blossoming reliably, dead things raked away. "In fact, I take that back," Lilia said aloud. Hetty's memory lane would be just like that: picture-perfect and unvisited.

Lilia's trip down memory lane was more of a wild hike. Even so, she had placed a few markers here and there. Think, Lilia, think. She knew she had not one but two letters from Roland. Ah, with the little tales her mother had written. Lilia went to her closet and searched, and when she couldn't locate the manila envelope, she thought again. Yes, the leather trunk, a wedding gift from Mr. and Mrs. Williamson. Aha, two manila envelopes tucked in the lining inside the lid, just as she remembered. One, marked IMPORTANT, included all the legal documents her children would need once she went poof. It had three rubber bands around it. Lilia pulled one. No longer elastic, it snapped unceremoniously. The other envelope was blank. Time to correct that, so in capital letters Lilia printed: TO BE BURNED BY LILIA HERSELF. IN CASE OF SUDDEN DEATH: MOLLY MURRAY-LAWSON AND KATHERINE A. TINGMAN MUST BOTH BE PRESENT TO RECEIVE THE ENVELOPE AND BURN IT TO-GETHER UNOPENED.

Better to give a task to two rivals to share. Neither would then peek out of curiosity.

12TH JULY, 1950.

Dear Lilia, I wonder if this letter will reach you. I suppose
you may be happily married by now, with a sweet nest and
a loving husband, a daughter pretty just like you, or a son
who is his father's pride. It is hard to imagine you as a
mother, Lilia. You yourself were not much older than a
child then, but who am I to protest the passing of time and
the changing of human hearts?

Well, Lilia, here is the reason I am writing you. I will be
in San Francisco from the 10th of August till the end of the
month. I wonder if I can pay you a friendly visit. Do say no
if this will cause any inconvenience, but it would be lovely
to see you in your present life. I always remember you as
the audacious girl with the golden-red curls from sun-
drenched California.

Roland did not mention that he was married, nor that his osten-
sible motivation was to meet a few rare-book dealers in San Francisco, though the real reason was to take a break from his wife and
recover from what he called "a bout of melancholy." All this Lilia
pieced together later, though only partially, from Roland's diary.
What did happen he had not recorded in detail. Roland could be
a pain. So much of what mattered was missing. Not one of the
stories he told was the full version.

Lilia opened the other letter, sent four years later but worded so
similarly that you would think Roland must have had a stack of
letters ready, waiting for him to fill in the name and date and a few
details (*sun-drenched California, golden-red curls*). Oh, Roland,
you silly goose of a man. If someone like him walked into Katherine's life, Lilia would pat white powder on his cheeks and smear
red paint on his nose. Clown on, she would say, let's see how long
this show will run.

In August of 1950, Lilia sent a note to the Fairmont, right before Roland's arrival. She would stop by on Wednesday afternoon, and if that was inconvenient, she wrote, she wished him a good stay in San Francisco and a happy life in Canada.

Had she worried about missing him? Lilia could not remember. Ah well, life never stops in the middle of a day or week for you to sort out all the memories. But there was plenty of time later. What she really needed to do now was to make a few calls. She could not afford stalling because Thanksgiving would soon be here.

She called Katherine after she had secured an invitation from Molly.

"Did you talk with Carol?" Katherine asked.

Carol lived in Southern California. That was eight hours minimum in holiday traffic. Molly was an hour away, an hour and a half at most. What part of the math did Katherine not understand? "I did," Lilia lied. "I even talked with Will. But if you don't want to go to Molly's I understand. I can go by myself."

"Who'd be driving you?"

"That's not for you to worry about," Lilia said. Lilia could see Katherine, wavering between wanting to love (her husband, her daughter, Lilia herself, even Molly) and wanting to be able to stop loving. Katherine had a muddled head around that *L* word. She took after Lucy, who had always loved indiscriminatingly until she had stopped loving, also indiscriminatingly. Oh, poor Lucy—was it why life was so hard for you?

"Listen, do what's best for you. I don't have to go to Molly's," Lilia said, feeling magnanimous in her pity for Katherine. And for Lucy.

"Shhhh, let me think," Katherine said.

"Think!" Lilia said. It was surprising how many people had the habit of saying "let me think" when they did not know how to think at all.

"Would it be cruel to leave Andy here by himself?"

"Shall we order him a few teddies so he won't have to cry himself to sleep?" Better to be cruel than to be receiving cruelty. That was the lesson Lucy had taught everyone by killing herself.

"What about—I know this is a lot to ask . . . ," Katherine said. "I'd be happy if you took Iola to Molly's. I can drive you there. I don't have to see anyone."

"Where are you going then? Back to Andy?"

"I can go out for a drive along the coast."

"Who are you visiting?"

"No one. I can spend a night in Arcata or Eureka. Just a day by myself, to clear my head."

Only the muddleheaded would say that spending some time by themselves would clear their heads. The clearheaded—they could be alone or they could be with others and it would not make a smidge of difference to their brains. Lilia wouldn't mind a befuddled Katherine. But how strange it was that she still kept her resolve to clear her head. Lilia would have applauded if Katherine said, Just a day by myself, to bask in my muddles.

"There're serial killers out there," Lilia said.

"You're being ridiculous."

"You never know," Lilia said. "I read in the paper a woman in Glen Hyde hired someone to make a barbecue pit in her backyard, and later the police found her husband's body cemented into it."

"Oh gosh, stop making up these horror stories."

"She told people her husband had gone away to visit relatives."

"So she killed him?"

"No, he died a natural death. Old age and sickness. And she didn't know what to do with his body, so she came up with this barbecue pit idea."

"Do you believe that? Some reporter must have dreamed it up in his bed."

"I saved the newspaper for you and Iola," Lilia said, which was a lie.

"Please don't show it to Iola."

Iola, Lilia wanted to say, couldn't read. "The reporter interviewed many neighbors. They all claimed that she was a nice lady, only confused. I'm telling you, people can be very confused."

"How did she make the worker bury the body?"

"She did it by herself. The worker only dug up the earth and unloaded the cement."

"I thought she was an old woman."

"Old women can surprise you," Lilia said.

"There're so many holes in the story," Katherine said. "Besides, are we talking about confused old people or serial killers?"

"Someone could put your life in danger, that's all I'm saying," Lilia said. "It's a miracle murders don't happen more often."

"Grandma, if someone else is listening to you, they'd think you're crazy yourself."

"The problem with some people is that they will never go crazy, no matter what," Lilia said. "I'm counting myself as one, and take my word, it's a good problem." Not like your mother. No, but no, Lilia thought, Lucy was not crazy, just confused.

LILIA UNDERSTOOD KATHERINE'S HESITATION ABOUT MOLLY. They came from different generations but were only six years apart in age. When Lilia and Gilbert had decided to take Katherine in, Molly, an accident-turned-princess, had not welcomed the idea. She was four when Lucy married, and after Lucy's death Molly, unlike her older siblings, saw little point in mourning or in letting their parents mourn.

Why can't Katherine stay with her dad? Molly had said. If she needs grandparents why can't they be Steve's parents?

I have not raised you to question my decisions, Lilia said. All children are selfish. That Lilia accepted, but Molly, unforgivably, did not know how to hide that selfishness.

Why can't I question? Molly said.

Because that'll lead you nowhere.

Did you say that to Lucy, too? Molly asked. Did she listen to you?

Molly deserved a slap. If Lilia did it right, it would make a crispy sound but not bruise that peachy face, and it would not be the pain but the sound that Molly would remember. The way she stared at Lilia so unblinkingly reminded her of Lucy. But Molly was not Lucy. No one was Lucy.

By all means continue your questioning, Lilia said. But just know I'm not obliged to answer you.

You're a meanie, Molly said.

Carol, who was to leave for college after that summer, had slipped into the room in the middle of the argument. She dragged Molly away, saying she had a few things she could not take to her dorm, and would Molly like to take a look to see if she wanted them in her room.

Carol reminded Lilia of her sister Margot. Softhearted, and

Lilia was not fond of softhearted people. Of all the children, Carol was closest to Gilbert. There were comforts Lilia could not give him that Carol could. They were like two hummingbirds, feeding on the nectar of love and kindness.

Lilia had never lost her composure. Sharp-tongued she was, and she took pride in that. Aloof sometimes, impatient at other times, but never had she allowed herself to be swept away by extreme feelings. What do you know about me, she could hear herself say to the world at the first sign of her urge to wreck everything around her. God knows she had enough reasons to want to do that, and plenty of times she was just about to. But then she remembered that the world was made up of people who knew nothing about her. She could afford to be nice to them.

Lilia wondered now if it was her very composure that had driven Lucy toward Steve's volatility. "How have I never thought of that?" she asked aloud. Steve had responded theatrically to Lucy's moods, sometimes with tears, sometimes with fists. Oh, Lucy did know how to provoke. There was no other way for her to be. She had not known that what she had considered her edge was merely brittleness. Brittleness could be used as a weapon only once in life, and in the end, when Lucy realized that, she had not hesitated to use it.

And what a weapon. What a clever girl.

LILIA DECIDED TO ASK MRS. NELSON TO HELP WITH LUCY and Timmy while she went to Roland's hotel that Wednesday afternoon. Always befriend your enemy—or better, Lilia thought, make your enemy your accomplice. Mrs. Nelson could do no wrong, and her innocence would exonerate Lilia.

She wanted to buy Gilbert a surprise present for their anniversary, Lilia explained to Mrs. Nelson. Of course, Mrs. Nelson said, exhilarated by her inclusion in a wife's secret. She asked Lilia how many years they had been married and Lilia said five. Mrs. Nelson brought out an album in which she kept the cuttings from a Miss Manners column.

Five years, Mrs. Nelson said. Wood. Something made of wood? A picture frame? Here it says silverware would do, too. But really it's Gilbert who should get you a present, don't you think?

It's also to celebrate his promotion, Lilia said. This is a special year for him.

Of course, Mrs. Nelson said, her eyes glancing at Lilia's midsection meaningfully, though Lilia was confident that she was not showing yet.

She'd better have something to show Mrs. Nelson at the end of the afternoon, Lilia thought when she entered the Fairmont's lobby. The shops inside looked even nicer than Emporium, but Lilia was confident that she could afford something. She was an efficient housekeeper, frugal when needed.

She had left neither address nor phone number in her note to Roland. He was at liberty not to be at the hotel, but there he was, and he showed little reservation when he invited Lilia up to his room. She had not allowed herself to imagine in advance what would happen, but in the elevator she found herself clutching her elbows, as though she felt nervous, and she had to keep her back to Roland so that she would not break out laughing or humming.

Lilia, you're not a kid anymore, Roland said when they entered his room.

Mrs. Murray, Lilia held out her hand to him. His glasses were not the ones she remembered, but the eyes behind were the same bluish gray. His hair, parted impeccably, did not show any sign of receding, unlike Gilbert's. Do men ever age in Roland's world? Lilia did not know what that world was like, but she imagined that there each day and each night were distinct, meaningful, memorable. In her own world there were days that were marked on the calendar—holidays, birthdays, anniversaries—but there were many more days that looked just like one another.

How do you do, Mrs. Murray? Roland said, and then asked if there was a child of Mr. and Mrs. Murray to whom he could send his regards.

Children, Lilia said.

Children? How many are we talking about?

Two, she said. A weaker soul would reveal that one of them belonged to him.

So I wasn't wrong, Lilia. I knew you would waste no time in getting married.

And with no trouble, either, but let's leave Mr. Murray out of this for the afternoon, shall we?

Fair enough.

Roland had made no effort to hide his wedding band. Tell me about Mrs. Bouley, Lilia said.

Let's leave her out, too, wouldn't you agree? Roland replied, leading Lilia into his bedroom with an almost fatherly gentleness.

Afterward Lilia asked about his wife again. She's not your Mrs. Ogden by any chance?

You have a good memory! I forgot I told you about Sidelle.

You don't talk about her often with your women? Do you talk

about her with your wife? How does Mrs. Bouley feel about Mrs. Ogden? Have they met? Are they friends?

Roland laughed. You haven't changed at all, Lilia.

How wrong he was, but she did not correct him. What made you write to the ranch? Lilia asked. If you thought I was already married, didn't you worry that the letter might never reach me?

It never hurts to send out a message in a bottle. And here we are, in any case.

But why?

Why I wrote you? Roland said. In fact, I don't know.

Was she to think that he came all the way to California on the same impulse that she went to his hotel five years ago? Or was he dismissing her with the easiest answer? I thought you always knew everything, Lilia said.

This, Roland said, is what I know. A man can love a woman like he loves his worst sin, and a man can also love a woman as his salvation. A man is lucky to have either kind of love, but if he has both, sometimes he must take a break.

So he sends out a random message in a bottle and hopes for the best?

Random? Have a little faith in yourself, Roland said. You and I get away with things, but you're more of a natural. If we were pickpockets I would be a well-trained one, I would perfect my skills, I would count my gain. But you, Lilia, you're not even self-taught. You could just take something away from one person and slip it into another person's pocket like it's nobody's business.

Is that a compliment?

Yes, Roland said. If only we lived closer.

Mrs. Ogden—is she still in England?

Yes.

Then it doesn't matter if we don't live so close, Lilia said.

With her it doesn't matter.

With me?

If we see each other once every five years, Roland said, what's the point?

He meant adultery performed once every five years could hardly be called adultery. What he needed was her infidelity to her own husband in his daily life.

Later they made love again. Lilia recognized some signs of his age. He must be over forty now. How old would that make Sidelle Ogden? When Lilia's mother had turned forty Lilia had thought of her as ancient.

What's on your mind? Roland said.

At least that was one thing he shared with Gilbert, as though a woman's thoughts after lovemaking became a man's property.

I wonder how it feels to be no longer young, she said.

Like you're talking on the phone, and before you can finish a sentence, the line clicks. You know all the things you want to say but you can't say them anymore.

Lilia was surprised by the melancholy in his tone. I'm asking about being old, she said. Not being dead.

When you are dead you don't have anything left to say.

Of course you do. I think most people die before they can say what they want to say.

Well then, once you are dead you can't want anymore, Roland said. That solves all problems. But getting old? Who will connect the line for you again?

Is that how you feel? That you want to say all these things but the line is already disconnected? Lilia asked.

Don't you have those feelings sometimes?

I'm not old, Lilia said.

How young you are, indeed.

Who do you want to say those things to? Lilia asked.

And what a good interrogator your youth makes you, Roland said.

Is that how Mrs. Ogden feels about growing old, too?

No, she never grows old. Mark my words, she'll die one day but not as an old woman.

Why are you so certain about that?

Because I've known her my entire adult life. Things happen because she makes them happen.

Lilia thought she could do that, too. Things happened because she wanted them to, didn't they? Here she was, a child of Gilbert inside her, and Roland back in her life. Never before had her two lives coexisted so peacefully. Look at all those politicians and diplomats who talked about world peace yet achieved nothing. If only they could learn a few things from her.

That night Lilia asked Gilbert, Do you remember what day it is tomorrow?

Of course, he said.

She told him there was something in the nightstand drawer for him. For tomorrow, she said.

Can I look now?

You have to wait.

The tie in the nightstand drawer—a new one—she had taken from Roland's closet before she left him. A memento? Roland had asked, watching her put the tie away in her purse. She had asked for it, knowing he would not say no.

Yes, Lilia said.

Are you not worried about your husband discovering it?

I thought we agreed to leave him out, Lilia had said.

Even Roland did not know how a woman kept her secrets. Perhaps no man knew.

K ATHERINE STOPPED THE CAR A BLOCK FROM MOLLY'S place, and Iola asked her again why she was not coming to the dinner party. Lilia reminded the girl that they had had this discussion for the duration of the drive. "They're your aunt and uncle and cousins," Lilia said. "They'll be happy to see you."

"I don't even know them," Iola said.

"You don't have to know them *well*," Lilia said.

Katherine turned around and fixed Iola's curls. "Listen, sweetie, sometimes going to a dinner party is like going to school. You don't have to like it. You just do it."

"You don't go to school during Thanksgiving break," Iola said.

"You can't take a break from living," Lilia said, and opened the car door. They could sit there for hours, talking in circles.

Katherine handed the pan of pumpkin brownies to Iola. "Tell everyone you helped me make them," she said.

Before Iola had time to protest and say she had not helped, Lilia cut her off. "Let me carry them," she said. "And make sure you come on time. We don't want to be stranded here."

"Stranded," Iola said. She liked to repeat words she did not understand, a habit that made Lilia pity the child. You could easily see the holes in her brain, like Swiss cheese. Any child would have a similar number of holes but a smarter one would at least know how to hide them.

"Iola has a condition," Lilia said to Katherine. "She repeats words."

"Do you mean echolalia? She doesn't. She's only expanding her vocabulary."

"Echolalia?" Iola said.

Lilia had asked Katherine several times where she was planning to spend the night, but she had avoided giving a definite answer.

Could she be cheating on Andy? Unlikely. Infidelity is too high an art.

The next morning, Katherine called and said she would be picking Lilia and Iola up at two o'clock. Lilia reminded Katherine to be on time—with the holiday traffic the drive might take them longer than usual to get back. Lilia did not want to miss dinner, which was at five. She wanted to be walking down the hallway with Iola and Katherine, so everyone could witness her homecoming.

"Still not here?" Molly asked Lilia, who had insisted on rolling the suitcase to the top of the driveway herself when Katherine hadn't shown up by five after two. They were like leftover kids whose parents had forgotten to pick them up from camp. Another disadvantage of growing old: You're reduced to the status of a six-year-old.

"Not everyone is as capable as you are," Lilia said. But it didn't sound sincere, so she added: "Quite a party you had yesterday."

"The more the merrier," Molly said.

The stale words, Lilia thought. How good Molly was at distributing them. The night before, other than Molly and Robert and their two children who had returned from college (Natalie, the oldest one, had stayed in Chicago with a friend's family), there were Robert's two siblings and their families. Molly had also invited her Israeli colleague and her two children (Where's your father? Lilia had asked both children, but neither gave her an answer), and two young couples, one from Brazil and one from Canada, who had something to do with Robert's research group. Lilia had taken an instant interest in the Canadians, but it turned out that they were from British Columbia. Had she been? they asked her, and she gave them the honest answer that British Columbia was not much of an attraction to anyone growing up in California. Had the couple come from Nova Scotia Lilia would have been more excited.

"Looks like it's going to rain soon," Molly said.

"Rain is what we need," Lilia said. "We've had a decade-long drought now."

"I mean there's no point getting wet outside," Molly said. "Too bad Jason and Amanda are out shopping and Iola has no one to play with."

How did Molly become so skilled in make-believe? Any observant person could see that Iola was not one of those indiscreet children who would welcome any random person into her world. She had met Jason and Amanda no more than five times in her life; they might as well be two strangers. Not to mention that they were college students now. To stay home and entertain a bratty little cousin? Lilia would think much less of them if they would do so willingly.

"No, the rain will just wait until we get into the car," Lilia said, and thanked Molly again for the dinner. Lilia had not explained Katherine's absence, and Molly had not asked. Staying clear of the many minefields, Lilia and Molly enjoyed each other reasonably. Lilia had never lapsed in sending birthday presents and Christmas presents to Molly and her family. Molly had not missed her biweekly check-in phone calls with Lilia, and her monthly visit.

Of Lilia's children, Molly was the most accomplished, the headmistress of an all-girls' school, and before that, the admissions officer for a prep school. It was typical of Katherine not to see the long-term benefits of being on friendly terms with Molly.

"Iola, send your parents our love," Molly said, and handed a bag of persimmons from her backyard to the girl. "And thank you for the pumpkin brownies you made."

"I didn't help making the brownies," Iola said.

"You helped eating them," Lilia said. "And you did a fabulous job with that."

Molly asked Iola to use the bathroom one more time. "I know you just went, sweetie, but it's a long drive." When the girl was out of their sight, Molly said, "Mom, you need to be nicer to Iola. And to Katherine, too."

"As if I'm an evil stepmother!"

"No, but people like Katherine and Iola are sensitive," Molly said.

Lilia did not like how Molly sounded. "Any girl can look trau-matized to you," Lilia said. "That's your occupational hazard."

"What I'm saying is, you have to make an extra effort with cer-tain people."

"You mean, Katherine and Iola are little dainty eggs that I should handle with extra care?"

"You can't deny their history."

"What history?"

"Well, Lucy."

"You don't even remember Lucy."

"Of course I do. A little, but we talked about Lucy later."

"Who is this 'we'?"

"Dad. Also Tim and Will and Carol."

"And what did you all conclude? That I mistreated her so she killed herself?"

"No, not that. We just thought Lucy might be more sensitive to things."

Lilia didn't speak right away.

"You've done so much for us," Molly said. "Nobody could change anything about Lucy, but it's not an easy situation for Kath-erine. We should all try our best for her and for Iola."

The girl, summoned, appeared from behind Molly soundlessly.

Lilia insisted that they wait by the curb. She had nothing more to say to Molly. Other than Roland's diaries and her own memo-ries, she did not probe people's recollections of the past. They could have their own histories, worthwhile or not, but they were like shop windows Lilia had no interest in studying. No, my dear, thank you but no.

"Where is Mommy?" Iola asked.

"Stop kicking," Lilia said, and moved the bag of persimmons away from the girl's toes. "Take a seat on the suitcase if you're tired."

"I'm not tired, I'm bored," Iola said.

Sometimes Lilia thought Iola had the ability to take a single look at the world and claim that god made a fundamental mistake when creating it: Everything is pointless, everything is boring. Are all children born with such a divine negation of life? Lilia could not remember her siblings or her children behaving this way. She herself had never found life boring for a moment.

"You always say that," Lilia said.

"Because I'm bored."

That's what she should do, Lilia thought. Before her death, she should make a list of the favorite sayings of her offspring and embroider a sampler for each of them. Iola would get a rainbow-colored one with the busiest pattern of twigs and flowers and butterflies and crab apples and squirrels and lizards, all surrounding that protest: I AM BORED. Molly would get one with ivory lace and fine feathers and cunning little wrens: WITH ALL DUE RESPECT.

"Can I have your phone?" Iola asked, despite having asked for it several times that morning and having been told that Lilia did not carry one with her.

"Want to hear a story?" Lilia asked.

Iola looked at Lilia as though she could not decide if it was a trick question.

"I mean it as a yes or no question. Do you want to hear a story?"

"That sounds babyish," Iola said.

"I'm not talking about baby stories," Lilia said. She had plenty of stories. The problem was she had never wanted to share them with her children, and now they seemed to have fabricated their own versions to make up for that loss. How could Molly think Lilia had mistreated Lucy and been responsible for her death?

"What do you know about your grandma?" Lilia asked. "No, not Grandma Paula, Grandma Lucy."

"Grandma Lucy?" Iola said. "Isn't she already dead?"

Lilia opened her mouth. She had no words. She had never before in her life been in a situation where she could not find any words.

Lilia decided to leave a record for Katherine and Iola. No, she wasn't thinking of Molly's accusation. Lilia had no interest in acquitting herself of unfounded charges. But Katherine and Iola deserved something more than confusion. They couldn't just have stories from Molly.

Lilia asked Nikko, the floor manager, for a composition book. "What color," Nikko asked, showing her a stack on the shelf. "Everyone needs a composition book these days."

"Give me two of them," Lilia said. "Black and red."

Katherine and Iola: I decided to leave something for the two of you, along with this book written by Lucy's birth father. His name is Roland Bouley, and here's his story, Lilia wrote on the first page of the composition book. She tried to make her letters stay between the lines. *I met Roland in 1945 and Lucy was born in 1946. I was a small part in his life, and Lucy was not in his life at all. But that's all right. Remember, only weak souls look for rewards from others. We're our own rewards.*

She then cut out the note and glued it carefully to the inside cover of Roland's diaries.

PART THREE

Noonday

...

[I embarked as a diarist on 12 November 1925, right before I turned fifteen. Rereading the first four years of my diary I experienced a not unpleasant giddiness, as though getting drunk on a wine too green. They were evidence that a boy's ego could be as colossal and fatalistic as a Greek tragedy. I stand by that ego but have enough humility not to burden readers. My real life, as seen here, began in the summer of 1929. — RB, 2 March 1989]

1 JULY 1929.

At teatime Aunt E joked about cousinhood being the only dangerous neighborhood, and I pretended that I did not notice Hetty's twisting fingers. There is plenty of time for her to outgrow her ardour for me. For now, she comes in handy. When she is here for the summer, the role of chaperone falls to Aunt E. To spend time with Hetty means to live nearer Aunt E than at any other time of the year. My cousinly duty to Hetty is a convenient pretext. My love for Aunt E, the context of my existence.

Reading Ovid last night, I wondered what plant or beast I deserved to be transformed into if I announced my passion. Will Aunt E remain my sole love? One must be careful not to place one's heart in a cage that can be unlocked by only one key.

I desire, however, for Aunt E to acknowledge my love. Accept it even? No matter, my poor dead parents would not have approved, nor would any of my relatives. Yet is this not the world's due to an orphan, who must be granted the rights to the uncommon, even the forbidden? One is not orphaned for nothing.

What a scandal we could make. I do believe I shall be able to make a great novel out of this love for Aunt E.

———

Aunt Evelyn is the widow of Uncle Albert, the eldest brother of my mother. He died from blood poisoning a year after my birth. The two daughters born in that marriage, Annabel and Dorothy, both chose marriages that allowed them to leave Halifax—Annabel to Toronto, Dorothy to Boston.

Uncle Victor married a good woman. He and Aunt Geraldine, with two sons, have saved the Fergusons from extinction, a misfortune that has befallen several old Nova Scotia families. George and Harold are both at school in England, and are spending the summer travelling to places still unknown to me. Emma, the eldest, is properly installed as the wife of a thriving solicitor in Halifax.

Uncle William is a bachelor, his romantic history unknown to me. A mistress abandoned and dying in an unheated room? A bastard son growing up in poverty? But Uncle William is a raging bore. One can hardly place him in a novel with even the most cliché plot.

My mother, Rosaline, married David Bouley from Boston, against her family's wishes. They were punished by untimely deaths, in a train crash. Marianne, Hetty's mother, married discerningly, to a surgeon whose patients come from all over the maritime provinces. They have four perfect children, and they lead a flawless life. Hetty is the eldest of the siblings, and two years younger than I am. Of all my cousins she is the closest to me in age and in friendship.

This house on the hill, overlooking Halifax Bay, is called
Elmsey. It is not beautiful but utilitarian, built in 1829 and
expanded when the Fergusons prospered. Relatives visit,
sometimes for an extended period, but none is a hanger-on
like me—poor relatives should never congregate. No novel
I have read features five orphans brought up in a house by
their benefactors. An orphan is a singular event. Had there
been five Rolands, where could we find the courage to
feign dignity when we competed to peck from the hands of
our patrons?

...

[While going through my diaries one last time, I have added some lines
to explain family relations and events. One can fabricate one's memories
when young; old age demands truthfulness at the cost of one's ego. —RB,
5 January 1990]

Lilia's notes taped next to the corresponding entries

A WARNING: THE FERGUSONS' family tree seems clear here but as
you will see later, cousins pop in and out, once removed or twice
removed or a hundred times removed. Had Roland been a big
name someone would have done the work, with the Fergusons and
the Bouleys traced back to however many generations. And we
could add Lucy, and you two, a precious branch. But what's a
branch to a tree? A tree has little remorse when it sheds a branch.

My own family—you're part of that, too. We have reliable roots.

They're starting a genealogy club. You see flyers everywhere.
"Meet twice a week. Led by Professor Roberta M. Lynch, a re-
nowned historian" with a list of her achievements. My theory: It's
designed as a competition to the memoir class, which Professor
Lynch calls an incubator for unhatchable eggs.

———

Later.

Hetty dropped in with a letter while I was in the middle of typing—my first novel, which is, in fact, my fourth, though this is going to be my first mature novel. Working on your writing, Hetty asked, and I could not help but joke that the book, once completed, would be dedicated to someone whom I have known all my life. She blushed (not knowing, of course, it is another woman I have in mind). If only she could stop that. No, I do not oppose the female virtue of blushing. What would I not give to see Aunt E blush? But Hetty's blushing has the effect of plain water. When one craves champagne.

I scanned the letter, which was from Arthur. He was talking about the coming term with what already seemed like nostalgia. Each day brings us closer to England, he wrote.

I discussed this with Hetty. Summer is so short, she said. Unbearably so, I agreed, and said perhaps some boy will capture her heart next term. She denied vehemently this possibility. No one at St. Mary's, she said, would fall for an Edgehill boy. What's wrong with them, I asked. They're still babies, she said.

I wonder if Aunt E would say that about me. Roland is only a baby, and will always be a baby: Roland the orphan, Roland the changeling, Roland whose only hope is to grow up into a decent enough man so he can marry Hetty.

No. That is not how my life will turn out. Roland Victor Sydney Bouley: You will become a man of fame and fortune through your own endeavours. You will not marry a woman out of obligation or convenience.

———

ROLAND MARRIED HETTY. THIS is hardly a spoiler.

Roland once introduced me to someone as his cousin. This was in 1954, the last time we met. He wrote to our Roosevelt Road address, which he said he had found in the telephone book. He was visiting someone at the navy base in Vallejo and asked if we could meet nearby.

It wasn't the first time he wrote me out of the blue. And I don't deceive myself that I was the only woman who'd received an unexpected letter from Roland. He might not have known what he wanted when he posted these letters. But when I agreed to see him, I knew what I wanted.

It was August, right before school started. Lucy was eight, and already difficult, more difficult than either Gilbert or I could understand. I told him that I would take Lucy out for a day by herself and have a serious talk with her. Gilbert looked nervous. What? I asked, and he said he was reminded of Hansel and Gretel. I laughed and said I wasn't a stepmother to my own children.

Timmy and Willie wanted to come, too. But I promised them toys or comics so they stayed home. I didn't want to bring Gilbert's sons with me. We met Roland at a beach in Benicia. Some fathers recognize their children right away. Roland was not one of them. He was patient and indifferent to Lucy, the way a man is with a neighbor's dog as long as the poor beast doesn't bark. Lucy could not be relied on to stay out of anyone's way, but on that day she mostly combed the beach, walking back and forth and mumbling to herself. I had given her plenty of warnings beforehand. Still, it amazed me that she did not clamor for my attention. Perhaps life began to defeat her right then, with a father who felt nothing for her.

Roland and I talked. We behaved with each other like former neighbors. When Lucy got bored we went to a diner. The waitress must have seen Roland there before. She looked at me with a nasty interest and studied Lucy's face rudely. Roland said I was his cousin from San Francisco. I knew the waitress saw through his lie and I could tell he didn't care.

Roland doesn't mention other women in California on this trip. He does write about our meeting. Only two lines. "L didn't come alone but with a child, a girl whose prettiness is marred by her moodiness. Shall we say this is the end of one Californian dream?"

We agreed to stay in touch, but he wasn't one to keep his promises. I wasn't feeling hopeful. I had thought when he asked about Lucy's age he might get an idea why I wanted them to meet. But bringing her was a mistake. What Roland and I had was like a kayak for two. Add one more person and it capsizes.

On the way home I told Lucy that she shouldn't mention to Gilbert or the boys about meeting my cousin. Why can't I? she asked, and I said she was welcome to tell them anything but then she shouldn't expect a new dress when school started. He's my cousin then, she said. Yes, I said. She shrugged and said she didn't understand why we had to come all the way to meet a cousin. Like father like daughter, I thought. They saw nothing in each other.

Who knew you can remember things better when you start to put them into words. If I keep this up, Roland's diary will be twice its thickness when I finish. It's like I'm getting this book pregnant. What about that, Roland?

———

2 JULY 1929.

> People from two races have a better chance for real
> romance. How else to explain the marriage between
> Mother and Father? Now that I have reached the age when
> I should start having a love life of my own, I have become
> obsessed with analysing marriages and love affairs. All

couples hold secrets that I have yet to learn. My poor parents of course are at the centre of my contemplations.

———

DO YOU NOT FIND it interesting that he called Canadians and Americans two races? But let me leave race and romance aside and tell you something entirely different. There are two kinds of people. The first kind, they need dreams like they need air and water. The second kind, they treat dreams like breadcrumbs or cobwebs. Take two people from these two different tribes, and they often end up in a long-lasting marriage.

For example, Roland and Hetty. There was a time in my life when the thought of Hetty made me grind my teeth, but I now understand Roland needed a woman who did not dream. When he burned a hole in the curtain with his cigarette or unsettled a dinner plate while daydreaming she was there to put things right again. He did just that. More than once. Intentionally, in my opinion. A mistress's letter laid out on his desk. A telegram from Sidelle left in the pocket of his pajamas. How else could he put up with Hetty?

My mother was a dreamer. She once wanted to become a writer and wrote some stories. Nothing came of that pursuit. But does a dream stop being a dream when it fails? My mother and Roland shared an ambition—it never occurred to me until now. So in a way my father and Hetty were dreamless comrades—imagine that!

Katherine: You know some of my siblings, but you haven't met my sister Lucille. She and I, we are both dreamers. Margot, Lucille's twin, lived in her shadow. Margot may have had some hand-me-down dreams. Our brothers inherited our father's dullness. It should be that way. Dreaming is a costly habit, especially for a man.

Roland was an expert in believing he had many lives. I don't have many lives, I don't deceive myself into thinking so, but I know how and when to dream.

Lucy inherited something from both Roland and me—you mix two dreamers and who knows what you get.

———

Later.

Cousin Petra visited on her way to Cape Breton. She feigned surprise at finding me grown into what she called a good-looking young man worth ten Lord Byrons combined. Of Hetty she said a dozen sonnets were in order.

I wonder, I said, if I would have turned out the same man had I been sent back to the Bouleys. I have learned not to mention Father's name in the house, but I thought Cousin Petra might offer some accidental insight into my parents' marriage.

She made an exaggerated sound. Like most of the family, she has to forgive my original sin of being born to an American father. We're far from the Loyalists, she said. The way she talks sounds as though the American Revolution were still going on outside our windows. History—be it a nation's or a person's—does not become the past for my mother's family.

No, it's not that we're for the Empire, Cousin Petra said. Roland, always be grateful to the Fergusons. Without them you'd have grown up a rude and crude American.

Canadians against Americans, yes, but really it is a clan against one man. Thank goodness I have inherited Father's looks. And like Mother I am drawn to forbidden romance.

Mother would have died from boredom rather than a train crash had she married into a Nova Scotian family as expected of her. Only a girl like Hetty would live in this

well-moulded world so uncomplainingly. Mother would
have found Hetty an unworthy match for her only son. You
must always keep this in mind, Roland. Her blood, reckless
and listless, runs in your veins.

...

[The Fergusons began in the milling business in Nova Scotia, providing
timber to the shipbuilding yards. When Grandpa Ferguson foresaw, after
a few fatal fires in town, that brick houses would soon replace wooden
houses, the family entered brick manufacturing. Later, he purchased a
plant that was said to be the first factory to produce ice skates on a large
scale in the New World, though his ambition reached beyond skates. By
the time Uncle Victor and his brothers entered the business the factory
had expanded to become a major manufacturer of nails and vault hinges
and an assortment of metal parts for bridges and ships.—RB 6 March
1989]

ROLAND'S MOTHER, IN THE EYES of her family, was the woman
who had married the wrong man and boarded the wrong train,
traveling toward death together. But aren't all marriages like that?
Though most of us go at a slower speed.

They were young and in love, so that was the silver lining. Not
that I believe in this silver lining business, invented by people who
can't accept that sometimes life is just bad, terrible, hopeless. At
Lucy's funeral, someone said to me, thank god you still have the
other children. I thank god for nothing, I said, and the woman only
exchanged a knowing look with a man next to her.

We don't know much about Roland's mother. He only mentioned her a few times, but she died young. Younger than Lucy. A
similar fate met his mother and his daughter, and he was not there
for either of them.

But there was one difference. Roland's mother didn't choose to die.

Those who spoke the nonsense about his mother—they must have lived and died in the same place, looking at every disaster befalling someone else as a punishment.

One thing my mother often said to us when we fought: No one says you have to like the people you love. I used to think she meant this: We were siblings, and we should love one another even if we didn't like one another. But maybe she was only telling herself that she didn't have to like us.

Whatever she meant, I can tell you that people often mess up between liking and loving. Katherine—your grandfather Gilbert believed that global peace was possible once the world's population found love for one another. He was young then so let us not laugh at his idea, but he was wrong, not because it was impossible for all those people to love one another. It was impossible for them to like one another. It's so damn hard for anyone to like anyone. But love comes easier. That's why you hear all these songs talking about loving someone, not liking someone.

Imagine if Roland's parents had stayed alive. Those uncles and aunts and cousins disliked Roland's father so much they would've extended that dislike to Roland. But bam, the person they disliked died. Now what should they do with Roland? Like him? No way. Love him? Why not. They kept Roland in that house, I think, to remind themselves how much they disliked Roland's father and how much they had overcome their dislike to love Roland.

People would be more consistent if they lived their lives based on their dislikes. Liking is so fussy. To turn like into dislike you just leave it like fresh milk on a summer day. To make dislike into like? That would beat the miracle of water turning to wine, don't you think?

---

6 JULY 1929.

Desmond said yesterday that I spent too much time
tackling the undesired self to justify my study of
hedonism. I was disheartened, though not by his criticism,
which is an honour. One fears his compliments, always
cutting and dismissive; even more fearful would be his
indifference.

Aunt E informed the family today that she was thinking
of taking a journey to the west. West where, Aunt Geraldine asked, but Aunt E was evasive. Why, she was pressed
(not by me—in my panic I had to gather all my courage to
look nonchalant), but she didn't answer, saying only that
she hadn't made the final decision. Typical of her to drop
one hint and withhold a thousand. What if I offered myself
as her travelling companion before the term starts. Would
she take me? Would she be willing to loan me the funds to
travel as her companion?

Would any woman pay a man to be in love with her?

Later I read a story told—made up?—by Seneca, about a
man who killed himself by abstaining from food for three
days and then sitting in his bath while his slaves kept refill-
ing the tub so he would not feel cold. But cold he must
have turned, as according to Seneca the man's soul drifted
away while he was enjoying his luxurious bath. One
wonders if that is what an inappropriate erotic interest is
like: pleasurable, timeless, fatal.

Last night I resolved not to dwell upon sex so much.
I wonder whether all men make such resolutions, and
whether all fail as wretchedly as I do. Does any man ever
make a name for himself by being oversexed?

———

MANY MEN HAVE DONE just that. Poor Roland, so inexperienced. He was eighteen here. Most people I knew—my siblings, myself, Gilbert—knew more about life at eighteen. But we must forgive him. Sometimes an orphan has a more sheltered life than a child with living parents.

What fascinates me is this: He would become more experienced, but he would never really stop being this young. How many people can be as consistent as that?

———

9 JULY 1929.

It turns out that of all places, Aunt E is planning a trip to Colorado. She revealed this information (and the date of departure—Tuesday week) after we returned from church. All of a sudden Bessie and Ethel, having not been told of the reason for the change of the atmosphere, served the food with more care. Behind them Lewis took on a claylike appearance.

Orphans and servants are human barometers—once again I am reminded that my lot is not far from that of Bessie, Ethel, and Lewis.

Why Colorado and why so sudden, Aunt Geraldine demanded to know, asking on behalf of Uncle Victor, who will not deign to speak when he feels in any way betrayed. And he is an easily betrayed man, always ready to punish. My cousins Annabel and Dorothy, by defecting in their marriages to places disapproved of by him, have become personae non grata. I too have learned valuable lessons, the earliest dating back to before school age—held responsible, I believe, for my mother's betrayal.

Colorado? Uncle William said. That's no place for you.

He sounded pitiful. There is something mysterious about Uncle William's attitude toward Aunt E, though in a household where everyone's past is constantly stirred up, this mystery has remained unprobed. I wonder if I alone can sense a secret that Aunt E and Uncle William have agreed to keep safe from familial scrutiny. My hypothesis is that Uncle William once proposed to Aunt E. Before her marriage to Uncle Albert or after Uncle Albert's death? Either possibility would add a plot twist to the novel I will be writing. If only Uncle William were a character ten times more interesting than he is. As he stands now, he is too minor a character, entirely dispensable.

I do not know much about Uncle Albert, only that he was closest to Mother and he opposed most vehemently her marriage to Father. After the marriage he and Mother never spoke to each other again.

Had Uncle Albert remained alive would I have had a less favourable position in this household? It was a miracle that he had not shipped me back to the Bouleys, care of Canadian National Railway and labelled FRAGILE. In any case those alive have the right to disturb the dead. If I declared my love to Aunt E, I could avenge Uncle Albert's mistreatment of my parents. Imagine Aunt E shedding Ferguson and taking up Bouley as her new name. Is there a law against one's marrying one's widowed aunt? I have never thought of looking into the matter.

To ease the tension Aunt E said that it was only to be a short trip.

It can't be a short trip if it's across a continent, Uncle William said. What's there in any case?

Foolish Americans, Uncle Victor said.

Aunt Geraldine touched her lips with the corner of her napkin. Hetty studied her pudding attentively. Poor Hetty. She does not have to be here all summer long as when we were younger. Jonathan and Thomas and Susie only come for a short visit at the beginning of the summer now. Hetty must have given convincing excuses for her stay. Or else they must have seen some rare qualities in me so as not to put a stop to what is so obvious to everyone.

It surprises me that I did not realise this earlier.

———

WHAT IF HETTY'S PARENTS were only being reasonable, because they thought this girlish crush would be over soon? I was being reasonable in thinking that once Lucy and Steve had had enough drama between them, the country-music kind, the head-spinning kind, the special-effect kind—I thought one day when Lucy went through them all she would say, enough is enough.

But no, reasonable parents make mistakes. Hetty's parents should've put their foot down and told her that there were a thousand reasons for her not to marry Roland. They should've married her off before her expiration date.

When Lucy married Steve, I wished first for a quick divorce, and then for both of them to calm down. I didn't keep my expectations high. Still, I wasn't prepared for what was coming. One of the first thoughts I had, right after Lucy died, was this: Now nobody will ever surprise me again.

———

Later.

Let me see if I can record everything as precisely as it happened, but with a novelist's distance and equanimity.

I went off to the stables before Aunt E and Hetty, pretending that I was sent to help get the horses ready. Freddie didn't mind. He definitely did not look his sober self.

When Aunt E and Hetty arrived, I behaved to Hetty like a lover, full of solicitations. Why, why, why do I have to be this caddish? Sometimes I have an odd feeling that I'm waiting for Hetty to surprise me. What if she would stick a spoon in the fire then press it red-hot to her arm, all the while watching me unblinkingly like one of those impassioned princesses in a Russian novel? What would I do if Hetty proved herself capable of such fervour? I would almost have to marry her for that spoon-shaped scar. Some would think that it was her money I was after. The decent ones would not say this to my face, but there are not many decent people in the world.

Alas, Hetty is not someone one lusts after. She is the kind of girl who uses a spoon as a mirror when distracted by her own thoughts. How tragic for a good-looking girl with a handsome income.

———

LUCY ONCE STOLE A safety razor from Gilbert's box. She was twelve. Back then we still counted everything because we were not wasteful people. Have I ever told you that we had the most detailed record of expense, down to every penny? Once in a while I told Gilbert that we should get rid of the account books that were a few years old, but he said it'd be fun to read them again. Some day when we are old, he said. Gilbert was like Roland that way. Any small thing from now could have ten times more meaning in the future. Forward-looking men, that's what they both were when young. Roland didn't change. He looked all the way ahead to his posterity.

We did our accounting every night, after the children went to bed. It was my favorite time of the day. Gilbert had the better penmanship, I did the addition and subtraction faster, and we talked and joked. About nothing special. Sometimes I wish I could go back and teach my mother a few things. Time in a marriage is something to be frittered away. When husband and wife do it well and do it together, that's happiness enough.

I used to have some wild notions about happiness. Any young girl would get them from movies. But a day in a life is longer than a life in a movie. I was a quick learner.

I didn't tell Gilbert about the missing razor. He might have broken one and forgotten to mention it to me. That was what I thought, until I was cleaning Lucy's room and found it, still in its wax wrapping paper, in the dollhouse under her doll's bed. A good hiding place, except the corner of the wax paper stuck out. I confiscated the razor and never said anything. She didn't ask me about it. For a while I watched her, trying to see if she knew I knew her secret. She knew. I thought any moment she would confess, but she never did. If I stared at her she simply stared back.

From then on, she must have known to buy the razors with her allowance. I wondered how Mr. Land never suspected anything. She probably lied sweetly and said she was sent by her father to buy them.

It was Regan Stoler's mother who alerted me. Regan was Lucy's friend at school. I forget if Mrs. Stoler noticed the scars herself or Regan told her about it. In any case I confronted Lucy and discovered the scars neatly lined up on her inner arm.

Nowadays people make a big fuss about such things, but I only warned her that she would look ugly in a summer dress if she kept doing it. She promised she would stop. No tears of remorse. No explanations. I didn't ask her why she did it. Nor did I tell Gilbert about it. You can't live a child's life for her—I've always believed that.

Sometimes I wonder what it would've been like to slide a razor across Hetty's pale wrist. She would have had little to bleed but good manners. If you could place Lucy and Hetty next to each other as young girls, they would be like day and night, yin and yang, a pot of bonsai and a field of wildflowers. Lucy had so much in her. She deserved a long life, don't you think?

Well, it doesn't really matter now.

———

I told Aunt E I was here to see if there was an extra horse today. I haven't been riding for a while, I said. That was not a lie.

And you now expect me to give away my horse, Aunt E said. I wonder if she has seen through my sham interest in Hetty.

As though on cue Hetty developed a headache. She told me to take Sahara, and said she would wait for us on the porch. Freddie, no longer indolent—he never is around Hetty—began a performance of dusting up the rocking chair and sending his boy to Lane's for cold orangeade.

Aunt E and I rode out toward the creek. After a period of silence I mustered the courage to ask her what she thought of my accompanying her on her trip. She looked sideways at me and said she was not a damsel in need of a knight.

Only I thought it would be a change of air, I said, for me, I mean.

Go to Boston, she said. You're old enough to make the trip. The Bouleys would be thrilled to see you.

And to don the pauper's clothes again? I said.

Their situation is not that meagre.

Then where did this reputation of my father being a schemer come from?

Men do worse things than marrying women for money, Aunt E said.

Like what?

Aunt E did not speak.

Like what? I asked again.

I don't want to disparage your father, she said. My position in this family is not that different from yours.

Except you are a Ferguson, I said. And you have your independence.

I live as one of the Fergusons and that's my independence, if you can call it that.

But you can leave freely. When you say you want to travel, none of them can stop you.

None of them will open the door if I ever come back, Aunt E said.

Why? I said.

You don't have to bite the hand that feeds you to betray it. If you dodge a petting gesture you've committed the sin of ingratitude.

I don't understand, I said.

I must have sounded pathetically young. When Aunt E spoke again it was no longer in her teasing tone. Roland, listen carefully, this is not where your future is.

Of course not, I thought. I've been talking about Oxford with my uncles, I said.

Oxford won't happen for you, Aunt E said.

Why not?

Because there's no longer the money for that.

What about my mother's money?

You can ask your uncles about finances. I'm only giving you a warning.

Did they send you as a messenger?

When do I ever do things at their behest, Roland?

Then why are you telling me these things?

(Writing this now, I feel ashamed to recall that I spoke with a hint of tears in my voice.)

I was fond of your parents, Aunt E said. They would be glad that I've treated you fairly.

What should I do, then? I said. Can I come with you to Colorado?

What would I do with you if I decided to get married out there? Aunt E asked.

It is a cliché when people say their hearts skipped a beat. But mine did just that. Get married? I asked. To whom?

(What's there for you in a marriage? What can a man give you that I cannot? Why are you abandoning me? I wish I had said all these things to her aloud.)

There's bound to be someone if one sets one's heart to it, Aunt E said.

What would Uncle Victor and Uncle William say?

I don't expect that you'd run back breaking the news to them?

No, I said. But don't you think they'd want to know?

It's been seventeen years. I can't wear my widow's weeds forever.

Why not, I thought, wait a few more years for me? How old is Aunt E? It surprised me that I never thought of that as a relevant question. With courage gathered from this heart-to-heart, I asked her.

Much older than you, Aunt E said.

How much older?

I'm thirty-nine, Roland.

And I am eighteen, almost a grown man—I wish I said that to her. I wish I made some confession. Instead I said cowardly, Oh.

───

THIRTY-NINE. STILL A SPRING CHICKEN. Gilbert often said the twentieth century was when the world began to become a better place. Here's at least something positive that supports his opinion. People stay spring chickens much longer now than sixty years ago.

On the other hand, Gilbert didn't see our twenty-first century. So far we've had many bad things, and they'll only get worse. The world is running out of good news, so maybe we'll all come to an end together, like that pastor in Oakland keeps warning us. I marked the date when I saw his bulletin board on the freeway. May 21, 2011. Let's see if the world will end in six months.

───

23 JULY 1929.

Aunt E left today. Hetty and I saw her off at the station. The rest of the family conducted a perfunctory farewell. Ethel and Bessie both seemed to grieve her departure genuinely. They, like the furniture in the house, can only be the witnesses of the comings and goings of those they serve. Ethel, I think, has been with the family long enough not to mind Uncle Victor's displeasure. And Bessie must be too young to believe that she might have to spend all her life in one house like Ethel.

───

I SHOULD TELL YOU about the stories my mother wrote. One of these days I will reread them. And perhaps you will like to read them, too.

My mother wasn't a great writer. Not even a good writer. All her stories were romances about the same traveling woman, and the different men she met. She called her Miss Myrtle. You couldn't tell where she was from or where she was going, but she was always on the move.

In one story Miss Myrtle walks into a salon and notices that the four-legged furniture is all standing on two or three legs. What happens before and after? Is it the same story in which she meets a Swede who is going to be executed because he stole his companion's gold and murdered him? Her romance in that story is not only with the doomed miner. The pastor summoned for the sinner's soul also falls for her. There is no salvation from lovesickness for either man.

I always thought that furniture was more interesting than Miss Myrtle and her lovers. I remember imagining our horses standing on only two or three of their legs all year round and thinking how funny it would be.

The idea of Miss Myrtle's traveling must have come from my great-grandmother Lucille. She trekked from Missouri to California with my great-grandfather Matthew, who was a physician, and they lived in Blanco Bar and Dutch Bar among the miners for two years. But Miss Myrtle is not interested in being a wife. She travels by herself and strikes up a conversation with any man in sight. And every man falls in love with her. In one story, some miners are celebrating July 4th with a reading of the Declaration of Independence, and when the document they special-ordered from Sacramento is not delivered in time, who is there to recite the whole thing but Miss Myrtle? All the miners fall madly in love with her, right there and then. In another story, she discusses the history of revolution with a few French miners and one of them writes a poem for her afterward in French. I don't know that my mother had any French. If she did, she certainly never told us. Even without it she had enough la-di-da for our father to laugh at.

And Miss Myrtle, you ask me, has she ever fallen in love? Almost, always almost, but then you reach the end of the story and she's setting out for the next camp or the next town, leaving broken hearts behind. My mother thought she'd given Miss Myrtle beauty and intelligence and freedom. What can men give that she doesn't already have? But my mother was wrong.

My mother must've dreamed of breaking a few hearts, too. But in reality she was like a piece of furniture that had to stand on two or three legs all her life. Writing those little tales must've been her way of polishing herself. But polish all she might, she was still like used furniture. Dented and scratched. And wobbly. Some women don't know how to make themselves treasured.

Do better than my mother, Katherine. Do better than Lucy, too.

———

Aunt E left me an address in New York City. She will be visiting a cousin of hers before travelling west. The cousin has spent much of the past decade as a companion to a woman who is a novelist and musician. Anyone I've heard of, I asked, and Aunt E said no, she supposed not. While we had tea at the station I asked more about them. Cousin Cliona had been trained as a concert pianist, but she had played too much and destroyed her hands. Like Schumann, Hetty said, and Aunt E said not exactly. Cousin Cliona did not have Schumann's madness. Of the other woman Aunt E did not say much.

So Aunt E has a life outside this house, with relatives

and friends unknown to me, and stories that she sees no point in sharing. What a fool I am to have imagined I am indispensable to her.

I also spoke with Hetty about my future. A professor told me last term I might qualify for Colonial Status for a fellowship at Oxford, I said, to which she replied that it must be welcome news to me. I wanted to remind her that I was supposed to go, fellowship or no, but she cut me off with a melancholy look.

Soon you will leave, too, she said. I wish Aunt Evelyn and you could both stay.

That look on Hetty's face: Where did she learn that expression?

Later.

There is, as Aunt E warned, no money to send me to England. Uncle Victor said they had been cautious with my money, but the economy has been volatile for months and a major part of the holdings Mother left, which were in wheat, has been greatly affected by the drought. What he meant, of course, was that I should remain grateful for what I do have.

The summer, already empty, became more so. There are plenty of girls in town, plenty of dances and picnics. The fleet will arrive, adding fresh navy officers. But Hetty and I, two old people living in our young shells, will let routine carry us. I am suffering from the internal bleeding caused by despair. Hetty, the anaemia caused by love.

———

THINK ABOUT THE SUMMER before the Great Depression. It's like the supper before the great earthquake in San Francisco. My father liked to tell about that meal, about his mother giving a piece of badly charred meat to calm the family dog, who went cuckoo as animals do before an earthquake. After the earthquake, the dog disappeared. My father wanted to search for it, but his parents wouldn't allow him. He was six then.

My father's family didn't pass down many stories. Just the opposite of my mother's family. The longer you live the more you appreciate those who bury their stories.

My father talked about that lost dog several times. His great-grandfather was a cobbler in Lithuania. The family saved everything to send their oldest son to America. He worked in a Chicago shipyard for a year before joining the forty-niners. That's all we knew of his family. Iola, you have a bit of Lithuanian blood in you. You should know where that country is on the map.

Who didn't suffer in the Great Depression? But it was impossible for Roland not to take it personally. He was like a farmer's wife, counting his lost chickens before they were hatched. My mother did that, too. People like them can never see there are other eggs that would become other chickens. There are never more beautiful chickens than the ones who refuse to be hatched. They cling to the unhatchable eggs.

Maybe that's why they both wanted to write books.

My mother used to drive me into a rage with the things she said. Every day gone is a day lost, she would say when she was doing the dishes. Lost to whom, or what? I wanted to ask, but she was only talking to herself, even when I was right next to her, drying the plates. She was the worst kind of pessimist. It's not a glass half empty or half full of water, but poison. The question she asked herself: Was there enough poison to kill someone?

There was a reason my father poked fun at her in front of others. How else could he have survived her pessimism? At least he got something out of her unhappiness.

I'm surprised that so few husbands and wives have murdered

each other. It still amazes me that my parents didn't. In grade school I thought they might do just that, though I wasn't sure who would be the killer, or how they would do it. An ax or a piece of rope in the shed or the rat poison in our cupboard? Firearms? My father once had to shoot a gelding that had got free in the night and eaten a whole sack of oats—he was so bloated there was no other way to free him from the pain. But the only crime my parents had the courage to commit was to go on with their marriage. She gave in first, but she got her revenge. What better way to forget someone than by dying on him? He lived on for some lonely years. When the target of his meanness was gone, he was doomed to remember her.

Now here's a lesson for you: It's foolish to love just one person, but it's more foolish to be nasty to just one person. If you want to be mean, it's better to be mean to many people. I've known a fair number of people, both men and women, who are like my father. Nice enough to everyone but one person—sometimes it's the spouse, sometimes it's a child, sometimes it's a friend.

———

24 JULY 1929.

Major Pilkington's niece arrived today. A dance party will be held in her honour, with cases of champagne that arrived on the same train. This gossip, having reached many ears within a few hours, reminds one of the paltriness of all this town has to offer. One imagines life carried out in a different manner in New York, or in sunny California where Pilkington's niece lives.

———

THIS IS THE FIRST TIME California is mentioned in Roland's diary. I'm not sure that young lady represented us well. I didn't have the good fortune to travel with cases of champagne, but I wouldn't want to trade places with Major Pilkington's niece. Some women have better luck even though they lack beauty or wit. And luck, if you ask me, makes a boring story.

I like to picture Roland at this age. So young! If I ask you to imagine me when I was sixteen, most likely you'd say, What's the point?

The point? Because you came from who I was then. You also came from who he was.

Jane was complaining this morning that all she could remember were the things before she turned ten and after she turned eighty. Where did those seventy years ago? she asked me.

Maybe those seventy years weren't real, I said.

That's not true, she said.

Maybe they didn't matter.

This afternoon I looked down at the street from my window and wanted to tell those people strutting around in their youth or middle age: Wait until you realize that these years you're living won't count.

---

26 JULY 1929.

> Dance at the Pilkingtons' last night. Almost everyone in
> town showed up. Miss Pilkington turned out to be a tre-
> mendous letdown: not much beauty, vulgarly loud, her
> teeth, however, flashily white.

Someone, whose name I didn't catch but who's from England and holidaying here, stayed close to Hetty. I should have felt relief but for the fact when Hetty was first whisked away, I, feeling pensive, watched the floor like an abandoned sweetheart.

Most of the young men at the dance will remain in Nova Scotia. They will inherit a business, marry, and have children, and their children will do the same. Am I too restless? I am, but one has to have something to one's name before claiming the right to be restless. Talent, or wealth. These things are given.

Later.

I would have ended today in a starker mood if not for Aunt E's telegram. She asked me if I would like to go to New York. I cannot help but think how truly fond of me she must be. She can't be doing this merely for my parents' sake.

———————

THERE WAS A TIME when I thought I would see many parts of the world, but after Molly's birth, I knew those places would have to wait for some time before they would see me.

And then Lucy died.

Katherine, for a few days after Lucy's death, your father talked about bringing you back to Alaska to his parents or giving you up for adoption. We never told you this. I don't think his parents were even interested in having you.

For a while we sent Steve a picture of you every year on your birthday and he sent us a check. Fifty dollars. Sometimes less. After a few years the checks stopped. I said we should stop sending him the pictures, but Gilbert said we shouldn't hold your pictures hostage. I said it would look like we were using your cute face to beg him for money. Eventually an envelope was returned as undeliverable, so end of argument.

Katherine: Yesterday I said you came from who Roland was, and who I was. You also came from who your parents were. "Your mother Lucy" — I've never said these words aloud. I've never said "my daughter Lucy" either. She's always been just Lucy.

At least when you read these words, I'm already dead.

Right after Lucy's death I thought of walking away permanently. Not because I didn't love my children, but other than Molly, they were old enough to be motherless, and Molly had a good father. Gilbert picked no favorite among his children. Everyone had his whole heart. I'm not like that. Love is like a savings account. You make a deposit, and use it here and there, sometimes subtracting an amount when you least expect it. You can say there is interest but that's not much to speak of. The account was more or less in the balance until Lucy died. When Lucy died everything was drained from it. Then nothing was left.

I asked my sister Margot about airplane tickets. Her husband Ralph was a travel agent. When I called her, the first thing she said was: Are you running away, too? I told her I needed a break, and she said that was what Lucille had said before she left for Australia.

When I gave birth to Lucy, Lucille and Margot came to visit. Lucille and I were not close. In fact, Margot always blamed me for driving Lucille away from the country and from her life. In any case that's a story for another day.

Lucy was five days old, and Lucille thanked me for giving the name to the baby. You're welcome, I said. I was so happy that I didn't bother to point out that in our family, in every generation there was a girl named after Great-grandmother Lucille. And then she said, It's wrong that you're not sharing anything Mother left us.

I was surprised. Our father was still healthy enough then. I told Lucille that our mother left nothing.

What about those papers you found in her trunk? Lucille asked.

I was sixteen and the twins thirteen when our mother died. I didn't believe they needed to read the stories our mother wrote. I still don't.

Father burned them, I said. With those letters from her friends.

You're lying, Lucille said. I asked Father.

In fact, I burned them, I said.

She told me I had no right to destroy anything our mother left us, and I said that she didn't leave them to us, and I imagine she would feel grateful that I had burned them. You don't know what Mother wanted, Lucille said, and I said I knew it more than anyone in the family. We went on quarreling, and Margot tried to stop us. In the end both she and baby Lucy started to cry. That was the last time Lucille and I fought. She left the country and eventually settled in Australia. She sent postcards and letters to all her siblings but me. She started a family there. Margot missed her dearly and went there to visit a few times.

In the end I didn't run away because you, Katherine, became the newest family member. And that's one thing I don't regret. But imagine, I could've traveled the world and knocked on Lucille's door!

Knock, knock.

Who's there.

Lilia.

Lilia who.

Lilia Liska from Benicia, California.

The last person to be expected at her door. She might've thought me a ghost. Or maybe we would have laughed together. Perhaps at the news of Lucy's death she would have cried. Though Lucille has the same hardness I do. We don't soak ourselves in tears.

If only Lucille and I hadn't been born into the same family. We would've respected each other. We would've stopped each other doing silly things. But the best qualities in a close friend are the most difficult to accept in a sister. Or in a child.

Well, I didn't run away. And I didn't see Lucille again until

Margot's funeral. I'm wrong to say I have few regrets in my life. Lucille is a regret. Any day they could send news of her death.

I wonder if she thinks of me this way, too. Neither of us will say, it's too late to do anything now. We'll only say, it is what it is.

Later. (I like how Roland often used this word.)

Is it a regret that I've never traveled? Julie signs up for one international tour a year. Julie is not much younger than me. After each trip she shares her photos. If I were a weaker soul I would sit next to her like those little women, *ooh*-ing and *ahh*-ing and thinking about all the places we've missed in the world.

But I have no interest in sitting on a coach with thirty other men and women, all of them with one foot in their graves. I have no interest in being shepherded and corralled in St. Petersburg or Barcelona or the Ring of Kerry. No, that wouldn't do for me. You should see the world with only one person, and to go away for so long that it stops being a mere holiday. A holiday is a dream, but even the best dream ends.

Katherine: Gilbert and I did what we could to make our family holidays special. Even if they were only at Russian River or Tomales Bay. They were good dreams. I hope they were for you, too.

The first time we drove to Oregon, Lucy conducted her siblings to count down as we were nearing the state border. Like going into a new year. She was the prettiest eleven-year-old girl on that day. So sunny her face was, not a wisp of moodiness. No one would believe that girl would do something to harm herself. I wish we could have kept her that way forever.

Not that I didn't welcome your birth, Katherine. But a mother's heart is like leavened dough. There can only be one perfect moment. That day, watching Lucy, so pretty, so lively, I thought: This is happiness. There's no more I would ask.

My heart is now stale bread. Good to be left on the windowsill for any greedy bird. A little longer and it'll harden into a rock, and you can knock a burglar out with it.

That trip was the first time we'd visited another state. Gilbert grinned behind the steering wheel like an old bear. I wouldn't trade this for any kingdom, he said aloud.

But no king would be interested in him and his brood of children chanting behind him. His small happiness.

I don't think Roland understood that kind of happiness. He had never had it. He would say he never wanted it. But that's like saying the food you've never tasted is not worth eating.

———

2 AUGUST 1929.

> No need to go into details about last week. To bite the
> hand that pets you is a worse sin than to bite the hand that
> feeds you. I commend myself for enduring humiliation
> with composure.
>
> ...

[A diarist's altruism is rarely understood by the world. All the moments in my life that are embarrassing, disheartening, and humiliating, can be found in my diary. If I am not always honest in life, I am among these pages, the honesty a pact between me and myself. Who can deny that someone reading my words—a young man arriving at a similar juncture in his life, or an older man taking a last, longing look at his youth—will not feel a momentary closeness to a kindred soul?

My triumph in life is that at an early age I developed the habit of saying to myself, "Look at that person who looks exactly like you, who is living your life, but much more stupidly. Aren't you happy you are not him?" To make a distinction between one's ego and one's exterior, to be always prepared to laugh at the latter, to never waver in one's tender care toward the former—these skills have stood me in good stead.—RB 26 March 1989]

———

LET'S FORGIVE ROLAND HIS BLUFFING. Let's enjoy it. Not every man's bluffing deserves admiration. Many men do it full-heartedly. Like women showing off their jewelry. No matter how expensive those stones and pearls are, you take one look and want to say to them: What would you do without them? The same with men who bluff, like those bodybuilders distorting their muscles onstage.

But not Roland. He wore his lies like tailored suits. And who could begrudge a man looking so dapper in his lies?

———

8 AUGUST 1929.

New York City. Last night it was near ten o'clock when I arrived in Greenwich Village. Nobody seemed to be sleeping, though some very old men and some rather young children were leaning against lampposts or crumpling in doorways. Streetcars and elevated trains and taxis and screaming people of all ages: It made me laugh to think that we were worried, back home, that a new branch of the railway, planned to run north of town, would disturb our peace.

Aunt E arranged my trip with the same efficiency that she had handled her own exodus. I am glad I proved myself able to rise to the occasion. She knew the obstacles I had to face back home. She did not ask, and there was no need to broadcast my courage. (Besides, I made my leave-taking sound provisional to Hetty and Aunt Geraldine. No need to go into that, either.)

Cousin Cliona and the woman she's a companion to—

Madame Zembocki—are planning to spend the next few weeks at the seaside. My job is to look after their parrot, Kotku.

I did not meet the two women until this morning. Being aware that they may be among the first real characters I can later use, I've studied them with my novelist's eyes.

Madame Z does not look foreign at all. She looks like someone out of a George Gissing novel. She wears a sage green dress of indescribable material and shape. She is not young. Neither is Cousin C, who is dressed out of fashion, too, but looks a less odd version of her patroness. Cousin C is warm toward me but has few words. Madame Z looks as though she is constantly listening to some music unheard by the rest of us.

In proximity to these two odd women, Aunt E has lost some of her sheen in my eyes. Perhaps it is New York City's doing. How many provincial affairs can survive the transplant to a metropolis?

. . .

[To contrast this arrival, dear reader, I would encourage you to look at the entry of 11 May 1969. On that day, I accompanied two Soviet artists from the Bolshoi Theatre to visit Madame Zembocki on her 100th birthday. Sidelle, the last living relative of Madame Zembocki, was too ill to travel, and had arranged that I take her place for this mission. Being sought out after years away from public attention, being followed by a camera crew—shall I say that was a brighter moment than a provincial youth's first expedition to New York?—RB 27 March 1989]

———

I APPROVE OF THESE two women. For one thing, they are quiet.

At lunch today, two fools from the eighth floor inserted themselves at our table and went on about their various theories—between them they offered six or maybe seven, I stopped counting—of the psychology of dieting. Enough knowledge to kill any wife. In any case, yada yada they went, so I cut a roll, smeared half of it with butter, and left the other half without. Here, I said to them, please give the roll a thorough psychoanalysis.

———

Later.

After breakfast I took a walk. People in the street act with certainty, the fruit peddlers claiming the space around their crates, the pedestrians purposeful in their hurried steps. Yet their faces, sweaty and weary, make one feel that whatever they do or whoever they are is only temporary. What is going to become of them? What is going to become of me?

New York City is like a prostitute past her prime. There is no way to peel off this ageing layer, greasy and grimy, to see the city in its original and pristine form. Can any metropolis ever have been virginal? Paris, which I have not yet visited, retains its allure for me, but it's the allure of an ageless courtesan.

This reminds me of the camping trip to Newfoundland last summer. One of Uncle William's friends, an amateur topographer whose day job is to drill holes in people's teeth, asked me to accompany him on a search for a small lake. After a day of trekking we found the lake, quite a distance away from where he had surmised it would be from the locals' descriptions. He was going to name it Lake Harriet, he said. Why Lake Harriet, I asked, thinking it must be his wife's name or an old lover's. He was working alphabetically, he explained, and told me he had named his last discovery Lake Georgiana.

One supposes, by the greatest luck, one might discover a crack in this city that is unseen by others. Crevice Cressida. Pothole Portia.

A young man arriving in New York City is always arriving too late. It is like seeing a beloved who has long been married off to a rich man, given birth to his offspring, and now gained the status of a dowager queen. And you can't even sidle up to the family members at a party and introduce yourself as one of their country cousins. Which doorman would allow you to cross the threshold?

Later.

It is hard to imagine how Cousin C and Madame Z pass their time in this house. It is not a dull house. It is full of all sorts of odd and useless objects, a bronze Buddha head mulling behind an umbrella stand, a plaque with indecipherable engravings lying belly up on the windowsill. Over the piano there is a framed drawing of a man, bald and morose. Stacks of music sheets are piled on the piano bench. A Japanese screen—heavy gold background with heavier-looking mountains depicted in an unsettling manner—separates the drawing room into two parts, making the room feel still darker and more crowded. The dining room, the hallway, the landing, the small guest room I am installed in—everywhere I look I see things better fit for a museum or a tomb. There is no dust, but time leaves indelible prints.

Imagine growing old in this house with a wife like Hetty.

Or any wife.

———

DID YOU REALLY IMAGINE this, Roland?

Hetty was the silk lining of finest quality for that coffin that was your marriage house. The objects in it were dusted daily. There was no other use for them. The vases were never empty of fresh flowers. What else could be filled in that house? I don't have to imagine these things to know. Imagination is an activity best saved for what you cannot see. I see your marriage well.

What I can't see, is how you went from being the Roland of San Francisco to the Roland of your marriage. I wonder if you understood it yourself.

...

[Here's the story of Madame Zembocki, the skeleton of it, some of which I learned from Aunt E, the rest pieced together. Elizabeth Nugent was born in Ireland to an English mother and an Anglo-Irish father. Like all interesting people she was orphaned—not at a tender age, but young enough to put her in the charge of an ill-fitted guardian, against whom she rebelled with the same passion required for any revolution in human history. When she gained her independence she travelled to the Continent, and spent a few years studying music in Prague. There she met Milos Zembocki, a man thirty years her senior—a Polish revolutionary who would soon be exiled to Siberia but not before he convinced his protégée of her noble obligation to his revolutionary cause and his personal happiness. Elizabeth Nugent, now Lyse Zembocki, did not follow her husband into exile. Rather, she moved to Moscow, first working as an English governess, and eventually, starting to publish stories and novels in Russian. Her literary career, however, was cut short when the news of Milos Zembocki's death reached her. Madame Zembocki returned to England, and then to Ireland, and from there she emigrated to America in 1912. She settled in New York and lived in the same building until her death at the age of 102.

It was said that her writing had been brought to the attention of Lenin by Maxim Gorky. After 1917, with both men's blessing, her books, hailed for their realistic portraits of revolutionaries in continental Europe and heralding a communist future for mankind, sold well and were taught in Soviet schools.—RB 4 April 1989]

10 AUGUST 1929.

Madame Z and Cousin C left for the seaside today. Aunt E has booked her trip to Chicago. She said now that she had seen Cliona and knew all was well, there was no reason for her to linger.

Why wouldn't things be well with her? I asked.

You have to understand there are people who're destined to be only one thing in life. Once they lose that prospect they live a rudderless life.

She doesn't seem rudderless, I said. (Madame Z composes song cycles, but not for publication or performance—this I'd learned from a conversation with Cousin C. Together they run a music society to educate working women and young girls without any means.)

If only you'd known her before, Aunt E said.

I wonder if I am one of those people who can be only one thing. What if this writing career doesn't bring me fame and profit? But what's the probability of that? Unlikely things happen—a train can derail, a future at Oxford can vanish, but those things are not within one's control. Putting words on the page is what I can do. I must not act out of defeatism.

Cousin C was affectionate toward me. She had met my parents once at some relative's wedding. They were not the youngest people there, she said, but they were the youngest-looking ones. Like a couple stepping out of a Bohemian folk song, she said.

To think of them as two dancing figures popping out of a music box . . . Had they been that fairy-tale couple they would have danced on forever, and the world would never have seen the birth of Roland Bouley.

Can one imagine one's own parents as virgins? This

question, once asked, cannot be unasked. Surely my father had other women before his marriage. The thought of this makes me feel agitated, especially since I have not yet seen a way to change my fate of being a virgin.

———

THERE ARE ENDLESS WAYS to group people. If you watch the news on television or read the newspapers, you'll see that's what people do all the time, and when they run out of labels they invent new ones. The more the merrier, and the smarter they think themselves. But sooner or later there will be more than enough labels to divide everyone from everyone. Then what? We all carry our own banners, no two alike. Every person has a reason to denounce the rest of the world. Maybe then we will fulfill Gilbert's belief that the world's population could be united. If we can't be united under love for one another, then hatred it would have to be, no?

Here's something I guarantee is more entertaining. I divide people into two groups. One group I can see their lovemaking and I will do so when I feel like it. The other group I cannot see them romantically engaged.

Like Roland, I've never been able to imagine my parents in their marriage bed. Children have a way of denying their parents such activities in their imagination. Those children who are charitable, I mean.

But here's a secret joy of mine. When I was old enough—twelve, thirteen—I started to make up love affairs for my mother. You know how young girls fantasize about having young men courting them? I used to search for a beau for her everywhere I turned. A ranch hand, a postman, a salesman, a clerk, a schoolteacher. All the way to the point where she would scheme an elopement with the man. I didn't go on thinking about them checking into an inn somewhere or settling in another town.

Maybe I was making stories for my mother the way she made stories for Miss Myrtle. Perhaps I was looking for a way to get her out of her marriage (and out of my life, too). But my stories only took place in my head. When you put words on the page, there'll always be someone like me who reads them. Sometimes against your wishes.

These notes to you are different. I know who they are for, and who will be reading them.

I have no trouble seeing my siblings in their marriages. Even in their bedrooms. A limb here and a piece of undergarment there. But unless someone puts a pistol to my head I won't go there! You shouldn't waste your vision on everyone you know, unless of course you have a perverted mind. Mine is not.

I don't have much interest in imagining Roland with Hetty in their bedroom. It must have been long and slow. Like the tasting menu Molly insisted I have for my eightieth birthday—known for "its exquisite presentation and poetic nuance"! It took me great self-discipline not to ask the waiter if someone old had ever died on him. "Mr. Smith suffered a heart attack while eating a poached quail egg." "Mrs. Smith choked on a piece of smoked artichoke and was not revived." Good stories for obits.

A tasting menu is not a meal to enjoy, but an exercise to keep your mind sharp. To stay awake I kept complimenting the waiter on his outfit. He wore a white jacket and a black bow tie. I wore a black dress with a white collar. I said had I been twenty years younger I'd elope with him. He asked me if I would allow him to flirt with other women, and I said only if he wouldn't mind my flirting with other men. When he returned with yet another course I found a classified ad I had cut and kept in my purse. Read it, I said to him, and he said he didn't have his reading glasses, so I read it aloud. "Choose me, foxy, sexy senior lady, well-educated, healthy, vivacious. Very clean and great dresser who is looking for a GEN-TLEMAN, age under 100, free of emotional baggage, well-off financially. Must be there for me. If you flirt with other women do not bother responding. My mindset is to be courted." The waiter said he was not qualified, and I said I was not the woman. We both agreed that we should wish her the best of luck. All the time you could hear Molly calculating the extra tips for what she later described to me as, "the constant and persistent harassment that gentleman had to endure."

Well? I thought. Perhaps she'll think twice from now on about ordering the tasting menu.

But I digress. No, no interest whatsoever in Roland and Hetty once they dim the bedroom light. But I do like to see them at their breakfast. Hetty stirring her coffee—I imagine she would count to the same number every morning, twenty, thirty, before raising the cup to her lips—and Roland, he would thank her for everything she placed in front of him, the whole time counting the words he had said. Once he had reached a decent number, he would open the newspaper.

When I think of his mistresses, I like to picture them in his bed, even though Roland never describes anyone in more than a sentence or two. Some must be long gone now. But the younger ones may still be alive. Dead or alive, they should all be grateful to me because I only see them in their best years and through a lover's eyes.

———

Later.

This evening, Aunt E said if there was anything I wanted to know I should ask her. Who knows when we will see each other next? she said. Hetty said something similar when she saw me off. Why do women like to sound so dramatic and morbid? Even Aunt E is not exempt from such sentimentality.

Oh, I'm following you west, I said.

No, don't, Aunt E said.

What do I do? I asked. Before leaving, through arguing and begging, I reached an agreement with Uncle Victor and Uncle William about managing part of my money until I turn twenty-one.

Stay in New York. Find some prospect here for yourself.

Aunt E gave me a list of people that I might contact. She also suggested that it wasn't a bad idea to get in touch with the Bouleys. I promised to do all she asked me to, but a young man's promise can stay an empty promise.

A telegram came today from Madame Z and Cousin C. A cousin of Madame Z's, Mrs. Sidelle Ogden, is visiting New York. Could I make myself available in case she needs hospitality? Heartening to think that within a week of arrival I can play host.

YOU CAN READ FROM this page on to the end and maybe you'll still feel as I do—I cannot picture Sidelle as Roland's lover. I hope this is not a spoiler for you. Yes, Sidelle and Roland were lovers for some years.

After Lucy died, I asked Mrs. Anderson, the librarian, about a poet named Sidelle Ogden. She couldn't find any poetry by Sidelle. I then asked my neighbor Holly's daughter, who was in graduate school. Roland mentioned Sidelle's name once, but I didn't know her story until I read this book, which happened much later.

When Lucy died, the women in my life—my sister Margot, my in-laws, friends and neighbors—they all tried hard to say the right things. But the right things are often the least helpful. I wondered then what Sidelle would've said—Roland had made her sound special.

Holly's daughter found a book in the university library for me. A biography of some woman poet who I can't remember now. She seemed much more famous than Sidelle but even that woman, Holly's daughter said, was out of fashion and no longer read.

Poets are not like movie stars. Had Roland had an affair with Joan Fontaine or Joan Crawford he would've become immortal. But he didn't get himself the right mistresses. He had this strange loyalty to Sidelle, as if nobody could be compared to her. So he chose other women he could forget easily, to sing and dance behind Sidelle like a chorus.

In that biography, there were a few pictures of a scrapbook the woman poet made of her friends. One page belonged to Sidelle, six photos. I should've taken the book to a copy shop and asked them to photograph that page for myself, but I was too prideful then. I didn't want to feel that I was becoming obsessed with Sidelle. I regret it now.

I don't remember the name of the poet, so I can't tell you where to look. The lesson: Things you talk yourselves out of now, one day they may be the exact things you want. I don't have many lessons to give, so pay attention whenever I offer one.

Without the pictures in front of me, I can only tell you what I remember of Sidelle. In one photo she was smoking, dark short hair, wearing a man's jacket. In another she wore a long dark robe with a fur collar, and a fur cape outside the robe. Eyes deep, nose narrow, chin pointed. A sharp woman. The other pictures were taken with friends, men and women. She wasn't smiling in any one of them.

Was she beautiful? Some people may think so, but that's not my concern. My problem is I can see Roland serving her a glass of wine or fetching her a fur coat or lighting her cigarette. I can see him walking with her in a park or sitting with her in a cab, and I can see him murmuring to her as in one of those scenes in an old Hollywood movie. But try as I may, I can't see them in bed.

Sidelle had this fierce look on her face that I liked. I have a similar look. Old Jonny, one of the hands on our ranch, used to say that a man would have to go to an ironsmith to get armor before marrying me. I was not older than seven or eight, or else I would have kicked him hard. Look at yourself in the mirror, he said. You look at everyone like you're going to pounce and kill them. Like a lion? I asked. Like a leopard, Old Jonny said.

That was when I started to study myself in the mirror. All my life I've known my face well.

On our second date I told Gilbert about Old Jonny's words, and Gilbert laughed. You're not a leopard, he said. You're a kitten. How genuinely he let himself be deceived. Sometimes I think I miss him quite a bit.

---

16 AUGUST 1929.

Once again Aunt E left. I now wonder if my so-called passion for her was only an outcome of living in the unnatural atmosphere of Elmsey. If a divine hand picked us up and placed us back there, would I still feel the same way for her?

I have not felt such disarming comfort with her as I felt in the past few days. We moved about, equally unimportant to the world at large yet equally central to our own worlds. Thus looked at we are not different from two goldfish in two tiny bowls, temporarily placed next to each other.

I was reminded of Anna Karenina when I watched Aunt E's train depart. All trains and all platforms remind me of the terror of romance. For a moment I wanted to ask the man next to me if the same thought ever occurred to him.

...

[When I came to know Sidelle better, this question about train stations arose in one of our conversations. No, it had never occurred to her that there was any terror in Anna's death, Sidelle said. It'd be a terror if Anna were left to live on. She then told an anecdote about meeting Constance Garnett at her countryside house. CG peeked at everyone through thick lenses. For someone who didn't know who she was, Sidelle said, she must have looked as benevolent and as dumb as the pumpkins in her garden.—RB, 5 April 1989]

Later.

I should record the conversation Aunt E and I had a few days ago, but before that I want to remind myself of this line I marked when I was reading the other day:

*Prosperum et felix scelus virtus vocatur.** [*Vice, when successful, is called virtue.]

I asked Aunt E about those things that were never discussed back at home, my parents particularly.

Your father was from a decent background, Aunt E said. What upset your uncles was that simplistic pride he had in being an American.

Was he a simple person? I asked.

No, far from it. But you see, that was the problem. The utmost American vice, as your uncles saw it, is that an American can hold on to his American-ness as though it's a magic spell.

But do you believe he had that vice? I asked Aunt E.

Anyone from a single culture falls victim to a certain silliness. People like you and me—you know my mother's side was American, people born to two races are better at being sceptics.

I didn't know Aunt E had an American mother. Is that where you're going to go, to see family on your mother's side? I asked.

I've stayed away for too long. They're more like strangers now.

Is that how I should treat the Bouleys?

You should try to establish a relationship with them. One of them may be able to help you. But don't set your expectations high. They didn't approve of your father.

Because he married my mother?

Because all his life he did worthless things that led him to pointless places. And you should take caution not to be like him, Aunt E said.

I tried not to look hurt. Should all sons be inoculated against their fathers? Is Aunt E doing this in my mother's stead?

This was the story Aunt E told me: Father met Mother at Port Royal, during the celebration of the 300th anniversary of French settlement. She was a schoolgirl then, travelling with her choir from Halifax. He crossed the border from America because he had nothing else to do at the time. How he had singled her out and made her fall in love with him god alone knows. When she came back home, she told her older brothers that she was planning to go to America to pursue a degree in Sanskrit, at Cornell University.

None of your uncles understood. What followed was, as you know, a marriage that nobody approved of, and a child. You should be glad that they didn't bring you with them on the trip.

Where did they leave me?

With a nanny in Ithaca. We sent for you right away. It took a while for the news to reach the Bouleys. And they didn't make any effort to get you back.

Aunt E didn't tell me much about her own marriage. Necessity creates opportunity, was all she said. I must remember that.

I OFTEN WONDER WHY Aunt E stayed in that house in Nova Scotia for so long. Yes, true, she had to raise her daughters, but she could have married and brought them with her. She could have made things happen if she wanted—that's how I like to think of her. Roland never considered that question. He was too busy thinking about himself. That's one drawback about reading his diaries. Everywhere you turn there is a question. It's a crowded book, like a crowded city. But all those questions you bump into, well, sooner or later they become dead ends.

What happened to Aunt E? There's not much more to learn from the rest of the book. Roland didn't forget her. Or else he wouldn't have kept the entries about her. But he remembered her and he kept her in the diaries because she made him look like an interesting young man. She was an interesting woman. This he forgot.

---

20 AUGUST 1929.

A sultry day, the kind of summer I've learned about from novels set in New York. To experience something that has long been known to me through words—oddly the effect is diluted.

I'm sitting here at the Biltmore, waiting for Mrs. Ogden. The grandiosity of the hotel is exactly as I imagined, and for that reason I decide that I am disappointed. Arrogant as I am, I don't think I possess a first-rate imagination. (First-rate observation I would allow myself.) I wonder if the whole world is not a second-rate production.

Later.

A memorable evening with a memorable woman.

Can Mrs. Ogden be called good-looking? I have little confidence in my judgement. Women endowed with beauty tend to carry themselves like Kitty in her exquisite dress. How many women can carry themselves with such striking ease as Mrs. Ogden, a remarkable Anna in an ordinary dress?

We had tea. Mrs. Ogden asked me questions about my family and my background. I embellished my story a little: Father and Mother's marriage against both families' wishes, my orphanhood, and me now, out by myself in the world. I did not say I was a prospectless man in New York. To see the world a little, I said when Mrs. Ogden asked me my plan. And to write. I made it sound as though I was a Hamlet sans irresolution, or a Quixote strengthened by cynicism. I even made fun of those books I would write one day.

Mrs. Ogden also asked me about Cousin C and Madame Z. I described them as I believe a great novelist would describe his favourite characters. I made a fond imitation of their parrot. I added a few lines about Aunt E. Like Tolstoy, not missing a single detail.

After tea we went up to the rooftop and took a stroll in the garden. I tried to show nonchalance. (But what will Hetty think, when she reads about such decadence in my letter?)

Imagine their thinking that they were building a Louvre here, I said. I have not been to the Louvre but I considered this a worldly comment.

We need to remember that there was a time when the Louvre itself was being built, Mrs. Ogden said. Anything we take for granted comes from something lesser.

Right away I regretted speaking too flippantly, but Mrs.

Ogden let it pass without further comment. She doesn't relish embarrassing people. She does not need to, because one feels embarrassed in front of her already.

She suggested that we meet again on Thursday. She is not as eccentric as Cousin C or Madame Z. She must have plenty of people to see in this city. Why me? Why again?

———

HERE'S THE DIFFERENCE BETWEEN Roland and me. I would never ask that question, Why me?

No law forbids disasters to happen to you. The flip side is that no law forbids happiness to happen to you. Another mother in my shoes could have wailed at the death of a child: Why me? The real question is: Why not me?

Katherine, you have heard your grandfather talk about meeting me at the UN conference. He visited the week after we met, and I liked him well enough to go on a date with him. He took me for a picnic on the Municipal Pier. We watched the fishermen, their heads wrapped in scarves or rags even though it was June. We tried to see the guards and prisoners on Alcatraz. Gilbert told a story about a man being imprisoned there for kidnapping a girl. He was an avid newspaper reader, he said. He then showed me an advertisement for the ranch. This is how I've found you, he said. I smiled and said nothing. He wouldn't have known where to look if I hadn't pointed the ad out at our first meeting. But it doesn't cost a woman to let a man feel proud.

What else did we do? We chatted. Parents, siblings, his nephews and nieces, the last movies we saw. Then a fisherman nearby, an old gentleman, asked if we wouldn't possibly mind moving farther down the pier. We thought our talking had frightened away his fish, but even before we could say anything, he apologized. He didn't intend to be rude, he explained, but he had worked all his life as a manservant. When you're a servant people expect that you don't listen unless you're spoken to, he said, but it's rather the opposite. My hearing was sharpened by my vocation. Now people don't think I can hear them because I'm old, but I happen to have exceedingly good hearing. I'm not proud of it.

I asked him about his work because I was always curious what people did for a living.

The man said he would have to start from the beginning, from the day he had been orphaned in Japan. He was writing a poem narrating his life, he said, a saga about his life. It would end when he was forced to be evacuated to the interior with other Japanese.

But your life is still going on, Gilbert said. You're free to do many things now. Don't finish the poem at a sad moment.

The old man said it was better to finish on a sad note than a hopeful one. I could see Gilbert wanted to disagree. I pinched him and asked the old man how long it would take him to finish the poem.

A few more months, he said. He recited a couplet. I forgot the exact words, but it had something to do with sailing to America with a heavy heart and a light wallet. He said he had only written to the part where he had started with his third employer, a woman he disliked because she had treated all her servants badly. What happened? I asked. Did you find a better place after?

The old man only smiled and asked me to be patient. He offered to post a copy to us. Gilbert wrote down his address for the man. We said goodbye to him and took a walk along the shoreline. Then Gilbert said something about the man that made me stop. You're not interested in reading the poem? I asked.

It doesn't hurt to make an old man happy, Gilbert said. It's important to make others feel good about themselves. I always laugh whenever someone tells a joke, even if it's not funny or I've heard it.

There is no law forbidding a man to be curious—but Gilbert didn't see it that way.

He then told me a story about a joke writer at a small-town

newspaper going to a big city, where all his jokes about pants and ants fell flat. Finally an old man handed him a dictionary and said, Unless you can make trousers rhyme with ants, this is no place for you.

What rhymes with trousers? I asked.

Gilbert made a show of thinking hard, and turned his face to me, looking long-faced and dejected. Schnauzers, he said.

It was then when I realized he might be more fun than I thought. So, when a man puts his heart into making a woman laugh, just say, Why not me?

———

22 AUGUST 1929.

> This morning I woke up with a heaviness on my chest. At
> first I blamed the oppressive heat and unbreathable air, the
> ceaseless whistling and honking and screaming from the
> street. I thought I would go to Central Park, which I had
> noted as a place where I could think real thoughts rather
> than trifles. But when I did eventually lie down in the
> shade, no breeze alleviated the heat, nor did any poetic
> thought enlighten my mind. I have been in New York City
> for a fortnight now. The letters I sent to the people on
> Aunt E's list remain unanswered. I imagine that all those
> who can help me are out of town at the moment. What am
> I going to do with myself when Madame Z and Cousin C
> return? Do I have the courage to trek back to Elmsey, pre-
> tending that I am ready to resume my life under that
> indifferent roof?
>
> But the day brightened up. I overheard two young
> women conversing in French. One insisted that the other
> had told a lie, which the latter denied, quoting someone

about truth, which I did not catch. I asked her to repeat the saying. They could laugh at my French but it is still better than most people can manage here. That I was eavesdropping turned them unfriendly, but I was able to charm them. The livelier one with dark hair and dark eyes, whose name is Yvette (the other one is Amelia, much plainer and shorter), asked my opinion.

Here their story goes:

They are dressmakers, previously apprenticed at some place in Paris. Yvette spoke of the fashion shop as though it were a household name, and I feigned familiarity and admiration. They arrived six months ago. They did not speak English, and worked for a shop on Twenty-third Street, where the forewoman speaks English but also takes a large part of their pay from them. Today Yvette and Amelia had taken the day off and, equipped with better English than when they arrived six months ago, went to peddle themselves on Fifth Avenue. The proprietress of the first shop they entered, upon hearing where they had apprenticed, was interested right away. She asked how much they were paid, and Yvette said twenty-four dollars a week.

The proprietress said, I'll pay you thirty a week if you come and work for me.

The whole time Yvette was narrating her triumph, Amelia was covering her cheeks with both hands. She lied, she said to me. They pay us each twelve dollars a week on Twenty-third Street.

Well, I said, she was not not telling the truth. Twenty-four was what you made.

Exactement, Yvette said.

We took a walk together. How did you decide to come to America, I asked them, and Yvette said that in the shop where they apprenticed, they saw a nice young woman, a regular patroness from America, whose father was said to own ten thousand miles of telegraph wires. Why can't we be rich like him, I thought. So we decided to come to America, Yvette said. Right? she said to Amelia.

Amelia nodded.

I asked them for their address, and in their glowing joy they did not hesitate to give it to me. Though now, thinking about it, I feel a tinge of envy, and a tinge of shame, too. They knew exactly how to find a prospect in a foreign country. What has stopped me?

———

NOT EVERYONE CAN SAIL the sea and discover a new continent. Not everyone can have a dynasty named after him. Some people are born to be settlers and pioneers. Some people are born to live a comfortable life on a couch. Roland's mother's side were settlers in Nova Scotia and his father's side were settlers in America. What I don't understand is why everything sounded so hard for him.

On the other hand, why am I complaining when my children and grandchildren are nothing like my mother or my grandmother or my great-grandmother?

———

23 AUGUST 1929.

Went to see Mrs. Ogden again this afternoon. Out of politeness I queried her well-being in the past few days. The heat has not abated.

No one has died so far, she said, in your absence.

I was so taken aback that I didn't know how to respond.

She smiled and said it was from a poem she had thought of writing.

I asked if I could have the honour of reading it when it is finished. Just then the manager arrived with a telegram on a silver tray. Mrs. Ogden gave it a cursory glance. For a moment I felt an odd jealousy, convinced that it came from a man who would send her multiple telegrams a day.

Her husband, she explained, was delayed by illness. They were to travel to the desert in the Southwest, but now the plan has to be postponed.

This is the first time Mr. Ogden has entered our conversation. I knew nothing of him, and Mrs. Ogden offered no more information. I decided that he must be one of those men with everything, who can always make a man like me feel wretched. (Last night I started reading *The Journal of a Disappointed Man,* and couldn't help but think perhaps one day I would publish a collection of these entries, under the title *The Journal of an Undistinguished Dreamer*—no, that has to wait until I become famous. Wretchedness itself is not interesting.)

———

NO ONE HAS DIED so far in your absence. Whoever Sidelle had in mind is lucky. Imagine those on their deathbeds holding their last breaths waiting for this person. Or maybe he's unlucky. The moment he shows up—ashes, ashes we all fall down!

I'm not a poetry reader. Roland recorded so many of Sidelle's words but only this one time about her poetry. Why? My theory is that her poetry was not about him.

She liked to talk about death. Did that make her attractive to him? He was the kind of man who wanted to live forever and have everything. Maybe he couldn't tear himself away because she played everyone's death on her finger like a puppet.

Roland didn't record many of Hetty's words. I imagine she would have talked about pressed flowers and cake recipes and goldfish and birds and wallpaper even when someone was dying next door. She might have been thinking of those things when she herself was lying there, dying, dying, and then dead.

Imagine them at your age, Iola. Hetty would be collecting butterflies and putting them into a killing jar for a quick execution, and then pinning them in neat rows. She would be careful about the wings and the antennas, and when she wrote down the names of the butterflies her handwriting would be as neat as the dead butterflies, all perfectly lined up.

Do people still collect butterflies? Gilbert used to work for a Mr. Dupree. When he died he left his collection of butterflies to Gilbert. Good wooden cases with glass tops, each shared by many butterflies. I said we should get rid of them. They occupied space and gathered dust. Gilbert said they were left to him by Mr. Dupree, so we must keep them. Besides, he said, we might not understand the value of such a collection.

Value, I thought to myself. What value is there with so many deaths? But I knew when to stop pestering him.

Sidelle would not collect butterflies. She would rip the wings off them.

You may think I was the kind of girl who would torture a bug or a frog, but the truth is that I've always known there is no point in making other creatures suffer because you occupy a higher place in the order of things.

(If you think the last sentence comes out of nowhere, this is what happened: Once a week Karen takes one of those IQ tests on the Internet. Yesterday she convinced Jinny to do it. Jinny didn't get a score as high as Karen. Jinny said it was because she was tired and so she started to choose the answers randomly. Fair enough, but what a big show Karen made of laughing at Jinny behind her back.)

———

I READ WHAT I wrote this morning, about Roland wanting everything, and remembered a day a long time ago. Lucy was three months old, and Gilbert and I took her out one evening for a walk. There was a full moon over the Bay Bridge. Round and golden, just as you'd see on a postcard. Gilbert said to Lucy, Look, the moon, and then kept pushing her forward. After a moment, he turned and asked me what was wrong. I was crying so hard the moon was all smeared in the sky.

I said that when Kenny was a baby my mother liked to take him out to see the moon. I said I missed my mother now I had a baby. Gilbert said he understood. Poor Gilbert, always ready to accept the easiest excuse. Roland would've said something better about the moon, like it belonged only to Lucy. He would make things sound special. By lying if he had to.

But don't all people lie when they call something or someone special? If not to others, then to themselves.

That was the first and last time I placed Gilbert and Roland side by side in my head. It was not fair to Gilbert. And not good for me, either.

Where did that collection of butterflies go, by the way?

———

24 AUGUST 1929.

Letter from Hetty the day before yesterday but I only now opened it. Picnics and dances, coming and goings of family and friends, melancholy and tedium masked by her elegant words and elegant penmanship. It would be dishonest to say I don't miss her, though only because she is the yardstick I can use to measure this new life against the old. My affection for my uncles and aunts fades quickly. Perhaps some feelings are written in vanishing ink. What if all feelings are?

I live like a Trappist monk at the moment. I have stopped greeting the parrot by its name. It has never harboured any goodwill toward me. I have not made friends in the city. (Does Mrs. Ogden count as a friend? Dream away, Roland.) I have spoken to no more than five people today, two of them the young brothers who sit on the stoop outside the building from early morning till late night. *There is not a fiercer hell than the failure in a great object.* But any failure is hell.

———

LUCY USED TO THREATEN ME that she would kill herself. From when she was young, eleven, twelve. She didn't try that on Gilbert. I didn't allow her to provoke me so I ignored her. I thought the threat would become a joke between us one day. She could be a furious girl, yes, but when she was not caught by rage she was the most joyful one among my children. Sometimes she laughed uncontrollably. About any little thing. She called it her magic laugh. Timmy and Willie and even Carol imitated her, but they didn't have the magic. You have to be able to let yourself go completely to laugh like that.

I didn't understand her rage, just as I didn't understand that laugh of hers. I thought my job was to be a lightning rod, or a circuit breaker. Was this a mother's failure? But how many mothers are not failures?

———

25 AUGUST 1929.

Sunday after a storm. My indolence washed off. On my morning walk I made a detour to West Twenty-fourth Street, arriving just too late to catch Yvette.

Yvette has arrangement on Sunday, Amelia told me. She insisted on speaking English to me. She wanted to practise the language, she said. Her struggle made her a bit more attractive. Any young woman looking hesitant in finding the right words has an air of coquetry, with just the perfect tinge of defencelessness.

Yvette holds a Sunday job as a model for a school of painters. The way Amelia said school made me resent the painters right away.

Why would she still stay in dressmaking? I asked. (Why not just live a life among parties and champagne, with soft fabric easily slipped off and shoulders thrown back, head tilted?)

The painters, they are poor, Amelia said. But Yvette likes to do something different so she can talk about it when we go back to France.

You plan to go back?

But yes, when we make enough money, Amelia said.

What's wrong with America? I asked.

People here don't really know anything about hats and dresses.

I didn't realise that a homely girl could be so judge-mental. That's harsh, no? I said.

Pah, Amelia said, people in Berlin and London and New York think they understand fashion. It's like one who doesn't have an ear . . .

Tone-deaf?

Yes, Amelia said. It's like tone-deaf people talking about music.

Beethoven was deaf.

He could hear even when he was deaf. Just like us—Yvette and I—we cannot afford the clothes we make, but we see things others don't see. And we know how to make women think they are stupid if they don't have the right clothes.

How?

We make things different every season, so anything six months old looks silly on a woman.

So that's how it works, I said. (Does Hetty know this? Does she follow each season's fashion? And Mrs. Ogden? Surely she knows everything.)

The conversation was more interesting than I expected, so I asked Amelia about her life in France. She was born in the countryside, close to a town called Besançon. It is near the border to Switzerland, and like most men living there her father was a watchmaker. They had a comfortable life until he went blind and could no longer work. She was six. There were five children in the house, and her two older brothers became apprentices to a watchmaker. Her mother planted vegetables. She used to read a lot of books, so peo-ple laughed at her, Amelia said, but when she started to sell her vegetables at the market they realised they had made a mistake. She is good at what she does.

Does she still do it?

Yes, with my younger sisters.

And your father?

He is still blind. My mother reads books to him, but she hasn't much time. She's busy with the garden, Amelia said.

The French countryside, what a romantic place. I would not mind settling down among the flowers and vegetables and the local girls, with a little cottage to myself, living a writer's life. Did you like growing vegetables? I asked.

I liked to go to the market. It was a fun day for us. We sat in the horse cart, on top of the vegetables, holding our lunch in napkins. Our dog Léon ran behind the cart, and no matter how loud we yelled at him and ordered him to go home, he always followed us.

I thought of making a clever comment about dogs and men, but did not do so when I saw Amelia's eyes grow misty. In her reverie she looked less plain. Perhaps memories are the best adornment for a woman.

After a few years, Amelia continued, her mother realised that she, Amelia, unlike her sisters, was not much help in the garden. She had the patience, as everyone does in her family, and her hands were far from clumsy, but she did not have a green thumb.

So you went into dressmaking?

Had she been a boy, she explained, she would have entered watchmaking, and she wouldn't have had to leave home. But to learn dressmaking she had to go to Paris. There she met Yvette, and they were the two youngest girls at the shop.

I asked about the shop's name, which I had pretended to be familiar with.

Rouff. Yvette's aunt worked there, Amelia said. She was always snappy, and she even made Yvette cry. Sometimes she would make clothes for the children and the poor women on their street. She prayed after she gave them the clothes. One day, she came down with a fever, and in a few days it was obvious she would die. She had been a wicked woman, she cried to the two girls. This early death was a punishment for her wickedness. The girls thought she was delirious, but the older woman said that the material she had used for the poor people had been stolen from the patrons. She had prayed often but not enough to make up for this sin. She died very unhappily.

That's when Yvette decided to come to America, Amelia said.

And you wanted to come, too? I asked.

She shrugged. I didn't mind.

How long will you work here before going back?

A few years, Amelia said. Sometimes I miss my maman. I used to think her arms were like the best radishes. When it was hot she put a cabbage leaf on her head. My sisters and I too wore cabbage leaves. My maman hemmed in some flowers from our garden at the edge of the leaves. We all looked wild and happy, not that we couldn't spare some money for proper hats.

I glanced at Amelia's arms, pale and even, though perhaps not as plump as her mother's. I tried to come up with something to say, and when I could not, she smiled at me forgivingly. People usually come to visit Yvette, she said. I don't mind that.

I like listening to you talking about your life.

Is that so? she asked. But of course you do. It's because we don't really know each other.

———

AMELIA WAS A PLAIN GIRL, but she made everything into a story. She knew in that way she would be remembered. People living in stories come across a little prettier than they are. And we're lenient toward people we remember. We forget many of their flaws.

What does it feel like to be born without much beauty to speak of? You must think I sound crazy, like a rich man wondering what it feels like to be poor. But what I mean is: I cannot imagine what kind of person I would have turned out to be if I had been born a plain girl. Or an ugly girl. Would I still be this Lilia? No one says a plain girl or an ugly girl can't make something out of her life.

One thing I'm certain about: I don't have to rely on telling stories to make myself feel special. That's what they're doing in that memoir class. Storytelling—they keep repeating the word like it's a magic spell. Show me one person who doesn't have a story. But it's how they emphasize the telling part that makes me laugh. With a fancy dress and the right amount of makeup, any story can pass as something more memorable. Someone could turn this little seamstress's story into a movie, and we'd all forget she was nothing to look at.

Actually, I must make a correction. Hetty didn't have a story to tell. She was not plain-looking. She was not poor. But can you cook over a toy oven and serve plastic food with tiny plastic utensils that wouldn't cut a baby's fingers? That was Hetty's life. No danger of anything or anyone getting burned or wounded or ruined.

If you think I'm being harsh on her, well, I am. And why shouldn't I be? Once you live to my age, you'll know there're some real pains in life. There's no getting around that. It's not like a minefield you see on TV, where people with special equipment mark the landmines, and then people with other special equipment get rid of them. Oh no, you don't know when and where something will happen to you, but it will, sooner or later. The only difference? You may not end up walking around with a missing limb. You look the same to the world.

Most people, even Roland, have to live with a few of those surprises. But not Hetty. She was so careful with her life that she probably never sprained her ankles or got caught in the rain. Accident-free, pain-free, no inconvenience whatsoever. No, it's not that I envy her. I pity Roland. He was afraid of being bored. And all he got himself in the end was a boring wife.

———

26 AUGUST 1929.

Mrs. Ogden asked me today if I wanted to accompany her on a trip to Pittsburgh. I assumed her husband's delay made it necessary for her to seek a male companion, but why me?

When? I asked.

Any time, she said. Unless your schedule doesn't allow it?

I pondered my life, which runs like a train without a timetable. How long will it take for that train to derail or crash?

Why me? I asked.

A young man should not doubt everything, she said.

I was only assessing my capacity to be a good companion.

There are a dozen men in this city willing to be what you call a good companion to me, she said. You don't have a dozen women in this city to offer your service, nor a dozen women willing to show you the world you haven't seen, do you?

What makes a woman think she knows a man better than he knows himself? I said, feigning equality between

Mrs. Ogden and me. Amelia would have stories about watchmakers and dressmakers were I to ask. Yvette might be willing to introduce me to the poor artists. But they're women with limited prospects. They cannot be my prospect.

You're a young man in search of a future, Mrs. Ogden said. The question you should ask yourself is how to get there, not why people do what they do to make it possible for you.

I've often thought what makes us human is that we do everything possible to stop others from having any kind of future, I said.

Mrs. Ogden looked at me, not willing, I resentfully thought, to engage in a conversation she deemed pointless. I pressed on. Isn't that true? Animals don't care about other animals' futures. They don't even care about their own, as long as they have food.

Mrs. Ogden smiled, then started talking about a sculptor she'd met for dinner the night before. I've noticed her doing this. She changes subjects when I begin to sound tiresome. Yet I cannot stop myself. She has that effect on me, changing me into someone stupider. Worse, not only do I have to rely on her to guide me out of that mire of foolishness, but I find some pleasure and reassurance in being thus led by her. She never makes a fuss about my gaffes. Never pauses to question me. I feel grateful for that, till when I can get free again to make another argument.

She continued talking about the dinner. She had gone because she was curious to see if the sculptor was still in love with a cousin of hers, who was said to have been Trotsky's lover once.

Is she Russian? I asked.

Part English, part continental, Mrs. Ogden said. We are, like all people, from everywhere.

Not me, I said. I'm a provincial boy from Nova Scotia.

You remind me of this cousin of mine. Once, at a house party, she sat down for five minutes and then, to everyone's horror, fetched her winter coat, which she'd just left with the maid. She wrapped herself tightly throughout the evening. She'd have been considered outright rude if not for her reputation of being an eccentric.

Perhaps she was cold? I said. Perhaps she had a chill?

The point is not how one feels but how one makes a hostess feel, Mrs. Ogden said.

I was stung by her words. I said that I didn't suppose I was in the position to make her feel anything.

It's my cousin Elizabeth I was telling you about, your Madame Zembocki.

Oh, what happened then?

I imagine she was forgiven in the end. People forgive her. Some people inspire admiration, others pity, others annoyance. She inspires forgiveness.

What about . . . ? I was going to say, what about you, or perhaps I was going to say, what about me. Either way I cut myself off in time.

The truly dangerous people are those who inspire a mix of everything—those are the people you must avoid.

Why?

When someone inspires a mix of things in you, you'd mistakenly think of yourself as being in love. Do you not agree?

I thought of Aunt E. I haven't had the good fortune of having fallen in love, I said.

I wouldn't call it a loss.

Not even at my age? I said. Immediately I knew that I had misspoken.

If a person hasn't thought through much of life by the age of thirteen or fourteen, I don't think he stands a chance, Mrs. Ogden said.

But what if, I said, someone does inspire everything? What if I do think of myself as falling in love?

In that case offer nothing.

Nothing will come of nothing?

How else does one manage a life?

Is that how you do it?

No, but I have my experience to rely on.

I have nothing to rely on? I asked.

You have my friendship.

Mrs. Ogden is not a better storyteller than Amelia, but she knows I listen to her with a ravenousness. She knows that I will always prefer one Mrs. Ogden to a thousand Amelias or even a thousand Yvettes. I resent her for knowing that, but I would resent it more if she didn't know.

Does this make me meek? No, it takes ten times more courage for one to stay close to a woman like Mrs. Ogden than to run away. I would be a meek man if I looked for comfort and love only among the Amelias and Yvettes of the world.

———

SIDELLE WAS RIGHT THAT the dangerous people are those who get you into a hodgepodge of feelings. Roland was fortunate to have that explained to him. Nobody warned me. I knew it by instinct.

They both did well, I mean Sidelle and Roland. For years I've been puzzled by something Roland wrote after Sidelle's death: "We, Sidelle and I, have been lifelong practitioners of that art of subtraction. Whatever has come up between us we agree we can do without. Show me one person who can rival my skills and hers. No one comes close. Not even Hetty."

But I think I understand it now. When two people decide that they could do without everything and anything, and they make that decision together, well, in the end they cannot do without each other. Things you don't need for your daily upkeep—they're the true luxury, what makes a difference to your life. Did Roland care for all those nights of listening to classical music next to Hetty on the sofa, or the dinners he had to attend with her when she served on this or that charity committee, or the trips they took, when they packed up their orderly life and unpacked it in a holiday house thousands of miles away? Do we remember every single piece of toast we eat for breakfast?

I once wanted a dream from Roland, and he did give me that. A lot more than that.

Imagine going to dear old Gilbert for a dream. It would be like searching a cereal box for a diamond.

---

29 AUGUST 1929.

> I paid a visit to Yvette and Amelia in the evening, catching them both in this time. I told them I was to be out of town for a few days. Yvette turned to Amelia with a knowing look, as though I was failing already, and in a way predicted by Yvette (or both?).
>
> The visit was short and lukewarm. Afterward, Amelia came downstairs to the door with me. When are you leaving? she asked.
>
> In the coming week, I said.
>
> A pause. Unnerved by her quietness I felt the need to say something. I asked her if she would not mind seeing a film together on Saturday.
>
> Oh, she said as though startled by the direction of the conversation. I was only looking at your shirt, she said, pointing to my sleeve. That button is coming loose. Do you

want me to get the needle and thread? It won't take a minute.

Something about Amelia alarmed me, that willingness to serve before one even asks. Another man may take advantage of such a trait, but am I that sordid? I told Amelia she need not worry about the button.

But who will take care of it? she asked.

I almost said Bessie. Oh, someone will, I said. The landlord's daughter, I lied.

Amelia looked at me with her grey eyes. So then, we'll see a film together on Saturday? she said, smudging the divide between a question and a statement.

———

LATER IN THIS BOOK Roland admits that he sometimes lies in his diary. Or changes the sequence of events. Exaggerates. Anything a man can do to make himself feel "first-rate." Do you think this may be a case of that?

———

31 AUGUST 1929.

I am no longer a virgin. Am I recording this in a celebratory or a mourning mood?

Yvette seduced me. No, I let her seduce me, and she made sure Amelia caught us. Did I act dishonourably, and if so, toward whom? I am banished from their little shared nest now. One imagines that whatever rift came between them would be fixed through a combination of Yvette's resourcefulness and Amelia's loyalty. Their friendship must flow on with the same smoothness as before, as if disturbed only momentarily by a fallen tree branch or an inconvenient boulder.

————

WHEN I WAS IN kindergarten, there was a teacher my best friend Amy and I both loved with a passion. Her name was Miss Corey. Was she a good teacher? I don't remember having learned much from her. What we loved most was her red hair, kept short, done with perfect finger waves.

Miss Corey had a habit of drawing little flowers and animals in our workbooks. She must have done it to make our work look better, even when we had the worst handwriting. But she never did it consistently. And you never knew whose workbook would be chosen on a given day. In the end, Amy and I both believed Miss Corey favored the other. I don't think Miss Corey even knew the damage she caused. The same with Roland, but I trust that the two French girls were smarter than Amy and me. He was right. They would remain friends, Roland or no Roland.

Here's a lesson: Don't become a casualty of other people's casual behavior. If someone puts his heart into hurting you or destroying you, you have to at least respect him. But more often people hurt others because they're thoughtless. They elbow and push you because it never occurs to them you can possibly exist in that space. Iola, you must remember this.

Thoughtlessness is the eighth deadly sin.

————

Dinner with Mrs. Ogden at her hotel. Cooler at the roof-top. Still, my collar was completely out of shape by the end of the night. I wonder if the waiters have been changing their collars every hour. They look sharp and pristine and unperturbed. All qualities that I associate with being a real, mature man. But then look at the service positions those good qualities have landed them.

Our talk started slowly like any languid summer conversation. By and by Mrs. Ogden was able to pry me open like a clam. Out spilled the story with Yvette and Amelia, hardly a pearl.

I don't see why this troubles you so, she said.

I explained that I felt unfairly used.

You didn't lose much, Mrs. Ogden said. This French girl, according to you, is a beauty.

I said I would not have lost *anything* had she had some genuine affection for me.

But the other girl is interested in you. Would you be happier had she been your lover?

I hesitated and then said no.

Because she is plain-looking?

Yes, I said.

Mrs. Ogden lit a cigarette. I am always a beat too late when I try to light it for her. I studied her face. Would she consider that as a criticism of herself? She is not a beautiful woman, though she is the last woman you would call plain.

Not only that, I added hastily. I don't harbour any romantic feeling toward her so it'd be ungentlemanly to engage her in any dishonourable manner.

You have a long life in front of you, Roland. Don't develop a habit of fretting over anything unnecessary.

What's necessary, then?

Living as best as we can. We have so little control over anything that it makes us pure fools if we fret. For instance, what if our train derailed between here and Pittsburgh tomorrow? Would you still be upset about your imperfect romance?

(At our first meeting I told Mrs. Ogden that my parents died in a train crash. Was she being forgetful, or intentionally cruel?)

Living well is an easier business for you, I said.

Do you mean living is an easier business for me?

You have what you want, I said.

But I also have what I don't want.

A queen can suffer from an imperfectly set ring, I suppose? A princess can lose sleep over a pea, I said.

Mrs. Ogden waved the smoke away from in front of her eyes. Think about it, Roland. Among the very first words we learn to say as children is no, but does our protest do us any good? We're still at the mercy of parents and nannies and governesses and then what? God? Fate? What if we say yes to everything?

Say yes to everything?

Good or bad, sweet or bitter, kind or cruel, Mrs. Ogden said, what's the difference?

The difference, I thought, is that if I lived by that creed I would never have left Halifax. That solid sameness I already have, in the form of Hetty. Like a lighthouse, she speaks of the unchanged and the unchangeable: Let the sky be stormy or be starry, and I see no reason to be different; the world is a dangerous place but I'll give you all the assurance within my capacity; yes, I'm here, come to me; yes, come to me and all will be well, but leave me, leave me at your own risk.

Thinking of a woman? Mrs. Ogden said, and when I

tried to deny it, she said she could tell when a man's attention had drifted to another woman. The absent one always finds a way to join the party, she said. Who is the lucky girl?

Oh, just a cousin, I said. We've grown up together.

Mrs. Ogden smiled. Many a marriage occurs between cousins, she said.

She's only a little girl, I said. We love each other like brother and sister, nothing more.

Many a marriage happens without the kind of love you believe to be a prerequisite.

Is that how it is with your marriage? I said. It was foolish always to be cornered by her.

Do you mean my marriage to Mr. Ogden, or the one before?

You were married before?

Widowed, too, she said.

Mrs. Ogden made it sound as though we were discussing someone toward whom we should only feel a clinical interest. I have always taken pride in being able to treat all things in life as potential material for the books I will write one day. But that pride vanishes in front of Mrs. Ogden. She has ten times more material, but she dismisses the past as easily as she dismisses my ambition.

I didn't . . . I'm sorry to hear.

You don't have to feel sorry. It happens to be a fact of my life. Yes, a young woman could marry a young man for love and happiness, but there is no guarantee that he could survive a war when several other millions died. Yes, she could marry again, to a man too old to be thrown into another war—there will be one, mark my words—but there's no guarantee that this man in his civilian clothes won't perish from disease.

Mr. Ogden, I don't— I stammered, I don't suppose his health problem is that dire?

No one knows death's mind when it comes to an older man, she said. Well, not when it comes to a child, either.

Did you . . . ?

Yes, I had a son. Not much younger than you. But perhaps it's better for a mother to lose a child than for a child to lose his parents. Hugh died before his father. Or, I should say, Charles went to the war to forget his son's death.

Being orphaned, I said, trying to find my voice, is not that difficult.

One supposes you're right. But you see what I mean, saying no won't stop illness or death or war or any of my little miseries.

But one can't possibly welcome these misfortunes with open arms, I said.

Not with open arms, but with indifference.

And then what?

You just live whatever life comes next. For instance, we might not have crossed paths if it weren't for my cousin. But would it matter? Hardly. I might be sitting here talking with another young man, and you with another woman.

I tried not to look hurt, but my face must have betrayed me.

———

I WISH SIDELLE AND I had met. It may sound unfair that someone has lived in your head for so long while you've never existed for her. But the truth is, I wouldn't want a stranger to know my life. Sidelle wouldn't have liked that, either, but she could do little about my knowing her.

She lost a child. So did I. You could say she lost her only child, but there is no good math in a child's death. She lost two husbands. I lost three. No good math there, either.

We're not in the habit of saying no to anything. Sidelle was right: Protest all you can and it gets you nowhere.

One thing I wish I knew better is what kind of mother Sidelle was. You may get an impression from Roland's diary that she wasn't a warm woman, but he never knew her as a mother. Possibly she didn't show that side to him.

Here's another possibility. Roland grew up without a mother, so the door to the world of mothers never opened itself to him. A different person might've got a sense of Sidelle as a mother. You don't have to see a woman with her child to know. Perhaps I've been wrong to think Hetty couldn't give him a child. Perhaps he couldn't give her a child because he couldn't imagine his wife as a mother. For once let's blame him instead of her.

For all the time Roland was infatuated with Sidelle, there would have been more things he didn't know about her than he did. I've made it a game to think about the things he didn't know. Some are big, some are little. It's the little ones that I still wonder about. Did she throw away a bouquet of flowers when the first petal dropped? (Hetty, I imagine, would only keep the freshest flowers in their house.) Did she wear a wig toward the end of her life? (Hetty would, don't you think?) Did she wiggle her toes when she was anxious? (This I still do, one of my very few weaknesses.) Did she have moments, like me, when she couldn't remember Roland's face? Or his voice? Or if not Roland, her two dead husbands? Did she miss her child and relive the days when he was alive? But he died young, and she didn't have that many years at her disposal.

A dead child doesn't grow old. Lucy was twenty-seven and she's still twenty-seven. I can't make up a life for her past that age, but I've relived those twenty-seven years many times.

Every morning since Lucy's death, I wake up and say to myself: Here's another day that Lucy refused to live. Not a day she gave up. If she gave up something I could give it up, too. But she refused flatly to have today, and tomorrow, and the next day, and the next day. All the more reason for me to live each day, to prove a point: I refuse to accept her refusal.

I didn't cry much when she died. I fought back more tears than I imagine any mother in my position would do. If there were an Olympic race for that, I could've won a gold medal. But not crying does strange things to a person. It's not like all those tears are held up behind a dike, and you live your life like a watchwoman on duty. Day and night. Making sure there's no crack, no leak, no danger of flooding. You would be doing everyone a good service if that were the case. But you watch that dike for years and one day you say to yourself: I would like to take a look at the water again. The dike says, What water, ma'am? So you climb to the top. What water indeed? It's a desert on the other side.

I would say—oh, I've never said this before: Lucy really broke my heart. She broke my heart in a way I never imagined a heart could be broken. Perhaps if I had shed those tears, they would have kept the broken pieces floating around in me. Not for mending, but it would have been good to keep the pieces in sight.

Well, no reason to cry over cracked eggs. Sidelle didn't cry over the death of her son, either. Don't ask me how I know it. I just do.

———

3 SEPTEMBER 1929.

Early morning. A ten-hour train ride with Mrs. Ogden coming. It will be the first time I share a journey this long with a woman. Not, of course, counting the family trips, bubbling with excitement that went flat too quickly. This will be different—intimacy that is not yet intimacy. A good wine that gives one's heart palpitations has to have the right degree of unfamiliarity.

Last night, even though it was late, I visited the couple

next door, Mr. and Mrs. Cotter. Cousin Cliona had said that in time of emergency I should seek help from the Cotters. My absence over the next few days and the parrot's welfare—this situation I counted as an emergency. The couple were obliging. Mrs. Cotter said that she would send their niece Eileen over twice a day to look after Kotku. I didn't know they had a niece in the house. I had only met their two young sons. Eileen is the one to trust, Mr. Cotter said, sending one of the boys to fetch the girl. Eileen, it turned out, is a more recent arrival in this city than I am. Her face would be beautiful if not for her stern eyebrows and harshly pressed lips. Perhaps they will be softened by this new world, though they could equally well be further hardened.

Afterward I thought about Eileen's future, feeling an authorial fondness toward the girl, whose fate in this unfriendly life remains unknown. What a grand feeling it gives one to think of all those tragedies awaiting a young soul. On the eve of a journey one often harbours tenderness toward those left behind, even if in this case it's only a stranger one has just met.

———

Night. William Penn Hotel.

Could this day be a new chapter in my life? But this cliché makes me laugh. No, Roland, you haven't lived enough to write even a page of prologue. A line or two of epigraph is all you have. And even that you have lifted out of Horace or Shakespeare.

But there will be more chapters after this. Perhaps it is finally the time for me to be serious about that masterpiece I am to write.

We left on the 8.05 train, in a compartment reserved for

two. For a while Mrs. Ogden, citing a headache, lounged on the sofa, which was not long enough, so she placed her feet up on the armrest. A fine model of a reclining woman, though I could not shake the feeling that there was a better artist who could capture her entire existence with eyes more critical, less enamoured.

I sat by the window, pretending to read. The countryside in its deepest summer green soon brought a fatigue to my eyes and my mind. A young man in his prime, travelling across a wealthy and vivacious land, in comfort and luxury, at someone else's expense—seen through the eyes of Eileen or Amelia or even Yvette I am a lucky man. But luck is the kind of possession that only accentuates what is lacking.

After we passed Philadelphia Mrs. Ogden joined me by the window. What are you reading? she asked.

I showed her the book, a novel by Ronald Firbank.

Oh, him, Mrs. Ogden said.

Did you know him? I asked.

Only a little, by being around. I wouldn't get too excited about him if I were you.

My cheeks felt warm. My taste is no less provincial than I am, I said.

Don't be absurd, Mrs. Ogden said. However, one Firbank would be enough use for the world.

What if, I thought, the world does not have any use for a single Roland Bouley?

I found him tiresome, though Charles called him a genius.

A dead husband is like a trap, and I am the kind of creature who jumps right into it. Did he . . . was he . . . ? How did he die?

Exactly? I don't know. I never want to know. War is a terrible, terrible thing, but that doesn't say much. Charles could've stayed out of the war like Firbank. But see, they are both dead now.

But you did love him, didn't you?

Why else did I marry him?

I wondered how a woman could refrain from wanting to know the exact details of a husband's death. But then I have never attempted to imagine my parents' death. Their living years, though, I often contemplate.

Death is a commonplace thing, Mrs. Ogden said. It happens to everyone. Yet most people don't understand that. We make it sound as though it were most extraordinary. The same with birth.

What's extraordinary, then? I asked. Nothing, I both expected and feared that she would reply.

I was reading Madame de Sévigné's letters last night, Mrs. Ogden said. She complained to her daughter about her son's love affair with an actress.

How very French, I said.

And when the actress was finally ready to receive the son, he could not consummate the intimacy, and Madame de Sévigné had quite a laugh out of the episode. If you were the man, it would be a most humiliating letter from your mother to your sister, don't you think? Except it was he who rushed to his mother's bedchamber and reported his mortification, right after his failure with the actress, all the time knowing too well that she would share this with his sister.

For a moment I had a bitter taste in my mouth. I remembered my talking about Amelia and Yvette with Mrs. Ogden. Perhaps I, too, gave her an opportunity for a laugh with someone.

Mrs. Ogden did not seem to notice my unease. One wonders what was going on between that mother and her two children, she said. That I would call extraordinary.

She sounds dreadful, I said.

We shouldn't denounce her. Had Hugh lived to be a grown man, who could guarantee I would not have been an equally appalling mother?

I could barely endure Mrs. Ogden's husbands, alive or dead. Her mention of a buried child brought a chill to this late summer day. We both have untimely deaths written into our histories, but between us there remains an abyss. To me the experience is no more than knowledge. I wish we could make a pact: I would never talk about my parents again, she her child.

———

WHEN SIDELLE SAID SHE didn't care about birth or death, it was because she couldn't do anything about them. So what, people say that all the time, I don't care. One of the biggest lies ever invented.

When I think about my life now, often I think about those births and deaths: the births of my children, and grandchildren, and you, Iola. You must feel a little special because I may not meet another great-grandchild—young people nowadays like to stay spring chickens and they put off laying eggs for as long as they can.

Each birth is like a message in a bottle. You want them to go far, and never return to you.

And those deaths in my life—they all started as messages sent by others—yes, I'm glad that they've reached me. All of them but Lucy's.

———

A couple just walked past my door, drunken with good wine or the prospect of imminent bliss. I am too young to have to listen to someone else's happiness in a lonely hotel room. Mrs. Ogden makes it sound as though nothing matters enough to perturb her. I can put up that façade, too. A performer sees through another performer.

It would not be a tedious task to uncover what matters to her, what perturbs her. Perhaps I would even be a part of it.

I shall rest for the night with this thought comforting me like a glass of warm milk.

———

ROLAND, WE DO AGREE sometimes.

———

4 SEPTEMBER 1929.

Mrs. Ogden and I had a touristy day in the least touristy parts of Pittsburgh today. The city is grimier and more oppressive than New York City. One almost has to admire the smoke bellowing out the chimneys. If this is the foundation of America, no wonder Mother's family set their hearts against it. No one wants to be engulfed by something so impersonal, but Americans seem to do better than people elsewhere at being engulfed.

Right after breakfast we were taken to visit the Heinz factory. Why Heinz, I asked Mrs. Ogden in the car. You're not by any chance writing an epic poem about pickles? I was being flippant, but I couldn't help it. I often sound flippant when I feel miserable. What if I become one of those people laughing out loud at a funeral, or worse, on my own deathbed?

KATHERINE: DO YOU RECOGNIZE YOURSELF in Roland, a little maybe? I don't mind if you laugh out loud at my funeral or my deathbed, but don't feel you're obliged to laugh when you feel miserable.

———

The stifling heat so early in the day, the haggard workers passing our car, just off the night shift most probably, white and colored, all looking grey against the blinding sun—all these make me miserable. I have always wanted to see the world. But is it necessary? If I were a bee, couldn't I just stay contented among the flowers I knew best? Nova Scotia is the meadow I left behind. For what, though—these steel-and-concrete Venus flytraps?

Mrs. Ogden ignored my ill disposition. As ever she steered the conversation toward strangers, when I wanted to be the subject. A friend of hers had been commissioned to do some artwork for the Heinzes, she said. He'd be glad to hear that she finally visited.

At the factory, a Mr. Smith led the tour. I must admit that it was entertaining to see the metal sheet coming down the conveying belt, cut and folded into a tin with lid and bottom all ready to go. Four minutes and fifteen seconds, Mr. Smith timed it. It's all about consistency, he said, everybody in his place, everything happening by the book. I watched him twisting his whiskers and could not help but feel disgust. Predictability and profit are the poisons of this century. I don't even need to be a socialist to denounce Mr. Smith.

Mrs. Ogden met with a few workers afterward, both men and women. She questioned them about their living and working conditions and took notes with a seriousness that baffled me. How does one connect this woman to the one lounging on the train? And what am I doing here, reading the ubiquitous Heinz 57 slogans when I should have been on an ocean liner, heading to Oxford.

I wandered off into an adjacent hall and studied the marble sculptures portraying workers at the factory. Are these the Herculeses of our time? The thought that a factory would have an artist commit such a banal thing as making pickles to eternity made me laugh loud.

· · ·

[Yet what is immortal? Few people remember Sidelle today, fewer know her poetry. Who will remember me after my death? Heinz, however, is immortal. As individuals, and as a human race, we are destined to be outlived by machines and pickles. — RB, 28 April 1989]

———

WELL, HERE I AM, remembering you. Who remembers the pickles at last night's dinner? Who remembers any pickle from any meal?

———

5 SEPTEMBER 1929.

We visited the U.S. Steel plant today. A negation rather than a celebration of human intelligence. The two men operating the gate to let the melted metal pour in—how I resented them, sweaty in their half-nakedness, their eyes no longer dazed by the phenomena that took our breaths away. Actors of the first-rate, holding ultimate contempt for us.

They were Czech, they later told us in broken English. Once removed from the noise and heat, they seemed less crazed, less devilish. Still, I resented them. There is no place for poetry or philosophy in their lives, but their bodies speak with such natural eloquence.

Yet one never wants to admit defeat. Is it for that reason that Mrs. Ogden—no, Sidelle—and I became lovers? Perhaps she is simply another flytrap. Should I have resisted? But she overwhelmed me more than the steel mills. I had no will to counter her will. A banal inevitability, surrender is.

Anything can happen on the road. Sidelle is my fellow traveller. Who is at home? Hetty. Oh, the thought of her makes me long for my lost youth.

Except not really.

PITTSBURGH: YOU WOULDN'T THINK of it as a romantic city. But romance happens everywhere. Had I known that they became lovers in Pittsburgh, I could have shown our Pittsburg to Roland. We could have lunched at the court of Los Medanos, sitting under the palm trees and clinking our wineglasses like two movie stars. I had the look. He had the air. We had the story between us.

Los Medanos—I wonder if it still stands there. Nice old place. My father once shared a business plan with the Williamsons, our neighbors, an inn and a ranch combined to attract tourists. It wasn't much of a success, but I did meet people during that time. Well, I say people, but what I really mean was I met Roland then. Yes, he came and stayed on our ranch for two days. And yes, I was only sixteen then, but for some people age doesn't matter. Look at Sidelle, old enough to be Roland's mother. But I've never judged her, so don't you judge me.

Before my father and Mr. Williamson started the business, they visited a few hotels and brought back free postcards. Of all the hotels they went to, I liked the look of Los Medanos the best. It's in Pittsburg, my father said. The town used to be called the New York of the Pacific. Is it as glamorous as New York, we asked, and he said of course not. Otherwise the name would have stuck.

They changed the name to Pittsburg because of the steel mills in town. They thought if the town could not be as fancy as New York it could at least be as rich as Pittsburgh. Like a woman from a family of status that lost its wealth getting married to a lesser man for money.

My Lithuanian great-grandfather worked in a Chicago shipyard, but he could've worked in a pickle factory or a steel mill in Pittsburgh. The workers Sidelle and Roland met, had they been born earlier they might have joined the forty-niners. These things didn't matter to Roland. But when I read his diaries I like to think about people from all the way back. Some of them made California. Some made us. If I think about life that way I don't find it disappointing. We've all done our share, and none of us is special.

Roland didn't understand this. I don't blame him. He lived in the days when he wrote these diaries. He had nothing to rely on. Sidelle and I, we have our experience.

---

7 SEPTEMBER 1929.

> Sidelle asked me tonight if I would like to travel with her in the coming months. Mr. Ogden, she said, will need to stay put. Stay put where, I wondered, but she did not say. Is she

paying for my trip, or is he? What am I, a secretary, a valet,
a spare while the damaged tyre awaits repairing?

...

[Sidelle and I travelled for the next seven months in midwestern America and southwestern America. From there we crossed the border and
travelled in Mexico before returning to California. Sidelle interviewed
industry workers and farmers for Harry Ogden, who was recovering from
tuberculosis at a sanatorium in France.

Harry never published the study with the information we had gathered. The documents we compiled are archived in three libraries: University of Pittsburgh, University of New Mexico, and California State
University at Fresno. An interested reader could seek them out, though I
wouldn't recommend it. The papers only offer a timeline and our geo-
graphical movements along the timeline. The real stories—only I know
them now.

We returned to New York in April 1930, and Sidelle sailed for England in August 1930.

The gap seen here is not my intention. Before Sidelle left for England, she asked that my diaries of our journey west and our sojourn in
New York be destroyed. It did not occur to me to disobey her wishes
then.

My memories of those months have not faded. But I don't feel that I
can re-create the entries. Hindsight doesn't always bring advantage.
What would I not give to reread those pages?—RB, 6 May 1989]

———

WHY? BECAUSE HE WROTE too much about their romantic journey? I wonder if Sidelle personally supervised the burning of his
diaries. I can see them sitting together, drinking, listening to some
music, and burning the pages one by one in a fireplace. How did

she persuade him to do it? What did he get in return? These things we will never know.

Poor Roland. He was not the kind of person who would easily part with any possession. My mother was like that, too. You should have seen the years of accumulation of postcards and letters she had saved. Some people live by what they accumulate. But they forget that what's accumulated can be destroyed in a moment by a flood or an earthquake or a fire. (My mother's accumulation was burned by my father.)

My rule of thumb: Whatever can be destroyed is not worth holding on to.

(And yes, anything can be destroyed, if you feel ready to hear this truth.)

I used to resent the fact that I couldn't read about that year in his life. But now I think, so what? A missing year is nothing. Everyone's life is like Swiss cheese.

(This has nothing to do with anything, but Clark, the new guy who for a week or so seemed interesting to me, insisted today on giving me a lecture on Swiss cheese. He said the Swiss cheese that doesn't have holes is called blind because those holes are called eyes. But blind people still have eyes, I said. Let's not be too literal, he said. There are a lot of good metaphors to live by. So I asked, What is metaphor? And he said, The thing that makes the world go around. I said, I thought money makes the world go around. He said, If you think about it, Lilia, money is one of the best metaphors we human beings have ever invented. I was afraid he would never stop so I said, That's good to know. And I left before he said anything more.)

19 NOVEMBER 1936.

I turned twenty today.

Happy birthday, Hetty said in the morning when I joined her at breakfast.

I didn't return to celebrate my birthday, though I was not surprised that Hetty remembered it. It's my third day back at Elmsey, half as houseguest, half as the hanger-on I once was. Why am I here, in any case? Nostalgia, perhaps, or one last effort to parse something that has never been— and perhaps never will be—understood. This house did not greet my birth and nor will it see my death. Whose child am I? Does not one need to figure out that question before one stops being anyone's child?

A quarter of my life gone, full of ignorance and misfortune, I said.

The next quarter is bound to be better, Hetty said.

Her faith in the right words as the remedy to fate's wrongdoing—had Hetty been Ovid no creature would have to be metamorphosed.

I said a better future to me sounds like truffles to the pigs. They search only out of instinct and what's their reward? What's the difference between me and a hog, in any case?

Hetty looked as unperturbed as a glass flower. Have you ever seen a truffle hog? she asked.

No, I said.

Neither have I, she said.

I said one suspected they were like any ordinary pig. Hetty said a school friend posed with a white truffle in a cage for a photograph. Where was that, I asked, and she said at a hotel lobby in Florence. It might not be a real one, I said. But it can't be a model truffle, she said, can it? I said why not, if there were mannequins and model train sets. She said, Ah, you do have a point, but isn't it odd to imagine the maker of a model truffle? He can't have much of a business going for him. Perhaps he has other models to make, I said. Who knows, the world may request more fake things than can be dreamt by you and me.

This is the kind of conversation Hetty and I are destined to have. With neither impatience or resentment between a long-married couple; nor passion, with the right proportion of misgiving and distrust and craze, between lovers. I can't even say I am bored. One is not going to end a conversation with Hetty in any place dangerous or thrilling. More likely one ends where one starts. From nowhere to nowhere.

My uncles' finances have improved. The Fergusons have always been lucky. But money will not salvage them from this existence they so stubbornly cling on to, and money certainly will not slow their journey to their demise. It is ungrateful of me to judge them so. But why not. They showed no curiosity about me. Their welcome, tepid, was not half of what Ethel and Bessie showed me. It is a big lie that blood is thicker than water. Blood can be thinned by leave-taking *and* reunion, betrayal *and* loyalty.

Hetty has changed, too, less prone to blushing. She left St. Mary's at the end of the spring but did not go to Switzerland as was always planned for her. Did the FitzGeralds lose the means to send her? But she looks happy enough so perhaps there are other reasons. A suitor? Several? A marriage in the making? I wish Aunt E were here to inform me.

It is odd that Aunt E is no longer part of Elmsey. Odder that I do not seem to miss her keenly. She married the owner of a silver mine in Colorado last year. I learned about the marriage from Hetty when I was in California.

For one day it hurt me to think that Aunt E did not send the news to me. I could have attended the wedding.

When Aunt Geraldine joined us, Hetty told her that it was my birthday. Many happy returns, Roland, Aunt G said a little absentmindedly. I broke her heart by leaving. She is the one to have raised me in the most consistent and conscientious manner. She would be happy to see Hetty and me marry, she would be thrilled to see us have a brood of children; and more than that, she would defend me, the penniless Roland, against any raised eyebrows or pursed lips. If that is not maternal love, I do not know what is.

Aunt G has not only found happiness in her own mediocre life but is also able to see happiness in other people's mediocre lives. Yet how dejected she looks now. Happy people should not be allowed to live past a certain age. Feeling guilty, I asked her about every one of my cousins. From her reply one would think they all live in fairy tales. Imagine her response when someone showed the scantest interest in me.

Aunt G asked what would come next for me. She did not want to know what had come before. Nobody in the house seemed to. Hetty alone has an idea of my migration across the continent, though I did not tell her about my short stint working as a clerk in an insurance company, enough for me to know that New York is not paved with gold. I had written her letters from the road, describing the scenery rather than the woman who shared that scenery with me. I left her the impression that I was travelling with a few men of my own age. I also hinted that such a journey should be kept secret from the family. She will never betray my trust.

I mentioned a possibility in London. Some connection at an advertising agency wrote me, I said, but I'm deciding between that and a post in Hong Kong.

Hong Kong, Roland? Aunt G said. Doing what there? It's a long way away.

I said all was not decided yet.

I'm sure your uncles can find you a good position in Halifax, she said.

Aunt G does not have a mind for irony, or else I would have laughed aloud at this suggestion. I don't mind travelling a little and seeing the world, I said.

Of course, there's a world out there we don't get to see, Aunt G said wistfully.

There's a world here that others don't get to see, either, Hetty said.

I was taken aback. There was a time when Hetty talked about going to the school in Switzerland with some enthusiasm. I can take a Hetty who is not interested in herself, but no curiosity whatsoever in the outside world? For a moment I thought how Sidelle could annihilate Hetty with a simple look. That thought terrifies me. They shall not meet. Of this I am certain, more certain than anything I have felt so far in my life.

Still, Aunt G said, some people pity us.

I wondered if she meant me. Or Aunt E.

Oh, Aunt Geraldine, nobody pities us, Hetty said. You're only in that mood of yours.

I did not know Aunt G had a mood of hers. This must be something new since last year.

Nobody dares to pity you, Aunt G said to Hetty. She then asked Hetty if she was still planning to visit the Reynars before the holidays. It is unlike Aunt G to exclude anyone present from a conversation. Such an abrupt shift must be her punishment for my disloyalty.

Hetty said she was postponing the trip. I told them Roland is back for a visit, she said.

I said there was no need for her to change her plans.

Oh, but family comes first, Aunt G said, speaking for Hetty.

How good we all are at pretending. Reynar. Must be a new addition to this part of the world. Who among them is courting Hetty?

_____

GILBERT TOOK ON THE responsibility of being a father to Lucy when he was twenty. I was a mother of two children at twenty. What was Lucy doing at twenty? Bouncing from one young man to another, many of them belonging to the group who burned their draft cards in Berkeley. Gilbert didn't say anything, but I knew he thought Lucy had got herself tangled up with the wrong crowd. One day she entertained us with the tale of her fist-fighting with an heiress at a party. She said the woman's name as though we should've heard of her. Who, I asked. She told us to take a trip to the Mountain View Cemetery. Find the grandest mausoleum, she said, and that's where her people are buried.

Gilbert was miserable then. He didn't feel any better when Lucy and her friends helped Timmy move across the border to Vancouver. Another war, and all those young people who refused to meet their responsibilities. Gilbert didn't understand that their dreams of love and peace were not that different from his own. Yes, love and peace never grow out of fashion.

But those miseries, what did they matter? Lucy died before the war ended. Born in peacetime and died in a war. That could fit on a tombstone, except it would tell the wrong story.

_____

21 NOVEMBER 1930.

A nice enough day. Hetty and I took a walk down toward the public garden. The first snow came and went, both quickly. Winter is late this year.

I can't tell what annoys me more—to run into old acquaintances who, having forgotten me (or pretending to have forgotten me?), need an explanation of who I am, or to greet those who claim to know me better than I know myself. Mr. O'Neil and I have never doubted you'd be back, Mrs. O'Neil said to me.

There was a kind of idle contentedness in Hetty, which made me feel discontented. My life is full of unclassified ambitions, and Hetty seems capable of brushing them aside like cobwebs. I felt a desire to rattle her.

You know you don't have to get stuck here, I said when we sat down at a less windy spot next to the water.

Oh, Hetty said. But I've never thought of myself as being stuck.

There's a world out there, and one has to see it.

Does one have to? Hetty said.

One ought to, I said.

She threw a piece of seaweed to an old gull nearby. We had been watching it for a while. With one claw permanently curled into a ball, the gull favoured the other leg yet would neither fly nor stay still. A limping man trapped in that bird, I thought, so defiant and unrelenting, not letting the world off the hook from witnessing his misery.

Did you enjoy seeing the world? Hetty asked.

Of course, I said.

But it was because you had friends with you, no?

I've been to places by myself, I said, which was mostly a lie. Being alone offers the most memorable experience.

I'm alone here, Hetty said, all the time.

I looked at her. She has parents and siblings. She has relatives who praise her beauty and virtue. She has admirers. She has money. She does not know what it means to be alone.

You're exaggerating, I said. You're in a mood.

I don't live a life that allows much of any mood. But it's a fine life as it is.

One sees Hetty at thirty or forty or seventy with the same depthless serenity. Is that what one should be looking for in a wife?

But, Roland, how can you be so certain that Hetty is still yours? Chances are, you will get a telegram next month that says she is getting married. No, impossible. I can tell where her heart is. A man always knows.

———

NO, ROLAND, YOU DON'T. A man like you never knows.

Hetty knew more than she liked, about life, about Roland, about herself even, but she made little fuss. Yes, I make fun of her, but there is one thing she got right: She didn't mind appearing dumb or blank. Most people live like hamsters in a wheel. There is always something to prove to the world. Hetty played possum. She might've secretly laughed at those proud hamsters in the spinning wheels. She had her reason to laugh.

I must be in a mood myself today. Had Hetty been born in our family she would have been like Margot.

Margot at least had children. And she was also lucky that they were all beside her bed, next to their father, when she died.

Once Margot said to me . . . I can't remember when this was, but during those years when our children were still little enough for us to think of ourselves as young mothers. She said, Do you find it strange that we can be mothers? I said, What do you mean? She said, Sometimes I wonder if Mother would be disappointed in us. Why, I asked her. Just a feeling, Margot said. She'd be happier if none of us married at all. Really, I said. Oh, I mean none of us girls, she said. Of course she wanted her sons married. Really, I said again.

Sometimes I think I'm just like her, she said. When Doug and Harrison grow up, I hope they have good wives, but I don't want Lynn or Ellie to be good wives for any man. It'd be fine if they decided not to marry.

I was startled. I wasn't used to a Margot who thought about anything, so I told her not to talk nonsense. What I meant was: Follow your script.

I take my words back. Hetty was no Margot. Going by Roland's diaries, she never made a slip and misspoke.

————

GOODNESS, HOW FAT THIS book is already becoming. Soon I will run out of pages in this notebook. And ink in this pen. And glue in this stick. Maybe Peter Wilson had a point about Roland's repetitiveness. I used to think that Wilson cut too much from Roland's diaries and left out many important things. But I now think Roland himself might be responsible. He just couldn't tell what was important, and what was not.

Sometimes as I read him, with all his whys about himself, and you want to say to him: Roland, enough of these questions! Why can't you give us some answers? Or, write more about other people. They'd help make you a more interesting man.

I mean, all of them but Hetty. If you think he becomes a bit boring in the second half of the book, let's blame Hetty. Even a little French seamstress is more fun to read about than her.

If you want to find out everything, read on slowly. Take a self-

guided tour. I'll meet you around the corner. I'll get some Post-its
and mark what's interesting to me. You may laugh at me, saying
I'm doing the same condensing work Peter Wilson did. But there
is a difference. I've been reading this book for a long time. Not
every day Roland recorded was worth recording. Not everyone deserved his attention. My job is to find the pages you will enjoy. I
don't want you to stop reading halfway.

I'll skip over Roland's words like a stone skimmed on the surface of a lake. That I can do.

———————

1 JANUARY 1931.

Dunlop stopped by in the evening and asked what I
thought of Mussolini's New Year address. I deliberately
chose not to tune in for it. I was working intensely on
Part II of my novel. Making a fresh start on New Year's
Day, that's more meaningful than contemplating humankind's common fate.

Dunlop found it unbelievable that I didn't listen to it.

Does he speak good English? I asked.

All politicians speak all tongues well. But how can you
be so impassive? We live in a historic time and we should
live every moment fully.

I said people living through the Great War must've felt
that, too. And those during the 1812 war. And those sailing
with Magellan. History is a cake, I said. Anyone can help
himself to a piece.

You're too young to be a cynic, Dunlop said.

You're too old to be a sentimentalist, I said.

I like Dunlop a great deal. He is in a similar situation,
momentarily stuck with this thankless job of writing adver-

tisements for things we cannot afford. He has set his heart
on a diplomatic career. He believes that the global future
lies in the hands of diplomats, and that this is the moment
to enter that game.

He asked me about the news from Hong Kong. No
news, I said, and he said if he were me he would take the
next ship out there, news or not. The war will break out in
no time, he said. The last thing you want is to get trapped
here.

I looked around. A year ago I would have given anything to be where I am now. A room. A job. In New York.
If this city is a trap it is a trap bigger than life.

Or enlist, he said.

In America?

Why not? But you're luckier, you can do that in Canada,
no? How I wish we could switch places. War doesn't happen every day. We can't let this train pass us by.

Dunlop is three years older than I am, but I can safely
say I am thirty years wiser. For one thing, he is desperately
in love with Millie, the little typist. Dunlop will never be
able to imagine a woman like Sidelle. Sometimes I feel that
I am like a millionaire who cannot really reveal my wealth
to anyone.

Later.

Letter from Sidelle. She said I should make up my mind
about coming to London. Why, because she is there?

―――――

ONLY A NOTE TO SAY this is the first time he didn't obey her.

―――――

10 MARCH 1931.

Hong Kong. Arrived yesterday afternoon. Alan Prismall is working at the Maritime Customs Service, and has promised to help secure a position for me, either here or in Shanghai.

Far East. Am I then a member of the "Far West" to the natives here? Far we are from one another, far from being equally human. From the dock to the Peninsula, the man who pulled the pedicab sweated profusely. Had he been a horse I would have halted the carriage and led him to a water trough. But everyone else seems to be at ease, those being transported and those transporting others on their backs. I tried out my minimal Cantonese on the pedicab driver and the bellhop, but both shook their heads disapprovingly and replied in pidgin English.

————

THIS REMINDS ME: I should have a chat with Cecilia. She moved in last month, and she keeps too much to herself to be healthy. She and her husband were from Hong Kong. They immigrated to America after they married, and he had a dental practice in San Francisco. One morning, as he was walking to the clinic, someone shot him dead from behind. Cecilia has never said anything about it. Elaine told us—she had followed the murder and the trial in the *Chronicle* back in the day, and she confirmed the story with Cecilia's children. She probably promised the children that she and her friends would take extra care of their mother. I pity anyone who trusts Elaine.

I should talk with Cecilia. Not about her husband's death, but about Hong Kong. Maybe she'll feel less sad if I ask her about the hotel Roland stayed in there.

———

25 MARCH 1931.

> On this island: Englishmen and their wives have their clubs and tea parties and picnics and dances, a society of their own; Scots and Welshmen and Irishmen enjoy a precarious brotherhood; and then there are the rest of us, an assortment of adventurers—New Zealanders, Aussies, Canadians, and of course Americans, who stand out just as much as the English. All of us float on top of a muddy current of native faces that look indistinguishable from one another. Perhaps Sidelle was right to say that I would find Hong Kong disappointing. Exoticism is like virginity. A more perverse mind may be able to make something out of it.
>
> If you are as rootless as you say, Sidelle wrote in her last letter, why not transplant yourself to where you belong?
>
> On the way to work, to fulfil my tedious task of representing Western civilisation, I stopped at a kiosk to read the headline of the *Tribune*. BHAGAT SINGH, RAJGURU AND SUKH-DEV EXECUTED. Executed. I felt that the situation called for my action. Buying a copy of the paper, at the least. But like a schoolboy refusing to deliver to a master the answer demanded, I stuck my hands in my pockets and walked away. In our time, news grows stale as fast as the vegetable leaves left behind by the roadside peddlers.
>
> Strangers' executions: Such stories are only pertinent when shared with someone close. I remember taking the train from Los Angeles to San Francisco, with Sidelle read-

ing aloud to me a French aristocrat's account of a French-
woman's execution. Court gossip and sensational
descriptions. The woman had poisoned her husband and
father-in-law (separately, so there was no mistaking her intention), and all the way up to the guillotine she was certain that she would be reprieved. Poor little murderess, so
miserable in her marriage that killing the husband alone
was not sufficient vengeance.

We colonists should remember that as a lesson. The natives are never married to us willingly.

———

BENJAMIN READ THE NEWS aloud at breakfast that his former colleagues at Stanford had discovered bacteria that can live on arsenic. Is that something worth celebrating? I asked. A mistake. It led
to a lecture. What I meant was, Should we congratulate the bacteria for being so peculiar in their diet? But, of course, Benjamin was
thinking of man's brilliance. I was so bored that I wrote on a piece
of toast with jam: arse. He looked it over. Arsenic, he said, showing
me the word in the paper like I didn't know how to spell. I told him
that there was not enough space on the toast. He took a second
piece and wrote the last three letters. Anything that is not complete
bothers him, he explained to me. Like I care!

People love to think themselves smarter than others. I let
them—until they try to enlighten me. I don't have any extra letters
attached to my name, but that doesn't stop me from ticking the
box saying I have an advanced degree. An advanced degree in living, that's what I have. I've educated myself about the world since
the days when Mr. Williamson subscribed to the newspapers for
the guests. Gilbert, too, was an avid reader of newspapers, but he
was looking for connections between himself and events. All his
life he followed the annual meeting of the UN in September, as if

he had contributed in some way, making it possible for all those politicians to gather. Wrong way to think about the news, if you ask me. I read the papers to see how many disasters I have escaped. All those fires and earthquakes and wars and assassinations and terrorist attacks, all those crashed trains and collapsed bridges and exploded gas tanks and contaminated lettuces, or those bankruptcies and stolen identities and losses of money or faces. Thank you but no thank you. Dear life, I have no interest in being any part of your drama. I can make my own drama if I want it.

Did you see today's news, someone walking into the Chapel of Chimes and stealing a backpack? Turned out there was a memorial service planned, and in the backpack was the urn containing the ashes. The family and the friends of the deceased, the police and the security monitor . . . so on and so forth, but I think the reporter missed one very crucial point. What disappointment for the thief when he opened the backpack. What bad luck. When a good deed is not rewarded we call life unfair, but at least it gives all those do-gooders an opportunity to feel martyred, to wail against injustice, to add something glorious to their histories. What do you call life when a bad deed, which is done purely for some gain, is not rewarded? When you steal but the only booty is a jar of ashes? When you set a bear trap and catch only an anteater? When a selfish man doesn't get what he wants? Don't call it justice. A slap in the face is a slap in the face. No, I'm not defending horrible people. All I'm saying is, life is unfair to everyone.

Roland's complaint about the news growing old was really about something else. All news grows old. It would be hilarious if it didn't, like a garden of flowers refusing to wither. It would be a garden of fake flowers.

What was difficult for Roland was that what he read in the newspaper had nothing to do with him. That's difficult for many men. Benjamin would've had much less to say had the overachieving bacteria not in some way been connected to his wife. Ohhhhh, I miswrote. I meant to say his life!

------

19 JUNE 1931.

I have lapsed in keeping this journal. No new pages added
to the novel since I left New York. No real friendship
formed on this island. (Or any island. It only recently
occurred to me that I have mostly lived an island life: Nova
Scotia, Manhattan, Hong Kong. England, too, if that is my
destination. The only time I wasn't on an island was when I
travelled with Sidelle.)

I have had no romantic encounter worth recording, unless one counts my expeditions to an opium den. A dispirit-
ing experience, in more than one sense. Someday I shall
entertain a woman with an account of my failure here. But
that day shall wait. That day can only exist on a foundation
of triumphs.

Later.

Triumphs. What triumphs, Roland?

A dark mood. Dark enough for me to look around and
see if there is a pistol lying by my hand.

For the past ten minutes I have been watching the mon-
grel dogs across the street. Two yellow and one black, lan-
guishing in the heat, tongues too long, too lopsided. And
the bare-butt baby sitting on the three-legged stool, with
his sister, four or five years old at most, guarding him, not
knowing that when the sun moves, they should move to
stay in the shade. Oh, dogs and children, creatures who
can't construe a way to escape their paltry existence. How I
envy you.

Sidelle has settled back into her marriage, dispatching
affectionate letters, seemingly out of friendship (or, possibly, maternal feelings?!). Hetty loyally sends news of Nova

Scotia. Nothing seems able to jolt me out of this apathy. Not even the news of my position in Shanghai, which seemed to induce a certain amount of jealousy among my fellow clerks.

...

[In August 1931, I took a post with the Maritime Customs Service in Shanghai. I believe it was in Shanghai that I started the habit of assigning only a single letter to most of the women with whom I had an encounter. In retrospect, this generosity, which equates to throwing veils indiscriminatingly over faces both meant to be remembered and meant to be forgotten, is among my regrets. I do wish, at times, to be able to remember a full name, a real person beyond a few sketched moments. — RB, 23 November 1989]

_____

WORDS ARE OF NO help if you want to remember something. I haven't put anything on the page until now. But everything I need to remember Lucy or Gilbert or Roland or the others by is with me. Ask me about any person in my life, and I can tell you a few stories. It's not just that I have a good memory. I keep people. Not out of greediness. And I'm not a hoarder. I keep people because I like living among them. They don't always know that. I have my pride.

What you don't forget makes who you are. Poor Roland — he kept his diary like a diligent farmer, never missing a season. But what did he reap but forgetfulness?

_____

2 SEPTEMBER 1931.

Met K at the party a few nights ago and already we have
seen each other twice. She is married to that bore LL. I do
not think she is in love with him at all.

With K to the Russian place for tea this afternoon. From
a certain angle her face can almost pass as beautiful. But
one looks again and wonders if the face, colourless, is truly
ugly. What a strange woman.

She was in Hoihow before Shanghai. There are only a
handful of Europeans there, she said, mostly missionaries,
fighting among themselves about religious doctrines. The
only thing that could unite them was me, she said, because
I'm an atheist.

Did they do anything to save you?

When I got sick they competed to feed me fresh milk
they could get hold of, K said. Fresh milk for an unsalvage-
able soul.

When K was too sick to stay on the island, they trans-
ferred LL to Shanghai so she could get access to Western
doctors. On the day we left, K said, I was so weak that the
Ukrainian harbourmaster had to carry me aboard. She described how she leaned onto the Ukrainian's shoulder and
watched LL walk in front of them onto the gangplank. I
thought to myself: If the harbourmaster misstepped and
we fell into the water together, it might not occur to my
husband to turn back and see what the havoc was about.

I asked her how she and LL met. She said she had left
England for Asia with the thought of becoming a travel
writer. She sold a few pieces in England and was able to get
a column with a newspaper in Singapore. Then I got sick,
she said. I'm not the marriageable type to start with, and
who wanted to marry a sick woman?

Certainly LL did.

Later when we were in bed I asked her if I was the only man outside her marriage to have held her in an immoral embrace. Oh, but there was that harbourmaster, she said. I kissed him on his mouth before he put me down on-board.

———

AN AFFAIR? IT DIDN'T sound like this woman was ever interested in any man, and she was dying now. Was she cheating on her husband or her death?

I suspect Roland sometimes revised his diaries for dramatic effect. Perhaps playing a rival to a husband was not enough for Roland. He had to create one episode in which he was more powerful than the grim reaper.

———

25 SEPTEMBER 1931.

The military tension in Manchuria, a daily topic here, seems to be largely unfelt in other continents. At least that is my impression from reading the English language newspapers. Of course there will be war, in Asia, in Europe, everywhere. Nothing has been learned since the last war. We as humans share a love of repetition. No one can refrain from joining the refrain when the music starts.

Later.

Dear lord. Matthews just came in with the news that K died last night. Dead? I was planning to see her later this week. Her death did not come as a surprise to anyone else.

Was I the last straw she grasped at, trying to hold on to
life?

———

YOU SEE WHAT I mean? I think Roland added things when he typed
out his diaries, making himself the last man in this woman's life.
Roland was good at rewarding himself through his own imagination. Well, who's not!

———

12 OCTOBER 1931.

How odd to have seen my name in the newspaper, even
though it was not my real name. The whole situation was
serendipitous. One's wish is that serendipity will bring joy
or wealth but neither was destined in this case. If anything,
simply a feeling of futility. I was at the Cathay for a drink
with Miller last week, and with him was a man named
Morris. Typical colonial material. While listening to them
argue about the imminent war, I doodled on a napkin.
Morris, who turned out to be a sub-editor at *The Shanghai
Evening Post*, asked me if I was interested in trying my
hand at political cartoons, as the *Post*'s chief cartoonist had
decided to return to London. I did not take the conversation seriously, as anything suggested over drinks should not
be. But the following day, after thinking things over, I
thought why not. Pencils and paper and time I have aplenty
at work. I sketched two drawings along the lines of John
Knott and two in my own style. To my surprise, Morris

liked the one with a Japanese sword and a Chinese silkworm, and the other one with a Chinese pedicab driver pulling a cart of globes, all haphazardly cut open and bleeding like wounded watermelons.

They ran the one with the watermelon globes in the paper today. They even gave me a Chinese name to go with the cartoon: 卜罗阑. I was told it sounds close to my English name, and with three well-chosen characters that are archaically poetic.

I have always wanted to make a name through my words, but it is my childish doodling that triumphed. The irony stings. In my novel I will not put any one of my characters through a war. A war is too facile a setting. Yet it is from the coming war that I have already profited. Well, there was no profit really, but one cannot discount any small achievement. A drink will be on me when I meet Miller tonight.

———

LUCY WAS GOOD AT drawing, too. I didn't know where she got that from until I read Roland's diary. It's never too late to solve a mystery.

I don't have a single drawing of hers. She chalked up fingers on the sidewalk and doodled in the margins of Gilbert's newspapers, but they were meant to be forgotten the next day. I was wrong yesterday to say I never forget. I don't remember what those drawings were like. They made her happy is what I know. Lucy was happiest when she could stay quiet and do something that took all of her concentration: drawing, sitting on the armrest of the sofa and reading the newspaper over Gilbert's shoulder, cutting and pinning old newspapers into dresses for her dolls or herself. But these moments were rare. More often she flitted around like a hummingbird. Have you watched a hummingbird for a long time? It makes you both tired and nervous.

I didn't have enough reason to worry then. But even if I had, what could I have done? You can't put a hummingbird in a cage and feed it sugar water.

———

12 DECEMBER 1931.

Yesterday morning, when I walked to the office I saw a little girl beggar, no older than six or seven, sitting outside the apothecary's. I've got used to seeing the other beggars coming to the International Settlement during the day and disappearing to their native habitat (wherever that is) at night. But this girl was new. I thought of stopping and asking what her story was, if she wanted money or the baguette I had just picked up at the bakery.

I did not, of course. There is not a shared language between us, and whatever I could have given her would not save her from this miserable existence.

This morning I didn't see her. I paused at the place where no one was standing with open palms. What if she had died overnight. The thought was surprisingly agonising.

———

I MARKED THIS FOR YOU because this may be the only time Roland experiences some paternal feelings. Isn't that extraordinary? Sometimes I wonder what happened to him that day.

———

12 MARCH 1932.

War is not for me. Perhaps for some people, war is a splendid banquet, a marvellously rare occurrence. Something to
relish. To prolong the night into day. To turn the day back
into night again. Me, I would rather my simple fare, water
and bread if need be. Dear mankind, thank you but no
thank you.

I cannot stop thinking about the League of Nations.
How did they fail so wretchedly with China? What is the
next country where they will fail humanity?

...

[I stayed through the January 28 incident and the six-week battle in
Shanghai, shaken by the bombardment and the carnage. The failure of
the Western powers to stop the Japanese invasion, the cease-fire badly
negotiated by the League of Nations, and the daily life scarred and
charred by war—all these precipitated my decision to leave for London.
If I have to witness a war, I thought, I want to do it with my own people.

A more dedicated chronicler of history would have kept a record of
those weeks. One with a heart more susceptible to suffering would have
found the images of the dead and the wounded etched in his memory. I
did not. And when I did write I only wrote about myself.

I drew a number of cartoons, though none of the originals survived
the war. I would encourage any interested reader to look through the
Post's archive in a library, presumably in Shanghai or Hong Kong. They
were my effort to reduce the horrors in the Far East into bite-size tid-
bits.

I gained nothing from my Shanghai experiences but an inoculation
against what was yet to come in Europe: When one walks down a street
and sees dozens of bodies, one does not look for anything in common

with them. I have no doubt that I loved my fellow human beings then. I still do. But I do not feel ashamed to admit that I love myself more. That's my magic trick. Rabbit after rabbit after rabbit out of my hat. A self sustaining itself: There will always be rabbits. And roses and silk handkerchiefs. — RB, 1 January 1990]

———

RABBIT AFTER RABBIT AFTER RABBIT. I'm glad I made this decision to skip a little in the book. I can't possibly comment on every page. It's like one person always writing too much in his letters, and the other running out of words to reply.

This morning I wondered whether another person reading Roland's diaries would be as patient with him as I am. But who would read him? Not a random stranger. Anyone who reads him would have already made some allowance for him.

Had Roland died before Hetty, she might have kept to his wishes and printed the three volumes as he had planned, rather than cutting them down. Would she have read them? Unlikely. Would she at least have done something to surprise the world? Like going through his address book and sending a copy of the diaries to every woman in it? Or making a bonfire of all the copies she printed?

There is no point in thinking about how Roland would look in a stranger's eyes. Just as I don't imagine people who didn't know Lucy would see anything in her pictures. They would think she was an innocent child and then an attractive woman. She was always good at pretending there was something loving and lovable in her eyes. I don't know where she got that. Did she think she could fool all those around her, or was her deception only meant for strangers, as her love was only for them?

She didn't deceive me. No, I loved her dearly. I still do. But what was in her eyes was something else — a wildness. I saw it, but

I didn't understand where it came from. That was why I had to bear the brunt of that storm called Lucy.

I wonder what it would've been like if that storm had raged longer. I suppose I would've become a storm shelter for the family. Or I would've become a storm myself! A hurricane. A tornado. A typhoon.

I'm telling you, the most deadly natural disaster that can befall anyone is family. And where can you look for a shelter when that disaster hits?

Those who didn't know Lucy well always liked her. Thought of her as witty and pretty. Even if she wasn't as pretty as I was at her age, she certainly outwitted me.

Roland once said happy people should not be allowed to live past a certain age. I disagree. Happy people should live as long as they want. It's the unhappy ones who should think twice before getting past forty or fifty. I must give Lucy that credit. Young people's unhappiness is like fireworks. As long as you're at a safe distance you may even enjoy the spectacle.

Unhappiness in middle age or old age: It's much worse. You become moldy and infect others. Sometimes it's more than dampness. It's humiliation. Like what Dorothy had to endure a few nights ago, when she got the bed wet and was too ashamed to summon an aide. A princess in her own pee, but there's nothing wrong with that when you're old. What was wrong was that she apologized the next morning, not only to the aides and the nurses but to anyone she thought might find it embarrassing on her behalf. You know that's one woman who has lived her life apologizing.

Generally speaking it's no fun to be my age, but I think I've done better than most. Here are a few tips about unhappiness. I hope you both learn from me.

First, don't mope. Unhappiness starts like water spilled or a manageable leak. But if you don't mop it up at once or fix the problem, what do you get? Water damage, mold infiltration, floor bending and creaking, going all the way down to the foundation.

If you want me to go on, I have the knowledge. I was married to Milt, a man who knew houses. After he retired, he liked to look through the inspection files he had kept. He showed me his notes, all in print. He talked about those houses like a father talking about his children attending college or finding a job or starting families of their own. Oh, Milt loved houses. Peter Wilson would think Milt repetitive, too. But Peter Wilson didn't understand that when you get older, anything you can put in between you and your final breath is not a waste of your breath. I bet he, too, repeats things to his wife: Maybe how he doesn't like the smell of the soap even though she's been buying the same brand for fifty years, or how he's annoyed by the creamed corn because the grits get into his dentures. I have a sense he is not a pleasant man. And Anne Wilson, she must be a wife in the same mold as Hetty Bouley. Why else did Hetty favor her among all her nieces?

Norman was a different case. Milt remembered all those houses lovingly, but Norman never talked about a single student from his forty-seven years of teaching driver's ed. They were all the same to him, the pumpkins and turnips and cabbages of each year's harvest, some handsome, some lopsided, some rotten from the beginning. What he couldn't let go of was the lawsuit Vallejo lost to Fairfield to be the county seat. In 1873! Who cares—anyone would say. But it was important to Norman, so I let him talk. Toward the end of Norman's life he said several times to me, Lilia, you're a patient woman. I'm not, I know, but I didn't demur when he said it. I'd simply performed an act of kindness.

A woman has to allow a man to live for something useless or something impossible: Milt's memory of those houses, Norman's obsession with county history, Gilbert's dream of world peace. In that way I was a good wife to all three of them.

Just a thought: Hetty was perhaps not as dumb as Roland and Sidelle thought she was. She let Roland be.

...

[In the summer of 1932, I left Shanghai for London. With Sidelle's help and with my experience in New York and the Far East, I secured a position in an advertising agency. For the next few years, I never orbited far from Sidelle. I met, through her, friends, liaisons, and acquaintances. I joined the Ogdens for a few holidays. I began to spend more time with Harry Ogden. He was convinced that there was an economic approach to preventing the war. I was convinced that he was wrong.

History has vindicated my pessimism. A war has to be fought. It has to be won or lost. But a war is not as interesting, in retrospect, as a garden party, a quick glance across the concert hall at an unfamiliar face, or a prolonged cab ride. With this as my guiding principle I have made the following selection from my diaries. History, the egotist that refuses to leave the centre stage of anyone's life, is, among these pages, banished to a prompter's corner.

In this way a man claims his final triumph over history, not by outliving it but by revision. — RB 4 April 1990]

---

1 JANUARY 1933.

Lord, have mercy on me.

Had I had a pistol by my hand I might have turned myself into a young Werther, but Sidelle is no Charlotte. She would raise an eyebrow at my graveside and say to the person next to her—and heaven knows there is always someone next to her—I don't see how adding a bad ending to a mediocre drama can make it less so.

Nothing is commoner to her than speaking of one's heart. How did I let her ambush me in my youth? How did I let myself slip and say the thing that I should never, ever, have said to any woman, let alone Sidelle?

Roland, you know the only person whom you can trust is yourself. Let us sift out all the things that drag you down, and let us, you and me, turn all these things into what will lift you up. Trust that our intelligence and willpower will act as the alchemist.

Lead to helium. Here we go.

What bothers you? That Sidelle has too many men and women around?

—It does not bother me that Sidelle is not a loyal wife. But I would like her to be a loyal mistress.

Loyal to whom?

—To me, of course.

Bravo, Roland. Such audacity. Are we to forget you have other lovers?

—She always comes before other women.

Harry Ogden, as you know, always comes before other men.

—Harry Ogden is harmless. He is like Count Bezukhov, except likely he will leave Sidelle a widow one day.

And you have set your heart on replacing him?

—I do not want to replace any husband.

Are you afraid that other men will replace you? No one is irreplaceable, if I may remind you. Even Sidelle.

—It is not about being replaceable. How many times do I have to say this?

Is there something you find lacking in her love for you?

—Her love? She is not a woman who loves.

Perhaps that is an unfair statement.

—A person who loves cannot remain unassailable as she does.

Have you undertaken any action to assail her?

—Yes.

By speaking your heart and demanding her to speak hers?

—One has to take a risk.

And now eating this bitter bread of banishment by
thyself?

—Self-banishment. She did not banish me.

What is the difference?

—One has to have some dignity.

Dignity is snake oil for the wounded soul. What do you
want from her, truly?

—The only thing I want is . . . everything.

Ah. Here we are nearer the truth. Wanting everything is
better than wanting nothing.

—Is it? This is, I think, what gives Sidelle the advantage
over me. She wants nothing.

From you, or anyone?

—I do not know! From me for sure.

And you want her to want something, Roland.

—I want her to want everything, Roland, and I want her
to want everything from no one but me.

———

WHAT'S WRONG WITH YOU, Roland? I've known only mothers
wanting what you want. From their children. And it's a horrible
thing, even for a mother.

Gilbert's mother was like that with him. My mother with Kenny,
too. A curse put on the last born. Some sons raised by mothers
greedy for love become greedy men. Like Kenny. But it's not always the case. Gilbert gave more than he received. It wasn't just
generosity. People can be demanding even if they're generous.
Some want so much because they think they should be awarded
especially for their generosity. They're often the bitterest souls.

A few days before Gilbert's mother died, he and I were in her
house with her. I was doing the dishes, and he was on the phone

with one of his siblings. And his mother said, What are you making all those noises for, Gilbert? I said, It's me, I'm in the kitchen. She said, What are you doing in my kitchen, Lilia? Whatever you're doing, you're doing it the wrong way.

To my surprise, I cried at her funeral. I didn't cry at my own mother's funeral. I thought it was the tears of Gilbert and his siblings and all those grandchildren that made my mind go weak. What a crocodile you are, I said to myself even as I was wiping my eyes.

Gilbert's mother was not fond of me. I was not a real person to her, only the woman her son married. Gilbert loved me, but had he married another woman he would've loved her as unselfishly as he loved me. My mother treated us well enough, but other than Kenny, we were just her children. Give her another set of children and she wouldn't have felt any difference. You see the pattern here? You can live a long life, surrounded by people, but you'll be darn lucky if one or two of them can take you as you are, not as who you are to them.

In our marriage Gilbert and I didn't make that mistake. We were always Gilbert and Lilia, not Gilbert's Lilia or Lilia's Gilbert.

Both Sidelle and Hetty took Roland as he was. What he was to them didn't matter. They saw through him. And they made a place in their lives for the person they saw through.

I see through him, too, but only now. Before his death and before reading his diaries I didn't take him for who he was, but for who he was to me, and to Lucy. Perhaps I also took Lucy as who she was to me, and to Roland, instead of who she was.

But who was Lucy?

2 JANUARY 1933.

Stayed in—calmer after a few drinks by myself. The intense emotions I have experienced in the past month feel like nothing but trifles.

I am like one of those people invited onstage by a magician. He deals the cards and says, Pick one. If I were smarter I would cross my arms and say, No, I cannot and I will not help you. Whatever card I pick is the card you have meant for me.

Yet I am an idiot. I am the person that any magician would use as a prop. I cannot *not* pick the card. I cannot *not* believe I have been chosen for a reason.

I start to think that my resentment of Sidelle is a resentment of her position: She is in control of her fate. I am not.

———

LUCY WAS IN CONTROL of her own fate, too. The woman Roland could not have in his life and the daughter he did not know was his—they both had what he wanted. I do, too.

But Sidelle did not like extreme feelings or actions. Neither do I. In a sense she and I are alike.

Lucy, or poor Lucy, she was in control of her fate but she, like Roland, could not live without extremes.

———

12 JANUARY 1933.

Waiting for M's arrival. She reminds me of Hetty, but with Hetty at least I do not have to make any effort. M is not as unruffled as Hetty. Perhaps it is for that reason I let myself stay interested in M. On the other hand, I do not have the respect for her I have for Hetty. Or call it pity.

Now I see a danger in Sidelle that I did not see two years ago. Most women are disproportional: Either their minds are too meagre to make their physical lustre last, or their bodies are miserably unfit to sustain their minds. Sidelle is the rare case where mind and body do not undermine each other.

Has Sidelle always been this way? Was she once as inexperienced as M? Did she ever deceive herself with a love interest that offered nothing in return, as Hetty insists on doing? When am I going to stop comparing everyone to her? It's unfair that one has to start with a woman like Sidelle. Nothing is crueller than telling a gambler that he has made the best bet of his life at the first try. The joy is to think that there will always be a bigger win.

I have not seen Sidelle since that disastrous conversation on New Year's Day. How long will this abstinence last?

In a sense M should be a perfect choice for me. She has enough love for me. We are compatible physically. I can imagine myself contentedly married to her. Infidelity may arise as an issue, but if neither of us thinks too much about it . . . She does not seem the kind who would make a good mother, but I have no interest in becoming a sire.

What if I proposed to M? I could show up at Sidelle's drawing room with the triumphant news.

———

PEOPLE OVERESTIMATE THEMSELVES, BUT not much harm comes from that if you know how to laugh about it. Do you think Sidelle would feel hurt if he proposed to any random woman?

The real harm comes from people who underestimate themselves. My mother convinced herself that she could not be a good wife and a good mother, and she acted accordingly. Lucy had the same conviction and she acted more absolutely. She was unhappy in a marriage like my mother and she died young like Roland's mother. Sometimes I find that odd.

I had vowed to have a different life long before I was old enough to think of marriage. I've done that, being all that my mother was not: a good wife, a good mother, a grandmother, and at the same time being myself, too. But all those lessons you learn from your mother don't mean you can save your daughter's life.

———

3 FEBRUARY 1933.

Back to Sidelle. The reunion began with a discussion of amputations in wartime and ended with an intimate afternoon in my bachelor's nest.

Rest assured you won't lose a limb in any war, Sidelle said afterward.

I asked her where the assurance came from.

You love yourself too much for that to happen.

What if I lost my life? I said. I might have been killed when they bombed Shanghai.

Bad luck then, she said. But to you losing a life is much less of a consequence than losing a limb.

I wondered if she was right. If one's love for oneself

could not be freed from one's love for one's physique in its perfect and intact form, then any alteration—the greying of hair, the weakening of legs, the waning of one's prowess, not to mention a wound, a scar, a permanent mark—would be a challenge to that love. Will I still love myself in this way sixty years down the line? A woman may love a man through his inevitable decline. At least one hopes that is the case. Does it mean that her love of him is less than his love of himself?

I remembered an oriental tale that Hetty once told me, a love story between the most beautiful lady of the empire and her royal fiancé. When some disaster deformed her face—fire? illness?—she wanted to break the engagement. He blinded himself so her heavenly voice alone would sustain his memory of her beauty. Thus they lived happily ever after. I recounted the story to Sidelle.

What a tiresome couple, she said.

Does such a tragedy not move you? I asked.

What's the point of him blinding himself when he already loves with blindness?

You don't see the beauty in such an extreme action?

I don't see any beauty in extremity. Losing a limb is a hideous business. Blinding yourself willingly is unsightly. Acting unnaturally in the name of love is a horrendous insult to love.

How does one act in the name of love? I said.

Sidelle stretched her legs out straight and crossed her feet, a ballerina in repose. When I leaned over to trace the contour of a knee, she said, We're not in a play. I'm not a theatrical woman.

The theatrical effect is all mine, then?

Do you behave this way with your other women?

I don't know, I replied. I don't think so.

One hopes not, Sidelle said.

Why, because this makes you cherish your command of my life?

I don't command, she said. It's you who has chosen to become commanded.

You should've thought twice before you picked me out of a pool of nobodies, I said. I suppose it won't take much for you to throw me back.

Roland, don't court unreal problems, Sidelle said.

You mean this—I gestured toward her and myself—this is not real life?

I don't deceive myself into thinking that you treat this as real, she said. Then: Is it real?

Is it not real to you? I asked.

Anything can be as real to me as I want to make it, but you, Roland, you take pride in making everything as unreal as you want, no?

I did not know—still do not know—if I should feel hurt or consoled by her words. Do I treat this life of mine as real? It is the only one I have.

———

DO YOU THINK IT'S a genetic trait that some people can't tell the real from the unreal?

One day when Lucy was three, she told me that she was planning to move out. Out to where, I asked, and she said to the pet store on Harrison Street. Nobody's there at night, I said. There're nighttime nannies there, she said. Really, I asked, for pets or for children? For anyone younger than five, she said. Where did you hear that? I asked. And she wouldn't say. She just smiled that smile of hers, meaning she was smarter than me. She had the same smile when she told me about a man giving birth to a baby in the park down the street. I thought that there must be a homeless man defecating where he should not. Turned out it was only a harmless old man peddling a few wooden dolls. Still, I confronted him about talking to unaccompanied girls. When he didn't show up again Lucy said the man had moved away with his baby.

I was disturbed. Children's fantasies, Gilbert insisted. All children have a phase. No doubt he was right. But the thing is, after a child dies, you can't stop thinking of those fantasies, as if they carried important messages. What made Lucy talk about leaving long before her time? Was Roland the man who gave birth to his daughter? He was theatrical. He wanted to be seen by many people. He gauged the world by what it did to him. Lucy had all those traits. But there was one thing he didn't pass on. He loved himself so much that he wouldn't risk even the smallest possibility of hurting himself. Why didn't Lucy inherit that?

I would not call myself a perfect mother, but I did give special attention to Lucy. Still, I knew that the moment people heard about Lucy's death, they would ask themselves: What did that mother do to that poor child? How did that mother fail so terribly?

When Lucy died people sent condolence cards and letters, calling it a tragedy. I didn't understand them. Her grandparents died in a train wreck, and yes, what a tragedy that was for a young couple. Is it so much of a tragedy if you live your life a little differently from most people? And choose to die in a different way than most people?

When Lucy died, I used the words that other people used. I said my heart was broken. That her death took something out of me. Can a broken heart have pumped blood steadily for thirty-six years, no, thirty-seven years now? A heart cannot break because none of our hearts is made of glass or porcelain. And a tragedy, does it tear you up like a monster with claws and teeth, or does it do so with a surgical knife or even something like what Nancy's daughter had for her eyes, some advanced technology involving lasers and computers? Sometimes when I hear people use those expressions I want to say: Show me your heart, show me where it's broken; and what has been taken from you, a kidney or a liver or several ribs?

Words are like grass. Like weeds. Having lived in this building—this life—long enough, I would not mind being a weed whacker. Chop chop whack whack. All those useless words gone. And then we could eat our meals in peace, like they always promise in their brochures.

But if I stopped saying things, even the simple words, they would think that I'd gone cuckoo. And they'd ask you for more money so they could pack me off to another unit. So you see, words are the most useless things that we cannot afford to lose. You can claim bankruptcy if you lose all your money. You can't do that with words.

We let go of so many important things because letting go, we are told, is a good, virtuous, courageous, and healthy thing to do. And all we end up holding on to are weedy words. As a lifelong gardener, I can guarantee you this: Few words are worth cultivating.

———

30 DECEMBER 1933.

I spent the evening with Sidelle and Mr. Ogden. If the curtains were not pulled close, if someone in the street looked at us longingly, perhaps we presented the perfect tableau: Sidelle reclining on the sofa; Mr. Ogden and me on two chairs drawn close, he having the full view of her sculpture-like head, me huddling near her leather-clad feet. At one point I had an urge to empty my brandy on her stocking and watch the liquid leave a trace in the fabric.

I have not figured out their marriage. It is a forbidden

topic. Mr. Ogden has only given her a chaste pat on the hands while I was around. Not even a kiss. Sidelle seems to have no qualms about her infidelity. In an early letter to me she wrote: "Of all the people in the world Harry is the only person I remain truly faithful to in my way." What this means she will never explain.

I made a toast to history, and Sidelle said every generation must have made the same toast.

May the future generations help enlighten us about this moment we live in, I said.

Aren't you happy none of us here has to think as a parent would? Sidelle said. To live with future generations in mind?

Yet she was a mother once. Mr. Ogden's only son had died in the Great War. There are also two grown daughters born to his first marriage. But if Sidelle had negated their existence and Mr. Ogden did not protest, I saw no point in bringing them up. With enough alcohol I could believe that we have all we need on this island made by the three of us: time, peace, beauty, harmony. Yes, there is a mainland or a continent out there, but from where we sit they may as well remain infinitely offshore.

Mr. Ogden informed me of his plan to buy a house in the countryside. I feigned interest, as it was not the first time I had heard of it. In the past few months he has begun to look weary. More than ever his presence makes me appreciate what I have: youth, energy, an appetite for life.

―――――

WHEN ROLAND WROTE THESE words he was younger than Lucy when she died. He had no idea what it would be like to have a child, or to think about the future with that child in mind. Lucy, on the other hand, thought of your future, Katherine. That's why she left that note. She didn't address it to anyone in particular. "Please take care of the baby for me. I'm too tired."

Katherine, we've never told you much about Lucy's death. It's okay for me to tell you now. By the time you read this I'll be as dead as a doornail. (By the way, why a doornail? Life is mostly made up of dead things. What's so special about a doornail? I'm not the kind to be hammered. Maybe I can say, I'll be as dead as a garden hose. Or a potholder, a clothespin. How about a shoe tree? I always love those dead things that go by the names of living things: a shoe tree, a drain snake, pigs in the blanket.)

Lucy walked out in the middle of the day. She left the note next to your bassinet, Katherine. It was Steve who found the note, and he didn't even think of calling us until two hours later. He thought Lucy might have gone out for a walk. He said it was not the first time he had come home and found you alone. You were a good sleeper. It was just like Steve to say later that if only you were one of those colicky babies, Lucy might not have taken off so easily.

When Steve called, I knew right away that Lucy was dead. I can't explain how. A mother knows. I didn't say anything immediately to Gilbert. You can call that an act of kindness. I didn't murder his hope when it seemed there was still reason to hope. Or you can call it an act of cruelty. I allowed him to go on believing something I knew to be false. Those two days I kept the secret: It was the only time I was truly disloyal to him, down to my last nerve. It was exhausting. Cheating on a husband always is, but cheating on a husband with death?

Poor Gilbert. He tried to stay optimistic. He tried so hard he started to sound like the newspaper articles during the UN peace conference. All those words like "future" and "temporary setback." I could tell that he was frightened and that he didn't know what he was frightened of. He raised Lucy and he loved her, but there was something in her that was beyond him. There is always something that makes people foreign to one another. Eighty percent of the world's population coming together to love and to live in peace? What a joke that UN conference was.

During those two days before they found Lucy, Tim called every day from Canada, asking if he should come home. All of a sudden he was not a boy anymore, but a grown man. We told him to stay where he was. We didn't want him to get into trouble. Will was working in the city then, and he left work early in the afternoon, taking Molly to the park, to the ice cream shop, and even bought her an expensive doll.

I was grateful to Tim, who called long distance, during the daytime, multiple times, even though I told him to only call at night to get the discount rate. I was grateful to Will. It didn't feel I had given him a lot, but he was like Gilbert, a goodhearted man. But I pitied them, too. You could see that they had that feeling that as long as they could do something, everything would be all right. I pitied them because I couldn't tell them that nothing would be all right in the end.

And then there was Carol. She skipped school and waited around, weeping, weeping, so I sent her to her friend Bonnie's house for an afternoon. That was when the police came. Had I had a choice, I would've had all my family there when the news arrived. Family reunion after a death is horrible. It is as though the death has to happen again. And the second time, someone has to act like a murderer.

It was me who called Tim, and it was me who sat Carol down when she came home.

Carol, oh, poor Carol. Of all my children she's the only one who's not equipped with something special. Lucy had her fierceness and her wildness (which served her well until she decided she had no further use for them). Will was a good kid and he turned out to be a solid man. He doesn't have a lot of ambitions, but he has more friends than my other children do. Tim is the smartest one. Molly is a bully and she uses that to her advantage. But Carol, I don't know. I used to think if there were an earthquake or wildfire she would be the first child I would lose. I could keep my eyes on her all the time, I could shackle her wrist to mine, but she would still simply melt like a candle when something unpleasant happened.

Poor Carol. At least she didn't marry badly. Chris may be the blandest man in the world, but a bland man is unlikely to cause a natural disaster at home. Do no harm, that should be the first requirement for any husband.

But why do I go on about the others when you're waiting to hear about your parents? Steve was with us in those two days. He had trouble returning to their apartment, and Gilbert said we must let him stay, he was part of the family. And I have to be fair to Steve for once, and tell you that during that time he shed more tears than any man I've known. Sure, we could blame him for many things, but what could you say to a rascal crying so uncontrollably? There had to be something real behind those tears.

When the police brought the news of Lucy's death, Gilbert started to sob while Steve's tears all of a sudden stopped. Oh, these men, crying for reasons they didn't understand, and because they didn't understand, when they stopped crying they thought they did something honorable or brave.

They found Lucy's body in the reservoir. She had always been a good swimmer.

I didn't cry. Crying is not my way. Arguing is. I haven't stopped arguing with Lucy for thirty-seven years. The children I've raised, the husbands I've seen die in their beds, my gardens, my reading Roland's diary—everything in my life is a part of that long argument with Lucy. She was my daughter. She shouldn't have quit so easily.

The first holiday season after Lucy's death was the most difficult. Any birthday, any holiday, any day with blue sky or rain is a reminder of the child who's decided to choose not to live in these days. But we had other children to take care of. We had you, Katherine. Gilbert's mother was in the hospital that fall, for some surgery. I made soup for Gilbert to take in a thermos to his mother and a second thermos to his father, who would not come to stay with us because of his pride. No, he didn't want to feel he was a burden to us. But what's the burden? I could chop up all the vegetables and meat in the world and I could feed an auditorium of mouths, but where was the burden in those things? For a while—ah, this would make you laugh—I couldn't make my mother's recipes of spinach dip or spinach pie. Spinach is a funny vegetable. You start with a giant bunch. There is never something called too much spinach for a family of seven, but you end up with a pitiful bowlful. So much easier to bake bread. Always rising! Baking bread makes you think that miracles might happen, and someday you could even raise the dead.

Oh, Lucy did something to me. Nothing felt like a weight to me after. Everything was light. Featherweight. I'd always known the term, but ever since Lucy's death it has nothing to do with boxing anymore. Feathers have weight, but to weigh the feathers you have to kill the bird and strip it and with so much ado you get a small handful of . . . nothing much. That's how I felt about Lucy when she died. Only so little of her left.

Oh, what nonsense. I see this is the danger of writing anything down. Happy people have no use for words. I've always been a happy person, but you see now that I've put these words down on the page I'm becoming a downer.

———

28 APRIL 1934.

A day with sunshine. Signs of spring everywhere. The tulips in the flower bed are like drunken dancers, dishevelled at just the right level but still beautiful, recovering from a long night of party-going that ends in the morning light. A girl walking past a magnolia tree picked up from the ground a fallen petal, which was large enough for one to write a short love poem on it. On a day like this it is hard to imagine that this marriage with life (yes, show me one living creature that is not wedded to life!) will disappoint one. We have trees and flowers and birds and fountains, we have poetry and music and youth and wine, and we will always have them, for better, for worse, for richer, for poorer, in sickness and in health. Who would make me a better bride than my life?

Later.

Out to picnic, just Sidelle and me, like new lovers, except we know each other so well, in a marriage of a kind, of our own making. Afterward we stopped at a small church. Let's see what's in store for humanity, she said, opening a random page of a Bible. Listen to this, she said. *Then Amnon hated her exceedingly; so that the hatred wherewith he hated her was greater than the love wherewith he had loved her.*

I'm glad neither of us is Amnon, I said.

Was I being honest? There have been times when I would have borrowed Amnon's lines and used them against Sidelle. No other woman has driven me to that extreme.

How do you know? she said, and held out a hand to me—an odd gesture. I kissed it.

Do we love each other so much that we're bound to hate each other one day? I said. I thought we were beyond that common error.

How meagre we are to each other, she said.

The day, still sunny, turned unkind.

Charles died nineteen years ago today, she said. In Gallipoli.

I never seem to be able to believe in the existence of her first husband. Or the child born in that marriage. Or even

Sidelle as a young wife. Her past matters so little to me that she might as well be a woman without one.

I was imagining today what Charles would be like as a middle-aged man, she said.

And?

I couldn't, just like I couldn't imagine Harry as a young man.

I thought that Harry Ogden would offer a model of a middle-aged man and eventually an old man for the dead first husband, but this I did not say. You don't always have to live through everything to know something, I said. You only need to live through something to know everything.

You missed the point, Sidelle said.

I know, I said, and I insist on doing so.

Why?

Oh, selfishness, I said. Unless the point you're making includes myself, I don't see why I should bother to meet that point.

You don't suffer from self-doubt as you used to, do you? Sidelle said.

Self-doubt is like truffles. I wouldn't mind flavouring my days with a sprinkle, but too much wouldn't do. Who wants to pay a hefty price for something so . . . dispensable? I said.

How sensible you sound.

Sensible, yes, and sensitive to my own need, too, I said. I then explained my recent theory concerning selfishness and sensitivity. People who are insensitively selfish and people who are unselfishly sensitive are equally demanding, and one should do what one can to avoid them in life. Insensitivity and unselfishness combined would make a hell for everyone. People who are selfish and sensitive, well, I said, wouldn't the world be a less boring place if they were the only ones left?

I suppose you're one of them, Sidelle asked.

I count you as one, too, I said. Mr. Ogden, I did not say, is selfish but insensitively so.

Sidelle did not reply, so I pressed her: Why, do you see a problem with my theory?

Oh, no, it's an ingenious theory, she said. At your age a man should always be building some sort of system.

How I resented her for that. What about someone at your age? I said. If she was unsympathetic enough to comment on my age why shouldn't I remind her of hers?

When one has lived through enough systems . . .

You stop believing in them? Start tearing them down?

One simply adapts oneself to wherever one settles.

So one system is as good as the next?

And as imperfect, she said.

No thing is more extraordinary than other things? And no one is more special than everyone else? I asked. That familiar bitterness gripped me again. I felt like a specimen she had come across, a bird with a rare defect that makes me sing better, or a fox with an odd pattern to its fur. She is interested in me, yes, but only till teatime.

Oh, we're both getting tiresome, she said. Let's take a walk down the lane. Wouldn't it be fun to catch sight of a fox.

It alarmed me, it touched me, it made me want to announce my love for her like a young man when our thoughts, coming from two directions, merged at the thought of a spring fox.

Later.

Is this what I am? Nobody special but someone Sidelle has known as a young man, whose every stage of life will unfurl before her eyes. Am I occupying the space of a husband who died too young, or a child lost too early?

It is a surprise that Sidelle has not written me off yet as a study, completed and ready to be filed away. But perhaps a superb specimen should be able to secure for itself a position of eternity in the heart of even the most demanding examiner.

———

DID SIDELLE REALLY MAKE Roland a specimen that was a combination of a husband and a son from a long-gone marriage? I don't think so. He was wrong most of the time when it came to women. Oh no, Roland, you don't explain a woman through the deaths that have happened in her life.

But I like Roland's system.

My father was selfish and insensitive. I imagine many bullies are. My brother Hayes, Milt (I know, none of you knows that side of him), Elaine, no need to go on.

My mother was sensitive and unselfish. A perfect example of those who make others miserable with their own misery.

Gilbert was insensitive and unselfish. I wouldn't say he made life a hell for anyone, but he avoided that by pure luck—by marrying me. If he had married someone else—say, my sister Lucille, his insensitiveness and his unselfishness would have made a monster out of her. She would have thrown tantrums because he was too good for her and because he was not good enough. If he had married a woman like my other sister, Margot, he would've smothered her with his kindness.

Sensitive and selfish people: Roland was one. I am one. Lucy, too. Pains in the neck, you might say, but imagine a world without people like us.

———

8 AUGUST 1934.

> Harry Ogden and Sidelle and a few friends are in Spain. I
> was half-heartedly invited even though she knew that I had
> committed to overseeing the department while Jenkins
> goes on holiday. One step closer to lifting yourself out of
> the pool of nobodies. All experience will come in handy in
> the end, once I succeed as a novelist. If not for this belief I
> would be sinking, not into a fatal despair but into a waist-
> deep, then chest-deep slush of self-hatred.
>
> And the women who stumble into my life: What are
> they but a few leaves floating on this pond called Roland's
> world?

————

I'VE ALWAYS THOUGHT ROLAND was exaggerating when he talked
about this hatred of himself, but I wonder now if he did mean it.
Can you love yourself as much as Roland did and still hate yourself? Maybe there is no difference between loving yourself with a
passion and hating yourself with a passion. You can't have one
without the other.

I don't suffer from self-hatred. But that's because I don't love
myself to an extreme.

Hate and love are funny words. You would think they're the
most serious of words but in fact, they are not. You could conduct
an experiment and count how many times a person says love in the
course of a day. I would do it, except I would lose my mind by nine
o'clock in the morning. You would think with so much love around,
the world would be a great place for everyone. O love, O love, O
love. We watched a cooking show the other day where a woman

dripped the salad "generously" with some "herb-infused oil." Yes, love is like that, you can drip it generously, in a greasy flood.

Hate is not any better. People use the word with even less care than love. At lunch someone grumbled, I hate broccoli. Really, I thought of turning around and asking her, Did a broccoli murder one of your ancestors? Did your husband take broccoli as a mistress?

I had a dream of Lucy last night. Odd that I still dream about her. She was in her teens, and I ran into her in an empty space, indoors—no windows, so there must have been some sort of lighting, but I couldn't tell. She was sitting on top of a painted block of wood, in a pink dress. When I saw her I said, Oh, Lucy. I was about to say something more but she looked at me furiously, with that angry look she used to give me, the look that said, I hate you, I hate you, I hate you.

Back then she often said those words to me. And gave me that look. In life I had never let her stop me from saying anything I wanted to say, but in my dream I paused. I became, truth be told, a little shy in my dream. Not feeling wrongly accused, or provoked, but shy. Like when you want to say something tender but can't find the right words. How many times in my life have I felt that way? Never.

I was sad when I first woke up that I hadn't said anything to her. But now I wonder if shyness in a dream is fine. Just as in real life, shyness is an underrated virtue. Imagine if people stopped dripping love and hurling hatred around, but achieved shyness instead. That's one thing that all those dignitaries and politicians have never thought of as an aim for a peace conference. Or for a brighter future for mankind.

I dream more often about Gilbert, and sometimes Norman and Milt, and once in a while my siblings. I rarely dream about my children. I think about them. What's better, to be thought of or to be dreamed of?

I wonder if Gilbert used to dream about Lucy. If he did, he

never told me. For the first months or perhaps the first year after Lucy died, he liked to talk about her—all sorts of things, from her infanthood to her marriage. I was the one to turn cold every time Lucy's name came up. No, I didn't want to live like that. I didn't want, every time I heard her name, to tell myself again, she's dead, she's dead, she's dead.

After a while, I said to Gilbert, Do me a favor, will you? Let's stop talking about Lucy.

He looked sad. But I don't want to forget her, he said.

We won't, I said. Even if we don't say her name for the rest of our lives we won't forget her for a moment.

He agreed. But now I wonder if it was because I refused to talk about Lucy with him that he went on talking about her with our children. Behind my back. He might have told the children more about Lucy when they were older. It was unlike Gilbert, but what did Molly mean when she said the other day that Dad told them more about Lucy than I did?

After Lucy's death I not only thought of walking out on my family, but also getting in touch with Roland. Not that he would offer any comfort. He would be the last one to do that. No, the reason was that I wanted to be with someone who had little space in his heart for another person.

I didn't contact Roland. I decided to remain loyal. Not only to my marriage and family. To my grief, really. People say grief this, grief that, but let me tell you, sometimes grief is the greediest lover. The moment you think of walking away you commit infidelity. Then what? Grief announces that you'd never have the right to it again. Grief turns its back to you. Grief is a good punisher.

I suppose in the end I wasn't brave enough.

But I did go to the library every year and ask Mrs. Anderson, my favorite librarian, if there was a book published under Roland's name. When I finally got this book, I regretted not having written him about Lucy's death. It would've made a difference to see her name in this book, and to read what he would've written.

Better late than never, people like to say. Sometimes I want to remind them, but no later than death, please.

———

10 OCTOBER 1934.

Hetty's letter today brought the news of the death of Aunt Geraldine. People die. On the ship to the Far East, an unobtrusive Japanese gentleman died unobtrusively, and we held a solemn gathering, letting the Pacific grant him final peace. In Hong Kong I once saw an old man, a load of bamboo poles carried on his severely bent back, collapse in the heat and never get up. In Shanghai people died from bombs, from coldness, from hunger. In the news last week a young woman's body was discovered in a canal, pregnant with a new life and an old despair. People die, but a harmless woman like Aunt G, so contented with life, why wouldn't she live forever? No one did better at holding on to life's mediocrities and making something of them. One would think all those weightless thoughts would make for her a permanent zeppelin, floating above the swamp called life and the whirlpool called death.

Some people only begin to live when they find a way to live their lives as tragedies. For the grander ones among these people—Hamlet, me, or even my mother—there is something delectable in that fate. But Aunt G should have been kept safe from even the most inevitable tragedy. How I hate to think of her death as a violation of that contract.

Later.

When is the funeral? Sidelle asked.

I don't think I can make it, I said.

What if we go together?

To Halifax?

I was thinking of going to America. You could meet me there after the funeral. We should travel while we can still do it freely.

Freedom is not a poor man's birthright, I said.

Neither is self-pity, she said.

That's precisely the reason I'm going to stay here, I thought, but I didn't say it. I didn't say that I wanted to make enough money to have a splendid flat, with expensive decorations, and with women who would not leave me feeling squalid about myself.

What about Harry? I said. Doesn't he want to travel with you?

Sidelle waved her cigarette without answering me.

———

THIS MORNING EAMON SAID to me, Breakfast is always my favorite meal of the day. I said, Is it? He said, Yes, guess why. I said, Why don't you tell me because whatever guesses I make, you'd say they're wrong. He said, It's a meal hard to brag about. I hate it when people talk about their dinners, the wine, the champagne, the different courses. Breakfast is easier to digest, harder to present, don't you think?

I thought to myself, You don't know the world half as well as I do. I read in the newspaper the other day that a mother is considered a failure these days if she doesn't serve two different kinds of fruit at breakfast for her children. Just someone's opinion, of course, but as a gardener I can tell you these opinions don't sprout for no reason.

You may start a new trend talking about breakfast, I said.

I'm sure all the trends we've thought of have already been started by someone else, he said.

I bet there's something no one has done yet, I said. Look at you and your friends, busy writing your memoirs. Not the most practical activity, if you ask me.

What's a practical activity?

A flower-arranging class so you can plan your own funeral display, I said.

Eamon looked pained and said, I don't know about that. Sounds rather morbid to me.

Why? Thinking about death doesn't make it come faster, I said. Once you have a design you love, you can leave instructions for the florists. Wouldn't that be nice? Or come up with a tasting menu for your own funeral reception. How about that?

You think differently from most of us, Eamon said.

———

WWII IS COMING. ROLAND'S war diaries are not as good as the war movies. The only thing we can learn is that not everyone dies in a war, not everyone is a hero, not everyone is a traitor, and not everyone suffers.

———

3 MARCH 1940.

> The war drags on like a half-hearted engagement, with no reason to dissolve and no wedding in sight.

———

THE WORST KIND OF engagement is not the one that should not have happened in the first place. No, the worst engagement is the one you know will fail but you still talk yourself into letting it happen. Here's something you should know, Katherine. When Steve came to Gilbert and asked for Lucy's hand, the only thing that kept us from saying no was that neither Steve nor Lucy would ever take no for an answer. Steve may change, Gilbert said. Gilbert was an optimist through and through.

I thought sooner or later Lucy would realize that the marriage wouldn't work out. I thought she would become the first person in our family to divorce. A record in itself. But I was also an optimist. I thought once things failed, Lucy would take action.

I never doubted her ability to do so. I wish that she had had the inability to take action. Indecisiveness is a virtue unappreciated. But I'm the one to blame. Roland was better at indecision. If the world were made up of men like Roland, we would be spared some catastrophes. Minor ones we can't avoid. In fact, some men are specialists in causing minor catastrophes. Like Roland, Steve, maybe my father, too.

Now, Katherine, let me hope by the time you read this you're free from that husband of yours. Andy is one of them.

If you can't marry the right man, at least marry a good man. Someone like Gilbert. I used to tell him that his heart was so large it was like one of those play structures in a park. The kids can play real-life chutes and ladders in your heart, I would say. What I didn't say was: All those secrets could go around and he would not catch any one of them. My secrets, I mean.

After Lucy and Steve were engaged, sometimes I would be cooking and all of a sudden feel jolted out of a bad dream. And then I would go back to chopping and stirring. She's your daughter, I would say to myself. You reap what you sow.

———

14 MAY 1940.

The war has begun again, more earnestly now. Belgium
and Holland are invaded, small countries on a small continent. Europe is still a stranger to me. One dismisses a
stranger's suffering easily.

Today Sidelle said, Harry and I could put our fingers on a
map with our eyes closed, and in any of the countries there
would be someone we know whom we may lose in this war.

I took that as a criticism but did not defend myself.

The memory of the frozen pond of Regent's Park last
December, when S and I huddled in the cold dampness. I
would rather live in that moment than this one, the refu-
gees popping up in this spring light like haphazardly trans-
planted flowers.

———

THIS MORNING WE WATCHED the news about the fire in Martinez,
in some old factories. The staff in the building ran around, making
sure all the windows were closed. The field trip to the Japanese
Garden was canceled. There are many disappointed souls, and I
count myself lucky not to be one among them. I don't mind being
in my room, remembering my own flowers growing in my own
gardens. What's the difference between loving the roses that bloom
now and loving the roses that bloomed fifty years ago?

The fire reminded me of a song that was passed down from my
great-grandmother Lucille. I could only recall this one line. "Bring
me back to old Mar-ti-nez." Such a sad line, and you know whoever was singing about old Martinez would never see it again.

But poor Martinez has come down a few pegs since then. Who sings about it these days? Who knows what kind of dreams the miners used to have about Martinez? Warm food, clean beds, women wishing them good luck and promising to marry them once they returned with gold? I wonder if Martinez is now half dead because all the men who once dreamed about it are gone. Imagine if all the people in the whole wide world stopped dreaming about Paris or London or New York. They would all be as dead as that city buried by the volcano, you know the one I'm talking about.

Great-grandmother Lucille could say something like this: If I point my finger at any of the mines on the map of the valley, I will find men from all those countries in Europe. Better than what Sidelle said, don't you think?

It's not peace that brings people together, but gold. I wish I could tell Gilbert.

———

18 JUNE 1940.

I have not been to France. I have not set a foot in Paris.
Now Paris has fallen, and I want to grab a passerby and say,
How can this be? How can we be duped into thinking that
the world is established to make us happy?

But even as I voice the same astonishment as everyone
else, I wonder if I am merely posing. I still think my life, to
me, is larger than Paris. I am mourning the end of a life
that I might have had. Indeed ought to have had.

Mr. Ogden believes that Britain will be invaded. He has
begun to talk about moving to America or Canada.

Unpatriotic, isn't it? I said to Sidelle today.

Sidelle reminded me that Mr. Ogden had sacrificed a son
for the Empire.

In Mr. Ogden's absence Sidelle always defends him. When Mr. Ogden is around, it's the opposite: I commend him for his farsightedness and Sidelle pokes fun at his caution.

Later.

Reading the news tonight I felt a pang for Yvette, the little French dressmaker. Did she and Amelia return to France? Or perhaps they both married in New York? Yvette would have had no trouble making any man marry her. Amelia? She has enough cunning to make up for her homeliness.

————

GILBERT WAS FINE-LOOKING WHEN he was young. He didn't have those movie-star qualities Roland had, but all the same he was handsome enough.

What if he had married someone like Amelia, that little dressmaker who probably looked like nothing but a radish? Would he still have been a husband with a giant heart? What if a plain and meek wife had made Gilbert into a different man?

Last week an author came to give a lecture, and I went along to hear if there was anything new about the world. And this woman said, We human beings don't change, we only become more ourselves as time passes.

What baloney. I have plenty of evidence that men change, oftentimes depending on whom they marry. For instance, Milt. Remember, Katherine, before I married him you all thought of the idea as a joke. Have a final fling if you want, Molly said to me, but we don't really need another set of stepsiblings, and you don't need another husband.

However, you were all so wrong. I married him for a reason.

Milt married my childhood friend, Maggie Williamson. He

was not a good husband to Maggie. There's no point going into details, but what I can say about that marriage is: Maggie was neither pretty nor fierce, and Milt took himself too seriously. (Maybe that's the problem with all bad marriages, a husband or a wife taking himself or herself too seriously.)

In any case Milt made Maggie suffer. I remember, when their four kids all had grown up, I told Maggie that she should get a divorce. She was horrified. I'm turning fifty next year, she said. What would I do with myself?

Fifty! Maggie should've listened to me. Anyone at fifty is still a babe. But she stuck it out in that marriage for twenty more years. Aren't you tired of him? I asked her often. And she only replied with the news of another grandchild on the way.

So why did I marry Milt if I wasn't crazy? I know that's what you're thinking. First of all, Milt might not have been such a good husband, but he mourned Maggie sincerely. You could see him age ten years overnight after the funeral. Just like my father. I have a soft spot for men who grow lost when they become widowers.

Norman had died the year before. And I said to myself: Lilia, you were lucky you married two good men. What if this time you go for someone who's not half as good as Gilbert or Norman? Maybe you'll put Milt in his place. Maybe he'll put you in your place.

The marriage with Milt surprised me. Ah yes, Milt and I, we had both learned a few things from life. Of my three husbands, he was the funniest. He wasn't that hilarious when he was married to Maggie. He never bothered to make her laugh, and my theory is that he saved that special talent for the last eight years of his life, for someone special like me.

A visitor said to me in the elevator the other day, "If only someone could be a grandmother first before she's a mother." I didn't have time to find out whose daughter the woman is. But yes, if only a man could be a widower first before marrying.

3 JULY 1940.

Mr. Ogden had decided to go to North America. I was able to convince him that Canada would be easier than the U.S.

Graham Harris from Canada House told me that their office was crammed with people wanting to send their children or themselves to Canada. I just received word from Alexander Bain, asking if I could help him find a way to enlist in the RAF. People rushing in both directions seeking safety, or glory, equally unreal.

If Mr. Ogden and Sidelle leave, should I follow them, too? Just as I have begun to like this job? I have a serviceable brain for public relations slogans. The skill of writing deceptive words is a highly sought one, in times of war and in times of peace. In that sense I am as indispensable as a barber, who will never be out of business unless the war wipes out the entirety of mankind. The only difference: A barber could do little with a bald head; with a few words I can make the head appear as though it sports an enviable haircut. Long live the propagandists.

WHAT IF ROLAND HAD persuaded Sidelle to leave with her husband? What if Roland had followed them onto that boat? There would've been no Roland in my life. No Lucy, either.

I'm ahead of the diary. It's hard not to rush when you've lived the years and reread his entries.

24 AUGUST 1940.

Sirens again this morning. But the bombing of Shanghai preempted everything I could feel about the bombing of London.

So it's settled that Mr. Ogden will sail to Canada, along with two of his Hungarian contacts.

Sidelle said she saw no reason to be rash.

Leaving a war zone doesn't seem rash at all, I said.

One should not be driven by external forces—that's what Sidelle meant, Mr. Ogden said to me. He has a habit of explaining Sidelle to me. How can she stand such a humourless husband? I tried to contain my frustration. What is Mr. Ogden but a verb in its past perfect tense?

And in case you haven't noticed, he continued, a war doesn't register as an emergency for Sidelle.

I do not deceive myself that, aside from Mr. Ogden, I am the only man in her life. I have not any solid proof, but I have suspected that she is developing a special fondness for that smooth-faced Eddie Legg. He writes poetry for her, and he has weak lungs. This is all Sidelle has told me. I asked to see his poems once, but she did not show even the slightest sign of having heard me.

Mr. Ogden rambled on a little longer about Sidelle's wilfulness and need for independence. But I think mostly to convince himself that he was not hurt by Sidelle's decision to stay.

———

WHEN LUCY WAS BORN, Gilbert's parents came to visit. His father took Gilbert out to a pub for a father-son talk, leaving his mother to explain to me about baby-tending. Now that you and Gilbert have a child, she said, you must get prepared for the next earthquake.

I said, What?

Sooner or later there's going to be another big one, she told me. She was five when the big earthquake hit San Francisco, and she and her siblings became separated from their parents. Eventually they found six of us, she said, but we never saw our littlest sister, Katie, again.

Oh my god, I said. Gilbert never told me. That's awful.

It was awful, she said. Gilbert didn't know.

You didn't tell him?

I didn't tell Jack, either, she said.

How odd that she's sharing that with me, I thought. She and I were never close. Maybe Katie was adopted by someone nice? I said.

Or maybe she died, Gilbert's mother replied. She was not two yet. You can't expect a tiny person like her to fend for herself.

I didn't know what to say. I didn't think it was right that Gilbert's mother had marched in with this horror story when Lucy was just a few days old.

When Jack and I started a family, she continued, I insisted on having a plan ready in the event of another earthquake. I sewed a tag with our names and address on the children's undershirts and underpants. And I kept doing this right up until Mike and Moe went into the army. Has Gilbert ever told you that?

No, I said.

Yes, I did, she said. Also, in the case of an earthquake, Jack was to get out of the house right away, whether he had time or not to help us. I wouldn't have been able to make enough money to raise the children.

What if you died because Jack didn't stay to save you?

We didn't die, did we? she said. We drilled the children and ourselves so we all knew what to do.

And you never told them about Katie?

Why make people sad when I don't have to?

So that's it, I thought. My mother-in-law wants me to promise to let her son live, even if everyone else will be crushed in the rubble. I'll talk about it with Gilbert, I said.

Just don't tell him about Katie, she said, then added that she had told her two daughters and Gilbert's two sisters-in-law when they had their firstborns. It's up to us women to be prepared.

Gilbert and I never got around to making that plan. But now that I think about Mr. Ogden, he must surely have been raised by a mother like Gilbert's. And in the house Mr. Ogden grew up in there was probably a sign on every door: GENTLEMEN FIRST.

---

18 SEPTEMBER 1940.

The news of the sinking of SS *City of Benares* arrived at midday. I went straightaway to Canada House. Rushing up the stairs I nearly knocked over the little secretary. Sorry, I yelled, and said a friend had gone down with the ship.

But there was not much more to learn there. Everyone was waiting for news, and parents and relatives had begun to arrive.

Mrs. Baker, Sidelle's cook, opened the door before I knocked. Mrs. Ogden told me to take the rest of the day off, she said. No, we haven't heard anything about Mr. Ogden.

I watched Mrs. Baker leave and hesitated at the foot of the stairs. Other men would have rushed up. Sidelle had been tossed into a void of waiting, just as those unfortunate passengers onboard were dumped into the sea. To lower a lifeboat, to battle the cold water, to hold out a firm hand: Is it a disgrace that I resent being called upon to act? I am not a brave man. My only decency is that I never pose as one.

Sidelle was magnificently calm. The moment I entered the sitting room she said she had already spoken to Harry's solicitor and his two daughters.

I've never met Mr. Ogden's daughters, I said.

They don't often visit, Sidelle said.

Are they not close to Mr. Ogden? (I hate to pry. No, that's a lie. I don't hate to pry. I hate not knowing.)

Oh, they're close to him, but they have their own lives.

I went on asking about the two daughters, and their marriages, all the while seeing too clearly that Sidelle had no interest in discussing them. The problem was, I did not know what else to say.

Why are you fretting so? Sidelle asked.

My hands and my feet did not look any different from their usual wringing or tapping selves. I replied that I had not yet known a person in my life who died on me unexpectedly.

Your parents? Sidelle said. But you were spared the shock.

I suppose I have plenty to learn in this war, I said.

I don't know what there is to learn, Sidelle said. People make such a big ado about death.

One has only one life—you can't argue with that?

One has only one fate, Sidelle corrected me. But before we are granted certainty, don't please let us subject ourselves to useless imaginings.

I would be hurt by her coolness if I were Mr. Ogden. Not having much to say in reply, I went to fetch a drink for her and for myself.

You don't have to stay here, she said. I'll ring if I hear anything.

I couldn't decide which would be better, to leave her alone or to insist on my rights to be next to her when—if—the news of Mr. Ogden's death arrives.

I think it is better that you go, she said.

On the tube I could not shake off two thoughts: How relieved I am that Sidelle did not decide to accompany Mr. Ogden; and how, if Mr. Ogden died, I would have in effect acted like a murderer, or at least an accomplice.

But Mr. Ogden is not dead yet. Some people survived after almost going down with the *Titanic*. Other people choke to death on a morsel of toast.

There is nothing good in any decent man's death. Mr. Ogden is a friend, not an enemy. He does not deserve to die. Between you and him, Roland, it is you who are of lesser use to the world.

———

I DON'T OFTEN COME to Roland's defense but for once I shall do so. Apples don't blossom in winter. Daffodils don't come out in July. There is an order of things. That's my definition of heaven. I would believe in a god if he lined up all the people in the world like a domino set, so the older ones always fell before the younger ones.

Roland was a young man and Harry Ogden was an older man. Let us not question why Harry Ogden died in the war, while Roland survived.

After Lucy died, a woman said to me, It doesn't feel right that a child should go before a parent. The world may never feel right to you again.

I didn't know if she thought she was doing me a favor, giving me a fair warning. People said all sorts of things when Lucy died. Most were kind, some less empty than others. But others were hilarious—

oh, they were so horrible they made me laugh. A teacher from Molly's old nursery school ran into me one day. You don't always have to wear black, you know? she said. Women these days don't have to wear black for long even when their husbands die. And one neighbor, Sally, a lovely lady, insisted on having me over for tea. I had a thousand tasks then, but I did stop by, thinking I would have a quick cup of tea with her. She baked scones and raspberry tarts and a lemon cake, plus a basket of chocolate chip cookies to send home with me. And for two hours she talked about a baby she and her husband lost to a drowning accident. It was almost fifty years ago, but how poor Sally wept.

You're not crying now but that's because you're in shock, she said. Just wait and see. She then told me that when her children, the ones they had after the first child died, asked for a puppy, her husband brought home a turtle, because a turtle lives forever!

The world would be a better place if we were lined up like dominoes in front of a giant turtle. What's your wish, my child? the turtle would whisper to me. (I imagine that's how a turtle talks. A turtle has all the patience god doesn't. God only rages.) I want all my children and grandchildren and great-grandchildren alive when it's time for me to go, I would say. I'll grant you this wish, he would whisper, and nudge me with his giant turtle toe. Down goes Lilia, knocking over the next person in line.

———

21 SEPTEMBER 1940.

The horror stories of survivors have begun to surface. It is almost a comfort to know that Mr. Ogden and his friends were lost immediately.

It's odd to think that with each war I lost a husband, Sidelle said to me this morning.

I have stayed over for the past two days. Surprisingly no sirens and no bombings at night. And both mornings I woke up with a feeling of euphoria. If only it took just one meaningful death for the war to end.

This is going to be a long war, I said emptily.

They both died early in the war, Sidelle said. Later these losses would feel more normal. Less conspicuous.

No death could be inconspicuous, but I was not in a mood to argue these days. I cannot say I'm grieving for Mr. Ogden.

Does Sidelle miss him? Can one mourn what one does not mind not having in life? She is blessed—or doomed— with a certain hardness. Deep down I suspect I am a senti- mental man. Last night I even went into Mr. Ogden's study to remind myself what his handwriting was like.

———

WHAT ROLAND DIDN'T UNDERSTAND is that Sidelle needed that hardness. How else could you live on after losing your only child?

Every girl in my family, in every generation, was taught this say- ing passed down from my great-grandmother Lucille: Pioneers are men, but pioneering is a woman's job.

My family came from a pioneering background. Roland's fam- ily, too. How many generations do you think it takes for that hard- ness in settler and pioneer genes to disappear?

———

26 SEPTEMBER 1940.

I met Mr. Ogden's daughters at his funeral. They struck me as outlandishly beautiful. Their mother must have been an uncommon woman. How odd that a raging bore like Mr. Ogden twice married covetable women.

Now that Sidelle is a widow, what change will it entail between us? Or, is there no point pondering the future?

———

I'VE NEVER SEEN A photograph of Mr. Ogden nor spent time picturing him, but I can tell you something I learned last week. Clark used to keep three mistresses—at the same time!—while he was married to his wife. Clark, that raisin of a man! "A retired actuary, a man loving his wife and mistresses equally, a good keeper of secrets"—if it were up to me, I would put that in his obituary.

Nancy was the one to find out, through her cousin's friend's cousin. The mistresses didn't know about each other but they knew about the wife, who knew about all three.

I've never had much interest in Clark, but now I feel tempted to tap him on his shoulder and say, Is it true about all those mistresses of yours? What did they see in you?

I think I know the answer. I've noticed that a man's ears don't change a lot when he gets older. Ears don't go bald, grow wrinkled, bend from osteoporosis. Sure, ears may go deaf, but I'm talking about the look of things. All that glitters is not gold, but all that glitters gets an idiom.

So, the look of things. Clark's ears are too large, too pointed, too out of place on his head. Imagine a man in a decent suit carrying a decent briefcase, with a decent wife in a decent house, yet all the while his ears look suspicious, as if mocking the man and his life.

Wouldn't you find those ears fascinating? Besides, that pair of ears makes him look ugly. When an ugly man has the boldness to chase after women, they may make the mistake of thinking more highly of him.

Harry Ogden must have had something about him. Roland didn't know what Sidelle saw in Harry Ogden, or what any woman saw in any man.

What did you see in Roland, you may want to ask me.

Last night I wondered: Would I have forgotten Roland if we had not produced a daughter?

I don't know. But I do know that you can't take Lucy out of this story.

———

...

[My war diaries: too many words, too little meaning. A consultation of any news clips or any other diarist's record from this period would reveal the same old story: bombs, fires, maimed bodies, the sound of glass being swept away in the early morning, a nation's courage, et cetera, et cetera. The selection here is a relevant account of what would change several people's lives in the long run. Though from where I sit now, across the bay from Elmsey, which has exchanged owners, a block from the house in which Hetty grew up, and a short walk to her grave, with Sidelle buried on the other shore of the Atlantic, all I can say is that relevance is but a fool's fortune. — RB, 2 February 1990]

———

ROLAND WAS BURIED NEXT to Hetty. Milt next to my friend Maggie. Norman next to his first wife, Christine. Gilbert near his parents. Lucy near my parents. A while ago we watched a documentary about water bugs. During the daytime they live in a giant group, thousands of them, milling around, exchanging gossip. But at night they slip away, floating alone. Then the day returns, and they do, too. It doesn't bother them whether they live among millions or float by themselves.

When we're alive we cannot exist without one another. Once we die, we are alone. But we're not as lucky as those water bugs. They would learn a few things about death each night and they would reconvene to compare notes in the morning. That kind of buggy loyalty is why war never breaks out among them.

Do we see people who've died before us when we die? I don't believe so, but how do I know either way, when I'm not dead yet. Someone's granddaughter visited the other day, and she told everyone that it was her seventh birthday. Seven! Elaine said. It's the best age, and you'll have a great year. The girl replied, I just turned seven so I can't tell you if it's going to be a great year. I roared with laughter. What a sensible seven-year-old.

I wouldn't mind not seeing Milt or Norman in the other world, or my folks. I would trust that they've all settled comfortably there. Lucy? I would like to catch a glimpse of her, but only from a distance. If we ran into each other I would ask if she regretted that she killed herself. The most useless question.

Roland? Even if I could find him, I'd be a stranger to him now. But perhaps I could play a trick on him. I could talk about his mistresses, a few details here and there. Who are you, he would ask. Someone who's known you better than yourself, I would say. Someone who's watched you all your life. Wouldn't it be funny if he said, Mother, is that you?

The one person I do want to see again is Gilbert. I want to ask him: Do you think we took each other for better people than we were?

---

23 FEBRUARY 1943.

> Quentin Jones told me about a possible opening at the
> Office of War Information,* in Washington. He thought
> someone with my experience would be a great fit. Do I
> want to go to the States now that I have found perfect
> peace, working at a perfect and boring job in a perfect and
> exhausting war?
>
> I told Sidelle about the opportunity, talking about it
> with more enthusiasm than I felt. Did she get the impres-
> sion that I wouldn't mind leaving her?

...

[*OWI was previously known as the Office of Facts and Figures. How I
wished I had worked for an agency called the Office of Facts and Figures. And lived a Life of Facts and Figures.

Sidelle and I sailed to America in the spring of 1943. I met Elmer
Davis's deputies in Washington, and secured a position in their London
division, working on psychological warfare. Throughout my career I had
the good habit of not keeping notes related to work. I can give a bare-
bones version of my professional journey. It was in the London office
that I befriended several card-carrying communists and their East European connections. In 1945, I left OWI and took on a job as a correspondent for the *Daily Worker*, but my ambition then was bigger than could
be contained by either of those positions. The assistance I gave the East
Europeans at the UN conference came from an honourable intention to
help out the small countries caught among superpowers. East Europe, I
thought then, would become a centre in the postwar Continent. I was
not wrong. And the news these days continuously proves my foresight.
The downfall of my professional fortune was caused not by my shortcom-
ings, but by a disloyal ally, who set up an inconvenient meeting between
me and one of his countrywomen. But there is no need to go into details.

All I can say is that my diplomatic vision, like my writer's career, was cut short by fate. —RB, 14 March 1990]

———

DO YOU THINK ROLAND was making up all these spy stories? But he was in California. And I did see him with the foreigners.

...

[June 1943: Sidelle and I travelled to Halifax from Washington, D.C. At her request. —RB 14 March 1990]

———

THIS PART IS MORE interesting. Don't skip!

———

8 JUNE 1943.

En route to Halifax, bringing my not-bride-to-be Sidelle.
On and off I have tried to get some sense out of her about our future.
Surely you aren't, she said, speaking of marriage?
What if I were? I asked.
Hugh was four years older than you are, Sidelle said.
Think what he would've said.
You never care about other people's opinions.
Not even my own son's?
A hypothetical son by now, though I did not point this

out to her. What if I wanted to be a married man? I said.
What if I wanted children?

Then you can find yourself a good wife to bear you
your children.

I regretted at once that I had given her an easy way out.
Well, perhaps I don't care for children, I said.

Then why are we talking about something that doesn't
concern either of us? We can't possibly end up in a marriage. Not—she studied me with her usual assessing look as
though I were a hat or a pair of gloves—if we can help it.

What if we can't help it?

You mean, what if you can't help it? Sidelle said. Then
marry a woman to end your folly. I don't think we'll be
doomed by anyone you marry. The real question is, how
much of our lives do we want to allocate to each other?

What she is not allocating to me—to whom do those
parts belong?

9 JUNE 1943.

Hetty is—what can I say, Hetty surprised me. I did not remember that she is able to leave a deep impression on me.
Perhaps I am becoming more impressionable? Or has she
acquired some sort of witchcraft? If Hetty wore a crown of
flowers she would be the opposite of Ophelia, with sweet
peas and daisies and lilies and Nordic poppies adorning her
hair, singing beguilingly simple tunes. Meticulous, sane,
immortal.

Perhaps it is these years of butterflying among women
that makes me see her in a new light. She is so sure of herself, so effortlessly sure.

Sidelle has taken a room at the Lord Nelson. I made a courteous visit at Elmsey but decided to stay with Hetty's family. Jonathan is away in the navy. Thomas is still at school. Let us hope the war ends before it is his turn.

Out to lunch with Sidelle and Hetty today. One cannot imagine a better-mannered girl than Hetty, or a smoother woman than Sidelle. Yet anyone watching from above would pity me, a poor man with two expensive dishes thrust upon him, neither of which he could quite afford.

It occurred to me, while I was studying the menu and listening in to their conversation—exquisite like bone china of the finest quality—that with a novelist's stroke of the pen, Hetty could have been married to Sidelle's son. They could have been in-laws vying for the same man's affection. The fact that the man had died would not have altered anything. They would have each maintained their exclusive rights to memories and mourning. Between an older woman and a younger woman there is bound to be a man.

And there I was, an almost-son to my lover, a brother to my almost-bride. How much easier it is for the novelist. How much more he can get away with. A novelist pays no hefty tax for his imagination as we do.

Next to Hetty, Sidelle looks her true age. That impermeable, marble quality of hers takes on a kind of coarseness. Subtle, yet still visible to a lover's eyes. This thought startled me at lunch, but now I feel a sense of vindictiveness.

And Hetty? Not a mote of dust seems able to settle on her.

Later.

Hetty and I stayed up late talking, two children without adult supervision once again. Much has changed at Elmsey. Ethel left to live with a nephew when her cataracts worsened. Bessie is not young anymore. Without much choice she married Freddie's grandson, who has now turned the livery stable into a mechanics' garage. In no time their three children will start helping in the workshop. Old Freddie is dead. Some of his horses are, too. Others have been sold. Uncle William died soon after Aunt Geraldine. Uncle Victor had a stroke last year. All our cousins are doing well. The men are good at business. The women marry sensibly.

Now that the best brain surgeons have been dispatched to England, Hetty's father has become unusually prosperous, his patients travelling from afar. Aunt Marianne has welcomed me with impeccable tepidness and has since remained more or less absent.

School friends and family friends: so many stories, so little difference. Marriage, children, enlistment, untimely deaths.

What is Mrs. Ogden's plan? Hetty asked when the stories from home ran dry.

I told Hetty that Sidelle had no definite plan. A war can be exhausting, I said. She needs a break.

What does she do?

Nothing much, I said. I did not know if I should say that Sidelle is a poet, as she does not talk about poetry these days.

What a funny question I asked, Hetty said. If people asked that about me I would have to say, Nothing really.

Mrs. Ogden helped Mr. Ogden make some business connections when he was alive, I said. She travelled with him often on business trips.

Now she can't even do that, Hetty said with a sigh. (Does she mean travelling is no longer available to Sidelle because there is a war, or there is not a husband anymore?)

It's only temporary, I said.

Hetty smiled a consent. I waited for the question that I wanted her to ask so I could give her a vague answer.

When she did not say anything I said, A woman doesn't always have to do something.

Yes, she said. I think we women are better off just to be.

I couldn't tell from Hetty's tone if she was being sarcastic, but I thought not.

You don't have just to be, I said. You could travel. What I didn't say was that travelling would be a sure way for Hetty to find a husband, as sitting in this house would not help.

There is a kind of indifference in Hetty that I do not remember being there before. Is this what she is becoming, a spinster who will someday peer at a bride driven down to the church and instantly redirect her attention to her knitting? Hetty is thirty-one now. Soon we will be two middle-aged cousins, sitting by the fireplace and reminiscing about dead ancestors.

Seeing Hetty again confirms what I vaguely felt when I was younger. There is something in her that frightens me. I have always expected more from life than it is willing to give me. Most people do. Even Sidelle expects certain things and does not settle for less. Hetty is different. It is not that Hetty does not want something—she wants a lot, including me. But the way she wants me is like the way she wants everything, not by desiring, not by seeking, not even by preempting, but by prophesying. If a little girl spreads her arms wide in front of the Public Gardens and says, This whole garden is mine, we will smile, indulging her dream of ownership because it does no harm to us. Then we will walk around her and enter the garden, forgetting her right away. If the same little girl points to a piece of marshland and says, Here's my garden, we can all agree that she is playing the same make-believe game, only in this case we have no desire to enter the garden. But what if we blink and then see that the marshland has become a garden, full of expensive cultivars and exotic imports? The girl only states something known to her as a fact. We cannot even say the word "witch" to that innocent face.

I have always wondered if the little girl Hetty looked at me once and said to herself, There is Roland, my future husband. The best I could do then is to vanish, leaving only a smile like the Cheshire cat.

We talk as though there were an urgent decision to be made about my life, Hetty said. I should really be asking you about that.

I told her about the position in Washington, and the possibility of transferring to London after the summer.

You're fulfilling your dreams, Roland.

My dreams? I asked.

Writing for a living. Seeing the world. Having an adventurous life.

If she were any other girl she would deserve a slap in the face.

10 JUNE 1943.

Hetty took me to visit Aunt Geraldine's grave. I had no tears to shed but got down on one knee to remove some moss from the headstone. Hetty stood behind me. Her shadow, elongated by the late afternoon sun, stretched beyond not one grave but many.

11 JUNE 1943.

I was thinking of your Hetty before you came, Sidelle said when I met her for tea.

Don't make fun of her, I said. She's the only one close to me from my family.

Yes, Sidelle said. We all reach that point, and the last one is often the person we hold on to like a buoy.

It's not as dire as that, I argued. Hetty and I can both marry someone, to double our holdings.

Why don't you suggest that to her? She should hurry. I was watching the buses leaving with the servicemen this morning. Imagine how many of them won't be returning. She won't compete with those girls who'll lose their sweethearts.

You're being unkind, I said.

Because I speak from practicality?

Hetty would've married long ago if practicality were ever a concern, I said.

I was reading Shakespeare earlier, Sidelle said. And I was imagining Hetty as poor Lavinia. Hetty wouldn't even have to have her hands cut off or tongue torn out, she would just be wordless as Lavinia, no?

I shivered. I had foreseen this years ago, and vowed that they should not meet, and yet I let it happen. Why are you talking about Hetty as though you hate her? I said.

Have you known me to hate anyone? Sidelle asked.

You've found pleasure imagining her in pain.

Do you realise that I'm only doing you and her a favour? Even being a speechless heroine in a tragedy is better than being a nobody. You're turning her into a nobody. And worse, she lets you.

Everyone is a nobody to you, I protested. Besides, I

don't think Hetty likes drama. She'll be just fine in her drama-less life.

Someday, Sidelle said, the cigarette smoke shrouding her face, someday, Roland, you will know you are a fool to think so.

...

[Sidelle was right. I was foolish not to keep my own counsel and to let another meeting take place. Perhaps I even schemed to make it happen. Did I do it out of boredom? Or out of curiosity, wanting to see what I could do to both women? One of the most dramatic moments of my life—no, let me revise—one of the most dramatic moments of my affair with Sidelle occurred then.

And the only dramatic moment in my marriage with Hetty.

How young we almost let ourselves become, when all three of us were no longer young.

I kept a record of those days but have decided not to include the entries. I have known humiliations well and I have no intention to spare myself. But that meeting in 1954 is better never to be exhumed.—RB 6 May 1990]

———

THIS HAPPENED THE YEAR when Roland visited and I took Lucy to meet him. He came to California to get away from both Hetty and Sidelle.

Elaine said today that everyone's life is a jigsaw puzzle, and only now, in their memoir class, was everyone finding "the wisdom and the courage" to fit the pieces together. Several people agreed. They all think they're creating masterpieces. Master pieces? More like pupil pieces.

If a life is a jigsaw puzzle, where all the pieces fit together, then it must be a boring life. What could be worse? A puzzle for babies.

A sheep into a slot for sheep, a dog into a slot for dog, a cow, a barn, a farmhouse. If I were forced to do that to my parents and siblings, my husbands and children and grandchildren, Roland and all the women in Roland's diaries I know by heart now — if I were given no choice but to fit them into the right slots, I might as well wish to be dead.

This is not to say I'm not curious about what happened between Roland, Sidelle, and Hetty. In my earlier readings I was mad at him. What did he destroy? How could he have done this? Now I'm over my anger. How could my mother have lived such a miserable life? How could Lucy have left us in such a cruel manner? How could anyone have done anything? People asking such questions are only trying to make life into a solvable puzzle. Real life? It misses important pieces and has useless extras.

I saw in the newspaper today that they were to start the trial of that murder case. A Russian mail-order bride was strangled last year, allegedly by her own husband, in their living room, seen by their only child. The husband said the wife was not an ordinary bride ordered online but a former KGB agent. Still working as a spy for the Russians. She was dead so she could not defend herself. And they're bringing that little boy back from his Russian grandparents for the trial. The only witness to the actual murder. Six years old last year, seven this year. How could his parents have allowed the marriage to deteriorate into a murder in front of their child? How could the judge think of letting the child relive the horror at the trial? But will these questions ever help anyone?

The word around is that Elaine went to Jean and asked if she could arrange a field trip for us to attend the trial.

Still, I have to say, it kills me not to know what happened at that meeting in 1954. Did Hetty slip poison into Sidelle's tea? Did Sidelle point a pistol at Hetty's heart? Did Roland beg both women to think of his happiness and reach a peace agreement? This is one time — okay, this is the only time — in my life that I can say I feel truly defeated. Whatever I can come up with would be what Roland would call a second-rate production.

———

16 JUNE 1943.

> Today we took the boat out to Georges Island. A cloudless
> summer day. Picnic under the lighthouse. Beautiful basket
> and neatly prepared food. I think Sidelle made a mistake.
> Hetty is not a nobody. She specialises in invisibility. Were
> she given a place in Greek mythology no god would ap-
> proach her, and no goddess be jealous of her.
>
> While we walked along the beach we passed a few
> young couples, the men wearing their bravery like the most
> spruce of uniforms, the girls their melancholy like the pret-
> tiest of dresses. So conscious of being together for what
> must feel like the last days of their togetherness that they
> all looked as if playacting. Everyone has an assigned role in
> a war. Everyone follows the script.
>
> On the way home we ran into a Mrs. Bye, who moved
> back to town from Toronto after she was widowed. Aunt
> Geraldine befriended her and now Hetty has inherited her
> as one of those brainless perennials. Mrs. Bye told me she
> liked her name. It makes it easier for people to part with
> her: Goodbye, Mrs. Bye. People love to say that to her and
> why not, she said, make a farewell less sad in this time of
> ours.
>
> Tomorrow Sidelle and I leave for New York. After all
> these years I still have not shaken off the notion that a train
> ride is a singular event. If a harmless trip on a train could
> kill my parents, it could happen to anyone. The Fergusons

used to treat every journey with solemnity, with all the family seeing off Uncle Victor or Uncle William on the platform even if it was a short business trip. So long, Godspeed, come back alive.

I asked Hetty not to come to the station. I was disappointed when she agreed so readily.

———

HETTY WAS GOOD AT small revenges. Refusing to see Roland off. Bringing Roland to a reunion with their cousins. Pleasant days and nights at home and abroad. Beautiful birthday presents. She would accumulate her revenges like a girl counting colored beads. Against Roland, but she also waited long enough to have her revenge against Sidelle.

Roland had his revenge, too, against both of them. He outlived them so he could have the last word. Some people live for the last word.

Sidelle did not have her revenge but she never needed it. Weak-minded people mistake people as life, and think they are hurt by this or that person. For Sidelle and for me: Only life hurts us. We don't take revenge against life.

I've outlived them all. But like Sidelle, I don't live for revenge.

———

17 JUNE 1943.

En route to New York. Sidelle's eyes closed elegantly. Sometimes I wonder if she ever thinks of peeking from behind half-closed lids to see what I am writing in my notebook. I always peek.

I used to think, when I was at St. Andrew's, that I was writing the most auspicious prologue to a prominent life; I had sketched out the chapters leading to success and fame, with romances, intrigues, and suspense sprinkled in. But it feels now as though I have only just reached the first semicolon of my life story; what has been achieved is not enough to fill a full sentence.

It occurred to me that since Malcolm Hobbs, I have not found any friends who can absorb my entire existence. Is friendship formed when young the only true connection? The women, in and out of my life, have never come close to reproducing this unconditional dedication. Those days when Malcolm and I lay in the meadow and read and talked: The birds sang more freely, the shafts of sunlight were more vibrant, our hearts more full of sweet yearning. If I go back to my early diaries I find page after page of such bliss, when one could feed on a single thought like a bee on nectar, when one's lust for life was kept alive not by one's flesh but by the very concept of living.

I now feel bad that I neglected to keep in closer touch with him. There is only my laziness to blame. When I get back to London I shall write him right away.

———

WE DID VISIT THE courthouse today, but we came to the drama too early. It will take another week for them to settle the jury selection. So we all trooped back like children brought to see a movie that's opening later. I include myself in this silliness.

But I forgive myself. I have a particular reason for wanting to watch the trial. Russian spies always make a good story. Roland, what would you have made of this? Russian spies in San Francisco again? In 2010? Wouldn't that be a good novel for you to write?

———

20. JUNE 1943.

The little household made up of Madame Zembocki and
Cousin Cliona has not changed. Thirteen years—can it be
true that it's been so long? They have aged, but like their
furniture, they have an aura of near immortality. That arrogant parrot is still present. But there is a greyer feeling than
when I was here last.

Madame Z's clothes may as well be the same outfits she
wore when I first met her, but back then they only looked
eccentric and dated, while now they are unquestionably
shabby. Her hair, still braided and coiled high on her head,
looks like hay. She was taciturn when Sidelle and I were invited to luncheon with them. Cousin Cliona did most of
the talking. Though never a talkative person herself, she
carried the conversation by posing question after question
to me. Sidelle looked reserved, not contributing much. I
felt as though I was put on a stage in front of three odd
women. How to charm even one of them seemed an impossible challenge.

But no, I was placed in front of three judges. None of
them seemed interested in delivering a verdict, especially a
favourable one.

Cousin Cliona said something about her work, I said to
Sidelle when I had dinner with her today. I thought they
were well-off. (Cousin Cliona told me that twice a week
she travels upstate to teach at a school of liturgical music.)

They are being cautious, Sidelle said. They may be
gifted but they're not so with their money. Besides, she
said, there's no way Lizzie can get her money out of the
Soviet Union now.

It took me a moment to realise Sidelle was talking about Madame Z—it's odd to hear her referred to by a young girl's name. So she has savings in the Soviet Union?

Her novels sell by the tens of thousands there, if not the millions.

Have you read her novels?

No, Sidelle said. She wrote them in Russian.

Surely someone would have translated them into English by now.

If there are translations, I don't want to know, she said. Lizzie is one person I've learned to avoid with reverence. You see, Lizzie is twelve years older, and before I could read she was already a prodigy. And with a seriousness that even a small child would recognise, she told me that there was no future for me in music. You could try poetry, she said. That's the closest you can get to music. Just like that, with one stroke of her finger.

I am in awe of people who have the confidence to take something away from another person, but I am more in awe of those who have the confidence to bestow something without the slightest worry of being mistaken.

Her blessing has made only a mediocre poet out of me, Sidelle said. But her real gift to me is common sense. I spent a life's ration of infatuation on her. After that I was cured once and for all.

When did she stop being a pianist?

When she got married.

Is domestic bliss worth such a sacrifice?

I suppose sometimes a marriage becomes a woman's ambition, Sidelle said.

But that didn't stop her from becoming a bestselling author in Russian, I said.

We don't know if her books have any merit. All I know is she used to be a great musician, and she's no longer one.

What a strange woman, I said. What I was really thinking was: Sidelle talks about Madame Z as though she were
already dead.

There is nothing strange. Lizzie is a single-minded
woman. I don't think people understand that she has succeeded because she lacks the kind of imagination you and I
and many others rely on for our sanity.

She has to have imagination to play music or write, no?
I said.

The predictable kind of imagination, Sidelle said. It
takes more than that for a person to live.

Later.

I ran into Cousin Cliona when I returned from the
travel agency. Dressed in a tweed suit and skirt, she looked
far less shabby than at the luncheon. She said that she was
on the way back from teaching.

Do you like teaching music? I asked, walking with her
toward her place.

I enjoy music, she said, but I'm afraid I'm not a good
teacher.

I said I was sure she's more than qualified. But it's an
awful amount of travelling, I said. Couldn't you teach at
home?

Cousin Cliona stopped abruptly. I wondered if the
thought of private lessons had never occurred to her. Oh
no, she said in terror. We can't possibly have that.

Why? I asked.

We don't want any music in the house, she said.

What an odd statement to make about a household
shared by two musicians.

I would have loved to have a longer conversation with
Cousin Cliona alone, away from the scrutinizing eyes of
Sidelle and the disinterested eyes of Madame Z. I want to

understand her, so willingly letting herself be subjugated by an eccentric.

I wonder if every woman I have met holds a key to my future. No, not every woman. There is that Isobel Cunningham at the Canada House. Pretty, but that is about it. The women holding my future hostage are those who could easily treat me as a nonentity. Even the kindhearted Cousin Cliona will forget me the moment I leave.

———

WHEN ROLAND REREAD ALL these years of diaries before passing them to Peter Wilson, could he still remember every single woman in his life? Of course not. Then why was he so afraid of being forgotten, when he himself invested so little in remembering others?

He was certainly not alone in that. Most people want to be rich but don't mind others being poor. They like good food but don't mind others staying hungry. Iola, I hope you get to learn this as early as possible. Most things people give you are those they can afford to lose. It's fine accepting them, but treat them like the Halloween candies and the cheap goody bags from birthday parties.

And in return, give only what you can afford to lose. My remembering Roland, as you must always know, is in that category.

———

21 JUNE 1943.

At Sidelle's request I joined her at a lunch meeting with a Mrs. Mildred Falk.

Mrs. Falk is not a pleasant-looking woman. Perhaps it is her eyebrows—thick, too masculine for my taste. Or her mouth, shapeless, full of contempt. The moment we sat down she started talking bluntly, explaining that she was part of an effort to cultivate a civilised Europe during wartime. She had tried to establish contact with Madame Zembocki, she said, as they would like to publish and perform her song cycles in Germany. Madame Zembocki, whom Mrs. Falk called a true European treasure, would appeal to many listeners.

I don't think she's a serious composer, Sidelle said.

That is for the composer herself to say, no?

I'm afraid I can't be of much help to you.

And you yourself, Mrs. Falk said, we've admired your poetry. We can publish your poems in the most beautiful German translation. I personally can guarantee that.

I admired Sidelle's coolness, as though Mrs. Falk had merely queried the possible sale of a piece of furniture. Whoever this ugly woman is, however she has managed to travel to America, I am sure she has learned about Mr. Ogden's death. Can one approach a woman whose husband one has just murdered and propose lovemaking? But that is what men do all the time. Is it not what, in the end, all dramas and all wars are about?

I interrupted. I may have missed it, but what did you say you and your husband do, Mrs. Falk?

We work in the cultural sphere.

That threatening vagueness: I imagined a globe into which they hurled all the artists and musicians and writers.

I don't see how my poetry is worth being read by anyone, Sidelle said. I would feel great pity for the person forced to translate it.

You're too harsh a judge of your own work, Mrs. Falk said.

Besides, my poetry is about trifles, Sidelle said.

Not every artist has the courage to admit that, Mrs. Falk said. Don't you think for that reason your poetry, like Madame Zembocki's music, deserves to be discovered and relished?

Sidelle smiled. Discretion, she said, is the better part of valour. Do you not agree, Mrs. Falk?

The waiter came for our orders. A natural pause, after which Mrs. Falk and Sidelle talked about common acquaintances and ski trips and plays that they had attended. I have never thought about the virtue of a woman's hysteria, but listening to them, one wonders if there is a point to war. Yes, so much will be annihilated, but at least one does not have to witness such iciness.

Later I asked Sidelle how she came to know Mrs. Falk.

Mr. Falk did some business with Harry's uncle, she said.

But who are these impertinent people?

You think they're impertinent? Mrs. Falk's father is German but her mother is English. England is to her as it is to me. Or even you. You and I may not be its most loyal subjects, but we have chosen a side. Mrs. Falk has, too.

So one has to always make a gamble one way or another.

We don't know the future, Roland. She might win this hand.

The thought that we could be on the losing side of this war had never occurred to me. Surely she should know she's on the wrong side, I said.

What's the difference between a winning side and a right side? Sidelle asked.

I must have looked appalled. She smiled and said, Rest assured. I still have a few principles.

I have always taken pride in not being a principled person. I have cultivated a stance of not abiding by any conventional values. I have been in positions that may sound

ignoble or immoral, and because of that I find a kind of
nobility and morality in myself. I cannot, however, picture
myself in the shoes of Mrs. Falk. Is treason such a para-
mount sin, like incest? Yet I would not mind defending incest from a philosophical or an aesthetical angle. Could I
defend treason similarly?

Had I been a novelist or a composer or a poet, and had
Mrs. Falk offered me the same deal, would I have been able
to say no?

...

[In the late 1950s, on a trip to West Germany, I saw a book at my host's
house, a list of names and condensed biographies of those who had
worked to undermine the Third Reich from inside and had been executed. Among the names was Mildred Falk (though not Alfred Falk).
The discovery stayed with me until a year later, when I happened to
mention it to an ex-communist friend (Malcolm Hobbs, who by then
had settled down in the countryside). The Falks, Malcolm said, worked
for the CPGB. It can't be, I said, recounting the meeting in New York.
Malcolm explained that those she had approached were either the ene-
mies/critics of the Communist Party or, like Madame Z, people who had
veered away from the party's cause.

I do not know how Mildred Falk was arrested, or what happened to
her husband. But even today, thinking about their scheme of coercing or
seducing some recluse like Madame Z into a notoriety embraced by the
Nazis—a scheme carried out in the name of a revolutionary cause—
I have no respect for Mrs. Falk's martyrdom.—RB, 22 May 1990]

IF YOU WERE PART of the muscle in the leg or some little valve in
the heart, how would you know that the brain is scheming to do

something harmful? Think of all those cells doing their jobs dutifully and wonderfully for that beautiful young body when Lucy killed herself.

They were like Madame Z, caught or not caught in a scheme, destroyed or not destroyed, all depending on luck.

Oh, luck. The most over-diligent chef ever. You can decline, saying you're full. Or you can cite a stomach bug. Or pout like a child and refuse to touch the food. Still, the chef brings you course after course. And truth be told, there is no leaving the table until you finish the last bite. And then, as you've paid your bill and are finally free to go, oh no, it's not over yet. Just like what happened when Molly took me to that tasting menu. Before we left, the very nice waiter brought a pretty bag to me. Here's a pumpkin bread for you, ma'am, baked with our special recipe.

Who among my children will serve that takeout pumpkin bread? It's not going to be Molly. I know that. Carol? She's like my sister Margot. There's no wildness in her. No thorns. No surprises. Tim and Will? No.

Katherine, I must be honest with you. I'm down to the last course now (finally!), and it's you I'm thinking of when I wonder about what luck is secretly baking for me.

———

29 AUGUST 1943.

Back to London. Sometimes I wonder how Hitler must feel about occupying everybody's thoughts in such a demanding way. When we all live like decks of cards being shuffled and reshuffled, all to his whim.

My current state: contentment with writing propaganda. Canada is my mother's country. America my father's. England, the mother country for both. It is rare that one can be loyal to all three of them, I told Sidelle today. It takes a war for this to happen.

Disloyalty is our privilege, Sidelle said. Don't throw it away.

Your privilege, I said. My generation cannot afford that or any luxury.

Every generation must feel the same way, she said. The world always owes the young more than it owes the old.

Not every generation. Look at us. It's as if we were finally old enough to sit down in a famous restaurant, but even before the hors d'oeuvres arrive a bomb has exploded nearby.

You could return another day, Sidelle said.

One comes back another day and the restaurant is no longer standing, I said.

Patience, Sidelle said. I would recommend that you have patience.

But for how long?

We win the war, or we lose. Either way the future will be clearer then.

There's no guarantee of any future for me even if the war ends tomorrow. And I do need one, I said. I'm still a young man.

And I'm not too old to marry.

I stared at her. My life is not really at the mercy of Hitler's whims, but a woman's.

You look as though I've insulted you, but all I just did was state a fact, she said.

Do you mean that I should marry you? I asked. I thought how my life would become much easier—I could settle down to write my books. We don't bore each other. We are neither of us anchored in one place. I remembered the first trip we took together. At one place in Arizona—or was it in New Mexico? somewhere in the desert—a man who served us food at an inn told us that there was little to see around there. Here even the jackrabbits carry their lunches with them, he said. But what is the difference between me and a jackrabbit, when all I have done in these years is carry an infatuation with me. I cannot possibly marry Sidelle. A man cannot just walk in one suit, eat one dish, make a life with one woman.

But you're right to hesitate, she said.

My heart sank a little.

On the way back, I heard someone call my name—a girl whose face and voice seemed so familiar that for a moment I panicked. I must have known her in an intimate manner, but it turned out I had only met her once in Thayer House, where she worked as a nurse. She is a Canadian brought up on the Continent. Let me call her D.

She said she was in London to say goodbye to a friend leaving for America—a Romanian friend from her school years. It had taken the friend and her family some trouble to get out of Romania, and they had lost all their possessions.

Another card shuffled out of the deck.

I asked D why she was not returning to Canada. Safer there, you know?

Duller too, she said.

But your parents, are they not worried?

Her sunny face turned less bright. I was almost certain that she would say she was an orphan. And I was ready to offer my own story so that she would feel closer to me immediately.

They're fine with the idea, she said. They're patriotic parents.

Are you the only one here?

My brother, too, she said. He's a pilot.

I asked to see her tomorrow. She is staying in London for a few days.

It is like a change in the weather. One always feels heartened when that happens.

———

HERE'S A THOUGHT. ROLAND never had a woman whose name starts with Z. From A to Z could never be his boast. Zoe, Zelda, Zsa Zsa, you name it, he missed them all.

This morning, at my eye checkup, Dr. Atler told me my vision was as beautiful as a 1958 Impala. I could see he was having a slow day. I told him that if he thought he could flirt with me, then he was wrong. Do the math, Doctor, I said to him. In 1958 I already had four children. He blushed! He said I was just like his mother. It's her job to embarrass you, I said, not mine.

No man should be dumb enough to talk about a woman with another woman. (I wonder if that was how Dr. Atler earned his divorce, praising a woman patient's vision to his wife.) But to go on talking about his mother with another mother . . . As though I cared!

May the poor woman rest in peace. What would she think if she knew her son talks about her all the time to his patients? I'm sure I'm not the only one who gets to hear about her in that dark office, reading the chart and trying to guess which option is better, one or two.

I won't bore you with too many of her stories, but today Dr. Atler got misty-eyed when he said she gave him a surprise gift when he turned fifty. He'd played clarinet throughout school, he said. His teacher thought he could go on as a professional musician, but his parents thought there was no money in music. He followed their advice, built a good practice, and on his fiftieth birthday his mother gave him a lamp made from his old clarinet.

He even showed me the picture on his phone. It's a nice-looking lamp, I said. Suits you well because you're not making music on it but making your patients see the light.

He thanked me as though I meant it as a compliment.

I feel bad for the clarinet. If there is a cemetery for old musical instruments the clarinet might prefer to go there. Who knows? The instruments might rise from their graves in the middle of the night and conduct themselves in a ghost symphony. All but this one.

Maybe after I'm gone, none of my children will become misty-eyed about any present I've given them. On the other hand, I've never taken something away from them and made it into a mummy for them.

———

2 SEPTEMBER 1943.

> Another date with D before she returns to her post at
> Thayer House. One has to acknowledge that, not having
> liberated anyone in this war yet, we at least have liberated
> ourselves.

———

THIS IS THE LAST woman I will mark for you. There are plenty more to come. I know them all by heart now, and reading about them again tires me out. It's amazing that Roland never seemed to get tired. Men are amazing. In the most predictable ways.

I decided not to attend the murder trial of the Russian mail-order bride/spy. Nancy told me that they put the boy on the witness stand. He curled up on the floor, to show what his mother looked like when he found her. You would think every adult in that courthouse should have enough sense not to make a child act that out. And they should have enough decency to close their eyes when he did.

People are born gawkers. You don't even want to hear about the days after Lucy's death.

Poor Lucy. Since she was a teenager she hated it when I came near her. Lucy, so headstrong, so good at pushing everyone away, but in the end she knew we would have to take care of what she left behind.

Last night I thought of the boy on the witness stand. If I were his mother I would rise from the grave and weep for him as I did not for Lucy.

———

10 OCTOBER 1943.

I went to Oakridge House for a weekend with Malcolm. He has not changed much since we last saw each other, when he sailed for Oxford. I suspect that I have not been keeping in touch out of jealousy.

But that is all water under the bridge now. One must credit the war, which can transform anything into water under the bridge. What remains is this precious life. By which I mean, my previous life.

We arrived in the evening. His uncle and aunt have no children. No doubt Malcolm is their heir. They certainly treat him as such.

After dinner, over a glass of port, Uncle Edmund began to sing "Rule Britannia!" Afterward Uncle Edmund said that during the war—it took me a moment to realise he was talking about the Boer War—people used to go to Buckingham Palace after dinner parties and sing patriotic songs outside. To cheer up Her Majesty, he said. One night, he said, it was foggy and cold, and some of us started a bonfire. And then one of the rooms lit up, and we all turned quiet. The French door to the balcony opened and out walked two guards, and in between a small black-clad figure.

Uncle Edmund's nostalgia was so poetic that I joined him afterward, singing "God Save the Queen." I expected Malcolm to mock us but he looked as though his mind was elsewhere.

Not many Englishmen, Malcolm said later, understand what the USSR is doing for us. We discuss postwar Europe and policy making as though we are winning this war by ourselves. But how many of us ask, what is the true meaning of this war? Perhaps in a hundred years people will say we lived at this turning point where the Nazis gave an opportunity for the rise of communism.

I would not be surprised if after this war some of us will be ready to pick up the hammer and sickle, Malcolm said. It's time for this island or even the whole world to turn red.

———

I WON'T PRETEND I know history well. But I do know it's only by the throw of the dice that Gilbert was not a communist. Young men dream in all colors. Gilbert's dream was in olive green and dove white, but he could've dreamed in red, and he would still be the same dear old Gilbert.

My little brother Kenny also dreamed in green, but money green, and when that dream led him astray he landed behind bars.

I don't know what colors his dreams were then, or after he came out of prison. We lost touch with him, but if he had died as a child, we would've always remembered him.

What colors were Roland's dreams? Maybe he himself wouldn't know. What are the colors of fame and success and immortality? Rainbow sprinkles?

Not long after Lucy died, Gilbert told me that the world felt too bright to him.

What do you mean? I asked. People often say the opposite, I thought. After someone dies the world loses some light. You see that in movies. Things turning gray.

He said the colors looked different. Red too red, green too green, blue too blue, white too white. Maybe you should have your eyes checked, I said. All those tears for Lucy must have done something funny to your eyes. Then Gilbert looked at me strangely and said, You really don't want to understand, Lilia. What don't I want to understand, I asked, but the truth was that I knew exactly what he meant.

Lucy died in May, at the end of the rainy season. Rain and fog would have suited us better that year. But in May it was sunshine again, with golden poppies popping out everywhere.

All my life, from then on, when I see golden poppies I think of Lucy.

Gilbert might have thought I wasn't mourning Lucy as a mother should. I wouldn't defend myself, not because I couldn't, but because no tears, no defense, nothing would bring her back.

Gilbert was so hard-hit by Lucy's death that I often think he lost twenty years due to a broken heart. You would think that it should've happened to me. You could say that Gilbert took a bullet for me. He was willing to do it from the very beginning. He even told me that when he was courting me, though he meant it differently then. Who knew that the bullet wouldn't come from a war, but from the daughter we raised together?

I'm all over the place today. I was trying to remember something else. But what is it?

———

14 OCTOBER 1943.

> Lunch with Malcolm. If not for his sarcasm I would think
> his interest in the USSR bodes ominously for his new politi-
> cal fervour.
>
> He said that the Russian Orthodox Church has been
> praying for the victory of the Soviet Union over Hitler, and
> the Archbishop of Canterbury looked for (or found?) Chris-
> tian seeds in communism. And mark this, he said, we're ob-
> sessed with talking about peace and postwar order as
> though we believe the Soviet Union will dutifully and virtu-
> ously leave Europe to us and go on tilling their socialist land.
>
> The last comment makes me think perhaps Malcolm is
> not so pro-Soviet as I feared.

...

[In retrospect, I would like to point out that Malcolm Hobbs changed the course of my life without suffering any substantial consequence. What can I say? He was an amateur dallying in politics because he could afford to do it. I, without a definite future at the time, seized any opportunity to advance my position. —RB, 6 June 1990]

———

NOW I REMEMBER WHAT I forgot to say. What did Molly mean when she said that Gilbert had talked with the children about

Lucy? Do they all think I killed Lucy? Do they think I've gone on with my life without suffering any consequences?

———

31 DECEMBER 1943.

What a year we have had, though this can be said of every year.

Spent the day with Sidelle, who was sentimental to-night. Illness or a glass of wine too many? Out of the blue—or after a glass too many—I asked her, Do you have other lovers?

Funny you would think so, she said.

Funny it's taken me so long to ask, I said.

You should know that by nature I am a lazy woman.

That might be the most insulting answer one could get from a woman. I tried to keep my voice even. We've known each other for some time, I said. What did you see in me in the first place—inexperience, youth, snobbishness, greed for your status and attention? What has made us carry on—habit, familiarity, obsession, or what?

Can't it be out of a little love? she said.

A little love, I said. You make us sound like an old couple, with nothing but a little love left.

Not many men can boast of a little love from me.

Some must have, I said. What did they do then? Fall on their knees and ask for your hand?

Roland, I've married twice, once for love and once for security. I've had enough.

So what you're really saying is, wouldn't it be nice to string me along because I'm a safe choice? No money, no status, no future, so you don't have to worry about being ensnared by me.

Why can't a woman want a man because she feels happy when she's with him, Sidelle said, clinking her glass on the edge of mine.

I have nothing to say about that, I said, though rather weakly.

Oh, Roland, we're a little happy together, aren't we?

I realised that Sidelle, who never gets drunk, must have got herself drunk because it suited her mood tonight. Sure, I said.

To the world we may look like two misers begrudging each other something better, Sidelle said. But we are our best selves when we don't give too much away. In that sense we are a perfect match. You have to trust me in this, as I'm so rarely wrong.

Is that so?

Why else, she said, do I not feel threatened at all by your army of lovers?

———

DID THEY STILL MAKE LOVE at this point in their affair? I hardly think so. What a pity for Sidelle.

———

1 JANUARY 1944.

Another year. The same war. Human casualties mounting like numbers on the scoreboard of a school game.

I've become involved in the International Labour Conference. I enjoy it more than writing propaganda. All the players, major or minor, treat the game as seriously as schoolboys on the rugby field. And the less experienced the player, the more fearless and desperate he is.

Yesterday Malcolm said that the Allies dreamed of Germany beating the Soviet Union and then simultaneously evaporating in its success. He gave me a copy of *The Art of War*, a perfect gift for my current pursuit. The translator, it turned out, was at Oxford with Malcolm's father.

———

I reread last year's diary. What a good liar I have become. Or what a lousy liar. Wouldn't anyone, reading these entries so packed with self-delusions, see through me?

Do other people lie in their diaries? They must.

———

ROLAND, DID YOU REALLY believe that people would one day read your diaries?

Sure, here I am, reading his diaries. But I'm only doing this by chance. Life has taken turns and led me here. I'm not surprised. But I wouldn't be surprised if life had taken different turns. Then I would've forgotten him. Or would've never known him in the first place.

But imagine him with his years of diaries. He would have to pack those notebooks every time he moved, and the suitcase would be getting heavier each year. He was almost homeless before his marriage to Hetty, and a homeless man unable to part with his words deserved some respect. What I don't quite understand is why he left Peter Wilson to finish the work for him. Toward the end of the book he said he arranged with a friend's press for the printing of his diaries. Why not do it then, so he could see the final product, three volumes instead of being reduced to one volume?

But it would've been hard for him not to go to the bookstores now and then and ask if anyone had bought a copy of his diaries. Maybe it's easier to imagine all those people getting to know him after his death.

————

4 MAY 1944·

Infidelity of any kind breeds a higher standard of loyalty. These days I find my new life more exhilarating. It used to be that I would imagine that everything I did was for the writing of those great novels that would bear my name. Now I convince myself that I am working for the future of America, of Europe, and of mankind. For the postwar order. It sounds terrific and glorifying.

Today Sidelle commented that I looked more purposeful. The thought of world peace must be doing you good, she said.

Something has to come along and disrupt the order of the old world, I said. Or else this war would be fought for nothing, and people would have died for nothing.

You sound like a socialist.

I thought about Malcolm. Interesting and alarming, how he can still influence my thinking.

And there's nothing wrong with your thinking that way for a day or two, Sidelle said. But trust me, you'd be equally bored if you joined that circle.

Which circle?

People who take great pleasure from dismantling the old order.

You think so?

Why else do you think I left poetry and painting?

You also painted? I asked. I never knew.

With even less talent than I wrote poetry.

Perhaps you're too modest.

Sometimes I think that I could write an old-fashioned novel in verse, about everyone I know, which nobody would care to read so nobody would know they are part of the novel.

Why not? I said. You could be the Pushkina of our time. Or an operetta?

With these modernist poets flipping and flapping across the stage? Just imagine Lizzie's horror, Sidelle said.

Lizzie?

I forgot. Your Madame Z.

———

I HAVE NEVER BOTHERED to ask Mrs. Anderson, the librarian, about Madame Z. Maybe she was a well-known writer, maybe she was little more than a nobody. What are the mathematics that determine how fast a person is forgotten? If I raised that question at breakfast, there would be quite a few men competing to give me answers. With long formulas and complicated graphics.

Sidelle only occupies a page in another poet's biography. How many people remembered her after she died? I wouldn't expect anything different after I myself die. We—I mean Sidelle and I— haven't lived to be remembered. We haven't even cared to change anyone's life. If people are influenced by us, for good or for bad, they themselves have to answer for that.

9 MAY 1944.

At lunch Malcolm said his doorman had been pestering him for his not-too-old suit.

Imagine if the Soviet Union won this war singlehandedly, I said. All the porters and doormen and waiters in London would demand what they would think of as theirs.

All the more reason we need to make sure such things don't happen in England. We need a progressive and fair system, not one to fight against Bolshevism. That fight would only cultivate Bolshevism.

I have a feeling I might have misread Malcolm. The Slavs are our hope, he said today, and then loaned me the Yugoslavia book by Rebecca West.

Later.

America, I imagine, I said when Sidelle asked me where I see myself after the war. Canada was my boyhood, I said. America will be my adulthood.

And England?

My romance, I said.

What a poetic trinity, Sidelle said.

This conversation took place after I spent an evening with her. Malcolm always makes me feel the urge to act, to take up a cause, to find higher meanings. Sidelle reminds me of the pleasure of making no commitment.

Still later.

A letter from Hetty, a timely reprimand. When was the last time I thought about her? When was the last time she appeared in these pages? Oh, Hetty. Really one of the most important people in my life, who slips from my mind so easily that no one would believe me if I say I do miss her.

TRUST ME, THE MOST important people in anyone's life are like air.

You can pick up a magazine and read those articles about marriage problems, problems between parents and children, between friends, and soon you realize that the one common complaint is that people feel they're being treated as empty air. Really, I always want to say, is that all the confidence you have in yourself? Your husband, your child, your best friend—if you truly are so important you should be exactly like air to them. If you want to be sure, take yourself away for a moment and see how they gasp for you.

I make fun of Hetty, but here's one thing she got right. She was perfectly fine with being just air to Roland. You may want to say the same thing about Gilbert, but we raised six children together. Children are a funny business. Each child is like a new season until you get used to it, and then another one comes along. Plenty of headaches along the way, but at the beginning of every season you think something new is happening, something different.

Gilbert and I were well seasoned together. Like a pair of salted fish with plenty of spices thrown in. Norman and Milt—they came to me already pickled.

I do have one question: What were Roland and Sidelle to each other? Certainly she was not just empty air to him. What about him to her? Ninety-nine out of a hundred people would think of him as a worthless man. But she alone knew his worth to her.

22 MAY 1944.

We are back to the early days, eating and sleeping for the war, drinking and revelling despite the war, making haphazard love because of the war. It's one of the few times that I wish I had enlisted. Sidelle points out that I would be the kind of soldier who gets shot before everyone else, who hangs on to my dear life when any other person would simply die. And then there would be those who have to sacrifice their lives for me, and in the end I would be the only one convalescing in a country house, waiting for my medal.

I said that her words would be taken by most men as an insult.

You don't think living an entirely selfish life requires some courage? Sidelle said.

Unless egotism is one's nature, I said.

You work so hard to make egotism your nature, Sidelle said. Trust me, egotistic people don't walk around with their egotism pinned to their hats. It's their virtues they want to display.

You often claim insights about me unknown to myself, I said.

Some have entertained angels unawares, Sidelle replied. Besides, you're made by me.

Having never heard this from her yet having always suspected it to be the case, I shivered.

No, you don't have to feel resentful, she said. We don't bore each other, and we have made this life together because neither of us wants to be bored. We can't undo this.

Why can't we?

You can't reproduce this with another woman, she said. I have no interest in reproducing this with another man.

Is that why people stay in a marriage? That getting unstuck takes too much time and effort? I said.

Oh, Roland, she said, what we have is better than any marriage.

———

WHAT KIND OF LIFE did Sidelle lead after Roland married Hetty? You can read on, but I bet you a hundred dollars that you won't find out, either. Because Roland himself didn't know. He claimed that she never took another lover. That I'm willing to believe. She had her loyalty, which was nobody's business.

Sidelle and I are made of the same material. It's a shame we never met. We wouldn't have been strangers. We would've understood each other. Men don't understand that all stories are, in the end, women's stories. That's why they start wars and make peace, so they can claim something for themselves.

The tale of Roland and Sidelle would make a good movie. A movie can skip a lot and go straight to the end. Shall I mark the page when Sidelle was on her deathbed? And Hetty on hers? It's not a spoiler that they both died, but it would be if I were to tell you what I think of their deaths.

We're getting closer to the UN conference. I don't have to re-read those pages. I met Roland. I met Gilbert. Gilbert and I married.

You can read and find a few lines about me in Roland's diaries. But I won't mark them for you. They're less important now, just as all those men's ambitions at the peace conference. Look at the wars coming after 1945. That peace conference achieved little, but changed some people's lives.

"One can very well do without a fate," there is a line like that somewhere in this book. Good wishful thinking. That is like saying one can very well do without a life.

...

[February 5, 1946, the *Queen Mary* sailed from Southampton to New York Harbour, carrying more than seventeen hundred British war brides and six hundred children to reunite with their GI husbands and fathers. A few men and I took the same transatlantic journey. — RB 2 April 1990]

———

I'M MARKING THIS PART for you.

Lucy was born while Roland was crossing the Atlantic. Put together a few shots of him on the ship and a few shots of baby Lucy and her new parents and add a soundtrack, it could be a movie clip. But movies are always bringing separate lives together. Real life does the opposite. Real life is all about growing apart.

Lucy was born before Roland's marriage. I didn't know it back then, but of course I wouldn't have done anything differently. I had my pride.

———

28 JANUARY 1946.

A telegram from Johnston arrived late yesterday. He's secured a cabin on *QM* for me, so I don't have to wait for *Mauretania*. A miracle or an omen? This morning when I told T, she reached over for my cigarette case. I filled her cigarette case last night. I will fill it again, so why this show of greediness as a childish protest?

A few days difference only, I said.

Typical of a man to change the departure date without consulting anyone, T said.

Why do I keep having these liaisons with inconvenient women? It is high time that I make an effort to be more principled in my affairs. Though this I must have said to myself hundreds of times in the past ten years.

Return date, I corrected her. I'm homebound.

Nothing more to say about T, but I've been thinking of my statement. Now that my diplomatic career is in the ashes, do I want to go back to work at a public relations firm, doing what I can do with my eyes closed? Or, should I have as a new ambition to make a home for myself?

30 JANUARY 1946.

Ventured out in the rain to lunch with Sidelle. Cold, grey, miserable. Just the kind of weather that makes one wonder for what reason we've fought hard to win a war. I would rather still be able to open the papers and read about battles and retreats, casualties foreign and domestic. Something that makes one feel thrilled to be among the living.

Sidelle listened to my change of travelling plan, unmoved, as if I were informing her of a weekend trip without her. (Even that, one wishes, would lead to a raised eyebrow or an inquiring look.) I thought her indifference was the cause of my many pointless affairs lately. Desperate for a conversation less deadened than the sky outside, I said as much to her. She listened with a smile as though I was trying to sell her some bogus goods and she was too generous to point this out directly.

But I do feel interested, she said when I faulted her for her apathy. I genuinely like to hear the details of your life.

Which parts? I asked.

Whichever parts you're willing to part with, she said.

Wouldn't it be more sensible if you're interested in what I cannot part with? I said.

The only woman you cannot part with is me. I'm not interested in myself.

I was startled. To hide it I laughed, the kind of mirthless, high-pitched laugh that draws other people's attention. A few patrons looked at us. I stared at one of them and he shrugged.

So my going back means nothing to you? I asked.

What do you want it to mean to me?

I wanted the farewell to hurt her. That the moment I turned to leave she would feel compelled to beg me to stay.

A farewell has many practical consequences, I said. What if I marry someone there? Say, Hetty.

What makes you think your marrying will change who we are to each other? You can't set that as a trap for yourself, and you can't expect me to submit myself to the trap.

One should not go into a marriage with the intention of being unfaithful, I said.

Unfaithful to whom? Sidelle said. What if I argue that your going into any marriage is being unfaithful to me? But fear not, I'm not going to make that case.

I would rather that you did, I said.

When you're not here, I'll miss you. A great deal I'll miss you. But I've spent much of my life missing many people. Should I lie and say that I'll feel your absence more keenly than the others'? Would you believe me?

The din in the café made me want to throw my fork at the mirror behind her. If she meant her two dead husbands and one dead son, I had no way to compete with them. Sidelle must have seen through my agitation. You're not, she said, thinking of returning to Canada permanently?

Suppose I am?

And you want me to make a case for your staying here?

Is there a case to be made? I asked. Staying here, doing what?

Doing what you do well, she said. You'll find a position here. Jenkins would gladly have you back.

I have told Sidelle a bare-bones version of my failure at the UN peace conference. A misstep with a wrong woman was how I presented it—many men have that in common. Sharing a story of a disgrace with Sidelle makes it sound like a joke. She is always good at taking some sting out of a situation.

Does London need one more moron devoting his life to public relations? I said. A man wants to make a difference.

Canada will let you do that?

I've had the suspicion, since returning from San Francisco, that somewhere, in London or in Washington, there is a dossier that has accumulated more information about me than I am comfortable with. Though perhaps that happens to all the people who showed up at the conference. Who was I but a correspondent for the *Daily Worker*? My conversations with people from different camps were only part of my job. Canada should have nothing against me.

At least I could make a difference to Hetty's life, I said. Can I make a difference to your life if I stay?

Sidelle gazed at me, and I read pity in her eyes.

4 FEBRUARY 1946.

Left London. Only a handful of us in the boat train, and by five o'clock in the afternoon I was settled in my cabin. No one saw me off at the Waterloo Station but Johnston, exchanging a final handshake, full of self-congratulations over his swift arrangement of my trip.

No one will see me off when we sail tomorrow.

By evening the bubble of serenity was burst, when seventeen hundred war brides and six hundred war babies boarded. Thinking back, Johnston did have an ambiguous

smile when he wished me Godspeed. He must have foreseen the chaos and had the good business sense not to
warn me.

5 FEBRUARY 1946.

The Lord Mayor of Southampton came onboard and bid
farewell to the war brides and their children. He reminded
them that they would be the kingdom's unofficial ambassadors. Unofficial ambassadors, I said to a man next to me.
I've never travelled with so many diplomats in my life.

He did not reply. To ease the awkwardness, I asked him
where he was travelling to. Australia via New York, he
said.

6 FEBRUARY 1946.

Anyone reading this diary: I dare you to imagine sailing
alongside all these war brides and war babies. The dramas
with nappies and nursing and meals and emergency boat
drills are enough to make each day feel like it lasts forty-
eight hours. I am trying to identify one, or more than one,
fragile soul among the male passengers who might be
driven to madness. A man throwing himself or, worse, a
baby tottering past him, to the sea—that could be the opening chapter of a novel.

So far, however, all the gentlemen have seemed sturdy
enough. I have observed several of them purchasing silk
stockings and perfume and chocolates among the war
brides at the shops, always three or four customers deep.

I bought some fragrant soaps for T. They may not reach her, but it's the intention that counts.

...

[To whom did I give the soaps? Someone onboard, I think, but there were too many women onboard. A few times in my life I have given them a moment of my thought. For many of them that crossing, free from their parents and husbands, must have been the apex of their lives. Imagine them scattered around the continent, to marriage, children, grandchildren, and then imagine that the ship had sunk on that journey. Who can say a long life provides anything but the tedium of length? Had we all gone down on that trip we would have all been immortal: young wives, angelic children, and a few men of great potential. —RB 4 April 1990]

7 FEBRUARY 1946.

I can see that after this journey, my desire for any progeny will be reduced to nil. I am looking for a wife who is not going to expand her ambitions to include motherhood. This much I know. For each child you send out to the world you are only waiting for the world to orphan him—and whose life would that boomerang take next but mine?

In that sense Sidelle would be a perfect wife. If I telegraphed her this proposal, what would she offer? Approval of my courage? Laughter at my impulse?

8 FEBRUARY 1946.

Never have I felt as bleak as I did this morning, watching the Atlantic and the sky above turn into the color of a new day as indifferent to me as any other day. It was freezing cold on the deck, but unless it is this early one cannot escape running into my fellow intrepid travellers. Yesterday was a day of seasickness, so it was quieter than the first two days. Still, a palpable excitement lives on, seasickness or not.

It's not that I don't find some of the war brides attractive. Why are they called that, as if they are each wed to their individual wars? Everywhere there are signs that say, FOR WAR BRIDES ONLY. Music is played for them. The ping-pong balls bounce around for them. The ocean splits itself for them.

Most of them are deliriously happy. One imagines those poor souls wandering out of a city into the forest in a Shakespeare play would feel happiness in the same abandoning manner. What will happen to them once solid land is beneath their feet again? When does a bride become simply a wife? Is it determined by time or by the corrosion of the husband's love?

After breakfast I handed a piece of chocolate to a little girl with more curls than teeth, who mistook my leg for something more stable than the deck chair. The young mother, biting half off for herself and handing the rest to the girl, smiled at me. A conversation duly followed. The young woman's name is Hilda, and she is nineteen. Her daughter is Ruby. They are from Cardiff, and they are going to join Earl, Hilda's husband, in Waterloo, Iowa. Very well.

I ran into Hilda a few times. I have charmed her. I have even charmed Ruby.

Poor Earl.

I do not find Hilda unattractive. Though, like any other woman onboard she is someone else's wife, saddled with someone else's issue.

So. Poor me.

9 FEBRUARY 1946.

Payton, the steward who likes to remind me every hour that I can find a quiet haven in the library, said to me this afternoon, I've never had so many children mistaking me as their father.

They must see something in you, I said.

No, it's them wild women. They won't allow their children to bother you gentlemen but won't stop them when they grab my legs.

They may be too tired. Don't hold it against the poor mothers.

Not when two of them said I was too old to be a father, Payton said darkly.

What if I abandon that long-past-due novel about myself and write one about Payton? A seafaring hero always provides adventures. Perhaps Payton's undistinguished bearing only conceals an unfathomable past with secrets and dramas.

10 FEBRUARY 1946.

Roland, let us be levelheaded and stop dodging the question you must answer.

Why has marriage become an urgency to you?

—One looks for a way out of any failure. I am not a man who believes that by going on failing I can succeed.

And what does marriage mean to you?

—A marriage to either Sidelle or Hetty would change my financial prospects.

Have you imagined what a marriage to Sidelle would be like?

—She would let me retain part of my freedom.

Hetty?

—I do not know.

Think not of now but ten years from today: Would you regret then not marrying either of them?

How about twenty years, or thirty years? One gambles with time when one comes to marriage. Sidelle will be seventy-six in twenty years. In thirty years she will likely be buried. Even if she wrote me into her will I'd be an impossible heir, not getting what I want from her. I never get what I want from her. I would be submitting myself to lifelong defeat if I married her.

Hetty? I want nothing from her.

12 FEBRUARY 1946.

Posterity, take notice: two telegrams dispatched today. One to Sidelle, saying I have made up my mind about my marriage, but all will be well. She will understand that nothing will change, as nothing is changeable between us.

The other to Hetty.

Between you and me, Hetty, let me always be the selfish one—but this I do not have to say to her.

———

LUCY WAS THREE DAYS old on this day. I've noticed that we often count days after a baby is born, or after a child dies. After anyone close dies, maybe.

Sidelle would disagree with me, but I still think we measure life by births and deaths.

...

[There used to be a book on Hetty's shelf: *A Girl's Guide to Amusing Yourself and Others*. Reading through my diary entries from during the war, it becomes obvious that I would have been the perfect man to pen the book: *A Coward's Guide to Surviving a World War*. Yet even a coward can be made a fool by his ambitions to have a place in history. Mine, dwarfed by the war, were inflated by the UN peace conference. Invested in the possibility of offering an alternative to a world whose fate was determined by those rogue superpowers, I did my share of diplomatic manoeuvres among the concerned parties. That endeavour, however, was cut short by a fallout with a Polish associate, who had introduced a blonde colleague to me to undermine my effort. But what do these things matter now? Stalin is dead, so is Truman. Sidelle is dead, so is Hetty. No, the book I should have written is not about war. I would be the perfect author for: *A Man's Guide to Surviving a Life of Disappointments*. — RB, 4 July 1990]

I DON'T HAVE ANY ambitions. And nobody will ask me to write a book. But if I could, what would mine be? A Woman's Guide to . . . what? To Life!

27 FEBRUARY 1946.

A blur of events, leading to the last day I am a bachelor.
Nova Scotia in winter, cold enough to preserve my youth.

On the way back here I felt like Chekhov in his coffin, transported in the oyster train. Except no crowd greeted me at my destination, no one mourned, no history was made.

Is this where I am going to be domesticated, to live a happy life with a wife and a number of offspring? Well, there will be no offspring, of that I am certain. Hetty is turning thirty-four.

All the relatives have been polite to me since my return. There is confusion among some of the oldest cousins, who thought Hetty and I had been engaged, and if not for the war would have married long ago.

The cousins on the Ferguson side, prosperous as ever, no longer intimidate me. If I do not have their wealth, I have made up for it by my worldliness. They have Nova Scotia on their side. I have America and Asia and Europe on mine.

Married life brings a list of practicalities, none too thrilling, but thank goodness Hetty is good with practicalities. We will wait to purchase a house, and for now we are renting Taftwood from the Gillises, fully furnished. I imagine Hetty imagining that one day we will move into our own house, bringing with her what she has accumulated through her maiden years. I feel like a pauper marrying into royalty, with only the shirt on my back. I am exaggerating, of course. How else can a deprived soul feel prodigious?

The question remains unanswered: What am I going to do after my marriage? Take a position at a provincial newspaper? Or become a clerk in a municipal office? Someone I met in town suggested that I enter local politics. Are you sure you or anyone in this town is ready for me? I almost asked. This pond is large enough for your pebbles, not, I am afraid, ready to be made into a meteor crater.

Hetty said I should take my time, and perhaps I could focus on a project I would like to pursue. It was charitable of her not to hint at that novel, now decades overdue. I am no novelist, I now realise, but I can certainly impersonate one, supported by his wife, working on a masterpiece to be discovered posthumously.

I told her I was mulling the possibility of starting a bookshop specializing in maps. The world is changing quickly and the borders are redrawn every day, I said, so that someone had better keep old maps for those who still want them.

Hetty listened with an attention that could turn any whimsy into sensibility. If I said I would have a shop selling dodo birds, would she applaud my ingeniousness?

Maybe it's only a niche interest for myself, I said.

But it's a brilliant idea, Hetty said, the way a spinster aunt would praise a baby whose toothless smile leaves an impression that ends only at the retina.

And botanical books, I said. Plants remain unchanged even if the borders get redrawn.

Maps and plants, Hetty said. The world will be well covered.

What about that, Roland. Do you want to dedicate the rest of your life to being a dealer of miscellanies? Trees and bushes, roses and violets—they are gone before we realise it, and they come back before we notice them. No wonder every Russian or English novel features an old tree. Split into halves by lightning, burned down by a careless fire. And yet they always revive themselves. Perhaps true immortality requires a root system. A pale existence in the darkest place on earth. No human has yet sprouted some roots between his toes. No human has yet sacrificed mobility for longevity.

Of course, there are always Julius Caesar, Napoleon,
Catherine the Great, immortalized by biographies. But
those books are just made of words, words, words. Words
are more rootless than we, the makers of words.

———

WORDS, WORDS, WORDS. SOMETIMES I pity Roland because he
didn't have the courage not to marry Hetty. Did Sidelle also pity
him?

What a marriage they were heading into! Convenient for him
because Hetty was as cold as marble and as malleable as clay. How
many times did she turn a blind eye to his love affairs? It's extraordinary to think she did have an explosion over Sidelle in 1954. We
don't know what kind of explosion, but all the same, Hetty picked
out one woman in the world to be her enemy. A world war by itself.

What did Roland want from Hetty? Nothing. What did she
want from him? Not much. With a marriage like that, you throw a
few ingredients you happen to have at hand into a cooking pot.
You don't expect a fancy dish. A tolerable stew would be fine, good
to feed a few hungry stomachs, and sometimes you even get something decent if you add a pinch of this and a pinch of that. (Hetty
didn't have a pinch of anything. Roland, on the other hand . . . you
could always count on him for that.)

The worst kind of marriage is the one that aims for happiness.
Don't tell me that every marriage should have that grand aspiration. A marriage reaching for happiness is like any average Joe'
wanting to make a cake as tall as Mount Everest and as colorful as
a tropical island. And on top of that, to make it edible. I'm not saying it's impossible. But tell me how many people can afford that
kind of happiness? We can make do with a sloppy cake as long as
it doesn't topple over. Cracked, fine. A bit dense, no problem.

Oversweetened, we can live with that. Underbaked, it won't kill you.

Once I watched a movie in which a woman baked a birthday cake for her husband. And then she thought it was not perfect, and she dumped it into the trash can. Oh, I laughed so hard someone had to shush me in the theater.

But people can be stubborn. I shouldn't have laughed at the woman in the movie. Lucy wanted her life to turn out like that perfect cake. It did not, so she dumped it, along with everything else.

Katherine, perhaps your marriage to Andy will still have some hope: if you both can learn to love a lopsided cake.

_____

31 MARCH 1946.

> While I am adapting to my serene, month-old marriage,
> the world is busy producing headlines. Stalin, Churchill,
> Truman; another war threatening the fragile peace; Nazi
> collaborators executed by firing squad in Eastern Europe;
> Greenwich, Connecticut, voting against becoming the site
> of the United Nations headquarters; the general assembly
> of Nova Scotia in place for their terms; war brides arriving
> in Halifax. The last piece of news induced in me a misty
> melancholy. Another man travelling on a ship full of the
> war brides might not have ended up in the same state of
> doomed bliss as me. This morning I studied my hairline for
> a long time. Is it my imagination, or am I losing my vitality,
> turning into an ape of idleness?

_____

ROLAND WILL CRY WOLF like this for the next forty years. Don't take him too seriously. The problem with idleness is not that it leads to sin. Most people don't understand what it means to be idle.

Here's a lesson for you in how to be idle wisely. I was never idle when I was keeping a house and raising my children. So much work! A weaker woman would dream about idleness, like a handmaiden dreaming about being a princess. But how often does that happen? I let idleness do the dreaming for me. Like when Lucy was two and Timmy was one. When I put them side by side and fed them soda crackers in the afternoon, I would say, One for you, Lucy, and one for you, Timmy. Children like things that can be repeated. But what I was really thinking when I handed the cracker to them was this: One for your daughter, Roland, and one for your son, Gilbert. Or, like when I did dishes at night. There was a special one that Lucy chipped when she was little, so for all the other dishes I washed and dried, I told myself the lovely things Gilbert did for me. I saved the chipped plate to the last, and when I did that I would remind myself of the words Roland said to me. No one looking at me—not even Gilbert's mother—could find any fault or say that I was idle. But I was, you see. I placed idleness in everything I did.

But don't let yourself be carried away. Once I asked Lucy—she must have been four or five—if she wanted children when she grew up. Yes, she said, seven children. Seven? I said. Why, that's a lot. And I asked what she would name them. That caught her unprepared. If you can't come up with seven names, maybe you don't want that many children, I teased her. And she started to cry. I said, I have a good name for you. How about Roland if you get a baby boy? That's a stupid name, she said. Still it's better than all the names you know, I said.

Oh my, she went into a tantrum. I waited for her to calm down, and after a few minutes, I thought I would just take Timmy and Willie out for a walk. When we got back, Lucy was still having a fit. I was amazed. I would've been exhausted if I had to cry even one-tenth of those tears.

When Gilbert returned from work, he asked Lucy why her face was all swollen like a red apple. Lucy said it was because she didn't like the name Roland. There's nothing wrong with not liking the name, Gilbert said. I don't like it, either.

That was the last time I ever said the name aloud to my family.

———

2 OCTOBER 1946.

A letter from Sidelle. The twenty-first since I married, but it is the first that has made me question my marriage.
I reread her previous letters to be certain. Until now Sidelle has sounded contented, her life run like a train with a reliable timetable, well-served by an engine of teas and dinner parties and theatres and concerts and weekend visits in the countryside and motoring trips in Ireland and Portugal. She seems a perfect model of someone who lives with the kind of pleasure that she never takes too seriously.

But this letter has a darker undertone. Sidelle has accompanied a friend to Paris for the peace conference. She mentioned his name, Michael Giles, in her last letter, but I did not think of him as anyone special. He is going to the conference as a journalist, and Sidelle said she was interested to see Paris in its current incarnation.

For some reason I do not imagine this Giles as much older than me. I wish she had gone with someone I knew.

A new name, without a face attached, crushes one with its unfamiliarity.

But it wasn't just the man that bothered me. She also sent a clip from *The Manchester Guardian,* which compared the peace conference to a Sartre play, a reference she found tasteless. "One supposes each generation has to remake the old hell as though it were unique to them," she wrote. It occurred to me that her generation must feel they are going out of fashion quickly. Soon this will be my generation.

In the letter she describes a concert at Notre Dame, observing the autumn equinox, which she attended alone. "Handel and Haydn, celestially rendered by the organist and the three vocalists yet giving little assurance. What a strange thing music is. In this world of ugliness, music can still give the pretence of beauty. Think of the abhorrence we feel when we see Goya's war prints. For some people, even reading the words describing such atrocities would be more than enough. But music, how cruelly it has deceived us."

Ugliness—such a crude word—is not in Sidelle's vocabulary. Her arguments were full of holes. Had I been next to her we would have had a debate. We would have stayed up all night, invigorated by the cold bath in the intellectual sea.

Is this darker mood of hers in any way connected to that faceless Giles?

Hetty and I have been to plays and concerts, too—provincial fare, soothing like the nice dry hands of a fair-minded nanny tucking one in at the end of the day.

At the concert in Paris, Sidelle wrote, she was unfortunately seated in front of a few loud Americans. "One voice, full of vulgar confidence, reminded me of the man we met in Santa Fe. Or do you think half of Americans would fit the bill? The women, talking and laughing as though in their chests they hosted a symphony, made me wonder if in your new life you are enjoying the same trait, that trait one only finds in a woman from the New Continent."

She knows Hetty is not that kind of loud woman, so why such unkindness? Or was she hinting at other women with whom I will cheat on my wife? I had thought we had an agreement that she will say nothing about my marriage, just as the agreement between Hetty and me is that she will never ask a single question about my past women. As far as Hetty is concerned my history has been cleansed by her diligent housekeeping.

And then, in Sidelle's letter: "Wouldn't it be beautiful if you were here, Roland. Paris is not good for ponderousness."

I wonder if Sidelle feels lonely. But she has so many friends to fill her days. The truly lonely one is this fool here, waiting for the clock to strike ten so I can pretend that I have had a fine evening of reading and then join my wife in our unruffled marriage bed.

———

DID SIDELLE FEEL LONELY? Did Roland feel lonely? Loneliness must be like a craving. I never craved anything when I was pregnant. But whenever the news of pregnancy comes up around here—a daughter, a daughter-in-law, a niece, a grandniece, a granddaughter, you name it, anytime it comes up—a few women will start comparing their pregnancy cravings. What's the big deal about wanting pickles for breakfast, or milkshakes for lunch, or fried green tomatoes for dinner? No one is going to be remembered by their cravings. Imagine the gravestone: HERE LIES ROSE-

MARY BETHANY WALKER, BELOVED WIFE, MOTHER, GRANDMOTHER, WHO LIKED TO CHEW JALAPEÑOS DURING HER PREGNANCIES.

Cravings—I have nothing to say about them. But I have a few words about loneliness. All those songs we used to listen to on the radio about loneliness when someone is in love, out of love, betrayed by love, stricken by love—why do people lump love and loneliness together? It's bad advertising for love. Or maybe love is a perfect commercial, selling loneliness that otherwise nobody would buy. If there is a higher power, maybe his job is to peddle all the loneliness of today before tomorrow's loneliness gets delivered.

When we moved to Orinda, Gilbert planted an olive tree for each of the children in the backyard. We started with two, for Lucy and Timmy, and soon we had three, and then four trees. We didn't plant one for Molly because by the time she was born, all the trees were infected with olive knots. They didn't die, but they didn't look pretty. Lonely people are like those olive trees. They don't have to say anything. Loneliness is written all over them.

We planted a flowering quince for Molly, which made her think she was special. I wish we had planted one for every child, instead of those sad trees. Or a hydrangea bush. Hydrangea is my favorite. Katherine, do you remember those bouquets we delivered to the public library and to Mrs. Yoshimatsu's shop? She gave you candies and made you small Japanese dolls. You may not have them anymore, but I have a pair of earrings in the shape of a sushi roll from her. After I die you should have them. I'll remember to make a note about that. And the gold ring from my great-grandmother Lucille. That's yours, and one day you can give it to Iola.

If only Lucy were the one to pass it to you.

Mrs. Yoshimatsu was a lonely woman. Remember the Japanese servant I told you about? That old man Gilbert and I met on our first date? His name was also Yoshimatsu, and later he had sent his epic poem to us. The copy we received was written in this beautiful calligraphy, one part in English, one part in Japanese. God knows how many copies he had sent out if he took the trouble to send one to us, two kid strangers. But Gilbert was never a stranger to anyone. He wrote back an effusive letter, and then he became friends with Mr. Yoshimatsu. How strange that people can meet this way and never part until one of them dies. Mr. Yoshimatsu died in 1952. When we moved to Orinda I noticed the flower shop in the village was called Yoshimatsu. It was run by a widow, Mrs. Yoshimatsu. She was not related to Gilbert's Mr. Yoshimatsu, but that didn't stop me from becoming her friend. Later I started supplying her with the hydrangeas from my garden, on the condition that she did not give me a penny in return. She died in 1985. A few years before that she could no longer manage the shop. Physically she was okay. But her brain began to go soft and she started to speak only in Japanese. Gilbert and I helped to find a place for her in Japantown. The florist's shop passed to another family, Chinese this time. I did not like them so I stopped sending the flowers to sell.

All those beautiful hydrangeas. Now they belong to someone else.

You don't have to be a widow or a widower to feel lonely. I know Gilbert felt lonely at times in our marriage. He never talked about it. He felt lonely not because I wasn't a good wife, or we didn't have good children, but because there was still so much he couldn't do for us. And there was a lot we couldn't give him, either.

Do I ever feel lonely? All I can say is that I'm not a keen customer for loneliness.

Once, after Lucy died, Gilbert mentioned feeling lonely "for no good reason." What do you mean for no good reason? I asked. We lost Lucy. No, it's not only about that, he insisted, though when I pressed he couldn't explain. After that, for a few months, he took up drinking. His father was a drinker, though not a criminally heavy one. His mother drank, too, and she thought it was a secret. So, to see Gilbert with his drink was alarming, and I said so. There's something in here, he thumped his chest, and I can't get it out. Drinking won't help you, I said. It helps a little, he said. This went on for a few weeks. Finally I put my foot down. Lucy is dead, I said. You can keep drinking to try to make yourself feel less sad, or you can put that bottle away and live with the fact that we'll just be sad for the rest of our lives.

She broke your heart, too, didn't she? Gilbert said.

For the first time after Lucy died my eyes felt heavy, so I said nobody's heart really got broken except in those silly songs. Gilbert nodded and then said, Lilia, of the two of us, you're the one who lives with pride.

I said I didn't know what he meant. But I did.

———

31 DECEMBER 1947.

Stocktaking time.

Marriage: serenely happy. Throw in a parasol and a walking stick and Hetty and I could be as eternal as a couple on a china dish or a bookplate. One imagines when most couples marry they commit themselves to the long journey ahead, wishing for smooth sailing—but always there is cold rain, scorching heat, seasickness, indigestible food. Some may be shipwrecked. Some may become food for cannibals. But how many people calculate the risks before they book the trip? Not my parents. Not Hetty's sister Susie, no less a polished product of their upbringing, who deserved every kind of happiness, yet died a year ago from cancer. One could even say Sidelle was not free from that fate. Hetty and I, on the other hand, have understood the futility of such an endeavour. No thank you, we are just fine where we are. If we want, we can take a stroll to the harbour and watch all those miniature Arks, each with a husband and a wife aboard, setting tiny sail with blind courage. So long, we wave at them. We wish you best of luck on your fatal journey.

Love: My friendship with Sidelle, as I have portrayed to Hetty, has been an ebb and a flow. If there are rules to it I do not see them clearly. Are we star-crossed lovers destined to live apart, or a pair of ageing pen pals? It doesn't do to ask these questions, Roland—I can hear her saying that. A lot of things wouldn't do, in Sidelle's book. She is not Sidelle Ogden for nothing.

In between love and marriage: J. She is perhaps a little plump and vulgar for my taste, though who can say that marriage does not change one's palate? Am I avenging Hetty or Sidelle with this pointless infidelity?

Profession: I can see I will always be an amateur in this business of book dealing. However, that shan't cast any shadow over my interest in it. I am also an amateur in cartooning and writing propaganda and negotiating world peace. Most amateurs want to be taken seriously, and the most amateurish among them always find ways to be taken seriously. That seems the hazard the world of today and the world of tomorrow will have to face. Gone are the good old days when people had the luxury to be themselves. One does not have to deal with amateurism when being oneself. But, of course, nowadays the question is: How to be someone else convincingly?

———

BY GROWING OLDER BY the day and becoming stupider by the day, Roland. Isn't that obvious?

Today they had the last memoir class. Dear me, what truths were shared, what tears were shed, what legacies were created. At lunch Nancy gave me a printed sheet. She's insisted on bringing

me the handouts. This one is especially good, she said. All the
great quotes that we can use when we think about our lives. I said
I couldn't really see the words because I didn't have my reading
glasses with me. She said, You can read them later, but can I share
the last line of my memoir with you? It's inspired by one of these
quotes. The teacher called my ending poignant and heartwarming
and perfect.

Your teacher makes a living by lying to innocent people, I
mumbled to myself.

What, Nancy said, but she's never good at hearing what she
doesn't want to hear. This is the last line I wrote today, she said. We
live to understand love, and we love to give meaning to life.

I looked at her. What's wrong, she said. I said I was glad I ate my
entrée because now, with her ending, I would have to skip the pudding. She looked horrified, but that's her problem! She had no
trouble finding someone to applaud her, but no, she wanted that
person to be me.

Lilia, you know you're not often a nice person, Nancy said.

Says who, I said.

Says everyone, she said.

Well, I agree. Has it occurred to you that I don't want to be a
nice person?

Elaine would've said something clever, thinking she'd hurt me,
but poor Nancy could only look at me with pity in her eyes. But
don't you ever want to be a nice person? she pleaded.

Not really, I said.

What makes us think we can be someone else now that we're all
knocking on the doors of our graves? Knock knock. Who's there.
Lilia Liska from Benicia, California, that's who I am. Always.

Don't misunderstand me. I'm also Gilbert's wife, and his children's mother, and his grandchildren's grandmother. If you throw
in Norman Imbody and Milt Harrison I'm more things. But do I
imagine writing a memoir with an inspirational last line? No, just
as I could never imagine pounding on the piano as a master pianist

or painting some apples and pears and milk jars as a real artist. You don't need to pretend to be an expert at something to be yourself. You don't have to be an expert at anything to be yourself.

Roland, if you think about him, got one thing right. He was always himself. Always the same age. Constant. It's a virtue, to be constant.

Katherine, all those classes you put Iola through — they may not be helping her. Not even the most skillful dancer can dance her way through life. Not even a master welder can mend a broken marriage. Not even the best computer engineer can program a perfect life.

There are a few things I can teach you. Practical things. If I had a patch of dirt I could make a garden for you. But as far as I can see, people don't care much about gardens these days. They care about properties. Molly called yesterday and said, as though she were chitchatting, Do you know the value of the house on Roosevelt Road? I said, No, I don't, and I don't want to know. It's someone else's house now. She said, It's going on the market. The listing price is 2.1 million. Dollars? I asked. What do you think, dimes, pennies? she said. You should've held on to it.

If 2.1 million dollars is the price of that house, this is not my time, I said. I've raised five children and a granddaughter in that house. I've made a garden for all of you. It's been a good run.

Well, this may please you, but the garden is no more, Molly said. Someone built an in-law unit there. I bet they're going to rent it out.

I thought to myself, I'm a three-time widow and I've lost a daughter. What's a garden to me? So I said, What does it matter? The garden wasn't there when we bought the house, and there's no law saying it should always be there.

I should've insisted that you keep the house in the family, Molly said. None of your siblings agreed with you, I reminded her. None of them lives in the Bay Area and understands this place anymore,

Molly said. How about Katherine, I said. She lives here, and she's never said anything to disagree with me.

Have you thought that that's exactly Katherine's problem? She doesn't know how to stand up for herself.

When she grew up with you, an aunt not much older but a bully all the time to her? I said. I'm not surprised.

I wasn't the bully, Molly said. You were.

To Katherine?

To her, to Dad, to all of us.

I said I had no idea what she was talking about. I could hear Molly take a deep breath. She has that dramatic sigh when she's ready to say something righteous. Sorry, Mom, that's neither here nor there. Let's just stay with Katherine. Has it occurred to you that you may have done Katherine a disservice?

By taking her in? By raising her?

By the way you raised her, Molly said.

I raised her the way I raised all of you, I said.

But we had parents.

What's the difference when Gilbert and I were there for her? I said.

Because you're not her parents, and you let her know they were not there for her. It wasn't good for a child to live with mysteries she didn't understand.

What options did we have? I asked. To pretend we were her parents? To give her up for adoption? Besides, we never kept anything secret. We told her Lucy killed herself and Steve was gone from her life. From the very beginning we explained those things. There was no mystery.

I can't make you see sense, Molly said.

You're the one not seeing sense. Everything makes sense to me.

Even Lucy's death? Molly said.

Now, that's what I call hitting below the belt, but I didn't say anything.

Then Molly said—I'm trying to remember everything and now I'm writing it down so I don't forget, not that I agree with her, not that I cannot defend myself.

This is how it went:

Molly said, Mom, do you know how guilty Dad felt about Lucy's death? It was nobody's fault, we kept telling him, but he said if something fails in life, someone should own up to the failure. Life was harder for Lucy than for you, he said to us, because whatever was in her always ran against the world. Someone had to watch out for her, get in between her and anything that would bruise her or injure her. Your mom didn't know that, he said. She couldn't see it because she runs into everything all the time, too, but she doesn't bruise easily. She can be as hard as life. Some people are born that way, and she thought Lucy should be like her. She thought everyone should be like her. But most people can get hurt. We don't know Lucy's father. Maybe he gets hurt easily, too.

I felt my blood turn cold then. Lucy's father, I said. What did he say about Lucy's father?

Not much, Molly said. Only that he was a man you met before you married Dad.

Did he tell Lucy, too?

I don't know, Mom. When he told us, we were all grown-ups.

Your father had the most honorable soul, I said. I don't think he'd ever have told Lucy.

Then he probably didn't, Molly said.

And thank you for enlightening me about a part of my marriage kept unknown to me, I said.

Mom, we all love you, and we all know how much you've done for us, Molly said.

The worst kind of sweet talk, I thought. People often say to their lovers before breaking up: I hope you know how much you've meant to me. A murderer might even say that before he carries out his murdering.

I've been thinking about Gilbert and Lucy since Molly's call.

Did Lucy inherit something from Roland that we didn't understand? Did Gilbert and I miss something? But any question you ask is like a white flag you wave on a battleground. No white flag can save us, however big it is and however long we wave it.

Late in Gilbert's life, when his cancer returned, he couldn't fall asleep one night so I sat up with him. I knew he wanted to talk. There were moments in our marriage when he wanted to do that, remember the past together, but I was always able to cut him off with a funny comment. What's the use of talking about the past? I wanted my mind to be sharp, and the past hammered and blunted it. I preferred to think about the weather and the trees and the flowers and what dinner I was planning to cook for the family.

But when Gilbert was so frail and we knew he was going to die, I thought to myself, from now on I will let him use his time in whatever way he wants. He asked me, Do you think we didn't love Lucy enough? I said, We've raised five other children. Let's talk about them first. He said, But we don't have to. We can see how they've turned out. I said, Then let's be happy for them. And Gilbert said, Do you think we failed to give Lucy the love she needed?

Nonsense, I said. That girl got more love from you and from me than anyone we know. He then said, We didn't give her a happy life, did we? I said, Happiness, parents can't give that. We only give children lives. And before he said any more I told him to stop. When you miss Lucy, I said, just look at Katherine.

Sometimes I see Steve in Katherine, too, he said.

No you don't, I said.

All children have genes from both parents, he said. Sometimes I think about our children and I can tell what they got from you and what they got from me. All except Lucy.

She took after me, I said.

That's what we decided to tell ourselves. You said it to make me feel better. I said it because I didn't know Lucy's father.

Of course you do, I said. You're her father.

Yes, I think I am, he said. Then he started to wipe away his tears. You and Lucy made me a good man, he said. Remember those hopes we had when we were young, the peace conference, the golden dawn for all the generations to come? When I saw you near the opera house for the first time, I thought how wonderful it would be to share the world with that beautiful girl.

Come on, I said, you sound like a mushy actor. He laughed. Lilia, thank you for putting up with me, he said. What do you mean? I said. You don't believe in those good things I believe in, he said. You old fool, I said. If I didn't believe in them I wouldn't be your wife. Don't you know me? Nobody can make me do anything.

I didn't ask Gilbert about the good things he thought I didn't believe in. Maybe I should have, and then he would've known he was wrong. They say when people are closer to death they want closure. But I'm not a sentimental person. I don't believe in closure. If you want to see some closure you can flip to the end of this book. Plenty of closure. You can skip the parts between this page and page 650, or you can read them. It wouldn't make a huge difference to Roland or to me.

Closure. I wonder if my great-grandmother Lucille ever thought about that. What's the point of closure when at any moment you could tumble off your mule into the valley and never see another day again? Or your best pal could hack you to death at night so he could run away with your two hundred dollars' worth of gold? Rattlesnakes and grizzly bears and floods and snowstorms—would they be so kind to wait until you find closure? And the man whom Great-grandmother Lucille took care of, both of his legs amputated, just lying there waiting for death, what use would he have had for that comforting word? There was this young Miwok mother, fourteen, really still a girl, when her white husband was crushed by a fallen tree and her tribe refused to take her and her baby back. Great-grandmother Lucille made a place for them in her household. When the baby died, the young mother returned to her tribe. Did she think about closure then? Did Great-grandmother Lucille, who was said to have treated the girl as her own daughter, the baby her grandchild?

Gilbert was right. I'm as hard as the hardest life. My love is as hard as I am. I came from a settler family. Like a settler I've lived through the bumps and wounds and amputations and deaths. I don't mope. Give me an ax and a hoe and I'll start a garden. Give me a good man and I'll build a family with him. Anything I can do, I do it with all my might, but I don't fight storms and floods and earthquakes. I don't deceive myself into thinking I can be who I am not.

But I was born a hundred years too late. We were settled people when I was born, everyone is settled now, and will be settled forever. Look at Molly, using those grand words like "communities" and "platforms" and "missions" and "progress" the way Gilbert talked about peace and eighty percent of the world's population loving one another, as though those pretty words were passwords to heaven. Look at Iola, with all those enrichment classes teaching her to skate like a bumbling swan, to play the violin like a carpenter with a bad saw, and to paint like paints don't cost a penny.

Sorry, Katherine. I'm not criticizing you or Molly or anyone. I just feel bad for you all. How quickly settled people forget how to live in the unsettled world! Life doesn't soften itself for anyone, but how we soften and pamper ourselves.

Roland and Hetty also came from settler families. I don't know their particular stories, but I once asked Mrs. Anderson, the librarian, for a book about the history of Nova Scotia. She wrote to a friend of hers in Vermont, who she said was a painter with a little place in Cape Breton. Mrs. Anderson's friend eventually sent a few books that she found in a local rummage sale.

In any case, the settlers in that part of the world didn't have any better a time of it than my folks. Maybe worse, with all those snowstorms and shipwrecks. Without the gold. I remember the story of a whole boat of people drowned in the middle of the night. They only had their pajamas on, and the town had to collect a huge amount of money to buy each body a new suit to be buried in. Decent people, were they not? But none of them, the living or the dead, would've been thinking about that word, closure.

———

31 DECEMBER 1956.

> Stocktaking time. Another year.
>   Marriage: heavenly. Mood: serene. Professional prospect: none whatsoever, though Hetty is a great manager of the household, and I can playact my book dealer's role like the best of amateur performers. What else do we need to keep this life going?
>   Sidelle: sixty-five letters from her in the last year; sixty-seven from me to her, which, as I've asked, were sent to the shop address. Soon I shall look into purchasing a second safe.

———

I'M ONLY MARKING THIS as a sample for you. Like one of those tiny bites of cheese they put out in a store to tempt you. The next two hundred pages, all are bits and pieces of cheese like this. In case you decide to skip, let me tell you what you'll be missing.

Roland and Hetty bought and moved into a house, across the bay from Halifax so Roland could feel "liberated" from his childhood shadow. (Imagine moving from San Francisco to Oakland to become a completely new person. Unlikely, but that is Roland all over, thinking unlikely thoughts.) Hetty died in the house (and I suppose Roland did, too, though Peter Wilson neglects to tell us). But I'm getting ahead of myself. They still had many years to live.

Roland had a shop on Garden Road, and occasionally a young woman would be hired as a helper, but these employees came and went like seasonal allergies. (No surprise there.) Weddings and funerals. Family reunions. Many charity dinners, because Hetty was a charitable lady. Holidays, mostly in Europe, but also to Asia a few times. You get the sense Hetty would rather have stayed in her garden, but she took the trouble of traveling with Roland so he could stay put as her POW for the rest of the time.

POW isn't my word, but Sidelle's. She used it once in a letter, and Roland recorded it alongside a long passage of analysis of the situation, as you can imagine. She must have been in what Roland called "that mood of Sidelle's." What kind of mood was that? She never meant to break up his marriage. She seemed fine with him living so far away. But somehow Roland made it sound like he had wounded Sidelle by marrying Hetty, and because of that wound, there had to be a flare-up once in a while. Can we trust him?

Ah yes, I remember now. Sidelle said something about him losing his own war of independence and becoming a POW. I would say that he would be on the losing side of that war in any case. Either he was Hetty's POW or Sidelle's. The question is: Which one would be a better jailor?

Sidelle, if you ask me—but we don't know what her life was really like in those years. It still kills me that we can only imagine it and that we may be so off the mark in our imaginings.

Roland claimed that he and Sidelle remained intimately connected even though they lived across the ocean from each other. That I believed. Sidelle said she was a loyal woman. And I believe her. She and I are alike in that way: We only say what we mean. And Roland, what else could he have to make him feel special but Sidelle's letters? They met up when Roland and Hetty holidayed in Europe, but it was different then. Roland was traveling with a wife. And Sidelle was an older woman.

Roland might have written another thousand pages, but his life would be nothing more than the earth rotating to make day and night, and the earth going around the sun to make summer and winter. Roland was that earth and Roland was that sun.

And then there were the South Pole and North Pole of his world: Hetty and Sidelle. Between the two poles there were other women. I was between those two poles, too, the little girl from California that he would never marry. But I've made a good use of my life. I won't say I don't have regrets. I do, but regrets are like weeds. You kill them before they grow and spread. Willpower is the strongest weed killer. And I have willpower.

------

19 NOVEMBER 1969.

London. The young men and young women in the street, hair too long, garments too loose, faces too vacant, make the city a foreigner to me. Had I been younger I would have strived to look like one of them—was it not how I felt forty years ago when I first arrived in New York City? Forty years move one a few steps on, to another place on the chessboard. When the girls walk by without sparing a moment of their attention on one, one belongs to the past. When the boys see no threat in one's existence, one becomes history.

But call me old-fashioned, or reactionary. The young people, blossoming in their delusions, made oblivious by cannabis, are only marching blindly onto a field of tomorrows. Whereas I am able to make use of the days last past. In that I am a millionaire and they, paupers.

For sure this same generation is sprouting around us at home, too. But Hetty is good at maintaining the moat between us and the army of nieces and nephews and their friends.

I arrived in the late evening. It was the soonest possible after I received the telegram from one of Mr. Ogden's daughters.

To London, I told Hetty as I was phoning the travel agency, Mrs. Ogden is dying. Right away Hetty went up to pack my suitcase, black suit and black tie ironed, socks rolled up like newborn black bunnies, handkerchiefs for tears, mufflers for the throat, pills for the heart, backup reading glasses, and an extra fountain pen.

Hetty's efficiency awed me. Perhaps what keeps me in this marriage is that I live in a state of perpetual awe. That the book entitled *Sidelle Ogden* is to end is a mere fact to Hetty. What kind of character I am in Sidelle's book is of no interest to Hetty. Perhaps when the book called *Roland Bouley* ends, she will accept it just as easily, allowing her eyes to pause at the word "Finis," but no more. If I were to die tomorrow she would pack up as efficiently as this, too. Perhaps she would even send me off to the morgue with a second pair of reading glasses, an extra pen, and a few coins. Blessed the man whose wife knows so well his habit of misplacing the trivial contents of his life.

Though, am I to die soon? If Hetty asked I would reassure her: No, darling, it's not time yet to let death do us part. I have no doubt that she would have all of the strength and courage to go on, but what would be the point of her outliving me? Hetty as a widow would be no different to Hetty as a wife. Nothing under the sun is new to her, so nothing gets old. I have not been a widower. That remains an unswum river, an untasted wine, an unmapped terrain, an unmet lover. I would not mind knowing what the experience is like. Oh dear lord, do all loving husbands and wives in long-lasting marriages harbour these secret, near-murderous, thoughts?

It seems I shall outlive Sidelle. No surprise there, unless

I drop dead this moment, or am hit by a car. But someone—
who? I don't think it was Sidelle—once told me that I was
not the kind of person to be run down by a car. Why? Does
that kind of tragedy only happen to people who are of the
indispensable kind?

———

ROLAND DIDN'T REMEMBER THAT it was me who told him that. But
at least he remembered my words.

After Lucy died, Gilbert once said that he didn't understand
how such a sad thing could have happened to us. What do you
mean? That we are too nice? I asked. He said, No, we're ordinary
people, and we should be allowed to live an ordinary life, without
this suffering. I thought to myself, who could grant us this? Someone with cancer might think, I don't deserve this. Someone who
lost a family member in a traffic accident would think, The world
is unfair. Someone who marries a woman like Lilia Liska should
ask himself, Why me? Someone who marries a woman like Hetty
Bouley should ask himself, Why on earth?

———

20 NOVEMBER 1969.

I rang the University College Hospital. It did not sound as
though Sidelle would be able to speak on the phone, but
the nurse said she would let her know of my arrival. I also
exchanged a call with Tessa Hutchinson, Mr. Ogden's elder
daughter. Likely it will be within a day or two, she said, and
I said I would keep my return plans open. Her unperturbed
tone, with so little curiosity in it, reminded me of Hetty.

What is the world going to do with itself without women like them?

After lunch I visited Sidelle and sat with her for as long as I could endure. The afternoon was empty of intruders. Had she informed people that she wanted to spend this time alone with me?

She looked insubstantial, but not as fatally near death as I imagined. The way she raised a hand slowly to me—and I duly held it and kissed it—reminded me of a moment years ago, when she was lounging on the sofa in her drawing room, a hand extended as a gesture of truce. I must have been in a frantic mood that day. Was it before the death of Harry Ogden, or after? It no longer matters. It happened so many times, and it always happened the same way: I wanted something from her, and she made it clear that I was making a fool of myself by wanting it. Perhaps if I still have the time to write that epic novel about my life, it should be titled *The Wrong Moods*.

Or, *The Wronged Moods*.

The only difference between Sidelle and life: She has always made the effort to appease me. Life, that bugger, never does.

Sidelle has lost her voice completely. Do other visitors, encouraged by her quiet reception, talk her ears off, or do they, unsettled by her wordless scrutiny, scuttle off after a decent quarter hour?

Even whispering seems to give her pain, but she has not lost her wit. The words she has difficulties saying aloud I can easily understand. The arrangement of our duet has changed, the essence not.

Hetty? she whispered.

No, she's not in London, I said. I came by myself.

She shook her head slightly, pitying me. No one is waiting at the hotel, then, was what her look said. In the past twenty years Sidelle and I have met, mostly in London, but also elsewhere in Europe, but I have always arrived as a tourist, accompanied by my dutiful wife. They do not meet. I do not even tell Hetty when I visit Sidelle. I do not have to. In the world of endless confrontations between countries, between ideologies, between religions—in a world where anything can cause a war, I have established an armistice between two remarkable women.

Peacemaking between a loyal wife and a mistress to whom one has dedicated lifelong loyalty—this is a higher art, and should be required for all future world leaders, policy makers, and diplomats. Perhaps my epitaph should be: Here rests an ambassador of human hearts.

You can't expect me to bring her this time, I said to Sidelle.

Still, pity in her eyes, but more good-humoured now. Then you will have to travel back alone after I die—that was what she would be saying to me. Or, too bad you didn't think that the return trip would be a little different. Who will accompany you home after the funeral?

I don't mind travelling alone, I said.

Brave, she whispered.

Am I? I would prefer to always travel alone, I said, had I had a choice.

She shook her head, seeing through my lie as easily as I had told it. Her greyish blue eyes looked nearer to youth than to death. A life with some tremendous losses, people will say so at her funeral, but what they don't know is this secret. All of us are fools in Sidelle's eyes, and she has lived a good life entertained by fools.

Besides, who can avoid journeying alone? I said, still protesting, still arguing. She is always able to turn me back into my twenty-year-old self. And what is my aloneness

even to myself? I said, pressing on as though she would answer me.

She shook her head, dismissing my digression. Ready
for business? she whispered.

For a moment I thought of her as one of those characters in a Russian novel, producing on her deathbed a secret
will, naming me her heir. Would that give me what I need
to secure a freedom from all that binds me to my current
life? I would feel no qualm to accept everything from her.
Though someone might come to challenge my bequest
after her death. Relatives from Mr. Ogden's side, perhaps.
Had we been ten times more socially prominent, we would
have made a splash of a scandal. But here we are, a mostly
forgotten poet and a provincial book dealer. No one would
know that we two have lived at the apex of human existence.

She pointed to a writing pad on the bedside table. On
the pad, written not in her penmanship, was an instruction.
"I have destroyed all the letters from you. Please destroy
my letters. Thank you."

It was that impersonal "thank you" that made me realise
that this was an instruction to all her friends. Still, I could
not for a moment recover from the cruelty of the message.
She was not leaving me anything. Giving she does not, taking she does. Yes, I kept a carbon copy of my letters to her,
so one could argue that there was no real loss. But that cold
gesture from the deathbed?

Can I not keep them? I said.

What's the point? her smile said.

The point is that the living need to live on, I said. And
the living need to hold on to things. You can't just take
them away with you.

What if I didn't obey her wish? She would never know.

I cannot be the first man in history to defy a woman's dying wish. A few weeks ago, I read in the news that a young couple, distraught lovers who could see no future, decided to jump from the balcony of a skyscraper together. They had both had plenty to drink, but when she stepped into the empty air he, all of a sudden, realised that there was not a trace of desire to die in him anymore. What if I were that man, looking down from a dazzling height, feeling no remorse or grief but instead an extreme relief that I hadn't taken that final step? I cannot stop Sidelle from dying, but I can stay safe on that solid ground built by her and myself, secured by all the letters we have written each other.

One rather likes a neat ending, she whispered.

You can't expect that I cut a limb off myself so that you can have your neat ending, I said.

She smiled. How I hate that mocking look in her eyes. Even dying doesn't soften her.

You're saying I exaggerate everything. And I'm being messy, vulgar, and sentimental, I said. She looked like she was ready to drift away from me. I put a hand on her lifeless hair. Sidelle, I said. You can't order me to destroy anything. What would I have to remember you by?

You yourself, she whispered. Enough, no?

You mean, I shall exist to the end of my days as a memento of your brilliance? I said. What an honour, what fortune. Let's all give a round of applause to Roland Bouley, created by the one and the only Sidelle Ogden.

She opened her eyes a little wider. Sympathy, mock sympathy.

Maybe I should congratulate myself, I said. Had I been a neurotic young man I might have died a long time ago for you. And then what? You would've gone on to find another young man, who'd have suited you just as well. Fortunately,

I've played whatever role you've assigned me. I've put my heart into it. Perhaps even surpassed your expectations. And now you say to me: Go back to your wife. I'm done with you.

Oh, Roland, Sidelle whispered.

I did not know what she meant by that, but I did not have time to figure it out. A woman, late middle-aged, plumpish, came in, presumably one of those female friends Sidelle has accumulated in the past twenty years. I greeted her and saw that her eyelids were puffy and red, the worst type of visitor at a hospital. She seemed surprised to find me there, and showed no recognition when I said my name. Her name was Mrs. Morse, and before Sidelle said anything she bent over to peck Sidelle on her cheek. Not a word, darling, she said. I'll come back later.

A sacrifice she had to make for me and for Sidelle, that the woman did not conceal. How can Sidelle have a woman like that as a friend, how can she permit a woman like that to contaminate the last days of her life? Perhaps even Sidelle had to allow herself some deterioration in her old age, letting miscellaneous people take hold of her attention. Stupid, stupid world.

Her son killed himself years ago, and she still writes one letter to him every day, Sidelle whispered.

It is interesting now to remember that all afternoon the longest sentence she spoke was about someone who is beyond intolerable.

Why doesn't she just die, then, if she's so eager to be with him? I said.

Your solution for everyone, she whispered. Here you are, her smile continued to speak. You're no less melodramatic than Mrs. Morse and I put up with you just fine.

There is never an only orphan, an only widow, an only widower, or an only sufferer, I said. Does she come to you because she thinks you can understand her loss? Or does she go to everyone because she's certain nobody can understand her loss and she must make this her one-woman crusade, to have her pains seen and heard and known? God bless her son's soul.

Sidelle closed her eyes. Exhausted by my tantrum, perhaps. When she opened them again I had the vague feeling that she would live on forever. Some people are not born to die.

Still not taking me seriously, are you? I said.

She smiled. Whatever you mean, that smile said, you're making a fool of yourself.

One wants to be taken seriously, I said emphatically.

Hetty? she whispered.

Sure, Hetty, I thought. She is the one woman who has never not taken me seriously. And then there are clients and acquaintances who in a way take this Roland seriously.

Has it occurred to you, I said, that perhaps one wants to be taken seriously only by one specific person?

Me?

Yes, why not.

The problem is, Sidelle's smile said, have you seen me take anyone or anything seriously?

I don't care about how you treat others, I said. What I don't understand is why on earth you cannot take me seriously. You said Hetty takes me seriously. Maybe she does. Maybe she doesn't. It's extraordinary, you can say, that I don't know if anything in my marriage truly matters to me, but it's also extraordinary that I don't care to know. What I do mind, however, is not knowing why you've never given me the one thing that I wanted. Had Hugh lived, would you have treated him this way, too? Perhaps you would have been one of those mothers who destroy the lives of their sons without any remorse. Perhaps he would have long fled from you. A son can do that. But I'm not your son. I've remained loyal to you.

A nurse entered, alerted by my raised voice. Sidelle indicated that all was well. She did not look like a person on the edge of death. What if they had made a mistake when they summoned me? What if my presence was somehow keeping her alive?

———

I just read what I wrote. Too much whiskey, too little clarity. My memory of the afternoon was longer than recorded here. What else was said? I don't seem to have grown a day older since I met Sidelle.

The front desk just rang and said there was a telegram for me. From Hetty. I told them to send it up tomorrow.

———

LUCY WAS HER FATHER'S daughter. All those tantrums, all those words, all those things they wanted but would never get—the world was a hurtful place for them, and no one could change it. But Roland was luckier than Lucy. Sidelle was not Roland's mother. I am Lucy's. That hardness in us makes us difficult mothers, but it makes us better women.

———

22 NOVEMBER 1969.

Sidelle died, at 16.13 by my watch, 16.16 as recorded by the nurse.

From yesterday morning on she did not regain consciousness. I was the only one who insisted on sitting with her. A few visitors came and went. I imagined her friends studying their calendars and train schedules. An outing would have to be cancelled, a dinner party postponed, a concert missed. But that is about all. The inconvenience her death causes will be minimal, just as Sidelle would have preferred. No fuss. A neat ending. And then onward with life.

I have no life here. Sidelle was my life in London. I wonder if I will ever return. In what form though? A black-clad man, old, frail, laying a bouquet of white lilies by a gravestone. That man would cut a melancholy figure on a film screen. That man would deserve a poem written for him, or a monologue in a play, or even an aria. But Sidelle is dead, and I see little point in keeping up with a performance that has always been partly for myself, partly for her. Was she truly the only audience, apart from myself, that I wanted to impress?

This afternoon, when Miss Otis, the nurse, came in to check on Sidelle, she told me perhaps it would be good for me to take a walk. You look pale, she said. Some fresh air will do you good. I refused, and she did not press further. The doctor said it would be likely today, she said. She told me to call her if there was any change.

There was nothing to do then. I thought of lying down next to Sidelle. Waiting for her death with her. But her bed was not much wider than a cot, so I pulled the chair closer and rested my head on the pillow, not quite touching hers.

I dozed off. I must have dozed off, because time passed. Then I was startled by her dying, which was not as smooth as I had imagined it would be. All human lives start with some sort of unsettlement, resistance, violence, so perhaps there is no surprise that a life may not want to leave without some resistance and violence, either. Subdued in her case, but not entirely peaceful.

I dispatched a telegram to Hetty. *Mrs. Ogden died. Awaiting funeral arrangements.*

According to Tessa Hutchinson and Sidelle's solicitor, everything is in order. A neat ending it is. She arranged her death just as she arranged my life. Well. Sensibly. Devastatingly so.

29 NOVEMBER 1969.

More people showed up at the funeral than I imagined would, though this was not really a surprise. What did surprise me, though, was that everyone sounded as though he or she had had the most special relationship with Sidelle. Did the crowd in that church gaze at one another, thinking, like me, of his or her own loss that could never be understood by the rest of the world?

————

How do you feel, Roland?

—Feel? Not feeling much.

Sad at least?

—Yes, yes, sad. But the baby bird that fell out of the nest this past spring and was devoured by Hetty's cat made me sad. A mediocre production of *Othello* Hetty and I went to last month made me sad. Reading some of my old diary entries makes me sad. But sadness is never a strong enough flavour for my emotional palate.

What is, then?

—Ah, but is that not my fatal problem? Nothing really is.

But do you want it: something stronger than nothing?

—The question is: Do I deserve something stronger than nothing? I used to think I would not be able to endure Sidelle's death, but here I am, with not a single strand of hair turned greyer. Imagine Hetty looking for the tearstains on my handkerchiefs when I return. How disappointed she will be.

Perhaps you overestimate yourself. What if Sidelle's death is too recent to make you feel its realness yet?

—She and I have put each other beyond the reach of death, don't you think?

Are you sure, Roland?

—How else am I to live my life now, Roland?

———

How long has it been since I fell into this lovely habit of having a conversation between one Roland and the other Roland.

———

IN THE EARLY YEARS of my marriage I often thought about Sidelle. I didn't know her at all back then, apart from the few things Roland had told me, but I thought of her as a competitor. I used to ask myself: What would Sidelle Ogden have done had she been in my shoes? Of course, I asked myself that when Lucy died, but I also asked it about smaller things. When Timmy fell from a swing and broke two baby teeth, I pressed the cotton ball to his mouth before taking him to the ER. In the waiting room I wondered, Would Sidelle Ogden feel disturbed by the sight of her child's blood? A lady waiting nearby asked if I needed help. I thanked her and said no, and she had to raise her voice above Timmy's crying to tell me that, had she been me, she would have broken down crying. I looked at her and thought, But you're not me—and you're not Sidelle Ogden, either.

I used to think she had something I didn't have. It was luck, and I wanted her luck. I used to think if she had been born a girl on a ranch and if I had been born as comfortably as she was, she would've been a little girl from California Roland didn't care to remember, and I would've had a free and glorious life.

But what is luck? It doesn't matter that Sidelle was never Lilia, or Lilia was never Sidelle. Luck is being born with all four limbs and a brain and a heart. Yes, there are some who're unlucky, but most of us have enough luck on our side. Not everyone can make the same something out of life. Sidelle and I, we are the kind of people who make the most out of any life. Luck is on my side as much as it was on her side. Roland and Hetty—now they were truly an unlucky couple.

When someone dies you feel sad for the life she will never get to have again, or you feel sad for yourself because that person will never be in your life again. I felt both things when Lucy died. Sometimes I couldn't tell which was which, if I wanted her to live on for us, or if I wanted her to live because of what I knew by then, that life could be cold and harsh but it was never psychopathic. When Gilbert died, I felt sad mostly for him. He had deserved a longer life, more days with his children and grandchildren. I was relieved that I didn't die before him. Not because I was selfish. But because if I died first, he would've been stuck thinking about his years without me, and about the life I missed. It'd have been like losing Lucy again for him.

I can always live without someone.

It was hard for Roland to feel sad when Sidelle died. He couldn't be sad for her because she had lived and missed nothing. He couldn't be sad for himself because—oh, Roland, let me be ungentle with you this once, but surely you already knew this: You were never really in Sidelle's life the way you imagined.

———

31 DECEMBER 1969.

> I have spent the past month rereading Sidelle's letters to me. Nearly four decades of them. I cannot see myself obey her wish. To destroy these letters would be, next to destroying my own diaries, the closest gesture to annul my life.

———

I HAVE NO DOUBT the letters survived Roland's death, but what happened to them after? Are they kept where his diaries are kept? And where that is, we'll never know. But sometimes I also wonder if Peter Wilson burned the letters. A tragedy for Roland, but not so much for Sidelle.

———

18 AUGUST 1987.

Henrietta Margaret Bouley, 2 February 1913 – 18 August 1987. Beloved wife of Roland V. S. Bouley. You did all you could, and were awarded a happy life.

Henrietta Margaret Bouley, 2 February 1913 – 18 August 1987. Beloved wife of Roland V. S. Bouley. We did all we could, and were awarded a happy marriage.

Henrietta Margaret Bouley, 2 February 1913 – 18 August 1987. Beloved wife of Roland V. S. Bouley. Of the world of thorns and weeds you cultivated a marriage as an ever-blooming flower.

Henrietta Margaret Bouley, 2 February 1913 – 18 August 1987. Beloved wife of Roland V. S. Bouley. No one's love cut deeper than yours. No one's life healed as yours did.

Henrietta Margaret Bouley, 2 February 1913 – 18 August 1987. Beloved wife of Roland V. S. Bouley. A woman without follies.

None of these can be carved on her headstone.

Perhaps I should keep it simple: Henrietta Margaret Bouley, 2 February 1913 – 18 August 1987.

Later.

Hetty died as she wished. At home, in her own bed, surrounded by no one, with her beloved husband under the same roof but not next to her.

In the past few months, she was increasingly resistant to admitting any visitor. Toward the end she allowed only the two nurses to see her in her less presentable state. Dr. Evans and I were spared the worst. Charitable patient, charitable wife.

This morning Marybeth, the younger one of the two nurses, said that she would call the doctor, while I should go to Hetty without delay. I went in. I thought of lying down next to her, being her husband for one last day. Just as I approached, she opened her eyes and stopped me from making myself a sentimental fool at her deathbed.

It looks like the fog will be gone soon, I said, pointing to the closed curtains. She shut and then opened her eyes, acknowledging the world that has sustained us all these years. I did not say more but sat with her, until she shut her eyes without opening them again, a sign that she wanted to be left alone.

I didn't see her again until the nurses told me she had died. 15.33.

Later.

Sleep is not coming. Earlier I took a few old books off Hetty's shelf, the ones she read when she was a schoolgirl. I randomly opened a book, and a few dried petals fell out. That sight startled me more than seeing her laid out, ready to be transported away from this life we have shared as husband and wife for forty-one years.

The book I opened and then closed for fear of intruding further upon the dead flowers is now on my desk. *A Girl's Guide to Amusing Yourself and Others.* A girlhood manual for a life of fulfilment. I wonder if Hetty, once a disciple of the book, had long ago succeeded in becoming a true master of that art.

Despite the animosity Sidelle had once shown toward Hetty (and vice versa, though Hetty was good at brushing it aside), I wonder if she would have applauded Hetty's life. Here was a woman of Sidelle's calibre, who, having lived a life of no fussiness, put a perfect full stop at the end of that book called *Hetty Bouley.* What it took her to be herself I shall never know.

One wonders if she was one of the last treasures of her generation. I say that as though I do not also belong to the same generation. But in a sense I am not of any generation, and that gives one the illusion of always being young. Hetty, so deeply rooted in the life known to our mothers, our aunts, their mother, their aunts, was old before her time. A man and a woman from two generations: Such was the secret of our long-lasting marriage, made not for romance but for happiness. Must you go, Hetty? But let me not ask the question that only a fool would ask. Fools we are not. We have done well by each other.

Rather, I would say this: Must I go?

———

POOR HETTY. ROLAND HAD only good words to say about her.

Do you think Hetty was the woman Roland thought she was? I don't. Hetty never needed Roland. She never needed anyone. Inside every Hetty there is always someone else, a woman like my mother or like Mrs. Williamson, and inside that woman you can find yet other women. Great-grandmother Lucille. My sister Lucille or Margot. A friend like Maggie. Sidelle. Lucy (how much of my life has been about Lucy—I only now understand it). My daughters and daughters-in-law. Like sets of Russian dolls. Infinite possibilities. How to entertain yourself and others—this is how: Always know that you have all those secret women inside you.

What about you two, Katherine and Iola. I don't know. You must work that out yourselves. I think I have only enough time left to figure out this doll called Lilia. Roland was right about one thing. When you start writing about yourself, it feels like you can go on living forever.

Gilbert said I was the one to live with pride. Perhaps I do. Posterity, take notice. I've never asked anyone, not even Lucy: Must you go?

And that question Roland lived with every day of his life—

I might as well order a gravestone with the question carved on it and have it delivered to his grave. Better late than never, don't you think?

ROLAND VICTOR SYDNEY BOULEY
19 NOVEMBER 1910—19 JANUARY 1991
MUST I GO?

Yes, Roland, yes. We all must.

ACKNOWLEDGMENTS

THE WRITING OF THIS NOVEL WAS INTERRUPTED BY LIFE, and the book could not have been finished without friends and supporters.

Sarah Chalfant: Your consistency and care sustain my writing. Charles Buchan and Jacqueline Ko and others at the Wylie Agency: Your attention makes many things possible.

Kate Medina and the Random House team: Thank you for your tireless work on my behalf.

Simon Prosser and the Hamish Hamilton team: Thank you for your extraordinary insight.

Friends whose kindness and generosity have lightened the dark days: the Hughes family, Gish Jen, Lan Samantha Chang, Isavane Samanna, Susan Wheeler, A. M. Homes, Tracy K. Smith, Jhumpa Lahiri, Cressida Leyshon, Joyce Carol Oates, Kirstin Valdez Quade, Noreen McAuliffe, Chen Reis, Sugi Ganeshananthan, Kerry Reilly, Patrick Cox, Rabih Alameddine, Benjamin Dreyer, Duchess Goldblatt, Taylor McNeil, Mary-Beth Hughes, Doris Ng, Hong-Sze Yu, Erin West, and many others.

Edmund White: Every minute spent with you is an antidote to life's terror, indifference, and tedium.

Mona Simpson: Friend and ally through thick and thin— LMWM, LMWM, LMWM!

Elizabeth McCracken: Dearest Elizabeth! Another three hundred pages won't be enough for all the love.

Amy Leach: Let kings assemble. Here you and I sit with our books; we have no other thrones.

Brigid Hughes: Anything I put down for you can only be a placeholder. Words do fall short.